Dexter in the Dark

Jeff Lindsay

D1342118

W F HOWES LTD

This large print edition published in 2008 by
W F Howes Ltd
Unit 4, Rearsby Business Park, Gaddesby Lane,
Rearsby, Leicester LE7 4YH

1 3 5 7 9 10 8 6 4 2

First published in the United Kingdom in 2007
by Orion Books

A CIP catalogue record for this book is available
from the British Library

ISBN 978 1 40741 720 2

Typeset by Palimpsest Book Production Limited,
Grangemouth, Stirlingshire
Printed and bound in Great Britain
by MPG Books Ltd, Bodmin, Cornwall

FSC
Mixed Sources
Product group from well-managed
forests and other controlled sources
Cert no. SGS-COC-2953
www.fsc.org
© 1996 Forest Stewardship Council

For Hilary, as always

ACKNOWLEDGMENTS

It is impossible to write in a vacuum. The air for this book was provided by Bear, Pookie, and Tink. My gratitude to Jason Kaufman and his aide de camp, Caleb, for their enormous help in shaping the manuscript.

And as ever, special thanks to Nick Ellison, who made it all happen.

IN THE BEGINNING

IT remembered a sense of surprise, and then falling, but that was all. Then IT just waited.

IT waited a very long time, but IT could wait easily because there was no memory and nothing had screamed yet. And so IT did not know IT was waiting. IT did not know it was anything at that point. IT just was, with no way to mark time, with no way even to have the idea of time.

So IT waited, and IT watched. There was not a great deal to see at first; fire, rocks, water, and eventually some little crawly things, which began to change and get bigger after a while. They didn't do very much except to eat each other and reproduce. But there was nothing to compare that to, so for a while that was enough.

Time passed. IT watched as the big things and the little things killed and ate one another aimlessly. There was no real joy in watching that, since there was nothing else to do and there were plenty more of them. But IT didn't seem able to do anything but watch. And so IT began to wonder: Why am I watching this?

IT could see no real point to anything that happened

and there was nothing IT could do, and yet there IT was, watching. IT thought about this a very long time, but came to no conclusions. There was still no way to think any of this through; the whole idea of purpose wasn't quite there yet. There was just IT and them.

There were lots of them, more all the time, busily killing and eating and copulating. But there was only one of IT, and IT did none of those things, and IT began to wonder why that was, too. Why was IT different? Why was IT so unlike everything else? What was IT, and if IT actually was something, was IT supposed to do something, too?

More time passed. The countless changing crawly things slowly got bigger and better at killing each other. Interesting at first, but only because of the subtle differences. They crawled, hopped, and slithered to kill one another – one actually flew through the air to kill. Very interesting – but so what?

IT began to feel uncomfortable with all this. What was the point? Was IT supposed to be a part of what IT watched? If not, then why was IT here watching?

IT became determined to find the reason IT was here, whatever that was. So now when IT studied the big things and the little things, IT studied the ways IT was different from them. All the other things needed to eat and drink or they died. And even if they ate and drank, they eventually died anyway. IT didn't die. IT just went on and on. IT didn't need to eat or drink. But gradually IT became aware that

IT did need . . . something – but what? IT could feel that somewhere there was a need, and the need was growing, but IT could not tell what it was; there was just the sense that something was missing.

No answers came as ages of scales and egg clutches paraded by. Kill and eat, kill and eat. What is the point here? Why do I have to watch all this when I can't do anything about it? IT began to feel just a little bit sour about the whole thing.

And then suddenly one day there was a brand-new thought: Where did I come from?

IT had figured out long ago that the eggs the others hatched from came from copulation. But IT had not come from an egg. Nothing at all had copulated to bring IT into existence. There had been nothing there to copulate when IT first became aware. IT had been there first and, seemingly, forever, except for the vague and disturbing memory of falling. But everything else had been hatched or born. IT had not. And with this thought the wall between IT and them seemed to grow vastly higher, stretching up impossibly tall, separating IT from them completely and eternally. IT was alone, completely alone forever, and that hurt. IT wanted to be a part of something. There was only one of IT – shouldn't there be a way for IT to copulate and make more, too?

And that began to seem infinitely more important, that thought: MORE of IT. Everything else made more. IT wanted to make more, too.

It suffered, watching the mindless things in their roiling riotous living. Resentment grew, turned into anger, and finally the anger turned into rage toward the stupid, pointless things and their endless, inane, insulting existence. And the rage grew and festered until one day IT couldn't stand it any longer. Without a pause to think what IT was doing, IT rose up and rushed at one of the lizards, wanting somehow to crush it. And a wonderful thing happened.

IT was inside the lizard.

Seeing what the lizard saw, feeling what it felt.

For a long while IT forgot rage altogether.

The lizard did not appear to notice it had a passenger. It went about its business of killing and copulating, and IT rode along. It was very interesting to be on board when the lizard killed one of the littler ones. As an experiment, IT moved into one of the little ones. Being in the one that killed was far more fun, but not enough to lead to any real purposeful ideas. Being in the one that died was very interesting and did lead to some ideas, but not very happy ones.

IT enjoyed these new experiences for a while. But although IT could feel their simple emotions, they never went beyond confusion. They still didn't notice IT, didn't have any idea that – well, they simply didn't have any idea. They didn't seem capable of having an idea. They were just so limited – and yet they were alive. They had life and didn't know it, didn't understand what to do with it. It didn't seem fair. And soon IT was bored once more, and growing angry all over again.

And finally one day the monkey things started to

show up. They didn't seem like much at first. They were small and cowardly and loud. But one tiny difference finally caught IT's attention: they had hands that let them do some amazing things. IT watched as they became aware of their hands, too, and began to use them. They used them for a great variety of brand-new things: masturbating, maiming one another, and taking food from the smaller of their own kind.

IT was fascinated and watched more closely. IT watched them hit each other and then run away and hide. IT watched them steal from one another, but only when no one was looking. IT watched them do horrible things to each other and then pretend that nothing had happened. And as IT watched, for the first time, something wonderful happened: IT laughed.

And as IT laughed, a thought was born, and grew into clarity wrapped in glee.

IT thought: I can work with this.

CHAPTER 1

What kind of moon is this? Not the bright, gleaming moon of slashing happiness, no indeed. Oh, it pulls and whines and shines in a cheap and guttering imitation of what it should do, but there is no edge to it. This moon has no wind in it to sail carnivores across the happy night sky and into slash-and-slice ecstasy. Instead this moon flickers shyly through a squeaky-clean window, onto a woman who perches all cheerful and perky on the edge of the couch and talks about flowers, canapés, and Paris.

Paris?

Yes, with moon-faced seriousness, Paris is what she is talking about in that far-spreading syrupy tone. She is talking about Paris. Again.

So what kind of moon can this possibly be, with its near-breathless smile and smirking lace around the edges? It batters feebly at the window, but it can't quite get in past all the sickly-sweet warbling. And what kind of Dark Avenger could simply sit across the room, as poor Dazed Dexter does now, pretending to listen while mooning blearily on his chair?

Why, this moon must be a honeymoon – unfurling its marital banner across the living-room night, signaling for all to rally round, sound the charge, once more into the church, dear friends – because Dexter of the Deadly Dimples is getting married. Hitched to the wagon of bliss pulled by the lovely Rita, who has turned out to have a life-long passion to see Paris.

Married, honeymoon in Paris . . . Do these words really belong in the same sentence as any reference at all to our Phantom Flenser?

Can we really see a suddenly sober and simpering slasher at the altar of an actual church, in Fred Astaire tie and tails, slipping the ring onto a white-wrapped finger while the congregation sniffles and beams? And then Demon Dexter in madras shorts, gawking at the Eiffel Tower and snarfing café au lait at the Arc de Triomphe? Holding hands and trundling giddily along the Seine, staring vacantly at every gaudy trinket in the Louvre?

Of course, I suppose I could make a pilgrimage to the Rue Morgue, a sacred site for serial slashers.

But let us be just a tiny bit serious for a moment: Dexter in Paris? For starters, are Americans still allowed to go to France? And for finishers, Dexter in Paris? On a *honeymoon*? How can someone of Dexter's midnight persuasions possibly consider anything so ordinary? How can someone who considers sex as interesting as deficit accounting enter into marriage? In short, how by all that is unholy, dark, and deadly can Dexter really mean to do this?

All wonderful questions, and very reasonable. And in truth, somewhat difficult to answer, even to myself. But here I am, enduring the Chinese water torture of Rita's expectations and wondering how Dexter can possibly go through with this.

Well then. Dexter can go through with this because he must, in part to maintain and even upgrade his necessary disguise, which prevents the world at large from seeing him for what he is, which is at best not something one would really like to have sitting across the table when the lights go out – especially if there is silverware present. And quite naturally, it takes a great deal of careful work to make sure it is not generally known that Dexter is driven by his Dark Passenger, a whispery-silk voice in the shaded backseat that from time to time climbs into the front seat to take the wheel and drive us to the Theme Park of the Unthinkable. It would never do to have the sheep see that Dexter is the wolf among them.

And so work we do, the Passenger and I, work very hard at our disguise. For the past several years we have had Dating Dexter, designed to present a cheerful and above all normal face to the world. This charming production featured Rita as the Girlfriend, and it was in many ways an ideal arrangement, since she was as uninterested in sex as I am, and yet wanted the companionship of an Understanding Gentleman. And Dexter really does understand. Not humans, romance, love, and all that gabble. No. What Dexter understands is the lethally grinning bottom line, how to find the utterly deserving among Miami's oh-so-many candidates for that final dark election to Dexter's modest Hall of Fame.

This does not absolutely guarantee that Dexter is a charming companion; the charm took years of practice, and it is the pure artificial product of great laboratory skill. But alas for poor Rita – battered by a terribly unfortunate and violent first marriage – she can't seem to tell the margarine from the butter.

All well and good. For two years Dexter and Rita cut a brilliant swathe across the Miami social scene, noticed and admired everywhere. But then, through a series of events that might well leave an enlightened observer somewhat skeptical, Dexter and Rita had become accidentally engaged. And the more I pondered on how to extricate myself from this ridiculous fate, the more I realized that it was a logical next step in the evolution of my disguise. A married Dexter – a Dexter with two ready-made children! – is surely a great deal further from seeming to be anything at all like what he really is. A quantum leap forward, onto a new level of human camouflage.

And then there are the two children.

It may seem strange that someone whose only passion is for human vivisection should actually enjoy Rita's children, but he does. I do. Mind you,

I don't get all weepy-eyed at the thought of a lost tooth, since that would require the ability to feel emotion, and I am quite happily without any such mutation. But on the whole, I find children a great deal more interesting than their elders, and I get particularly irritable with those who cause them harm. In fact, I occasionally search them out. And when I track these predators down, and when I am very sure that they have actually done what they have been doing, I make sure they are quite unable to do it ever again – and with a very happy hand, unspoiled by conscience.

So the fact that Rita had two children from her disastrous first marriage was far from repellent, particularly when it became apparent that they needed Dexter's special parenting touch to keep their own fledgling Dark Passengers strapped into a safe, snug Dark Car Seat until they could learn how to drive for themselves. For presumably as a result of the emotional and even physical damage inflicted on Cody and Astor by their drug-addled biological father, they too had turned to the Dark Side, just like me. And now they were to be my children, legally as well as spiritually. It was almost enough to make me feel that there was some guiding purpose to life after all.

And so there were several very good reasons for Dexter to go through with this – but Paris? I don't know where it came from, this idea that Paris is romantic. Aside from the French, has anyone but Lawrence Welk ever thought an accordion was sexy? And wasn't it by now clear that they don't like us there? And they insist on speaking French, of all things?

Perhaps Rita had been brainwashed by an old movie, something with a perky-plucky blonde and a romantic dark-haired man, modernist music playing as they pursue each other around the Eiffel Tower and laugh at the quaint hostility of the dirty, Gauloise-smoking man in the beret. Or maybe she had heard a Jacques Brel record once and decided it spoke to her soul. Who can say? But somehow Rita had the notion firmly welded into her steel-trap brain that Paris was the capital of sophisticated romance, and the idea would not come out without major surgery.

So on top of the endless debates about chicken versus fish and wine versus cash bar, a series of monomaniacal rambling monologues about Paris began to emerge. Surely we could afford a whole week, that would give us time to see the Jardin des Tuileries *and* the Louvre – and maybe something by Molière at the Comédie-Française. I had to applaud the depth of her research. For my part, my interest in Paris had faded away completely long ago when I learned that it was in France.

Luckily for us, I was saved from the necessity of finding a politic way of telling her all this when Cody and Astor made their subtle entrance. They don't barrel into a room with guns blazing as most children of seven and ten do. As I have said, they

were somewhat damaged by their dear old biological dad, and one consequence is that you never
see them come and go: they enter the room by
osmosis. One moment they are nowhere to be seen
and the next they are standing quietly beside you,
waiting to be noticed.

'We want to play kick the can,' Astor said. She
was the spokesperson for the pair; Cody never put
more than four words together in a single day. He
was not stupid, very far from it. He simply
preferred not to speak most of the time. Now he
just looked at me and nodded.

'Oh,' said Rita, pausing in her reflections on the
land of Rousseau, Candide, and Jerry Lewis, 'well
then, why don't you—'

'We want to play kick the can with *Dexter*,' Astor
added, and Cody nodded very loudly.

Rita frowned. 'I guess we should have talked
about this before, but don't you think Cody and
Astor – I mean, shouldn't they start to call you
something more, I don't know – but just Dexter?
It seems kind of—'

'How about mon papere?' I asked. 'Or Monsieur
le Comte?'

'How about, I don't think so?' muttered Astor.

'I just think—' said Rita.

'Dexter is fine,' I said. 'They're used to it.'

'It doesn't seem respectful,' she said.

I looked down at Astor. 'Show your mother you
can say 'Dexter' respectfully,' I told her.

She rolled her eyes. 'Puh-*leeeeeze*,' she said.

13

I smiled at Rita. 'See? She's ten years old. She can't say *anything* respectfully.'

'Well, yes, but—' Rita said.

'It's okay. They're okay,' I said. 'But Paris—'

'Let's go outside,' said Cody, and I looked at him with surprise. Four entire syllables – for him it was practically an oration.

'All right,' said Rita. 'If you really think—'

'I almost never think,' I said. 'It gets in the way of the mental process.'

'That doesn't make any sense,' Astor said.

'It doesn't have to make sense. It's true,' I said.

Cody shook his head. 'Kick the can,' he said. And rather than break in on his talking jag, I simply followed him out into the yard.

CHAPTER 2

Of course, even with Rita's glorious plans unfolding, life was not all jubilation and strawberries. There was real work to do, too. And because Dexter is nothing if not conscientious, I had been doing it. I had spent the past two weeks dabbing on the last few brushstrokes of a brand-new canvas. The young gentleman who served as my inspiration had inherited a great deal of money, and he had apparently been using it for the kind of dreadful homicidal escapades that made me wish I was rich, too. Alexander Macauley was his name, though he called himself 'Zander,' which seemed somewhat preppy to me, but perhaps that was the point. He was a dyed-in-the-wool trust-fund hippie, after all, someone who had never done any real work, devoting himself entirely to lighthearted amusement of the kind that would have made my hollow heart go pitter-pat, if only Zander had shown slightly better taste in choosing his victims.

The Macauley family's money came from vast hordes of cattle, endless citrus groves, and dumping phosphates into Lake Okeechobee. Zander came frequently to the poor areas of town to pour out his largesse across the city's homeless. And the favored few he really wished to encourage he reportedly brought back to the family ranch and gave employment, as I learned from a teary-eyed and admiring newspaper article.

Of course Dexter always applauds the charitable spirit. But in general, I am so very much in favor of it because it is nearly always a warning sign that something nefarious, wicked, and playful is going on behind the Mother Teresa mask. Not that I would ever doubt that somewhere in the depths of the human heart there really and truly does live a spirit of kind and caring charity, mingled with the love of fellow man. Of course it does. I mean, I'm sure it must be in there somewhere. I've just never seen it. And since I lack both humanity and real heart, I am forced to rely on experience, which tells me that charity begins at home, and almost always ends there, too.

So when I see a young, wealthy, handsome, and otherwise normal-appearing young man lavishing his resources on the vile downtrodden of the earth, I find it difficult to accept the altruism at face value, no matter how beautifully presented. After all, I am fairly good at presenting a charming and innocent picture of myself, and we know how accurate that is, don't we?

Happily for my consistent worldview, Zander was no different – just a lot richer. And his in-herited money had made him a little bit sloppy.

Because in the meticulous tax records I uncovered, the family ranch appeared to be unoccupied and idle, which clearly meant that wherever he was taking his dear dirty friends, it was not to a healthy and happy life of country labor.

Even better for my purposes, wherever they went with their new friend Zander, they were going barefoot. Because in a special room at his lovely Coral Gables home, guarded by some very cunning and expensive locks that took me almost five full minutes to pick, Zander had saved some souvenirs. It's a foolish risk for a monster to take; I know this full well, since I do it myself. But if someday a hardworking investigator comes across my little box of memories, he will find no more than some glass slides, each with a single drop of blood preserved upon it, and no way ever to prove that any of them is anything sinister at all.

Zander was not quite so clever. He had saved a shoe from each of his victims, and counted on too much money and a locked door to keep his secrets safe.

Well really. No wonder monsters get such a bad reputation. It was just too naive for words – and shoes? Seriously, shoes, by all that's unholy? I try to be tolerant and understanding of the foibles of others, but this was a bit much. What could possibly be the attraction in a sweaty, slime-encrusted, twenty-year-old sneaker? And then to leave them right out in the open like that, too. It was almost insulting.

Of course, Zander probably thought that if he was ever caught he could count on buying the best legal care in the world, who would surely get him off with only community service – a little ironic, since that was how it had all started. But one thing he had not counted on was being caught by Dexter instead of the police. And his trial would take place in the Traffic Court of the Dark Passenger, in which there are no lawyers – although I certainly hope to catch one someday soon – and the verdict is always absolutely final.

But was a shoe really enough proof? I had no doubt of Zander's guilt. Even if the Dark Passenger hadn't been singing arias the entire time I looked at the shoes, I knew very well what the collection meant – left to his own devices, Zander would collect more shoes. I was quite sure that he was a bad man, and I wanted very much to have a moonlight discussion with him and give him some pointed comments. But I had to be absolutely sure – that was the Harry Code.

I had always followed the careful rules laid down by Harry, my cop foster father, who taught me how to be what I am with modesty and exactness. He had shown me how to leave a crime scene clean as only a cop can, and he had taught me to use the same kind of thoroughness in selecting my partner for the dance. If there was any doubt at all, I could not call Zander out to play.

And now? No court in the world would convict Zander of anything beyond unsanitary fetishism based on his display of footwear – but no court in the world had the expert testimony of the Dark Passenger, either, that soft, urgent inner voice that demanded action and was never wrong. And with that sibilance mounting in my interior ear it was difficult to stay calm and impartial. I wanted to claim Zander for the Final Dance the way I wanted my next breath.

I wanted, I was sure – but I knew what Harry would say. It wasn't enough. He taught me that it's good to see bodies in order to be certain, and Zander had managed to hide all of them well enough to keep me from finding them. And without a body, no amount of wanting it would make it right.

I went back to my research to find out where he might be stashing a short row of pickled corpses. His home was out of the question. I had been in it and had not had a hint of anything other than the shoe museum, and the Dark Passenger is normally quite good at nosing out cadaver collections. Besides, there was no place to put them at the house – there are no basements in Florida, and it was a neighborhood where he could not dig in the yard or carry in bodies without being observed. And a short consultation with the Passenger convinced me that someone who mounted his souvenirs on walnut plaques would certainly dispose of the leftovers neatly.

The ranch was an excellent possibility, but a quick trip to the old place revealed no traces at all. It had clearly been abandoned for some time; even the driveway was overgrown.

I dug deeper: Zander owned a condo in Maui, but that was much too far away. He had a few acres in North Carolina – possible, but the thought of driving twelve hours with a body in the car made it seem unlikely. He owned stock in a company that was trying to develop Toro Key, a small island south of Cape Florida. But a corporate site was certainly out of the question – too many people might wander in and poke around. In any case, I remembered trying to land on Toro Key when I was younger, and it had armed guards strolling about to keep people away. It had to be somewhere else.

Among his many portfolios and assets, the only thing that made any sense at all was Zander's boat, a forty-five-foot Cigarette. I knew from my experience with a previous monster that a boat provided wonderful opportunities for disposing of leftovers. Simply wire the body to a weight, flip it over the rail, and wave bye-bye. Neat, clean, tidy; no fuss, no muss, no evidence.

And no way for me to get my proof, either. Zander kept his boat at the most exclusive private marina in Coconut Grove, the Royal Bay Yacht Club. Their security was very good, too good for Dexter to sneak in with a lock pick and a smile. It was a full-service marina for the terminally rich, the kind of place where they cleaned and polished your bowline when you brought the boat in. You didn't even have to fuel up your own boat; just call ahead and it would be ready for you, down to chilled champagne in the cockpit. And happily smiling armed guards infested the grounds night and day, tipping their hats at the Quality and shooting anyone who climbed the fence.

The boat was unreachable. I was as certain as I could be that Zander was using it to dispose of the bodies, and so was the Dark Passenger, which counts for even more. But there was no way to get to it.

It was annoying, even frustrating, to picture Zander with his latest trophy – probably bundled neatly into a gold-plated ice chest – calling cheerfully ahead to the dockmaster and ordering the boat fueled, and then strolling nonchalantly down the dock while two grunting Wackenhuts put the chest on board his boat and waved a respectful good-bye. But I could not get to the boat and prove it. Without this final proof, the Harry Code would not allow me to proceed.

Certain as I was, what did that leave me? I could try to catch Zander in the act the next time. But there was no way to be sure when that would be, and I couldn't watch him all the time. I did have to show up at work now and then, and make my token appearances at home, and go through all the motions of maintaining a normal-seeming life. And so at some point in the next weeks or so if the pattern held, Zander would call the dockmaster and order his boat prepared, and—

And the dockmaster, because he was an efficient employee at a rich man's club, would make a note of exactly what he did to the boat and when: how much fuel he put in, what kind of champagne, and how much Windex he used on the windscreen. He would put all that in the file marked 'Macauley,' and store it on his computer.

And suddenly we were back in Dexter's world again, with the Passenger hissing certainty and urging me to the keyboard.

Dexter is modest, even self-effacing, and certainly aware of the limits of his considerable talent. But if there was a limit to what I could discover on the computer, I had not found it yet. I sat back down and went to work.

It took me less than half an hour to hack into the club's computers and find the records. Sure enough, there was a thorough service record. I checked it against the meetings of the board of Zander's favorite charity, One World Mission of Divine Light, which was on the edge of Liberty City. On February 14, the board was delighted to announce that Wynton Allen would be moving out of the den of iniquity that is Miami and onto Zander's ranch to be rehabilitated by honest labor. And on February 15, Zander had taken a boat trip that used thirty-five gallons of fuel.

On March 11, Tyrone Meeks had been granted similar happiness. And on March 12, Zander took a boat ride.

And so it went; each time some lucky homeless

person was chosen for a life of bucolic joy, Zander placed a service order on his boat within twenty-four hours.

This was not seeing the bodies – but the Harry Code had been set up to operate in the cracks of the system, in the shadow areas of perfect justice rather than perfect law. I was sure, the Passenger was sure, and this was enough proof to satisfy all of us.

Zander would go on a different kind of moonlight cruise, and not all of his money would keep him afloat.

CHAPTER 3

So on a night like many others, when the moon flung down chords of manic melody onto its happily bloodthirsty children, I was humming along and preparing to go out for a sharp frolic. All the work was done and it was playtime now for Dexter. It should have been a matter of mere moments to gather my simple toys and head out the door for my appointment with the trust-fund troublemaker. But of course, with marriage looming, nothing at all was simple anymore. I began to wonder, in fact, if anything would ever be simple again.

Of course, I was building a perfect and nearly impenetrable facade of gleaming antiseptic steel and glass to cement onto the front of the Gothic horror of Castle Dexter. So I was very willing to cooperate in retiring the Old Dexter, and therefore I had been in the process of 'consolidating our lives,' as Rita put it. In this case that meant moving out of my comfy little nook on the edge of Coconut Grove and into Rita's three-bedroom house father south, as this was the 'sensible' thing to do. Of course, aside from being sensible it was also a Monster Inconvenience. Under the new regime there was no way I could keep anything even slightly private if I should want to. Which of course I did. Every dedicated, responsible ogre has his secrets, and there were things that I did not wish to see the light of day in anyone's hands but my own.

There was, for example, a certain amount of research on potential playmates; and there was also the small wooden box, very dear to me, that contained forty-one glass slides, each with a single drop of dried blood preserved in the center, each drop representing a single less-than-human life that had ended at my hands – the entire scrap-book of my inner life. Because I do not leave great heaps of decaying flesh lying about. I am not a slovenly, slipshod, madly slashing fiend. I am an extremely tidy, madly slashing fiend. I am always very careful indeed to get rid of my leftovers, and even some cruel implacable foe bent on proving me the vile ogre that I am would be hard-pressed to say what my little slides really were.

Still, explaining them might raise questions that could eventually prove awkward, even to a doting wife – and even more so to some fearsome nemesis passionately devoted to my destruction. There had been one such recently, a Miami cop named Sergeant Doakes. And although he was technically still alive, I had begun to think of him in the past tense, since his recent misadventures had cost him both his feet and hands, as well as his tongue.

He was certainly in no shape to bring me to well-deserved justice. But I knew enough to know that if there had been one like him, there would sooner or later be another.

And so privacy seemed important – not that I had ever been a show-off where my personal affairs were concerned. As far as I knew, no one had ever seen into my little slide box. But I had never had a fiancée cleaning up for me, nor two very inquisitive kids sniffing around my things so they could learn to be much more like Dark Daddy Dexter.

Rita seemed to appreciate my need for a bit of personal space, if not the reasons for it, and she had sacrificed her sewing room, turning it into something she called Dexter's study. Eventually this would house my computer and my few books and CDs and, I suppose, my little rosewood box of slides. But how could I possibly leave it in here? I could explain it to Cody and Astor easily enough – but what to tell Rita? Should I try to hide it? Build a secret passage behind a fake bookcase leading down a winding stairway to my dark lair? Put the box in the bottom of a fake can of shaving cream, perhaps? It was something of a problem.

So far I had avoided needing to find a solution by hanging on to my apartment. But I still kept a few simple things in my study, like my fillet knives and duct tape, which could readily be explained away by my love for fishing and air-conditioning. The solution could come later. Right now I felt icy fingers prodding and tickling at my spine, and I had an urgent need to keep an appointment with a spoiled young man.

And so into my study I went, in search of a navy blue nylon gym bag I had been saving for a formal occasion, to hold my knife and tape. I pulled it from the closet, a sharp taste of anticipation building on my tongue, and put in my party toys: a new roll of duct tape, a fillet knife, gloves, my silk mask, and a coil of nylon rope for emergencies. All set. I could feel my veins gleaming with steely excitement, the wild music rising in my inner ears, the roaring of the Passenger's pulse urging me on, out, into it. I turned to go—

And ran into a matched pair of solemn children, staring up at me with expectation.

'He wants to go,' Astor said, and Cody nodded, looking at me with large unblinking eyes.

I honestly believe that those who know me would say I have a glib tongue and a ready wit, but as I mentally played back what Astor had said and tried again to find a way to make it mean something else, all I could manage was a very human sound, something like, 'He muh whu hoo?'

'With you,' Astor said patiently, as if speaking to a mentally challenged chambermaid. 'Cody wants to go with you tonight.'

In retrospect, it's easy to see that this problem would come up sooner or later. And to be perfectly fair to me, which I think is very important, I had expected it – but later. Not now. Not on the edge of my Night of Need. Not when every hair on my neck was standing straight up and screeching with the pure and urgent compulsion to slither into the night in cold, stainless-steel fury—

The situation clearly called for some serious pondering, but all my nerves were clamoring for me to leap out the window and be off into the night – but there they were, and so somehow I took a deep breath and pondered the two of them.

The sharp and shiny tin soul of Dexter the Avenger was forged from a childhood trauma so violent that I had blocked it out completely. It had made me what I am, and I am sure I would sniffle and feel unhappy about that if I was able to feel at all. And these two, Cody and Astor, had been scarred the same way, beaten and savaged by a violent drug-addicted father until they, too, were turned forever away from sunlight and lollipops. As my wise foster father had known in raising me, there was no way to take that away, no way to put the serpent back in the egg.

But it could be trained. Harry had trained me, shaped me into something that hunted only the other dark predators, the other monsters and ghouls who dressed in human skin and prowled the game trails of the city. I had the indelible urge to kill, unchangeable and forever, but Harry had taught me to find and dispose of only those who, by his rigorous cop standards, truly needed it.

When I discovered that Cody was the same way, I had promised myself that I would carry on the Harry Way, pass on what I had learned to the boy, raise him up in Dark Righteousness. But this was an entire galaxy of complications, explanations, and teachings. It had taken Harry nearly ten years to cram it all into me before he allowed me to play with anything more complicated than stray animals. I had not even started with Cody – and although it made me feel like I was trying to be a Jedi Master, I could not possibly start with him now. I knew that Cody must someday come to terms with being like me, and I truly meant to help him – but not tonight. Not with the moon calling so playfully just outside the window, pulling at me like a soft yellow freight train hitched to my brain.

'I'm not, uh—' I started to say, meaning to deny everything. But they looked up at me with such an endearing expression of cold certainty that I stopped. 'No,' I said at last. 'He's much too young.'

They exchanged a quick glance, no more, but there was an entire conversation in it. 'I told him you would say that,' Astor said.

'You were right,' I said.

'But Dexter,' she said, 'you said you would show us stuff.'

'I will,' I said, feeling the shadowy fingers crawl slowly up my spine and prodding for control, urging me out the door, 'but not now.'

'When?' Astor demanded.

I looked at the two of them and felt the oddest combination of wild impatience to be off and cutting mixed with an urge to wrap them both in a soft blanket and kill anything that came near them. And nibbling at the edges, just to round out the blend, a desire to smack their thick little heads together.

Was this fatherhood at last?

The entire surface of my body was tingling with cold fire from my need to be gone, to begin, to do the mighty unmentionable, but instead I took a very deep breath and put on a neutral face. 'This is a school night,' I said, 'and it is almost your bedtime.'

They looked at me as if I had betrayed them, and I supposed I had by changing the rules and playing Daddy Dexter when they thought they were talking to Demon Dexter. Still, it was true enough. One really can't take small children along on a late-night evisceration and expect them to remember their ABCs the next day. It was hard enough for me to show up at work the morning after one of my little adventures, and I had the advantage of all the Cuban coffee I wanted. Besides, they really were much too young.

'Now you're just being a grown-up,' Astor said with a withering ten-year-old sneer.

'But I am a grown-up,' I said. 'And I am trying to be the right one for you.' Even though I said it with my teeth hurting from fighting back the rising need, I meant it – which did nothing at all to soften the identical looks of bleak contempt I got from both of them.

'We thought you were different,' she said.

'I can't imagine how I could be any more different and still look human,' I said.

'Not fair,' Cody said, and I locked eyes with him, seeing a tiny dark beast raise its head and roar at me.

'No, it's not fair,' I said. 'Nothing in life is fair. Fair is a dirty word and I'll thank you not to use that language around me.'

Cody looked hard at me for a moment, a look of disappointed calculation I had never seen from him before, and I didn't know if I wanted to swat him or give him a cookie.

'Not fair,' he repeated.

'Listen,' I said, 'this is something I know about. And this is the first lesson. Normal children go to bed on time on school nights.'

'Not normal,' he said, sticking his lower lip out far enough to hold his schoolbooks.

'Exactly the point,' I told him. 'That's why you always have to *look* normal, *act* normal, make everyone else think you *are* normal. And the other thing you have to do is exactly what I tell you, or I won't do this.' He didn't look quite convinced, but he was weakening. 'Cody,' I said. 'You have to trust me, and you have to do it my way.'

'*Have* to,' he said.

'Yes,' I said. 'Have to.'

He looked at me for a very long moment, then switched his stare to his sister, who looked back at him. It was a marvel of sub-vocal communication; I could tell that they were having a long, very intricate conversation, but they didn't make a sound until Astor shrugged and turned back to me. 'You have to promise,' she said to me.

'All right,' I said. 'Promise what?'

'That you'll start teaching us,' she said, and Cody nodded. 'Soon.'

I took a deep breath. I had never really had any chance of going to what I consider a very hypothetical heaven, even before this. But to go through with this, agreeing to turn these ragged little monsters into neat, well-schooled little monsters – well, I would certainly hope I was right about the hypothetical part. 'I promise,' I said. They looked at each other, looked at me, and left.

And there I was with a bag full of toys, a pressing engagement, and a somewhat shriveled sense of urgency.

Is family life like this for everyone? If so, how does anyone survive it? Why do people have more than one child, or any at all? Here I was with an important and fulfilling goal in front of me, and suddenly I get blindsided by something no soccer mom ever had to face and it was nearly impossible to remember what I was thinking only moments ago. Even with an impatient growl from the Dark Passenger – strangely muted, as if just a little confused – it took me several moments to pull myself together, from Dazed Daddy Dexter back to the Cold Avenger once again. I found it difficult to call back the icy edge of readiness and danger; it was difficult, in fact, to remember where I had left my car keys.

Somehow I found them and stumbled out of my study, and after mumbling some heartfelt nothing to Rita, I was out the door and into the night at last.

CHAPTER 4

I had followed Zander long enough to know his routine, and since this was Thursday night, I knew exactly where he would be. He spent every Thursday evening at One World Mission of Divine Light, presumably inspecting the livestock. After about ninety minutes of smiling at the staff and listening to a brief service he would write a check for the pastor, a huge black man who had once played in the NFL. The pastor would smile and thank him, and Zander would slip quietly out the back door to his modest SUV and drive humbly to his house, all aglow with the virtuous feeling that comes only from true good works.

But tonight, he would not drive alone.

Tonight Dexter and his Dark Passenger would go along for the ride and steer him to a brand-new kind of journey.

But first the cold and careful approach, the payoff to the weeks of stealthy stalking.

I parked my car only a few miles from Rita's house at a large old shopping area called Dadeland and walked to the nearby Metrorail station. The train was seldom crowded, even at rush hour, but there were enough people around that no one paid any attention to me. Just a nice man in fashionably dark clothes carrying a gym bag.

I got off one stop past downtown and walked six blocks to the mission, feeling the keen edge sharpening itself within me, moving me back to the readiness I needed. We would think about Cody and Astor later. Right now, on this street, I was all hard, hidden brightness. The blinding orange-pink glare of the special crime-fighting streetlights could not wash away the darkness I wrapped tighter around me as I walked.

The mission sat on the corner of a medium-busy street, in a converted storefront. There was a small crowd gathered in front – no real surprise, since they gave out food and clothing, and all you had to do to get it was to spend a few moments of your rum-soaked time listening to the good reverend explain why you were going to hell. It seemed like a pretty good bargain, even to me, but I wasn't hungry. I moved on past, around back to the parking lot.

Although it was slightly dimmer here, the parking lot was still far too bright for me, almost too bright even to see the moon, although I could feel it there in the sky, smirking down on our tiny squirming fragile life, festooned as it was with monsters who lived only to take that life away in large, pain-filled mouthfuls. Monsters like me, and like Zander. But tonight there would be one less.

I walked one time around the perimeter of the

parking lot. It appeared to be safe. There was no one in sight, no one sitting or dozing in any of the cars. The only window with a view into the area was a small one, high up on the back wall of the mission, fitted with opaque glass – the restroom. I circled closer to Zander's car, a blue Dodge Durango nosed in next to the back door, and tried the door handle – locked. Parked next to it was an old Chrysler, the pastor's venerable ride. I moved to the far side of the Chrysler and began my wait.

From my gym bag I pulled a white silk mask and dropped it over my face, settling the eyeholes snugly. Then I took out a loop of fifty-pound-test fishing line and I was ready. Very soon now it would begin, the Dark Dance. Zander strolling all unknowing into a predator's night, a night of sharp surprises, a final and savage darkness pierced with fierce fulfillment. So very soon, he would amble calmly out of his life and into mine. And then—

Had Cody remembered to brush his teeth? He had been forgetting lately, and Rita was reluctant to get him out of bed once he was settled in. But it was important to set him on the path of good habits now, and brushing was important.

I flicked my noose, letting it settle onto my knees. Tomorrow was photo day at Astor's school. She was supposed to wear her Easter dress from last year to look nice for the picture. Had she set it out so she wouldn't forget in the morning? Of course she wouldn't smile for the picture, but she should at least wear the good dress.

Could I really be crouched here in the night, noose in hand and waiting to pounce, and thinking about such things? How was it possible for my anticipation to be filled with these thoughts instead of the fang-sharpening eagerness of turning the Dark Passenger loose on an oh-so-deserving playmate? Was this a foretaste of Dexter's shiny new married life?

I breathed in carefully, feeling a great sympathy for W.C. Fields. I couldn't work with kids, either. I closed my eyes, felt myself fill with dark night air, and let it out again, feeling the frigid readiness return. Slowly Dexter receded and the Dark Passenger took back the controls.

And not a moment too soon.

The back door clattered open and we could hear the sound of horrible animal noises blatting and bleating away inside, a truly awful rendering of 'Just a Closer Walk with Thee,' the sound of it enough to send anyone back to the bottle. And enough to propel Zander out the door. He paused in the doorway, turned to give the room a cheery wave and a smirk, and then the door slammed shut and he came around his car to the driver's side and he was ours.

Zander fumbled for his keys and the lock clicked open and we were around the car and behind him. Before he knew what was happening the noose whistled through the air and slipped around his neck and we yanked hard enough to pull him off his feet, hard enough to bring him to his knees with his breath stopped and his face turning dark and it was good.

'Not a sound,' we said, cold and perfect. 'Do exactly as we say, not a single word or sound, and you will live a little longer,' we told him, and we tightened the noose just a bit to let him know he belonged to us and must do as we said.

Zander responded in a most gratifying way by slipping forward onto his face and he was not smirking now. Drool leaked from the corner of his mouth and he clawed at the noose, but we held it far too tight for him to get a finger under the line. When he was very close to passing out we eased the pressure, just enough to let him crackle in a single painful breath. 'On your feet now,' we said gently, pulling upward on the noose so he would do as he was told. And slowly, clawing his way up the side of his car, Zander obeyed.

'Good,' we said. 'Get in the car.' We switched the noose to my left hand and opened the door of the car, then reached around the door post and took it again in my right as we climbed in the backseat behind him. 'Drive,' we said in our dark and icy command voice.

'Where?' Zander said in his voice, now a hoarse whisper from our little reminders with the noose.

We pulled the line tight again to remind him not to talk out of turn. When we thought he had received the message we loosened it again. 'West,' we said. 'No more talk. Drive.'

He put the car in gear and, with a few small tugs

on the noose, I steered him west and up onto the Dolphin Expressway. For a while Zander did exactly as we said. He would look at us in the mirror from time to time, but a very slight twitch of the noose kept him extremely cooperative until we took him onto the Palmetto Expressway and north.

'Listen,' he said suddenly, as we drove past the airport, 'I am like really rich. I can give you what-ever you want.'

'Yes, you can,' we said, 'and you will,' and he did not understand what we wanted, because he relaxed just a little bit.

'Okay,' he said, voice still rough from the noose, 'so how much do you want?'

We locked eyes with him in the mirror and slowly, very slowly so he would begin to under-stand, we tightened the line around his neck. When he could barely breathe, we held it like that for a moment. 'Everything,' we said. 'We will have everything.' We loosened the noose, just a little. 'Drive,' we said.

Zander drove. He was very quiet the rest of the way, but he did not seem as frightened as he should have been. Of course, he must believe that this was not really happening to him, could not possibly happen, not to him, living forever in his impenetrable cocoon of money. Everything had a price, and he could always afford it. Soon he would negotiate. Then he would buy his way out.

And he would. Eventually he would buy his way

out. But not with money. And never out of this noose.

It was not a terribly long drive and we were quiet all the way to the Hialeah exit we had chosen. But when Zander slowed for the off-ramp, he glanced at me in the mirror with fear in his eyes, the climbing terror of a monster in a trap, ready to chew off his leg to escape, and the tangible bite of his panic sparked a warm glow in the Dark Passenger and made us very glad and strong. 'You don't – there, there isn't – where are we going?' he stammered, weak and pitiful and sounding more human all the time, which made us angry and we yanked too hard until he swerved onto the shoulder momentarily and we had to grant him some slack in the noose. Zander steered back onto the road and the bottom of the ramp.

'Turn right,' we said, and he did, the unlovely breath rasping in and out through his spit-flecked lips. But he did just as we told him to do, all the way down the street and left onto a small, dark lane of old warehouses.

He parked his car where we told him, by the rusty door of a dark unused building. A partially rotted sign with the end lopped off still said JONE PLASTI. 'Park,' we said, and as he fumbled the gear lever into park we were out the door and yanking him after us and onto the ground, pulling tight and watching him thrash for a moment before we jerked him up to his feet. The spit had caked around his mouth, and there was some small bit

40

of belief in his eyes now as he stood there ugly and disgusting in the lovely moonlight, all atremble with some terrible mistake I had made against his money, and the growing notion that perhaps he was no different from the ones he had done exactly this to washed over him and left him weak. We let him stand and breathe for just a moment, then pushed him toward the door. He put one hand out, palm against the concrete-block wall. 'Listen,' he said, and there was a quaver of pure human in his voice now. 'I can get you a ton of money. Whatever you want.'

We said nothing. Zander licked his lips. 'All right,' he said, and his voice now was dry, shredded, and desperate. 'So what do you want from me?'

'Exactly what you took from the others,' we said with an extrasharp twitch of the noose. 'Except the shoe.'

He stared and his mouth sagged and he peed in his pants. 'I didn't,' he said. 'That's not—'

'You did,' we told him. 'It is.' And pulling back hard on the leash we pushed him forward and through the door, into the carefully prepared space. There were a few shattered clumps of PVC pipe swept off to the sides and, more important for Zander, two fifty-gallon drums of hydrochloric acid, left behind by Jone Plasti when they had gone out of business.

It was easy enough for us to get Zander up onto the work space we had cleared for him, and in just a few moments we had him taped and tied into place and we were very eager to begin. We cut the noose off and he gasped as the knife nicked his throat.

'Jesus!' he said. 'Listen, you're making a big mistake.'

We said nothing; there was work to do and we prepared for it, slowly cutting away his clothing and dropping it carefully into one of the drums of acid.

'Oh, fuck, please,' he said. 'Seriously, it's not what you think – you don't know what you're about to do.'

We were ready and we held up the knife for him to see that actually we knew very well what we were doing, and we were about to do it.

'Dude, please,' he said. The fear in him was far beyond anything he thought possible, beyond the humiliation of wetting his pants and begging, beyond anything he had ever imagined.

And then he grew surprisingly still. He looked right into my eyes with an uncalled-for clarity and in a voice I had not heard from him before he said, 'He'll find you.'

We stopped for a moment to consider what this meant. But we were quite sure that it was his last hopeful bluff, and it blunted the delicious taste of his terror and made us angry and we taped his mouth shut and went to work.

And when we were done there was nothing left except for one of his shoes. We thought about having it mounted, but of course that would be untidy, so it went into the barrel of acid with the rest of Zander.

This was not good, the Watcher thought. They had been inside the abandoned warehouse far too long, and there could be no doubt that whatever they were doing in there, it was not a social occasion.

Nor was the meeting he had been scheduled to have with Zander. Their meetings had always been strictly business, although Zander obviously thought of them in different terms. The awe on his face at their rare encounters spoke volumes on what the young fool thought and felt. He was so proud of the small contribution he made, so eager to be near the cold, massive power.

The Watcher did not regret anything that might happen to Zander – he was easy enough to replace: the real concern was why this was happening tonight, and what it might mean.

And he was glad now that he had not interfered, had simply hung back and followed. He could easily have moved in and taken the brash young man who had taken Zander, crushed him completely. Even now he felt the vast power murmuring within himself, a power that could roar out and sweep away anything that stood before it – but no.

The Watcher also had patience, and this, too, was a strength. If this other was truly a threat, it was better to wait and to watch, and when he knew enough about the danger, he would strike – swiftly, overwhelmingly, and finally.

So he watched. It was several hours before the other came out and got into Zander's car. The Watcher stayed well back, with his headlights off at first, tailing the blue Durango easily in the late-night traffic. And when the other parked the car in the lot at a Metrorail station and got on the train, he stepped on, too, just as the doors slid closed, and sat at the far end, studying the reflection of the face for the first time.

Surprisingly young and even handsome. An air of innocent charm. Not the sort of face you might expect, but they never were.

The Watcher followed when the other got off at Dadeland and walked toward one of the many parked cars. It was late and there were no people in the lot. He knew he could make it happen now, so easily, just slip up behind the other and let the power flow through him, out into his hands, and release the other into the darkness. He could feel the slow, majestic rise of the strength inside as he closed the distance, almost taste the great and silent roar of the kill—

And then he stopped suddenly in his tracks and slowly moved away down a different aisle.

Because the other's car had a very noticeable placard lying on the dashboard.

A police parking permit.

He was very glad he had been patient. If the other was with the police . . . This could be a much bigger problem than he had expected. Not good at all. This would take some careful planning. And a great deal more observation.

And so the Watcher slipped quietly back into the night to prepare, and to watch.

CHAPTER 5

Somebody once said that there's no rest for the wicked, and they were almost certainly talking about me, because for several days after I sent dear little Zander on to his just reward poor Dogged Dexter was very busy indeed. Even as Rita's frenetic planning kicked into high gear, my job followed suit. We seemed to have hit one of those periodic spells Miami gets every now and then in which murder just seems like a good idea, and I was up to my eyeballs in blood spatter for three days.

But on the fourth day, things actually got a little bit worse. I had brought in doughnuts, as is my habit from time to time – especially in the days following my playdates. For some reason, not only do I feel more relaxed for several days after the Passenger and I have a night encounter, but I also feel quite hungry. I'm sure that fact is filled with deep psychological significance, but I am far more interested in making sure I get one or two of the jelly doughnuts before the savage predators in Forensics shred them all to pieces. Significance can wait when doughnuts are on the line.

But this morning I barely managed to grab one raspberry-filled doughnut – and I was lucky not to lose a finger in the process. The whole floor was buzzing with preparation for a trip to a crime scene, and the tone of the buzz let me know that it was a particularly heinous one, which did not please me. That meant longer hours, stuck some-where far from civilization and Cuban sandwiches. Who knew what I would end up with for lunch? Considering that I had been short-changed on the doughnuts, lunch could prove to be a very import-ant meal, and for all I knew I would be forced to work right through it.

I grabbed my handy blood-spatter kit and headed out the door with Vince Masuoka, who despite his small size had somehow grabbed two of the very valuable filled doughnuts – including the Bavarian cream with the chocolate frosting. 'You have done a little too well, Mighty Hunter,' I told him with a nod at his plundered loot.

'The gods of the forest have been good,' he said, and took a large bite. 'My people will not starve this season.'

'No, but I will,' I said.

He gave me his terrible phony smile, which looked like something he had learned to do by studying a government manual on facial expres-sions. 'The ways of the jungle are hard, Grasshopper,' he said.

'Yes, I know,' I said. 'First you must learn to think like a doughnut.'

'Ha,' Vince said. His laugh was even phonier than his smile, sounding like he was reading aloud from a phonetic spelling of laughter. 'Ah, ha ha ha!' he said. The poor guy seemed to be faking everything about being human, just like me. But wasn't as good at it as I was. No wonder I was comfortable with him. That and the fact that he quite often took a turn bringing the doughnuts.

'You need better camouflage,' he said, nodding at my shirt, a bright pink-and-green Hawaiian pattern complete with hula girls. 'Or at least better taste.'

'It was on sale,' I said.

'Ha,' he said again. 'Well, pretty soon Rita will be picking your clothes.' And then abruptly dropping his terrible artificial jollity, he said, 'Listen, I think I have found the perfect caterer.'

'Does he do jelly doughnuts?' I said, truthfully hoping that the whole subject of my impending matrimonial bliss would simply go away. But I had asked Vince to be my best man, and he was taking the job seriously.

'The guy is very big,' Vince said. 'He did the MTV Awards, and all those showbiz parties and stuff.'

'He sounds delightfully expensive,' I said.

'Well, he owes me a favor,' Vince said. 'I think we can get him down on the price. Maybe like a hundred and fifty bucks a plate.'

'Actually, Vince, I had hoped we could afford more than one plate.'

'He was in that South Beach magazine,' he said, sounding a little hurt. 'You should at least talk to him.'

'To be honest,' I said, which of course meant I was lying, 'I think Rita wants something simple. Like a buffet.'

Vince was definitely sulking now. 'At least talk to him,' he repeated.

'I'll talk to Rita about it,' I said, wishing that would make the whole thing go away. And during the trip to the crime scene Vince said no more about it, so maybe it had.

The scene turned out to be a lot easier for me than I had anticipated, and I cheered up quite a bit when I got there. In the first place, it was on the University of Miami campus, which was my dear old alma mater, and in keeping with my life-long attempt to appear human, I always tried to remember to pretend I felt a warm, fuzzy fondness for the place when I was there. Secondly, there was apparently very little raw blood to deal with, which might mean that I could be done with it in a reasonable amount of time. It also meant freedom from the nasty wet red stuff – I really don't like blood, which may seem odd, but there it is. I do, however, find great satisfaction in organizing it at a crime scene, forcing it to fit a decent pattern and behave itself. In this case, from what I learned on the way there, that would hardly be a challenge.

And so it was with my usual cheerful good spirits

that I sauntered over toward the yellow crime-scene tape, certain of a charming interlude in a hectic workday—

And came to a dead stop with one foot just inside the tape.

For a moment the world turned bright yellow and there was a sickening sensation of lurching weightless through space. I could see nothing except the knife-edged glare. There was a silent sound from the dark backseat, the feeling of subliminal nausea mixed with the blind panic of a butcher knife squealing across a chalkboard. A skittering, a nervousness, a wild certainty that something was very badly wrong, and no hint of what or where it was.

My sight came back and I looked around me. I saw nothing I didn't expect to see at a crime scene: a small crowd gathered at the yellow tape, some uniforms guarding the perimeter, a few cheap-suited detectives, and my team, the forensic geeks, scrabbling through the bushes on their hands and knees. All perfectly normal to the naked eye. And so I turned to my infallible fully clothed interior eye for an answer.

What is it? I asked silently, closing my eyes again and searching for some answer from the Passenger to this unprecedented display of discomfort. I was accustomed to commentary from my Dark Associate, and quite often my first sight of a crime scene would be punctuated by sly whispers of admiration or amusement, but this – it was clearly a sound of distress, and I did not know what to make of it.

What? I asked again. But there was no answer beyond the uneasy rustle of invisible wings, so I shook it off and walked over to the site.

The two bodies had clearly been burned somewhere else, since there was no sign of any barbecue large enough to bake two medium-size females quite so thoroughly. They had been dumped beside the lake that runs through the UM campus, just off the path that ran around it, and discovered by a pair of early-morning joggers. It was my opinion from the state of the small amount of blood evidence I found that the heads had been removed after the two had burned to death.

One small detail gave me pause. The bodies were laid out neatly, almost reverently, with the charred arms folded across the chests. And in place of the severed heads, a ceramic bull's head had been carefully placed at the top of each torso.

This is exactly the kind of loving touch that always brings some type of comment from the Dark Passenger – generally speaking, an amused whisper, a small chuckle, even a twinge of jealousy. But this time, as Dexter said to himself, *Aha, a bull's head! What do we think about that?*, the Passenger responded immediately and forcefully with—

Nothing?

Not a whisper, not a sigh?

I sent an irritated demand for answers, and got

no more than a worried scuttling, as if the Passenger were ducking down behind anything that might provide cover, and hoping to ride out the storm without being noticed.

I opened my eyes, as much from startlement as anything else. I could not remember any time when the Passenger had nothing to say on some example of our favorite subject, and yet here he was, not merely subdued but hiding.

I looked back at the two charred bodies with new respect. I had no clue as to what this might mean, but since it had never happened before, it seemed like a good idea to find out.

Angel Batista-no-relation was on his hands and knees on the far side of the path, very carefully examining things I couldn't see and didn't really care about. 'Did you find it yet?' I asked him.

He didn't look up. 'Find what?' he said.

'I don't have any idea,' I said. 'But it must be here somewhere.'

He reached out with a pair of tweezers and plucked a single blade of grass, staring hard at it and then stuffing it into a plastic baggie as he spoke. 'Why,' he said, 'would somebody put a ceramic bull head?'

'Because chocolate would melt,' I said.

He nodded without looking up. 'Your sister thinks it's a Santeria thing.'

'Really,' I said. That possibility had not occurred to me, and I felt a little miffed that it hadn't. After all, this was Miami; anytime we encountered something that looked like a ritual and involved animal heads, Santeria should have been the first thing all of us thought. An Afro-Cuban religion that combined Yoruba animism with Catholicism, Santeria was widespread in Miami. Animal sacrifice and symbolism were common for its devotees, which would explain the bull heads. And although a relatively small number of people actually practiced Santeria, most homes in the city had one or two small saint candles or cowrie-shell necklaces bought at a botanica. The prevailing attitude around town was that even if you didn't believe in it, it didn't hurt to pay it some respect.

As I said, it should have occurred to me at once. But my foster sister, now a full sergeant in homicide, had thought of it first, even though I was supposed to be the clever one.

I had been relieved to learn that Deborah was assigned to the case, since it meant that there would be a minimum of bone-numbing stupidity. It would also, I hoped, give her something better to do with her time than she had appeared to have lately. She had been spending all hours of the day and night hovering around her damaged boyfriend, Kyle Chutsky, who had lost one or two minor limbs in his recent encounter with a deranged freelance surgeon who specialized in turning human beings into squealing potatoes – the same villain who had artfully trimmed away so many unnecessary parts from Sergeant Doakes. He had not had the time to finish with Kyle, but

Debs had taken the whole thing rather personally and, after fatally shooting the good doctor, she had devoted herself to nursing Chutsky back to vigorous manhood.

I'm sure she had racked up numberless points on the ethical scoreboard, no matter who was keeping track, but in truth all the time off had done her no good with the department, and even worse, poor lonely Dexter had felt keenly the uncalled-for neglect from his only living relative.

So it was very good news all around to have Deborah assigned to the case, and on the far side of the path she was talking to her boss, Captain Matthews, no doubt giving him a little ammunition for his ongoing war with the press, who simply refused to take his picture from his good side.

The press vans were, in fact, already rolling up and spewing out crews to tape background shots of the area. A couple of the local bloodhounds were standing there, solemnly clutching their microphones and intoning mournful sentences about the tragedy of two lives so brutally ended. As always, I felt reverently grateful to live in a free society, where the press had a sacred right to show footage of dead people on the evening news.

Captain Matthews carefully brushed his already perfect hair with the heel of his hand, clapped Deborah on the shoulder, and marched over to talk to the press. And I marched over to my sister. She stood where Matthews had left her, watching his back as he began to speak to Rick

Sangre, one of the true gurus of it-it-bleeds-it-leads reporting. 'Well, Sis,' I said. 'Welcome back to the real world.'

She shook her head. 'Hip hooray,' she said.

'How is Kyle doing?' I asked her, since my training told me that was the right thing to ask about.

'Physically?' she said. 'He's fine. But he just feels *useless* all the time. And those assholes in Washington won't let him go back to work.'

It was difficult for me to judge Chutsky's ability to get back to work, since no one had ever said exactly what work he did. I knew it was vaguely connected to some part of the government and was also something clandestine, but beyond that I didn't know. 'Well,' I said, searching for the proper cliché, 'I'm sure it just needs some time.'

'Yeah,' she said. 'I'm sure.' She looked back at the place where the two charred bodies lay. 'Anyhow, this is a great way to get my mind off it.'

'The rumor mill tells me you think it's Santeria,' I said, and her head swiveled rapidly around to face me.

'You think it's *not*?' she demanded.

'Oh, no, it might well be,' I said.

'But?' she said sharply.

'No buts at all,' I said.

'Damn it, Dexter,' she said. 'What do you know about this?' And it was probably a fair question. I had been known on occasion to offer a pretty fair guess about some of the more gruesome

55

murders we worked on. I had gained a small reputation for my insight into the way the twisted homicidal sickos thought and operated – natural enough, since, unknown to everyone but Deborah, I was a twisted homicidal sicko myself.

But even though Deborah had only recently become aware of my true nature, she had not been shy about taking advantage of it to help her in her work. I didn't mind; glad to help. What else is family for? And I didn't really care if my fellow monsters paid their debt to society in Old Sparky – unless, of course, it was somebody I was saving for my own innocent pleasure.

But in this case, I had nothing whatsoever to tell Deborah. I had, in fact, been hoping she might have some small crumb of information to give to me, something that might explain the Dark Passenger's peculiar and uncharacteristic shrinking act. That, of course, was not the sort of thing I really felt comfortable telling Deborah about. But no matter what I said about this burned double offering, she wouldn't believe me. She would be sure I had information and some kind of angle that made me want to keep it all to myself. The only thing more suspicious than a sibling is a sibling who happens to be a cop.

Sure enough, she was convinced I was holding out on her. 'Come on, Dexter,' she said. 'Out with it. Tell me what you know about this.'

'Dear Sis, I am at a total loss,' I said.

'Bullshit,' she said, apparently unaware of the irony. 'You're holding something back.'

'Never in life,' I said. 'Would I lie to my only sister?'

She glared at me. 'So it isn't Santeria?'

'I have no idea,' I said, as soothingly as possible. 'It seems like a really good place to start. But—'

'I knew it,' she snapped. 'But what?'

'Well,' I started. And truly it had just occurred to me, and probably it meant nothing at all, but here I was in mid-sentence already, so I went on with it. 'Have you ever heard of a *santero* using ceramics? And bulls – don't they have a thing for *goat* heads?'

She looked at me very hard for a minute, then shook her head. 'That's it? That's what you got?'

'I told you, Debs, I don't got anything. It was only a thought, something that just now came to me.'

'Well,' she said. 'If you're telling me the truth—'

'Of course I am,' I protested.

'Then, you've got doodly-squat,' she said and looked away, back to where Captain Matthews was answering questions with his solemn, manly jaw jutting out. 'Which is only slightly less than the horsepucky I got,' she said.

I had never before grasped that doodly-squat was less than horsepucky, but it's always nice to learn something new. And yet even this startling revelation did very little to answer the real question here: Why had the Dark Passenger pulled a duck and cover? In the course of my job and my hobby I have seen some things that most people can't even imagine, unless they have watched several of those movies they show at traffic school for driving drunk. And in every case I had ever encountered, no matter how grisly, my shadow companion had some kind of pithy comment on the proceedings, even if it was only a yawn.

But now, confronted by nothing more sinister than two charred bodies and some amateur pottery, the Dark Passenger chose to scuttle away like a scared spider and leave me without guidance – a brand-new feeling for me, and I discovered I did not like it at all.

Still, what was I to do? I knew of no one I could talk to about something like the Dark Passenger; at least, not if I wanted to stay at liberty, which I very much did. As far as I was aware, there were no experts on the subject, other than me. But what did I really know about my boon companion? Was I really that knowledgeable, merely because I had shared space with it for so long? The fact that it had chosen to scuttle into the cellar was making me very edgy, as if I found myself walking through my office with no pants on. When it came down to the nub of things, I had no idea what the Dark Passenger was or where it came from, and that had never seemed all that important.

For some reason, now it did.

A modest crowd had gathered by the yellow tape barrier the police had put up. Enough people so that the Watcher could stand in the middle of the group without sticking out in any way.

He watched with a cold hunger that did not show on his face – nothing showed on his face; it was merely a mask he wore for the time being, a way to hide the coiled power stored inside. Yet somehow the people around him seemed to sense it, glancing his way nervously from time to time, as if they had heard a tiger growling nearby.

The Watcher enjoyed their discomfort, enjoyed the way they stared in stupid fear at what he had done. It was all part of the joy of this power, and part of the reason he liked to watch.

But he watched with a purpose right now, carefully and deliberately, even as he watched them scrabble around like ants and felt the power surge and flex inside him. *Walking meat*, he thought. *Less than sheep, and we are the shepherd.*

As he gloated at their pathetic reaction to his display he felt another presence tickle at the edge of his predator's senses. He turned his head slowly along the line of yellow tape—

There. That was him, the one in the bright Hawaiian shirt. He really was with the police.

The Watcher reached a careful tendril out toward the other, and as it touched he watched the other stop cold in his tracks and close his eyes, as if asking a silent question – yes. It all made sense now. The other had felt the subtle reach of senses; he was powerful, that was certain.

But what was his purpose?

He watched as the other straightened up, looked around, and then seemingly shrugged it off and crossed the police line.

We are stronger, he thought. *Stronger than all of them. And they will discover this, to their very great sorrow.*

He could feel the hunger growing – but he needed to know more, and he would wait until the right time. Wait and watch.

For now.

CHAPTER 6

A homicide scene with no blood splattered should have been a real holiday outing for me, but somehow I couldn't get into the lighthearted frame of mind to enjoy it. I lurked around for a while, going in and out of the taped-off area, but there was very little for me to do. And Deborah seemed to have said all she had to say to me, which left me somewhat alone and unoccupied.

A reasonable being might very well be pardoned for sulking just a tiny bit, but I had never claimed to be reasonable, and that left me with very few options. Perhaps the best thing to do would be to get on with life and think about the many important things that demanded my attention – the kids, the caterer, Paris, lunch . . . Considering my laundry list of things to worry about, it was no wonder the Passenger was proving a wee bit shy.

I looked at the two overcooked bodies again. They were not doing anything sinister. They were still dead. But the Dark Passenger was still silent.

I wandered back over to where Deborah stood, talking to Angel-no-relation. They both looked at me expectantly, but I had no readily available wit to offer, which was very much out of character. Happily for my world-famous reputation for permanently cheerful stoicism, before I could really turn gloomy, Deborah looked over my shoulder and snorted. 'About fucking time.'

I followed her gaze to a patrol car that had just pulled up and watched a man dressed all in white climb out.

The official City of Miami *babalao* had arrived.

Our fair city exists in a permanent blinding haze of cronyism and corruption that would make Boss Tweed jealous, and every year millions of dollars are thrown away on imaginary consulting jobs, cost overruns on projects that haven't begun because they were awarded to someone's mother-in-law, and other special items of great civic importance, like new luxury cars for political supporters. So it should be no surprise at all that the city pays a Santeria priest a salary and benefits.

The surprise is that he earns his money.

Every morning at sunrise, the *babalao* arrives at the courthouse, where he usually finds one or two small animal sacrifices left by people with important legal cases pending. No Miami citizen in his right mind would touch these things, but of course it would be very bad form to leave dead animals littered about Miami's great temple of justice. So the *babalao* removes the sacrifices, cowrie shells, feathers, beads, charms, and pictures in a way that will not offend the *orishas*, the guiding spirits of Santeria.

He is also called upon from time to time to cast spells for other important civic items, like blessing a new overpass built by a low-bid contractor or putting a curse on the New York Jets. And he had apparently been called upon this time by my sister, Deborah.

The official city *babalao* was a black man of about fifty, six feet tall with very long fingernails and a considerable paunch. He was dressed in white pants, a white guayabera, and sandals. He came plodding over from the patrol car that had brought him, with the cranky expression of a minor bureaucrat whose important filing work had been interrupted. As he walked he polished a pair of black horn-rimmed glasses on the tail of his shirt. He put them on as he approached the bodies and, when he did, what he saw stopped him dead.

For a long moment he just stared. Then, with his eyes still glued to the bodies, he backed away. At about thirty feet away, he turned around and walked back to the patrol car and climbed in.

'What the fuck,' Deborah said, and I agreed that she had summed things up nicely. The *babalao* slammed the car door and sat there in the front seat, staring straight ahead through the windshield without moving. After a moment Deborah muttered, 'Shit,' and went over to the car. And because like all inquiring minds I want to know, I followed.

When I got to the car Deborah was tapping on

the glass of the passenger-side window and the *babalao* was still staring straight ahead, jaw clenched, grimly pretending not to see her. Debs knocked harder; he shook his head. 'Open the door,' she said in her best police-issue put-down-the-gun voice. He shook his head harder. She knocked on the window harder. 'Open it!' she said.

Finally he rolled down the window. 'This is nothing to do with me,' he said.

'Then what is it?' Deborah asked him.

He just shook his head. 'I need to get back to work,' he said.

'Is it Palo Mayombe?' I asked him, and Debs glared at me for interrupting, but it seemed like a fair question. Palo Mayombe was a somewhat darker offshoot of Santeria, and although I knew almost nothing about it, there had been rumors of some very wicked rituals that had piqued my interest.

But the *babalao* shook his head. 'Listen,' he said. 'There's stuff out there, you guys got no idea, and you don't wanna know.'

'Is this one of those things?' I asked.

'I dunno,' he said. 'Might be.'

'What can you tell us about it?' Deborah demanded.

'I can't tell you nothing 'cause I don't know nothing,' he said. 'But I don't like it and I don't want anything to do with it. I got important stuff to do today – tell the cop I gotta go.' And he rolled the window up again.

'Shit,' Deborah said, and she looked at me accusingly.

'Well I didn't do anything,' I said.

'Shit,' she said again. 'What the hell does that mean?'

'I am completely in the dark,' I said.

'Uh-huh,' she said, and she looked entirely unconvinced, which was a little ironic. I mean, people believe me all the time when I'm being somewhat less than perfectly truthful – and yet here was my own foster flesh and blood, refusing to believe that I was, in fact, completely in the dark. Aside from the fact that the *babalao* seemed to be having the same reaction as the Passenger – and what should I make of that?

Before I could pursue that fascinating line of thought, I realized that Deborah was still staring at me with an exceedingly unpleasant expression on her face.

'Did you find the heads?' I asked, quite helpfully I thought. 'We might get a feel for the ritual if we saw what he did to the heads.'

'No, we haven't found the heads. I haven't found anything except a brother who's holding out on me.'

'Deborah, really, this permanent air of nasty suspicion is not good for your face muscles. You'll get frown lines.'

'Maybe I'll get a killer, too,' she said, and walked back to the two charred bodies.

Since my usefulness was apparently at an end, at least as far as my sister was concerned, there was really not a great deal more for me to do on-site. I finished up with my blood kit, taking small samples of the dried black stuff caked around the two necks, and headed back to the lab in plenty of time for a late lunch.

But alas, poor Dauntless Dexter obviously had a target painted on his back, because my troubles had barely begun. Just as I was tidying up my desk and getting ready to take part in the cheerfully homicidal rush-hour traffic, Vince Masuoka came skipping into my office. 'I just talked to Manny,' he said. 'He can see us tomorrow morning at ten.'

'That's wonderful news,' I said. 'The only thing that could possibly make it any better would be to know who Manny is and why he wants to see us.'

Vince actually looked a little hurt, one of the few genuine expressions I had ever seen on his face. 'Manny Borque,' he said. 'The caterer.'

'The one from MTV?'

'Yeah, that's right,' Vince said. 'The guy that's won all the awards, and he's been written up in *Gourmet* magazine.'

'Oh, yes,' I said, stalling for time in the hope that some brilliant flash of inspiration would hit to help me dodge this terrible fate. 'The award-winning caterer.'

'Dexter, this guy is big. He could make your whole wedding.'

'Well, Vince, I think that's terrific, but—'

'Listen,' he said, with an air of firm command that I had never heard from him before, 'you said

66

you would talk to Rita about this and let her decide.'

'I said that?'

'Yes, you did. And I am not going to let you throw away a wonderful opportunity like this, not when it's something that I know Rita would really love to have.'

I wasn't sure how he could be so positive about that. After all, I was actually engaged to the woman, and I had no idea what sort of caterer might fill her with shock and awe. But I didn't think this was the time to ask him how he knew what Rita would and would not love. Then again, a man who dressed up as Carmen Miranda for Halloween might very well have a keener insight than mine into my fiancée's innermost culinary desires.

'Well,' I said, at last deciding that procrastinating long enough to escape was the best answer, 'in that case, I'll go home and talk to Rita about it.'

'Do that,' he said. And he did not storm out, but if there had been a door to slam, he might have slammed it.

I finished tidying up and trundled on out into the evening traffic. On the way home a middle-aged man in a Toyota SUV got right behind me and started honking the horn for some reason. After five or six blocks he pulled around me and, as he flipped me off, juked his steering wheel slightly to frighten me into running up on the sidewalk. Although I admired his spirit and would have loved to oblige him, I stayed on the road. There is never any point in trying to make sense of the way Miami drivers go about getting from one place to another. You just have to relax and enjoy the violence – and of course, that part was never a problem for me. So I smiled and waved, and he stomped on his accelerator and disappeared into traffic at about sixty miles per hour over the speed limit.

Normally I find the chaotic mayhem of the evening drive home to be the perfect way to end the day. Seeing all the anger and lust to kill relaxes me, makes me feel at one with my hometown and its spritely inhabitants. But tonight I found it difficult to summon up any good cheer at all. I never for a moment thought it could ever happen, but I was worried.

Worse still, I didn't know what I was actually worried about, only that the Dark Passenger had used the silent treatment on me at a scene of creative homicide. This had never happened, and I could only believe that something unusual and possibly Dexter-threatening had caused it now. But what? And how could I be sure, when I didn't really know the first thing about the Passenger itself, except that it had always been there to offer happy insight and commentary. We had seen burned bodies before, and pottery aplenty, with never a twitch or a tweet. Was it the combination? Or something specific to these two bodies? Or was it entirely coincidental and had nothing whatever to do with what we had seen?

The more I thought about it, the less I knew, but the traffic swirled around me in its soothing homicidal patterns, and by the time I got to Rita's house I had almost convinced myself that there was really nothing to worry about.

Rita, Cody, and Astor were already home when I got there. Rita worked much closer to the house than I did, and the kids were in an after-school program at a nearby park, so they had all been waiting for at least half an hour for the opportunity to torment me out of my hard-won peace of mind.

'It was on the news,' Astor whispered as I opened the door, and Cody nodded and said, 'Gross,' in his soft, hoarse voice.

'What was on the news?' I said, struggling to get past them and into the house without trampling on them.

'You *burned* them!' Astor hissed at me, and Cody looked at me with a complete lack of expression that somehow conveyed disapproval.

'I what? Who did I—'

'Those two people they found at the college,' she said. 'We don't want to learn *that*,' she added emphatically, and Cody nodded again.

'At the – you mean at the university? I didn't—'

'A university is a college,' Astor said with the underlined certainty of a ten-year-old girl. 'And we think burning is just gross.'

It began to dawn on me what they had seen on the news – a report from the scene where I had spent my morning collecting dry-roasted blood samples from two charred bodies. And somehow, merely because they knew I had been out to play the other night, they had decided that this was how I had spent my time. Even without the Dark Passenger's strange retreat, I agreed that it was completely gross, and I found it highly annoying that they thought I was capable of something like that. 'Listen,' I said sternly, 'that was not—'

'Dexter? Is that you?' Rita yodeled from the kitchen.

'I'm not sure,' I called back. 'Let me check my wallet.'

Rita bustled in beaming and before I could protect myself she wrapped herself around me, apparently intent on squeezing hard enough to interfere with my breathing. 'Hi, handsome,' she said. 'How was your day?'

'Gross,' muttered Astor.

'Absolutely wonderful,' I said, fighting for breath. 'Plenty of corpses for everybody today. And I got to use my cotton swabs, too.'

Rita made a face. 'Ugh. That's – I don't know if you should talk like that around the children. What if they get bad dreams?'

If I had been a completely honest person, I would have told her that her children were far more likely to cause someone else bad dreams than to get them, but since I am not hampered by any need to tell the truth, I just patted her and said, 'They hear worse than that on the cartoons every day. Isn't that right, kids?'

'No,' said Cody softly, and I looked at him with surprise. He rarely said anything, and to have him not only speak but actually contradict me was disturbing. In fact, the whole day was turning out to be wildly askew, from the panicked flight of the Dark Passenger this morning and continuing on through Vince's catering tirade – and now this. What in the name of all that is dark and dreadful was going on? Was my aura out of balance? Had the moons of Jupiter aligned against me in Sagittarius?

'Cody,' I said. And I do hope some hurt showed in my voice. 'You're not going to have bad dreams about this, are you?'

'He doesn't have bad dreams,' Astor said, as if everyone who was not severely mentally challenged ought to know that. 'He doesn't have any dreams at *all*.'

'Good to know,' I said, since I almost never dream myself, either, and for some reason it seemed important to have as much as possible in common with Cody. But Rita was having none of it.

'Really, Astor, don't be silly,' she said. 'Of course Cody has dreams. Everybody has dreams.'

'I don't,' Cody insisted. Now he was not only standing up to both of us, he was practically breaking his own record for chattiness at the same time. And even though I didn't have a heart, except for circulatory purposes, I felt an affection for him and wanted to come down on his side.

'Good for you,' I said. 'Stick with it. Dreams are very overrated. Interfere with getting a good night's sleep.'

'Dexter, really,' Rita said. 'I don't think we should encourage this.'

'Of course we should,' I said, winking at Cody. 'He's showing fire, spunk, and imagination.'

'Am not,' he said, and I absolutely marveled at his verbal outpouring.

'Of course you're not,' I said to him, lowering my voice. 'But we have to say stuff like that to your mom, or she gets worried.'

'For Pete's sake,' Rita said. 'I give up with you two. Run outside and play, kids.'

'We wanna play with Dexter,' Astor pouted.

'I'll be along in a few minutes,' I said.

'You better,' she said darkly. They vanished down the hall toward the back door, and as they left I took a deep breath, happy that the vicious and unwarranted attacks against me were over for now. Of course, I should have known better.

'Come in here,' Rita said, and she led me by the hand to the sofa. 'Vince called a little while ago,' she said as we settled onto the cushions.

'Did he?' I said, and a sudden thrill of danger ripped through me at the idea of what he might have said to Rita. 'What did he say?'

She shook her head. 'He was very mysterious. He said to let him know as soon as we had talked it over. And when I asked him talked what over he wouldn't say. He just said you would tell me.'

I barely managed to stop myself from the unthinkable conversational blunder of saying, 'Did he?' again. In my defense, I have to admit that my brain was whirling, not only with the panicked notion that I had to flee to some place of safety but also with the thought that before I fled I needed to find time to visit Vince with my little bag of toys. But before I could mentally choose the correct blade, Rita went on.

'Honestly, Dexter, you're very lucky to have a friend like Vince. He really does take his duties as best man seriously, and he has wonderful taste.'

'Wonderfully expensive, too,' I said – and perhaps I was still recovering from my near-gaffe with almost repeating 'Did he?' but I knew the moment it was out of my mouth that it was absolutely the wrong thing to say. And sure enough, Rita lit up like a Christmas tree.

'Really?' she said. 'Well, I suppose he would, after all. I mean, it most often goes together, doesn't it? You really do get what you pay for, usually.'

'Yes, but it's a question of how much you have to pay,' I said.

'How much for what?' Rita said, and there it was. I was stuck.

'Well,' I said, 'Vince has this crazy idea that we should hire this South Beach caterer, a very pricey guy who does a lot of celebrity events and things.'

Rita clapped her hands under her chin and looked radiantly happy. 'Not Manny Borqu!' she cried. 'Vince knows Manny Borque?'

Of course it was all over right there, but Dauntless Dexter does not go down without a fight, no matter how feeble. 'Did I mention that he's very expensive?' I said hopefully.

'Oh, Dexter, you can't worry about money at a time like this,' she said.

'I can too. I am.'

'Not if there's a chance to get Manny Borque,' she said, and there was a surprisingly strong note in her voice that I had never heard before except when she was angry with Cody and Astor.

'Yes, but Rita,' I said, 'it doesn't make sense to spend a ton of money just for the caterer.'

'Sense has nothing to do with it,' she said, and I admit that I agreed with her there. 'If we can get Manny Borque to cater our wedding, we'd be crazy not to do it.'

'But,' I said, and there I stopped, because beyond the fact that it seemed idiotic to pay a king's ransom for crackers with endives hand-painted with rhubarb juice and sculpted to look like Jennifer Lopez, I could not think of any other objection. I mean, wasn't that enough?

Apparently not. 'Dexter,' she said. 'How many times will we get married?' And to my great credit I was still alert enough to clamp down on the urge to say, 'At least twice, in your case,' which I think was probably very wise.

I quickly changed course, diving straight into tactics learned from pretending to be human for so many years. 'Rita,' I said, 'the important part of the wedding is when I slip the ring on your finger. I don't care what we eat afterward.'

'That's so sweet,' she said. 'Then you don't mind if we hire Manny Borque?'

Once again I found myself losing an argument before I even knew which side I was on. I became aware of a dryness in my mouth – caused, no doubt, by the fact that my mouth was hanging open as my brain struggled to make sense of what had just happened, and then to find something clever to say to get things back onto dry land.

But it was far too late. 'I'll call Vince back,' she said, and she leaned over to give me a kiss on the cheek. 'Oh, this is so exciting. Thank you, Dexter.'

Well, after all, isn't marriage about compromise?

CHAPTER 7

Naturally enough, Manny Borque lived in South Beach. He was on the top floor of one of the new high-rise buildings that spring up around Miami like mushrooms after a heavy rain. This one sat on what was once a deserted beach where Harry used to take Debs and me beachcombing early on Saturday mornings. We would find old life preservers, mysterious wooden chunks of some unfortunate boat, lobster-pot buoys, pieces of fishnet, and on one thrilling morning, an exceedingly dead human body rolling in the surf. It was a treasured boyhood memory, and I resented extremely that someone had built this shiny flimsy tower on the site.

The next morning at ten Vince and I left work together and drove over to the horrible new building that had replaced the scene of my youthful joy. I rode the elevator to the top in silence, watching Vince fidget and blink. Why he should be nervous about facing someone who sculpted chopped liver for a living, I don't know, but he clearly was. A drop of sweat rolled down his cheek and he swallowed convulsively, twice.

'He's a caterer, Vince,' I told him. 'He isn't dangerous. He can't even revoke your library card.'

Vince looked at me and swallowed again. 'He's got a real temper,' he said. 'He can be very demanding.'

'Well, then,' I said with great good cheer, 'let's go find somebody else more reasonable.'

He set his jaw like a man facing a firing squad and shook his head. 'No,' he said bravely, 'we're going to go through with this.' And the elevator door slid open, right on cue. He squared his shoulders, nodded, and said, 'Come on.'

We went down to the end of the hall, and Vince stopped in front of the last door. He took a deep breath, raised his fist, and, after a slight hesitation, knocked on the door. After a long moment in which nothing happened, he looked at me and blinked, his hand still raised. 'Maybe,' he said.

The door opened. 'Hello Vic!' the thing in the doorway warbled, and Vince responded by blushing and stammering, 'I only hi.' Then he shifted his weight from one foot to the other, stammered something that sounded like, 'Er wellah,' and took a half step backward.

It was a remarkable and thoroughly engaging performance, and I was not the only one who seemed to enjoy it. The manikin who had answered the door watched with a smile that suggested he might enjoy being in the audience for any kind of human suffering, and he let Vince squirm for several long moments before he finally said, 'Well come *in*!'

Manny Borque, if this was really him and not some strange hologram from *Star Wars*, stood a full five foot six inches tall, from the bottom of his embroidered high-heeled silver boots to the top of his dyed orange head. His hair was cut short, except for black bangs which parted on his forehead like a swallow's tail and draped down over a pair of enormous rhinestone-studded eyeglasses. He was dressed in a long, bright-red dashiki, and apparently nothing else, and it swirled around him as he stepped back from the door to motion us in, and then walked in rapid little steps toward a huge picture window that looked out on the water.

'Come over here and we'll have a little talk,' he said, sidestepping a pedestal holding an enormous object that looked like a giant ball of animal vomit dipped in plastic and spray-painted with Day-Glo graffiti. He led the way to a glass table by the window, around which sat four things that were probably supposed to be chairs but could easily have been mistaken for bronze camel saddles welded onto stilts. 'Sit,' he said, with an expansive wave of his hand, and I took the chair-thing nearest the window. Vince hesitated for a moment, then sat next to me, and Manny hopped up onto the seat directly across from him. 'Well,' he said. 'How have you been, Vic? Would you like some coffee?' and without waiting for an answer he swiveled his head to his left and called, 'Eduardo!'

Beside me Vince took a ragged breath, but before

he could do anything with it Manny whipped back around and faced me. 'And *you* must be the blushing bridegroom!' he said.

'Dexter Morgan,' I said. 'But I'm not a very good blusher.'

'Oh, well, I think Vic is doing enough for both of you,' he said. And sure enough, Vince obligingly turned just as scarlet as his complexion would allow him to do. Since I was still more than a little peeved at being subjected to this ordeal, I decided not to come to his aid by offering Manny a withering remark, or even correcting him on the subject of Vince's actual identity as 'Vince,' not 'Vic.' I was sure he knew the right name quite well and was simply tormenting Vince. And that was fine with me: let Vince squirm – it served him right for going over my head to Rita and getting me into this.

Eduardo bustled in holding a vintage Fiestaware coffee service in several bright colors, balanced on a clear plastic tray. He was a stocky young man about twice the size of Manny, and he, too, seemed very anxious to please the little troll. He set a yellow cup in front of Manny, and then moved to put the blue one in front of Vince when he was stopped by Manny, who laid a finger on his arm.

'Eduardo,' he said in a silky voice, and the boy froze. 'Yellow? Don't we remember? Manny gets the blue cup.'

Eduardo practically fell over himself grinding into reverse, nearly dropping the tray in his haste

79

to remove the offensive yellow coffee cup and replace it with the proper blue one.

'Thank you, Eduardo,' Manny said, and Eduardo paused for a moment, apparently to see if Manny really meant it or if he had done something else wrong. But Manny just patted him on the arm and said, 'Serve our guests now, please,' and Eduardo nodded and moved around the table.

As it turned out, I got the yellow cup, which was fine with me, although I wondered if it meant that they didn't like me. When he had poured the coffee, Eduardo hustled back to the kitchen and re-turned with a small plate holding half a dozen *pastelitos*. And although they were not, in fact, shaped like Jennifer Lopez's derriere, they might as well have been. They looked like little cream-filled porcupines – dark brown lumps bristling with quills that were either chocolate or taken from a sea anemone. The center was open, revealing a blob of orange-colored custardy-type stuff, and each blob had a dab of green, blue, or brown on top.

Eduardo put the plate in the center of the table, and we all just looked at it for a moment. Manny seemed to be admiring them, and Vince was apparently feeling some kind of religious awe, as he swallowed a few more times and made a sound that may have been a gasp. For my part, I wasn't sure if we were supposed to eat the things or use them for some bizarre, bloody Aztec ritual, so I simply studied the plate, hoping for a clue.

It was finally provided by Vince. 'My God,' he blurted.

Manny nodded. 'They're wonderful, aren't they?' he said. 'But so-o-o-o last year.' He picked one up, the one with the blue top, and gazed at it with a kind of aloof fondness. 'The color palette really got tired, and that horrible old hotel over by Indian Creek started to copy them. Still,' he said with a shrug, and he popped it into his mouth. I was glad to see that it didn't seem to cause any major bleeding. 'One does grow fond of one's own little tricks.' He turned and winked at Eduardo. 'Perhaps a little too fond sometimes.' Eduardo went pale and fled to the kitchen, and Manny turned back to us with a huge crocodile smile. 'Do try one, though, won't you?'

'I'm afraid to bite one,' Vince said. 'They're so *perfect*.'

'And I'm afraid they might bite back,' I said.

Manny showed off a few dozen teeth. 'If I could teach them that,' he said, 'I would never be lonely.' He nudged the plate in my direction. 'Go ahead,' he said.

'Would you serve these at my wedding?' I asked, thinking perhaps somebody ought to find some kind of point in all this.

Vince elbowed me, hard, but it was apparently too late. Manny's eyes had narrowed to little slits, although his impressive dental work was still on display. 'I do not serve,' he said. 'I *present*. And I *present* whatever seems best to *me*.'

'Shouldn't I have some idea ahead of time what that might be?' I asked, 'I mean, suppose the bride is allergic to wasabi-basted arugula aspic?'

Manny tightened his fists so hard I could hear the knuckles creak. For a moment I had a small thrill of hope at the thought that I might have clevered myself out of a caterer. But then Manny relaxed and laughed. 'I like your friend, Vic,' he said. 'He's very brave.'

Vince favored us both with a smile and started to breathe again, and Manny began to doodle with a pad and paper, and that is how I ended up with the great Manny Borque agreeing to cater my wedding at the special discounted price of only $250 a plate.

It seemed a bit high. But after all, I had been specifically instructed not to worry about money. I was sure Rita would think of some way to make it work, perhaps by inviting only two or three people. In any case, I didn't get a great deal of time to worry about mere finances, as my cell phone began its happy little dirge almost immediately, and when I answered I heard Deborah say, without even attempting to match my cheery hello, 'I need you here right away.'

'I'm awfully busy with some very important canapés,' I told her. 'Can I borrow twenty thousand dollars?'

She made a noise in her throat and said, 'I don't have time for bullshit, Dexter. The twenty-four hours starts in twenty minutes and I need you there for it.' It was the custom in Homicide to convene everybody involved in a case twenty-four hours after the work began, to make sure everything was organized and everyone was on the same page. And Debs obviously felt that I had some kind of shrewd insight to offer – very thoughtful really, but untrue. With the Dark Passenger apparently still on hiatus, I didn't think the great light of insight would come flooding in anytime soon.

'Debs, I really don't have any thought at all on this one,' I said.

'Just get over here,' she told me, and hung up.

CHAPTER 8

The traffic on the 836 was backed up for half a mile right after the 395 from Miami Beach poured into it. We inched forward between exits until we could see the problem: a truckload of watermelons had emptied out onto the highway. There was a streak of red-and-green goo six inches thick across the road, dotted with a sprinkling of cars in various stages of destruction. An ambulance went past on the shoulder, followed by a procession of cars driven by people too important to wait in a traffic jam. Horns honked all along the line, people yelled and waved their fists, and somewhere ahead I heard a single gunshot. It was good to be back to normal life.

By the time we fought our way through the traffic and onto surface streets, we had lost fifteen minutes and it took another fifteen to get back to work. Vince and I rode the elevator to the second floor in silence, but as the doors slid open and we stepped out, he stopped me. 'You're doing the right thing,' he said.

'Yes, I am,' I said. 'But if I don't do it quickly Deborah will kill me.'

84

He grabbed my arm. 'I mean about Manny,' he said. 'You're going to love what he does. It will really make a difference.'

I was already aware that it would really make a difference in my bank account, but beyond that I still didn't see the point. Would everyone truly have a better time if they were served a series of apparently alien objects of uncertain use and origin instead of cold cuts? There is a great deal I don't understand about human beings, but this really seemed to take the cake – assuming we would have a cake at all, which in my opinion was not a sure thing.

There was one thing I understood quite well, however, and that was Deborah's attitude about punctuality. It was handed down from our father, and it said that lateness was disrespect and there were no excuses. So I pried Vince's fingers off my arm and shook his hand. 'I'm sure we're all going to be very happy with the food,' I said.

He held on to my hand. 'It's more than that,' he said.

'Vince—'

'You're making a statement about the rest of your life,' he said. 'A really *good* statement, that your and Rita's life together—'

'My life is in danger if I don't go, Vince,' I said.

'I'm really happy about this,' he said, and it was so unnerving to see him display an apparently authentic emotion that there was actually a little bit of panic to my flight away from him and down the hall to the conference room.

The room was full, since this was becoming a somewhat high-profile case after the hysterical news stories of the evening before about two young women found burned and headless. Deborah glared at me as I slipped in and stood by the door, and I gave her what I hoped was a disarming smile. She cut off the speaker, one of the patrolmen who had been first on the scene.

'All right,' she said. 'We know we're not going to find the heads on the scene.'

I had thought that my late entrance and Deborah's vicious glare at me would certainly win the award for Most Dramatic Entrance, but I was dead wrong. Because just as Debs tried to get the meeting moving again, I was upstaged as thoroughly as a candle at a fire-bombing.

'Come on, people,' Sergeant Sister said. 'Let's have some ideas about this.'

'We could drag the lake,' Camilla Figg said. She was a thirty-five-year-old forensics geek and usually kept quiet, and it was rather surprising to hear her speak. Apparently some people preferred it that way, because a thin, intense cop named Corrigan jumped on her right away.

'Bullshit,' said Corrigan. 'Heads float.'

'They don't float – they're solid bone,' Camilla insisted.

'Some of 'em are,' Corrigan said, and he got his little laugh.

Deborah frowned, and was about to step in with an authoritative word or two, when a noise in the hall stopped her.

CLUMP.

Not that loud, but somehow it commanded all the attention there was in the room.

CLUMP.

Closer, a little louder, for all the world approaching us now like something from a low-budget horror movie . . .

CLUMP.

For some reason I couldn't hope to explain, everyone in the room seemed to hold their breath and turn slowly toward the door. And if only because I wanted to fit in, I began to turn for a peek into the hall myself, when I was stopped by the smallest possible interior tickle, just a hint of a twitch, and so I closed my eyes and listened. *Hello?* I said mentally, and after a very short pause there was a small, slightly hesitant sound, almost a clearing of the mental throat, and then—

Somebody in the room muttered, 'Holy sweet Jesus,' with the kind of reverent horror that was always guaranteed to pique my interest, and the small not-quite-sound within purred just a bit and then subsided. I opened my eyes.

I can only say that I had been so happy to feel the Passenger stirring in the dark backseat that for a moment I had tuned out everything around me. This is always a dangerous slip, especially for artificial humans like me, and the point was driven home with an absolutely stunning impact when I opened my eyes.

It was indeed low-budget horror, *Night of the Living Dead*, but in the flesh and not a movie at all, because standing in the doorway, just to my right, staring at me, was a man who was really supposed to be dead.

Sergeant Doakes.

Doakes had never liked me. He seemed to be the only cop on the entire force who suspected that I might be what, in fact, I was. I had always thought he could see through my disguise because he was somewhat the same thing himself, a cold killer. He had tried and failed to prove that I was guilty of almost anything, and that failure had also failed to endear me to him.

The last time I had seen Doakes the paramedics had been loading him into an ambulance. He had been unconscious, partly as the result of the shock and pain of having his tongue, feet, and hands removed by a very talented amateur surgeon who thought Doakes had done him wrong. Now it was true that I had gently encouraged that notion with the part-time doctor, but I had at least had the decency to persuade Doakes first to go along with the plan, in order to catch the inhuman fiend. And I had also very nearly saved Doakes at considerable risk to my own precious and irreplaceable life and limbs. I hadn't quite pulled off the dashing and timely rescue I'm sure Doakes had hoped for, but I had tried, and it was really and truly not my fault that he had been more dead than alive when they hauled him away.

So I didn't think it was asking too much for some small acknowledgment of the great hazard I had exposed myself to on his behalf. I didn't need flowers, or a medal, or even a box of chocolates, but perhaps something along the lines of a hearty clap on the back and a murmured, 'Thanks, old fellow.' Of course he would have some trouble murmuring coherently without a tongue, and the clap on the back with one of his new metal hands could prove painful, but he might at least try. Was that so unreasonable?

Apparently it was. Doakes stared at me as if he was the hungriest dog in the world and I was the very last steak. I had thought that he used to look at me with enough venom to lay low the entire endangered species list. But that had been the gentle laughter of a tousle-haired child on a sunny day compared to the way he was looking at me now. And I knew what had made the Dark Passenger clear its throat – it had been the scent of a familiar predator. I felt the slow flex of interior wings, coming back to full roaring life, rising to the challenge in Doakes's eyes. And behind those dark eyes his own inner monster snarled and spat at mine. We stood like that for a long moment, on the outside simply staring but on the inside two predatory shadows screeching out a challenge.

Someone was speaking, but the world had narrowed to just me and Doakes and the two black shadows inside us calling for battle, and neither one of us heard a word, just an annoying drone in the background.

Deborah's voice cut through the fog at last. 'Sergeant Doakes,' she said, somewhat forcefully. Finally Doakes turned to face her and the spell was broken. And feeling somewhat smug in the power – joy and bliss! – of the Passenger, as well as the petty victory of having Doakes turn away first, I faded into the wallpaper, taking a small step back to survey the leftovers of my once-mighty nemesis.

Sergeant Doakes still held the department record for bench press, but he did not look like he would defend his record anytime soon. He was gaunt and, except for the fire smoldering behind his eyes, he looked almost weak. He stood stiffly on his two prosthetic feet, his arms hanging straight down by his sides, with gleaming silver things that looked like a complicated kind of vise grip protruding from each wrist.

I could hear the others in the room breathing, but aside from that there was not a sound. Everyone simply stared at the thing that had once been Doakes, and he stared at Deborah, who licked her lips, apparently trying to think of something coherent to say, and finally came up with, 'Have a seat, Doakes. Um. I'll bring you up to date?'

Doakes looked at her for a long moment. Then he turned awkwardly around, glared at me, and clumped out of the room, his strange, measured footsteps echoing down the hall until they were gone.

On the whole, cops don't like to give the impression that they are ever impressed or intimidated, so it was several seconds before anyone risked giving away any unwanted emotion by breathing again. Naturally enough, it was Deborah who finally broke the unnatural silence. 'All right,' she said, and suddenly everyone was clearing their throats and shifting in their chairs.

'All right,' she repeated, 'so we won't find the heads at the scene.'

'Heads don't float,' Camilla Figg insisted scornfully, and we were back to where we had been before the sudden semi-appearance of Sergeant Doakes. And they droned on for another ten minutes or so, tirelessly fighting crime by arguing about who was supposed to fill out the paperwork, when we were rudely interrupted once again by the door beside me swinging open.

'Sorry to interrupt,' Captain Matthews said. 'I've got some – ah – really great news, I think.' He looked around the room frowning, which even I could have told him was not the proper face for delivering great news. 'It's, uh, ahem. Sergeant Doakes has come back, and he's, uh – It's important for you people to realize that he's been badly, uh, damaged. He has only a couple of years left before he's eligible for full pension, so the lawyers, ah – we thought, under the circumstances, um . . .'

He trailed off and looked around the room. 'Did somebody already tell you people?'

'Sergeant Doakes was just here,' Deborah said.

'Oh,' Matthews said. 'Well, then—' He shrugged. 'That's fine. All right then. I'll let you get on with the meeting then. Anything to report?'

'No real progress yet, Captain,' Deborah said.

'Well, I'm sure you'll get this thing wrapped up before the press – I mean, in a timely fashion.'

'Yes, sir,' she said.

'All right then,' he said again. And he looked around the room once, squared his shoulders, and left the room.

'Heads don't float,' somebody else said, and a small snort of laughter went around the room.

'Jesus,' Deborah said. 'Can we focus on this, please? We got two bodies here.'

And more to come, I thought, and the Dark Passenger quivered slightly, as if trying very bravely not to run away, but that was all, and I thought no more about it.

CHAPTER 9

I don't dream. I mean, I'm sure that at some point during my normal sleep, there must be images and fragments of nonsense parading through my subconscious. After all, they tell me that happens with everyone. But I never seem to remember dreams if I do have them, which they tell me happens to nobody at all. So I assume that I do not dream.

It was therefore something of a shock to discover myself late that night, cradled in Rita's arms, shouting something I could not quite hear; just the echo of my own strangled voice coming back at me out of the cottony dark, and Rita's cool hand on my forehead, her voice murmuring, 'All right, sweetheart, I won't leave you.'

'Thank you very much,' I said in a croaking voice. I cleared my throat and sat up.

'You had a bad dream,' she told me.

'Really? What was it?' I still didn't remember anything but my shouting and a vague sense of danger crowding in on me, and me all alone.

'I don't know,' Rita said. 'You were shouting, "Come back! Don't leave me alone."' She cleared her throat. 'Dexter – I know you're feeling some stress about our wedding—'

'Not at all,' I said.

'But I want you to know. I will never leave you.' She reached for my hand again. 'This is forever with me, big man. I am holding on to you.' She scooted over and put her head on my shoulder. 'Don't worry. I won't ever leave you, Dexter.'

Even though I lack experience with dreams, I was fairly sure that my subconscious was not terribly worried about Rita leaving me. I mean, it hadn't occurred to me that she would, which was not really a sign of trust on my part. I just hadn't thought about it. Truly, I had no idea why she wanted to hang on to me in the first place, so any hypothetical leave-taking was just as mysterious.

No, this was my subconscious. If it was crying out in pain at the threat of abandonment, I knew exactly what it feared losing: the Dark Passenger. My bosom buddy, my constant companion on my journey through life's sorrows and sharp pleasures. That was the fear behind the dream: losing the thing that had been so very much a part of me, had actually defined me, for my whole life.

When it scuttled into hiding at the university crime scene it had clearly shaken me badly, more than I had known at the time. The sudden and very scary reappearance of 65 percent of Sergeant Doakes supplied the sense of danger, and the rest was easy. My subconscious had kicked in and supplied a dream on the subject.

Perfectly clear – Psych 101, a textbook case, nothing to worry about.

So why was I still worrying?

Because the Passenger had never even flinched before, and I still didn't know why it had chosen now. Was Rita right about the stress of the approaching wedding? Or was there really something about the two headless bodies by the university lake that just plain scared the Dark out of me?

I didn't know – and, since it seemed like Rita's ideas about comforting me had begun to take a more active turn, it did not look like I was going to find out anytime soon.

'Come here, baby,' Rita whispered.

And after all, there really isn't any place to run in a queen-size bed, is there? The next morning found Deborah obsessed with finding the missing heads from the two bodies at the university. Somehow word had leaked out to the press that the department was interested in finding a couple of skulls that had wandered away. This was Miami, and I really would have thought that a missing head would get less press coverage than a traffic tie-up on I-95, but something about the fact that there were two of them, and that they apparently belonged to young women, created quite a stir. Captain Matthews was a man who knew the value of being mentioned in the press, but even he was not pleased with the note of surly hysteria that attached itself to this story.

And so pressure came down on all of us from

above; from the captain to Deborah, who wasted no time passing it on down to the rest of us. Vince Masuoka became convinced that he could provide Deborah with the key to the whole matter by finding out which bizarre religious sect was responsible. This led to him sticking his head in my door that morning and, without any kind of warning, giving me his best fake smile and saying, firmly and distinctly, 'Candomblé.'

'Shame on you,' I said. 'This is no time for that kind of language.'

'Ha,' he said, with his terrible artificial laugh. 'But it is, I'm sure of it. Candomblé is like Santeria, but it's Brazilian.'

'Vince, I have no reason to doubt you on that. My question is, what the hell are you talking about?'

He came two steps into the room in a kind of prance, as if his body wanted to take off and he couldn't quite fight it down. 'They have a thing about animal heads in some of their rituals,' he said. 'It's on the Internet.'

'Really,' I said. 'Does it say on the Internet that this Brazilian thing barbecues humans, cuts off their heads, and replaces them with ceramic bulls' heads?'

Vince wilted just a bit. 'No,' he admitted, and he raised his eyebrows hopefully. 'But they use animals.'

'How do they use them, Vince?' I asked.

'Well,' he said, and he looked around my little

96

room, possibly for another topic of conversation. 'Sometimes they, you know, offer a part to the gods, and then they eat the rest.'

'Vince,' I said, 'are you suggesting that some-body ate the missing heads?'

'No,' he said, turning sullen, almost like Cody and Astor might have done. 'But they could have.'

'It would be very crunchy, wouldn't it?'

'All right,' he said, exceedingly sulky now. 'I'm just trying to help.' And he stalked away, without even a small fake smile.

But the chaos had only begun. As my unwanted trip to dreamland indicated, I was already under enough pressure without the added strain of a rampaging sister. But only a few minutes later, my small oasis of peace was ripped asunder once again, this time by Deborah, who came roaring into my office as if pursued by killer bees.

'Come on,' she snarled at me.

'Come on where?' I asked, quite a reasonable question, I thought, but you would have thought I had asked her to shave her head and paint her skull blue.

'Just get in gear, and come on!' she said, so I came on and followed her down to the parking lot and into her car.

'I swear to God,' she fumed as she hammered her car through the traffic, 'I have never seen Matthews this pissed before. And now it's my fault!' She banged on the horn for emphasis and swerved in front of a van that said PALMVIEW

97

ASSISTED LIVING on the side. 'All because some asshole leaked the heads to the press.'

'Well, Debs,' I said, with all the reasonable soothing I could muster, 'I'm sure the heads will turn up.'

'You're goddamned right they will,' she said, narrowly missing a fat man on a bicycle that had huge saddlebags stuffed with scrap metal. 'Because I am going to find out which cult the son of a bitch belongs to, and then I'm going to nail the bastard.'

I paused in mid-soothe. Apparently my dear demented sister, just like Vince, had gotten hold of the idea that finding the appropriate alternative religion would yield a killer. 'Ah, all right,' I said. 'And where are we going to do that?'

She slid the car out onto Biscayne Boulevard and into a parking space at the curb without answering, and got out of the car. And so I found myself patiently following her into the Centre for Inner Enhancement, a clearinghouse for all the wonderfully useful things that have the words 'holistic,' 'herbal,' or 'aura' in them.

The Centre was a small and shabby building in an area of Biscayne Boulevard that had apparently been designated by treaty as a kind of reservation for prostitutes and crack dealers. There were enormous bars on the storefront windows and more of them on the door, which was locked. Deborah pounded on it and after a moment it gave an annoying buzz. She pushed, and finally it clicked and swung open.

We stepped in. A suffocating cloud of sickly sweet incense rolled over me, and I could tell that my inner enhancement had begun with a complete overhaul of my lungs. Through the smoke I could dimly see a large yellow silk banner hung along one wall that stated WE ARE ALL ONE. It did not say one of what. A recording played softly, the sound of someone who seemed to be fighting off an overdose of downers by occasionally ringing a series of small bells. A waterfall murmured in the background and I am sure that my spirit would have soared, if only I had one. Since I didn't, I found the whole thing just a bit irritating.

But of course, we weren't here for pleasure, or even inner enhancement. And Sergeant Sister was, of course, all business all the time. She marched over to the counter, where there stood a middle-aged woman wearing a full-length tie-dyed dress that seemed to be made out of old crepe paper. Her graying hair radiated out from her head in a kind of random mess, and she was frowning. Of course, it may have been a beatific frown of enlightenment.

'Can I help you?' she said, in a gravelly voice that seemed to suggest we were beyond help.

Deborah held up her badge. Before she could say anything the woman reached over and plucked it from her hand.

'All right, Sergeant Morgan,' the woman said, tossing the badge on the counter. 'It seems to be genuine.'

'Couldn't you just read her aura and tell that?' I suggested. Neither of them seemed ready to give that remark any of the appreciation it deserved, so I shrugged and listened as Deborah began her grueling interrogation.

'I'd like to ask you a few questions, please,' Deborah said, leaning forward to scoop up her badge.

'About what?' the woman demanded. She frowned even harder, and Deborah frowned back, and it began to look like we were in for a good old-fashioned country frown-off, with the winner getting free Botox treatments to freeze her face into a permanent scowl.

'There have been some murders,' Deborah said, and the woman shrugged.

'What's that got to do with me?' she asked.

I applauded her reasoning, but after all, I did have to play for my own team now and then.

'It's because we are all one,' I said. 'That's the basis of all police work.'

She swiveled her frown to me and blinked at me in a very aggressive way. 'Who the hell are you?' she demanded. 'Lemme see your badge.'

'I'm her backup,' I said. 'In case she's attacked by bad karma.'

The woman snorted, but at least she didn't shoot me. 'Cops in this town,' she said, 'are *swimming* in bad karma. I was at the FTAA rally, and I know what you people are like.'

'Maybe we are,' Deborah said, 'but the other

side is even worse, so could you just answer a few questions?'

The woman looked back at Deborah, still frowning, and shrugged. 'Okay, I guess,' she said. 'But I don't see how I can help. And I call my lawyer if you get out of line.'

'Fine,' Deborah said. 'We're looking for a lead on somebody who might be connected to a local alternative religious group that has a thing for bulls.'

For a second I thought the woman was almost going to smile, but she caught herself just in time. 'Bulls? Jesus, who doesn't have a thing for bulls. Goes all the way back to Sumer, Crete, all those old cradle-of-civilization places. Lots of people have worshipped them. I mean, aside from the huge cocks, they're very powerful.'

If the woman thought she was going to embarrass Deborah, she didn't know as much about Miami cops as she thought she did. My sister didn't even blink. 'Do you know of any group in particular that might be local?' Debs said.

'I dunno,' she said. 'What kind of group?'

'Candomblé?' I said, briefly grateful to Vince for supplying a word. 'Palo Mayombe? Or even Wicca.'

'The Spanish stuff, you gotta go over to Eleggua on Eighth Street. I wouldn't know about that. We sell some stuff to the Wicca people, but I'm not gonna tell you about it without a warrant. Anyway, they don't do bulls.' She snorted. 'They just stand around in the Everglades naked, waiting for their power to come.'

101

'Is there anybody else?' Debs insisted.

The woman just shook her head. 'I dunno. I mean, I know about most of the groups in town, and nothing like that I can think of.' She shrugged. 'Maybe the Druids, they got a spring event coming up. They used to do human sacrifice.'

Deborah frowned even more intensely. 'When was that?' she said.

This time the woman actually did smile, just a little, with one corner of her mouth. 'About two thousand years ago. You're a little late on that one, Sherlock.'

'Is there anything else you can think of that might help?' Deborah asked.

The woman shook her head. 'Help with what? There might be some psycho loser out there who read Aleister Crowley and lives on a dairy farm. How would I know?'

Deborah looked at her for a moment, as if trying to decide if she had been offensive enough to arrest, and then apparently decided against it. 'Thank you for your time,' she said, and she flipped her business card on the counter. 'If you think of anything that might be helpful, please give me a call.'

'Yeah, sure,' the woman said, without even glancing at the card. Deborah glared at her for a moment longer and then stalked out of the door. The woman stared at me and I smiled.

'I really like vegetables,' I said. Then I gave the woman the peace sign and followed my sister out.

'That was a stupid idea,' Deborah said as we walked rapidly back to her car.

'Oh, I wouldn't say that,' I said. And it was quite true, I wouldn't say it. Of course, it really was a stupid idea, but to say so would have been to invite one of Debs's vicious arm punches. 'If nothing else, we eliminated a few possibilities.'

'Sure,' she said sourly. 'We know it probably wasn't a bunch of naked fruits, unless they did it two thousand years ago.'

She did have a point, but I see it as my job in life to help all those around me maintain a positive attitude. 'It's still progress,' I said. 'Shall we check out the place on Eighth Street? I'll translate for you.' In spite of being a Miami native, Debs had whimsically insisted on studying French in school, and she could barely order lunch in Spanish.

She shook her head. 'Waste of time,' she said. 'I'll tell Angel to ask around, but it won't go anywhere.'

And she was right. Angel came back late that afternoon with a very nice candle that had a prayer to St Jude on it in Spanish, but other than that his trip to the place on Eighth Street was a waste of time, just as Debs had predicted.

We were left with nothing, except two bodies, no heads, and a very bad feeling.

That was about to change.

CHAPTER 10

The next day passed uneventfully and we got no closer to any kind of hint about the two murders at the university. And life being the kind of lopsided, grotesque affair that it is, Deborah blamed our lack of progress on me. She was still convinced that I had special magical powers and had used them to see straight into the dark heart of the killings, and that I was keeping vital information from her for petty personal reasons.

Very flattering, but totally untrue. The only insight I had into the matter was that something about it had scared the Dark Passenger, and I did not want that to happen again. I decided to stay away from the case, and since there was almost no blood work involved, that should have been easy in a logical and well-ordered universe.

But alas, we do not live in any such place. Our universe is ruled by random whim, inhabited by people who laugh at logic. At the moment, the chief of these was my sister. Late the following morning she cornered me in my little cubbyhole and dragged me away to lunch with her boyfriend,

Kyle Chutsky. I had no real objections to Chutsky, other than his permanent attitude of knowing the real truth about everything. Aside from that, he was just as pleasant and amiable as a cold killer can be, and it would have been hypocritical for me to object to his personality on those grounds. And since he seemed to make my sister happy, I did not object on any other grounds, either.

So off I went to lunch, since in the first place she was my sister, and in the second, the mighty machine that is my body needs almost constant fuel.

The fuel it craves most often is a *medianoche* sandwich, usually with a side of fried *plátanos* and a *mamey* milk shake. I don't know why this simple, hearty meal plays such a transcendent chord on the strings of my being, but there is nothing else like it. Prepared properly, it takes me as close to ecstasy as I can get. And no one prepares it quite as properly as Café Relampago, a storefront place not far from police HQ, where the Morgans have been eating since time out of mind. It was so good even Deborah's perpetual grumpiness couldn't spoil it.

'Goodamn it!' she said to me through a mouthful of sandwich. It was certainly far from a novel phrase coming from her, but she said it with a viciousness that left me lightly spattered with bread crumbs. I took a sip of my excellent *batido de mamey* and waited for her to expand on her argument, but instead she simply said it again. 'Goddamn it!'

'You're covering up your feelings again,' I said. 'But because I am your brother, I can tell something is bothering you.'

Chutsky snorted as he sawed at his Cuban steak. 'No shit,' he said. He was about to say more, but the fork clamped in his prosthetic left hand slipped sideways. 'Goddamn it,' he said, and I realized that they had a great deal more in common than I had thought. Deborah leaned over and helped him straighten the fork. 'Thanks,' he said, and shoveled in a large bite of the pounded-flat meat.

'There, you see?' I said brightly. 'All you needed was something to take your mind off your own problems.'

We were sitting at a table where we had probably eaten a hundred times. But Deborah was rarely troubled by sentiment; she straightened up and slapped the battered Formica tabletop hard enough to make the sugar bowl jump.

'I want to know who talked to that asshole Rick Sangre!' she said. Sangre was a local TV reporter who believed that the gorier a story was, the more vital it was for people to have a free press that could fill them in on as many gruesome details as possible. From the tone of her voice, Deborah was apparently convinced that Rick was my new best friend.

'Well, it wasn't me,' I said. 'And I don't think it was Doakes.'

'Ouch,' said Chutsky.

'*And*,' she said, 'I want to find those fucking heads!'

'I don't have them, either,' I said. 'Did you check lost and found?'

'You know something, Dexter,' she said. 'Come on, why are you holding out on me?'

Chutsky looked up and swallowed. 'Why should he know something you don't?' he asked. 'Was there a lot of spatter?'

'No spatter at all,' I said. 'The bodies were cooked, nice and dry.'

Chutsky nodded and managed to scoop some rice and beans onto his fork. 'You're a sick bastard, aren't you?'

'He's worse than sick,' Deborah said. 'He's holding out something.'

'Oh,' Chutsky said through a mouthful of food. 'Is this his amateur profiling thing again?' It was a small fiction; we had told him that my hobby was actually analytical, rather than hands-on.

'It is,' Deborah said. 'And he won't tell me what he's figured out.'

'It might be hard to believe, Sis, but I know nothing about this. Just . . .' I shrugged, but she was already pouncing.

'What! Come on, please?'

I hesitated again. There was no good way to tell her that the Dark Passenger had reacted to these killings in a brand-new and totally unsettling way. 'I just get a feeling,' I said. 'Something is a little off with this one.'

She snorted. 'Two burned headless bodies, and

107

he says something's a little off. Didn't you used to be smart?'

I took a bite of my sandwich as Deborah frittered away her precious eating time by frowning. 'Have you identified the bodies yet?' I asked.

'Come on, Dexter. There's no heads, so we got no dental records. The bodies were burned, so there's no fingerprints. Shit, we don't even know what color their hair was. What do you want me to do?'

'I could probably help, you know,' Chutsky said. He speared a chunk of fried *maduras* and popped it into his mouth. 'I have a few resources I can call on.'

'I don't need your help,' she said and he shrugged.

'You take Dexter's help,' he said.

'That's different.'

'How is that different?' he asked, and it seemed like a reasonable question.

'Because he gives me *help*,' she said. 'You want to solve it for me.'

They locked eyes and didn't speak for a long moment. I'd seen them do it before, and it was eerily reminiscent of the nonverbal conversations Cody and Astor had. It was nice to see them so clearly welded together as a couple, even though it reminded me that I had a wedding of my own to worry about, complete with an apparently insane high-class caterer. Happily, just before I could begin to gnash my teeth, Debs broke the eerie silence.

'I won't be one of those women who needs help,' she said.

'But I can get you information that you can't get,' he said, putting his good hand on her arm.

'Like what?' I asked him. I'll admit I had been curious for some time about what Chutsky was, or had been before his accidental amputations. I knew that he had worked for some government agency which he referred to as the OGA, but I still didn't know what that stood for.

He turned to face me obligingly. 'I have friends and sources in a lot of places,' he said. 'Something like this might have left some kind of trail some-where else, and I could call around and find out.'

'You mean call your buddies at the OGA?' I said.

He smiled. 'Something like that,' he said.

'For Christ's sake, Dexter,' Deborah said. 'OGA just means other government agency. There's no such agency, it's an in-joke.'

'Nice to be in at last,' I said. 'And you can still get access to their files?'

He shrugged. 'Technically I'm on convalescent leave,' he said.

'From doing what?' I asked.

He gave me a mechanical smile. 'You don't really want to know,' he said. 'The point is, they haven't decided yet whether I'm any fucking good anymore.' He looked at the fork clamped in his steel hand, turning his arm over to see it move. 'Shit,' he said.

And because I could feel that one of those awkward moments was upon us, I did what I could to move things back onto a sociable footing. 'Didn't you find anything at the kiln?' I asked. 'Some kind of jewelry or something?'

'What the fuck is that?' she said.

'The kiln,' I said. 'Where the bodies were burned.'

'Haven't you been paying attention? We haven't found where the bodies were burned.'

'Oh,' I said. 'I assumed it was done right there on campus, in the ceramic studio.'

By the suddenly frozen look on her face, I realized that either she was experiencing massive indigestion or she did not know about the ceramic studio. 'It's just half a mile from the lake where the bodies were found,' I said. 'You know, the kiln. Where they make pottery?'

Deborah stared at me for a moment longer, and then jumped up from the table. I thought it was a wonderfully creative and dramatic way to end a conversation, and it took a moment before I could do more than blink after her.

'I guess she didn't know about that,' Chutsky said.

'That's my first guess,' I said. 'Shall we follow?'

He shrugged and speared the last chunk of his steak. 'I'm gonna have some flan, and a *cafecita*. Then I'll get a cab, since I'm not allowed to help,' he said. He scooped up some rice and beans and nodded at me. 'You go ahead, unless you want to walk back to work.'

I did not, in fact, have any desire to walk back to work. On the other hand, I still had almost half a milk shake and I did not want to leave that, either. I stood up and followed, but I softened the blow by grabbing the uneaten half of Deborah's sandwich and taking it with me as I lurched out the door after her.

Soon we were rolling through the front gate of the university campus. Deborah spent part of the ride talking on the radio and arranging for people to meet us at the kilns, and the rest of the ride clenching her teeth and muttering.

We turned left after the gate and headed down the winding road that leads to the ceramic and pottery area. I had taken a class in pottery there my junior year in an effort to widen my horizons, and found out that I was good at making very regular-looking vases but not terribly successful at creating original works of art, at least not in that medium. In my own area, I flatter myself that I can be creative, as I had recently demonstrated with Zander.

Angel-no-relation was already there, carefully and patiently looking through the first kiln for any sign of practically anything. Deborah went over and squatted beside him, leaving me alone with the last three bites of her sandwich. I took the first bite. A crowd was beginning to gather by the yellow tape. Perhaps they were hoping to see something too terrible to look at: I never knew why they gathered like that, but they always did.

Deborah was now on the ground beside Angel, who had his head inside the first of the kilns. This would probably be a long wait.

I had barely put the last bite of sandwich into my mouth when I became aware that I was being watched. Of course I was being *looked at*, anyone on the business side of the yellow tape always was. But I was also being *watched* – the Dark Passenger clamored at me that I had been singled out by something with an unhealthy interest in special wonderful me, and I did not like the feeling. As I swallowed the last of the sandwich and turned to look, the whisper inside me hissed something that sounded like confusion . . . and then settled into silence.

And as it did I felt again the wave of panicked nausea and the bright yellow edge of blindness, and I stumbled for a moment, all my senses crying out that there was danger but my ability to do anything about it completely gone. It lasted only a second. I fought my way back to the surface and looked harder at my surroundings – nothing had changed. A handful of people stood looking on, the sun shone brightly, and a gentle wind riffled through the trees. Just another perfect Miami day, but somewhere in paradise the snake had reared its head. I closed my eyes and listened hard, hoping for some hint about the nature of the menace, but there was nothing but the echo of clawed feet scrabbling away.

I opened my eyes and looked around again.

There was a crowd of perhaps fifteen people pretending not to be fascinated by the hope of seeing gore, but none of them stood out in any way. None of them were skulking or staring evilly or trying to hide a bazooka under their shirt. In any normal time, I might have expected my Passenger to see a dark shadow around an obvious predator, but there was no such assistance now. As far as I could see, nothing sinister loomed in the crowd. So what had set off the Passenger's fire alarm? I knew so little about it; it was just there, a presence filled with wicked amusement and sharp suggestions. It had never showed confusion before, not until it saw the two bodies by the lake. And now it was repeating its vague uncertainty, only half a mile from the first spot.

Was it something in the water? Or was there some connection to the two burned bodies here at the kilns?

I wandered over to where Deborah and Angel-no-relation were working. They didn't seem to be finding anything particularly alarming, and there were no jolts of panic roiling out from the kiln to the place where the Dark Passenger was hiding.

If this second retreat was not caused by something in front of me, then what caused it? What if it was some kind of weird interior erosion? Perhaps my new status of impending husband-hood and stepfather-ness was overwhelming my Passenger. Was I becoming too nice to be a proper host? This would be a fate worse than someone else's death.

I became aware that I was standing just inside the yellow crime-scene tape, and a large form was lurking in front of me.

'Uh, hello?' he said. He was a big, well-muscled young specimen with longish, lank hair and the look of someone who believed in breathing through the mouth.

'How can I help you, citizen?' I said.

'Are you, uh, you know,' he said, 'like a cop?'

'A little bit like one,' I said.

He nodded and thought about that for a moment, looking around behind him as if there might be something there he could eat. On the back of his neck was one of those unfortunate tattoos that have become so popular, an Oriental character of some kind. It probably spelled out 'slow learner.' He rubbed the tattoo as if he could hear me thinking about it, then turned around to me and blurted out, 'I was wondering about Jessica.'

'Of course you were,' I said. 'Who wouldn't?'

'Do they know if it's her?' he said. 'I'm like her boyfriend.'

The young gentleman had now succeeded in grabbing my professional attention. 'Is Jessica missing?' I asked him.

He nodded. 'She was, you know, supposed to work out with me? Like every morning, you know. Around the track, and then some abs. But yesterday she doesn't show up. And same thing this morning. So I started thinking, uh . . .' He

114

frowned, apparently at the effort of thinking, and his speech trickled to a halt.

'What's your name?' I asked him.

'Kurt,' he said. 'Kurt Wagner. What's yours?'

'Dexter,' I said. 'Wait here a moment, Kurt.' I hurried over to Deborah before the strain of trying to think again proved too much for the boy.

'Deborah,' I said, 'we may have a small break here.'

'Well, it isn't your damned pot ovens,' she snarled. 'They're too small for a body.'

'No,' I said. 'But the young man over there is missing a girlfriend.'

Her head jerked up and she rose to standing almost on point like a hunting dog. She stared over at Jessica's like-boyfriend, who looked back and shifted his weight from foot to foot. 'About fucking time,' she said, and she headed for him.

I looked at Angel. He shrugged and stood up. For a moment, he looked like he was going to say something. But then he shook his head, dusted off his hands, and followed Debs over to hear what Kurt had to say, leaving me really and truly all alone with my dark thoughts.

Just to watch; sometimes it was enough. Of course there was the sure knowledge that watching would lead inevitably to the surging heat and glorious flow of blood, the overwhelming pulse of emotions throbbing from the victims, the rising music of the ordered madness as the sacrifice flew into

115

wonderful death . . . All this would come. For now, it was enough for the Watcher to observe and soak in the delicious feeling of anonymous, ultimate power. He could feel the unease of the other. That unease would grow, rising through the musical range into fear, then panic, and at last full-fledged terror. It would all come in good time.

The Watcher saw the other scanning the crowd, flailing about for some clue to the source of the blossoming sense of danger that tickled at his senses. He would find nothing, of course. Not yet. Not until *he* determined that the time was right. Not until *he* had run the other into dull mindless panic. Only then would he stop watching and begin to take final action.

And until then – it was time to let the other begin to hear the music of fear.

CHAPTER 11

Her name was Jessica Ortega. She was a junior and lived in one of the nearby residence halls. We got the room number from Kurt, and Deborah left Angel to wait at the kilns until a squad car arrived to take over.

I never knew why they were called residence halls instead of dormitories. Perhaps it was because they looked so much like hotels nowadays. There were no ivy-covered walls bedecking the hallowed halls here, the lobby had lots of glass and potted plants, and the halls were carpeted and clean and new-looking.

We stopped at the door of Jessica's room. It had a small, neat card taped at eye level that read ARIEL GOLDMAN & JESSICA ORTEGA. Below that in smaller print it said INTOXICANTS REQUIRED FOR ENTRY. Someone had underlined 'Entry' and scrawled below it YOU THINK?

Deborah raised an eyebrow at me. 'Party girls,' she said.

'Somebody has to do it,' I said.

She snorted and knocked on the door. There

was no answer, and Debs waited a full three seconds before knocking again, much harder.

I heard a door open behind me and turned to see a reed-thin girl with short blond hair and glasses looking at us. 'They're not here,' she said with clear disapproval. 'For like a couple of days. First quiet I've had all semester.'

'Do you know where they went?' Deborah asked her.

The girl rolled her eyes. 'Must be a major kegger somewhere,' she said.

'When was the last time you saw them?' Deborah said.

The girl shrugged. 'With those two it's not seeing them, it's hearing them. Loud music and laughing all night, okay? Major pain in the butt for somebody who actually studies and goes to class.'

She shook her head, and her short hair riffled around her face. 'I mean, please.'

'So when was the last time you heard them?' I asked her.

She looked at me. 'Are you like cops or something? What did they do now?'

'What have they done before?' Debs asked.

She sighed. 'Parking tickets. I mean, lots of them. DUI once. Hey, I don't want to sound like I'm ratting them out or something.'

'Would you say it's unusual for them to be away like this?' I said.

'What's unusual is if they show up to class. I don't know how they pass anything. I mean,' she gave us half a smirk, 'I can probably *guess* how they pass, but . . .' She shrugged. She did not share her guess with us, unless you counted her smirk.

'What classes do they have together?' Deborah asked.

The girl shrugged again and shook her head. 'You'd have to check like the registrar,' she said.

It was not a terribly long walk to see like the registrar, especially at the pace Deborah set. I managed to keep up with her and still have enough breath to ask her a pointed question or two. 'Why does it matter what classes they had together?'

Deborah made an impatient gesture with her hand. 'If that girl is right, Jessica and her roommate—'

'Ariel Goldman,' I said.

'Right. So if they are trading sex for good grades, that makes me want to talk to their professors.'

On the surface, that made sense. Sex is one of the most common motives for murder, which does not seem to fit in with the fact that it is often rumored to be connected to love. But there was one small thing that did not make sense. 'Why would a professor cook them and cut off their heads like that? Why not just strangle them and throw the bodies in a Dumpster?'

Deborah shook her head. 'It's not important how he did it. What matters is whether he did.'

'All right,' I said. 'And how sure are we that these two are the victims?'

'Sure enough to talk to their teachers,' she said. 'It's a start.'

We arrived at the registrar's office, and when Debs flashed her badge we were shown right in. But it was a good thirty minutes of Deborah pacing and muttering while I went through the computer records with the registrar's assistant. Jessica and Ariel were, in fact, in several of the same classes, and I printed out the names, office numbers, and home addresses of the professors. Deborah glanced at the list and nodded. 'These two guys, Bukovich and Halpern, have office hours now,' she said. 'We can start with them.'

Once again Deborah and I stepped out into the muggy day for a stroll across campus.

'It's nice to be back on campus, isn't it?' I said, in my always futile effort to keep a pleasant flow of conversation going.

Deborah snorted. 'What's nice is if we can get a definite ID on the bodies and maybe move a little closer to grabbing the guy who did this.'

I did not think that identifying the bodies would really move us closer to identifying the killer, but I have been wrong before, and in any case police work is powered by routine and custom, and one of the proud traditions of our craft was that it was good to know the dead person's name. So I willingly trundled along with Deborah to the office building where the two professors waited.

Professor Halpern's office was on the ground floor just inside the main entrance, and before the outer door could swing shut Debs was already knocking on his door. There was no answer. Deborah tried the knob. It was locked, so she thumped on the door again with the same lack of result.

A man came strolling along the hall and stopped at the office next door, glancing at us with a raised eyebrow. 'Looking for Jerry Halpern?' he said. 'I don't think he's in today.'

'Do you know where he is?' Deborah said.

He gave us a slight smile. 'I imagine he's home, at his apartment, since he's not here. Why do you ask?'

Debs pulled out her badge and showed it to him. He didn't seem impressed. 'I see,' he said. 'Does this have anything to do with the two dead bodies across campus?'

'Do you have any reason to think it would?' Deborah said.

'N-n-n-o,' he said, 'not really.'

Deborah looked at him and waited, but he didn't say anything more. 'Can I ask your name, sir?' she said at last.

'I'm Dr Wilkins,' he said, nodding toward the door he stood in front of. 'This is my office.'

'Dr Wilkins,' Deborah said. 'Could you please tell me what your remark about Professor Halpern means?'

Wilkins pursed his lips. 'Well,' he said, hesitating, 'Jerry's a nice enough guy, but if this is a murder investigation . . .' He let it hang for a moment. So did Deborah. 'Well,' he said at last, 'I believe it was last Wednesday I heard a disturbance in his office.' He shook his head. 'These walls are not terribly thick.'

'What kind of disturbance?' Deborah asked.

'Shouting,' he said. 'Perhaps a little bit of scuffling? Anyway, I peeked out the door and saw a student, a young woman, stagger out of Halpern's office and run away. She was, ah – her shirt was torn.'

'By any chance did you recognize the young woman?' Deborah asked.

'Yes,' Wilkins said. 'I had her in a class last semester. Her name is Ariel Goldman. Lovely girl, but not much of a student.'

Deborah glanced at me and I nodded encouragingly. 'Do you think Halpern tried to force himself on Ariel Goldman?' Deborah said.

Wilkins tilted his head to one side and held up one hand. 'I couldn't say for sure. That's what it looked like, though.'

Deborah looked at Wilkins, but he didn't have anything to add, so she nodded and said, 'Thank you, Dr Wilkins. You've been very helpful.'

'I hope so,' he said, and he turned away to open his door and enter his office. Debs was already looking at the printout from the registrar.

'Helpern lives just a mile or so away,' she said, and headed toward the doors. Once again I found myself hurrying to catch up to her.

'Which theory are we giving up?' I asked her. 'The one that says Ariel tried to seduce Halpern? Or that he tried to rape her?'

'We're not giving up anything,' she said. 'Not until we talk to Halpern.'

CHAPTER 12

Dr Jerry Halpern had an apartment less than two miles from the campus, in a two-story building that had probably been very nice forty years ago. He answered the door right away when Deborah knocked, blinking at us as the sunlight hit his face. He was in his mid-thirties and thin without looking fit, and he hadn't shaved for a few days. 'Yes?' he said, in a querulous tone of voice that would have been just right for an eighty-year-old scholar. He cleared his throat and tried again. 'What is it?'

Deborah held up her badge and said, 'Can we come in, please?'

Halpern goggled at the badge and seemed to sag a little. 'I didn't – what, what – why come in?' he said.

'We'd like to ask you a few questions,' Deborah said. 'About Ariel Goldman.'

Halpern fainted.

I don't get to see my sister look surprised very often – her control is too good. So it was quite rewarding to see her with her mouth hanging open as Halpern hit the floor. I manufactured a suitable matching expression, and bent over to feel for a pulse.

'His heart is still going,' I said.

'Let's get him inside,' Deborah said, and I dragged him into the apartment.

The apartment was probably not as small as it looked, but the walls were lined with overflowing bookshelves, a worktable stacked high with papers and more books. In the small remaining space there was a battered, mean-looking two-seater couch and an overstuffed chair with a lamp behind it. I managed to heft Halpern up and onto the couch, which creaked and sank alarmingly under him.

I stood up and nearly bumped into Deborah, who was already hovering and glaring down at Halpern. 'You better wait for him to wake up before you intimidate him,' I said.

'This son of a bitch knows something,' she said. 'Why else would he flop like that?'

'Poor nutrition?' I said.

'Wake him up,' she said.

I looked at her to see if she was kidding, but of course she was dead serious. 'What would you suggest?' I said. 'I forgot to bring smelling salts.'

'We can't just stand around and wait,' she said. And she leaned forward as if she was going to shake him, or maybe punch him in the nose.

Happily for Halpern, however, he chose just that moment to return to consciousness. His eyes fluttered a few times and then stayed open, and as

124

he looked up at us his whole body tensed. 'What do you want?' he said.

'Promise not to faint again?' I said. Deborah elbowed me aside.

'Ariel Goldman,' she said.

'Oh God,' Halpern whined. 'I knew this would happen.'

'You were right,' I said.

'You have to believe me,' he said, struggling to sit up. 'I didn't do it.'

'All right,' Debs said. 'Then who did it?'

'She did it herself,' he said.

Deborah looked at me, perhaps to see if I could tell her why Halpern was so clearly insane. Unfortunately, I could not, so she looked back at him. 'She did it herself,' she said, her voice loaded with cop doubt.

'Yes,' he insisted. 'She wanted to make it look like I did it, so I would have to give her a good grade.'

'She burned herself,' Deborah said, very deliberately, like she was talking to a three-year-old. 'And then she cut off her own head. So you would give her a good grade.'

'I hope you gave her at least a B for all that work,' I said.

Halpern goggled at us, his jaw hanging open and jerking spasmodically, as if it was trying to close but lacked a tendon. 'Wha,' he said finally. 'What are you talking about?'

'Ariel Goldman,' Debs said. 'And her roommate,

Jessica Ortega. Burned to death. Heads cut off. What can you tell us about that, Jerry?'

Halpern twitched and didn't say anything for a long time. 'I, I – are they dead?' he finally whispered.

'Jerry,' said Deborah, 'their heads were cut off. What do you think?'

I watched with great interest as Halpern's face slid through a whole variety of expressions portraying different kinds of blankness, and finally, when the nickel dropped, it settled on the unhinged-jaw look again. 'You – you think I – you can't—'

'I'm afraid I can, Jerry,' Deborah said. 'Unless you can tell me why I shouldn't.'

'But that's – I would never,' he said.

'Somebody did,' I said.

'Yes, but, my God,' he said.

'Jerry,' Deborah said, 'what did you think we wanted to ask about?'

'The, the rape,' he said. 'When I didn't rape her.'

Somewhere there's a world where everything makes sense, but obviously we were not in it. 'When you *didn't* rape her,' Deborah said.

'Yes, that's – she wanted me to, ah,' he said.

'She wanted you to rape her?' I said.

'She, she,' he said, and he began to blush. 'She offered me, um, sex. For a good grade,' he said, looking at the floor. 'And I refused.'

'And that's when she asked you to rape her?' I said. Deborah hit me with her elbow.

'So you told her no, Jerry?' Deborah said. 'A pretty girl like that?'

'That's when she, um,' he said, 'she said she'd get an A one way or the other. And she reached up and ripped her own shirt and then started to scream.' He gulped, but he didn't look up.

'Go on,' said Deborah.

'And she waved at me,' he said, holding up his hand and waving bye-bye. 'And then she ran out into the hall.' He looked up at last. 'I'm up for tenure this year,' he said. 'If word about something like this got around, my career would be over.'

'I understand,' Debs said very understandingly. 'So you killed her to save your career.'

'What? No!' he sputtered. 'I didn't kill her!'

'Then who did, Jerry?' Deborah asked.

'I don't know!' he said, and he sounded almost petulant, as if we had accused him of taking the last cookie. Deborah just stared at him, and he stared back, flicking his gaze from her to me and back again. 'I didn't!' he insisted.

'I'd like to believe you, Jerry,' Deborah said. 'But it's really not up to me.'

'What do you mean?' he said.

'I'm going to have to ask you to come with me,' she said.

'You're *arresting* me?' he said.

'I'm taking you down to the station to answer a few questions, that's all,' she said reassuringly.

'Oh my God,' he said. 'You're arresting me. That's – no. No.'

'Let's do this the easy way, Professor,' Deborah said. 'We don't need the handcuffs, do we?'

He looked at her for a long moment and then suddenly jumped up to his feet and ran for the door. But unfortunately for him and his masterful escape plan, he had to get past me, and Dexter is widely and justly praised for his lightning reflexes. I stuck a foot in the professor's way, and he went down onto his face and slid head-first into the door.

'Ow,' he said.

I smiled at Deborah. 'I guess you do need the cuffs,' I said.

CHAPTER 13

I am not really paranoid. I don't believe that I am surrounded by mysterious enemies who seek to trap me, torture me, kill me. Of course, I know very well that if I allow my disguise to slip and reveal me for what I am, then this entire society will join together in calling for my slow and painful death, but this is not paranoia – this is a calm, clearheaded view of consensus reality, and I am not frightened by it. I simply try to be careful so it doesn't happen.

But a very large piece of my carefulness had always been listening to the subtle whisperings of the Dark Passenger, and it was still being strangely shy about sharing its thoughts. And so I faced a new and unsettling inner silence, and that made me very edgy, sending out a little ripple of uneasiness. It had started with that feeling of being watched, even stalked, at the kilns. And then, as we drove back to headquarters, I could not shake the idea that a car seemed to be following us. Was it really? Did it have sinister intent? And if so, was it toward me or Deborah, or was it just random Miami driver spookiness?

I watched the car, a white Toyota Avalon, in the side mirror. It stayed with us all the way until Deborah turned into the parking lot, and then it simply drove by without slowing or the driver appearing to stare, but I could not lose my ridiculous notion that it had indeed been following us. Still, I could not be sure unless the Passenger told me, which it did not – it merely gave a sort of sibilant throat-clearing, and so it seemed beyond stupid for me to say anything to Deborah about it.

And then later, when I came out of the building to my own car to go home for the night, I had the same feeling once again, that someone or something was watching – but it was a *feeling*. Not a warning, not an interior whisper from the shadows, not a get-ready flutter of invisible black wings – a *feeling*. And that made me nervous. When the Passenger speaks, I listen. I act. But it was not speaking now, merely squirming, and I had no idea what to do given that message. So in the absence of any more definite idea, I kept my eyes on my rearview mirror as I headed south for home.

Was this what it was like to be human? To walk through life with the perpetual feeling that you were meat on the hoof, stumbling down the game trail with tigers sniffing at your heels? If so, it would certainly go a long way toward explaining human behavior. As a predator myself, I knew very well the powerful feeling of strolling in disguise through the herds of potential prey, knowing that

I could at any moment cut one of them from the herd. But without any word from the Passenger I did not merely blend in; I was actually part of the herd, vulnerable. I was prey, and I did not like it. It made me a great deal more watchful.

And when I came down off the expressway, my watching revealed a white Toyota Avalon following me.

Of course there are lots of white Toyota Avalons in the world. After all, the Japanese lost the war and that gives them the right to dominate our car market. And certainly many of these Avalons could reasonably be heading for home along the same crowded route I took. Logically speaking, there are only so many directions in which to go, and it made perfect sense for a white Avalon to go in any one of them. And it was not logical to assume that anyone would want to follow me. What had I done? I mean, that anybody could prove?

And so it was perfectly illogical of me to feel that I was being followed, which does not explain why I made a sudden right turn off U.S. 1 and down a side street.

It also does not explain why the white Avalon followed.

The car kept well back, as any predator would do to avoid spooking its chosen prey – or as any normal person might do if they just happened to take the same turn by coincidence. And so with the same uncharacteristic lack of logic, I zigged again, this time to the left, down a small residential street.

A moment later the other car followed.

As mentioned, Dashing Dexter does not know the meaning of fear. That would have to mean that the roaring thump of my heart, the parching of my mouth, and the sweat pouring out of my hands was no more than massive uneasiness.

I did not enjoy the feeling. I was no longer the Knight of the Knife. My blade and my armor were in some subbasement of the castle, and I was on the field of battle without them, a suddenly soft and tasty victim, and for no reason I could name I was sure that something had my scent in its ravening nostrils.

I turned right again – and noticed only as I went by it the sign that said NO OUTLET.

I had turned down a cul-de-sac. I was trapped.

For some reason, I slowed and waited for the other car to follow me. I suppose I just wanted to be sure that the white Avalon was really there. It was. I continued to the end of the street, where the road widened into a small circle for turning around. There were no cars in the driveway of the house at the top of the circle. I pulled in and stopped my engine, waiting, amazed by the crashing of my heart and my inability to do anything more than sit and wait for the inevitable teeth and claws of whatever was chasing me.

The white car came closer. It slowed as it reached the circle, slowed as it approached me . . .

And it went past me, around the circle, back up the street, and into the Miami sunset.

I watched it go, and as its taillights disappeared around the corner I suddenly remembered how to breathe. I took advantage of this rediscovered knowledge, and it felt very good. Once I had restored my oxygen content and settled back into being me, I began to feel like a very stupid me. What, after all, had really happened? A car had appeared to follow me. Then it had gone away. There were a million reasons why it might have taken the same route as I had, most of them summed up by the one word: coincidence. And then, as poor Dithering Dexter sat sweating in his seat, what had the big bad car done? It had gone past. It had not paused to stare, snarl, or throw a hand grenade. It had just gone by and left me in a puddle of my own absurd fear.

There was a knock on my window and I bumped my head on the ceiling of the car.

I turned to look. A middle-aged man with a mustache and bad acne scars was bent over, looking in at me. I had not noticed him until now, further proof that I was alone and unprotected.

I rolled down the window. 'Can I help you with something?' the man said.

'No, thank you,' I told him, somewhat puzzled as to what help he thought he could offer. But he did not keep me guessing.

'You're in my driveway,' he said.

'Oh,' I said, and it occurred to me that I probably was and some explanation was called for. 'I was looking for Vinny,' I said. Not brilliant, but serviceable under the circumstances.

'You got the wrong place,' the man said with a certain mean triumph that almost cheered me up again.

'Sorry,' I said. I rolled up the window and backed out of the driveway, and the man stood and watched me go, presumably to be sure that I did not suddenly leap out and attack him with a machete. In just a few moments I was back in the bloodthirsty chaos of U.S. 1. And as the routine violence of the traffic closed around me like a warm blanket, I felt myself slowly sinking back into myself. Home again, behind the crumbling walls of Castle Dexter, vacant basement and all.

I had never felt so stupid – which is to say, I felt as close to being a real human being as it was possible for me to feel. What on earth had I been thinking? I had not, in truth, been thinking at all, merely reacting to a bizarre twitch of panic. It was all too ridiculous, too patently human and laughable, if only I had been a real human who could really laugh. Ah, well. At least I was really ridiculous.

I drove the last few miles thinking of insulting things to call myself for such a timid overreaction, and by the time I pulled into the driveway at Rita's house I was thoroughly soaked in my own abuse, which made me feel much better. I got out of my car with something very close to a real smile on my face, generated by my joy in the true depth of Dexter Dunderhead. And as I took one step away from the car, half turning to head for the front door, a car drove slowly by.

A white Avalon, of course.

If there is such a thing in the world as justice, then this was surely one of the moments it had arranged just for me. Because many times I had enjoyed the sight of a person standing with their mouth hanging open, completely incapacitated by surprise and fear, and now here was Dexter in the same stupid pose. Frozen in place, unable to move even to wipe away my own drool, I watched the car drive slowly past, and the only thought I could muster was that I must look very, very stupid.

Naturally, I would have looked a great deal stupider if whoever was in the white car did anything other than drive past slowly, but happily for the many people who know and love me – at least two, including myself – the car went by without pausing. For a moment I thought I could see a face looking at me from the driver's seat. And then he accelerated, turning slightly away into the middle of the street so that the light gleamed for an instant off the silver bull's head Toyota emblem, and the car was gone.

And I could think of nothing at all to do but eventually close my mouth, scratch my head, and stumble into the house.

There was a soft but very deep and powerful drumbeat, and gladness surged up, born from relief and anticipation of what was to come. And then the horns sounded, and it was very close now, only a matter of moments before it came and then everything would begin and happen again at last, and as the gladness rose into a melody that climbed until it seemed to come from everywhere, I felt my feet taking me to where the voices promised bliss, filling everything with that joy that was on the way, that overwhelming fulfillment that would lift us into ecstasy—

And I woke up with my heart pounding and a sense of relief that was certainly not justified and that I did not understand at all. Because it was not merely the relief of a sip of water when you are thirsty or resting when you are tired, although it was those things, too.

But – far beyond puzzling, deep into disturbing – it was also the relief that comes after one of my playdates with the wicked; the relief that says you have fulfilled the deep longings of your innermost self and now you may relax and be content for a while.

And this could not be. It was impossible for me to feel that most private and personal of feelings while lying in bed asleep.

I looked at the clock beside the bed: five minutes past midnight, not a time for Dexter to be up and about, not on a night when he had planned only to sleep.

On the other side of the bed Rita snored softly, twitching slightly like a dog who dreamed of chasing a rabbit.

And on my side of the bed, one terribly confused Dexter. Something had come into my dreamless night and made waves across the tranquil sea of my soulless sleep. I did not know what that something was, but it had made me very glad for no reason I could name, and I did not like that at all. My moonlight hobby made me glad in my own emotionless way and that was all. Nothing else had ever been allowed into that corner of the dark subbasement of Dexter. That was the way I preferred it to be. I had my own small, well-guarded space inside, marked off and locked down, where I felt my own particular joy – on those nights only and at no other time. Nothing else made sense for me.

So what had invaded, knocked down the door, and flooded the cellar with this uncalled-for and unwanted feeling? What in all the world possibly *could* climb in with such overwhelming ease?

I lay down, determined to go back to sleep and prove to myself that I was still in charge here, that nothing had happened, and certainly wouldn't happen again. This was Dexterland, and I was king. Nothing else was permitted inside. And I closed my eyes and turned for confirmation to the voice of authority on the inside, the inarguable master of the shadowy corners of all that is me, the Dark Passenger, and I waited for it to agree, to hiss a soothing phrase to put the jangling music and its geyser of feeling into its place, out of the dark and into the outside. And I waited for it to say something, anything, and it did not.

And I poked at it with a very hard and irritated thought, thinking, *Wake up! Show some teeth in there!*

And it said nothing.

I hurried myself into all the corners of me, hollering with increasing concern, calling for the Passenger, but the place it had been was empty, swept clean, room to rent. It was gone as if it had never been there at all.

In the place where it used to be I could still hear an echo of the music, bouncing off the hard walls of an unfurnished apartment and rolling through a sudden, very painful emptiness.

The Dark Passenger was gone.

CHAPTER 14

I spent the next day in a lather of uncertainty, hoping that the Passenger would return and somehow sure it would not. And as the day wore on, this dreary certainty got bigger and bleaker.

There was a large, brittle empty spot inside me and I had no real way to think about it or cope with the gaping hollowness that I had never felt before. I would certainly not claim to feel anguish, which has always struck me as a very self-indulgent thing to experience, but I was acutely uneasy and I lived the whole day in a thick syrup of anxious dread.

Where had my Passenger gone, and why? Would it come back? And these questions pulled me inevitably down into even more alarming speculation: What was the Passenger and why had it come to me in the first place?

It was somewhat sobering to realize just how deeply I had defined myself by something that was not actually me – or was it? Perhaps the entire persona of the Dark Passenger was no more than the sick construct of a damaged mind, a web spun to catch tiny glimmers of filtered reality and protect me from the awful truth of what I really am. It was possible. I am well aware of basic psychology, and I have assumed for quite some time that I am somewhere off the charts. That's fine with me; I get along very well without any shred of normal humanity to my name.

Or I had until now. But suddenly I was all alone in there, and things did not seem quite so hard-edged and certain. And for the first time, I truly needed to know.

Of course, few jobs provide paid time off for introspection, even on a topic as important as missing Dark Passengers. No, Dexter must still lift that bale. Especially with Deborah cracking the whip.

Happily, it was mostly routine. I spent the morning with my fellow geeks combing through Halpern's apartment for some concrete residue of his guilt. Even more happily, the evidence was so abundant that very little real work was necessary.

In the back of his closet we found a sock with several drops of blood on it. Under the couch was a white canvas shoe with a matching blotch on top. In a plastic bag in the bathroom was a pair of pants with a singed cuff and even more blood, small dots of spray that had been heat-hardened.

It was probably a good thing that there was so much of it out in the open, because Dexter was truly not his usual bright and eager self today. I found myself drifting in an anxious gray mist and wondering if the Passenger was coming home, only to jerk back to the present, standing there in the closet holding a dirty, blood-spattered sock. If any real investigation had been necessary, I am not sure I could have performed up to my own very high standards.

Luckily, it wasn't needed. I had never before seen such an outpouring of clear and obvious evidence from somebody who had, after all, had several days to clean up. When I indulge in my own little hobby I am neat and tidy and forensic- ally innocent within minutes; Halpern had let several days go by without taking even the most elementary precautions. It was almost too easy, and when we checked his car I dropped the 'almost.' Clearly displayed on the central armrest of the front seat was a thumbprint of dried blood.

Of course, it was still possible that our lab work would show that it was chicken blood, and Halpern had simply been indulging in an inno- cent pastime, perhaps as an amateur poultry butcher. Somehow, I doubted it. It seemed over- whelmingly clear that Halpern had done something truly unkind to someone.

And yet, the small nagging thought tugged at me that it was, just as overwhelmingly so, too easy. Something was not quite right here. But since I had no Passenger to point me in the right direc- tion, I kept it to myself. It would have been cruel, in any case, to burst Deborah's happy balloon. She was very nearly glowing with satisfaction as the results came in and Halpern looked more and more like our demented catch of the day.

Deborah was actually humming when she dragged me along to interview Halpern, which took my unease to a new level. I watched her as we went into the room where Halpern was waiting. I could not remember the last time she had seemed so happy. She even forgot to wear her expression of perpetual disapproval. It was very unsettling, a complete violation of natural law, as if everyone on I-95 suddenly decided to drive slowly and carefully.

'Well, Jerry,' she said cheerfully as we settled into chairs facing Halpern. 'Would you like to talk about those two girls?'

'There's nothing to talk about,' he said. He was very pale, almost greenish, but he looked a lot more determined than he had when we brought him in. 'You've made a mistake,' he said. 'I didn't do anything.'

Deborah looked at me with a smile and shook her head. 'He didn't do anything,' she said happily.

'It's possible,' I said. 'Somebody else might have put the bloody clothes in his apartment while he was watching Letterman.'

'Is that what happened, Jerry?' she said. 'Did somebody else put those bloody clothes in your place?'

If possible, he looked even greener. 'What – bloody – what are you talking about?'

She smiled at him. 'Jerry. We found a pair of

your pants with blood on 'em. It matches the victims' blood. We found a shoe and a sock, same story. And we found a bloody fingerprint in your car. Your fingerprint, their blood.' Deborah leaned back in her chair and folded her arms. 'Does that jog your memory at all, Jerry?'

Halpern had started shaking his head while Deborah was talking, and he continued to do so, as if it was some kind of weird reflex and he didn't know he was doing it. 'No,' he said. 'No. That isn't even— No.'

'No, Jerry?' Deborah said. 'What does that mean, no?'

He was still shaking his head. A drop of sweat flew off and plopped on the table and I could hear him trying very hard to breathe. 'Please,' he said. 'This is crazy. I didn't do anything. Why are you— This is pure Kafka, I didn't do anything.'

Deborah turned to me and raised an eyebrow. 'Kafka?' she said.

'He thinks he's a cockroach,' I told her.

'I'm just a dumb cop, Jerry,' she said. 'I don't know about Kafka. But I know solid evidence when I see it. And you know what, Jerry? I'm seeing it all over your apartment.'

'But I didn't *do* anything,' he pleaded.

'Okay,' said Deborah with a shrug. 'Then help me out here. How did all that stuff get into your place?'

'Wilkins did it,' he said, and he looked surprised, as if someone else had said it.

'Wilkins?' Deborah said, looking at me.

143

'The professor in the office next door?' I said.

'Yes, that's right,' Halpern said, suddenly gathering steam and leaning forward. 'It was Wilkins – it had to be.'

'Wilkins did it,' Deborah said. 'He put on your clothes, killed the girls, and then put the clothes back in your apartment.'

'Yes, that's right.'

'Why would he do that?'

'We're both up for tenure,' he said. 'Only one of us will get it.'

Deborah stared at him as if he had suggested dancing naked. 'Tenure,' she said at last, and there was wonder in her voice.

'That's right,' he said defensively. 'It's the most important moment in any academic career.'

'Important enough to kill somebody?' I asked.

He just stared at a spot on the table. 'It was Wilkins,' he said.

Deborah stared at him for a full minute, with the expression of a fond aunt watching her favorite nephew. He looked at her for a few seconds, and then blinked, glanced down at the table, over to me, and back down to the table again. When the silence continued, he finally looked back up at Deborah. 'All right, Jerry,' she said. 'If that's the best you can do, I think it might be time for you to call your lawyer.'

He goggled at her, but seemed unable to think of anything to say, so Deborah stood up and headed for the door, and I followed.

'Got him,' she said in the hallway. 'That son of a bitch is *cooked*. Game, set, point.'

And she was so positively sunny that I couldn't help saying, 'If it was him.'

She absolutely beamed at me. 'Of course it was him, Dex. Jesus, don't knock yourself. You did some great work here, and for once we got the right guy first time out.'

'I guess so,' I said.

She cocked her head to one side and stared at me, still smirking in a completely self-satisfied way. 'Whatsa matter, Dex,' she said. 'Got your shorts in a knot about the wedding?'

'Nothing's the matter,' I said. 'Life on earth has never before been so completely harmonious and satisfying. I just—' And here I hesitated, because I didn't really know what I just. There was only this unshakable and unreasonable feeling that something was not right.

'I know, Dex,' she said in a kindly voice that somehow made it feel even worse. 'It seems way too easy, right? But think of all the shit we go through every day, with every other case. It stands to reason that now and then we get an easy one, doesn't it?'

'I don't know,' I said. 'This just doesn't *feel* right.'

She snorted. 'With the amount of hard evidence we got on this guy, nobody's going to give a shit how it *feels*, Dex,' she said. 'Why don't you lighten up and enjoy a good day's work?'

I'm sure it was excellent advice, but I could not

take it. Even though I had no familiar whisper to feed me my cues, I had to say something. 'He doesn't act like he's lying,' I said, rather feebly.

Deborah shrugged. 'He's a nut job. Not my problem. He did it.'

'But if he's psychotic in some way, why would it just burst out all of a sudden? I mean, he's thirty-something years old, and this is the first time he's done anything? That doesn't fit.'

She actually patted my shoulder and smiled again. 'Good point, Dex. Why don't you get on your computer and check his background? I bet we find something.' She glanced at her watch. 'You can do that right after the press conference, okay? Come on, can't be late.'

And I followed along dutifully, wondering how I always seemed to volunteer for extra work.

Deborah had, in fact, been granted the priceless boon of a press conference, something Captain Matthews did not give out lightly. It was her first as lead detective on a major case with its own media frenzy, and she had clearly studied up on how to look and speak for the evening news. She lost her smile and any other visible trace of emotion and spoke flat sentences of perfect cop-ese. Only someone who knew her as well as I did could tell that great and uncharacteristic happiness was burbling behind her wooden face.

So I stood at the back of the room and watched as my sister made a series of radiantly mechanical statements adding up to her belief that she had arrested a suspect in the heinous murders at the university, and as soon as she knew if he was guilty her dear friends in the media would be among the first to know it. She was clearly proud and happy and it had been pure meanness on my part even to hint that something was not quite righteous with Halpern's guilt, especially since I did not know what that might be – or even if.

She was almost certainly right – Halpern was guilty and I was being stupid and grumpy, thrown off the trolley of pure reason by my missing Passenger. It was the echo of its absence that made me uneasy, and not any kind of doubt about the suspect in a case that really meant absolutely nothing to me anyway. Almost certainly—

And there was that almost again. I had lived my life until now in absolutes – I had no experience with 'almost,' and it was unsettling, deeply disturbing not to have that voice of certainty to tell me what was what with no dithering and no doubt. I began to realize just how helpless I was without the Dark Passenger. Even in my day job, nothing was simple anymore.

Back in my cubicle I sat in my chair and leaned back with my eyes closed. *Anybody there?* I asked hopefully. Nobody was. Just an empty spot that was beginning to hurt as the number wonder wore off. With the distraction of work over, there was nothing to keep me from self-absorbed self-pity. I was alone in a dark, mean world full of terrible things like me. Or at least, the me I used to be.

Where had the Passenger gone, and why had it gone there? If something had truly scared it away, what could that something be? What could frighten a thing that lived for darkness, that really came to life only when the knives were out?

And this brought a brand-new thought that was most unwelcome: If this hypothetical something had scared away the Passenger, had it followed it into exile? Or was it still sniffing at my trail? Was I in danger with no way left to protect myself – with no way of knowing whether some lethal threat was right behind me until its drool actually fell on my neck?

I have always heard that new experiences are a good thing, but this one was pure torture. The more I thought about it, the less I understood what was happening to me, and the more it hurt.

Well, there was one sure remedy for misery, and that was good hard work on something completely pointless. I swiveled around to face my computer and got busy.

In only a few minutes I had opened up the entire life and history of Dr Gerald Halpern, Ph.D. Of course, it was a little trickier than simply searching Halpern's name on Google. There was, for example, the matter of the sealed court records, which took me almost five full minutes to open. But when I did, it was certainly worth the effort, and I found myself thinking, *Well, well, well* . . . And because at the moment I was tragically alone on the inside, with no one to hear my pensive remarks, I said it aloud, too. 'Well, well, well,' I said.

The foster-care records would have been interesting enough – not because I felt any bond with Halpern from my own parentless past. I had been more than adequately provided with a home and family by Harry, Doris, and Deborah, unlike Halpern, who had flitted from foster home to foster home until finally landing at Syracuse University.

Far more interesting, however, was the file that no one was supposed to open without a warrant, a court order, and a stone tablet direct from the hand of God. And when I had read through it a second time, my reaction was even more profound. 'Well, well, well, *well*,' I said, mildly unsettled at the way the words bounced off the walls of my empty little office. And since profound revelations are always more dramatic with an audience, I reached for the phone and called my sister.

In just a few minutes she pushed into my cubicle and sat on the folding chair. 'What did you find?' she said.

'Dr Gerald Halpern has A Past,' I said, carefully pronouncing the capital letters so she wouldn't leap across the desk and hug me.

'I knew it,' she said. 'What did he do?'

'It's not so much what he did,' I said. 'At this point, it's more like what was done to him.'

'Quit screwing around,' she said. 'What is it?'

'To begin with, he's apparently an orphan.'

'Come on, Dex, cut to the chase.'

I held up a hand to try to calm her down, but it clearly didn't work very well, because she started tapping her knuckles on the desktop. 'I am trying to paint a subtle canvas here, Sis,' I said.

'Paint faster,' she said.

'All right. Halpern went into the foster-care system in upstate New York when they found him living in a box under the freeway. They found his parents, who were unfortunately dead of recent and unpleasant violence. It seems to have been very well-deserved violence.'

'What the fuck does that mean?'

'His parents were pimping him out to pedophiles,' I said.

'Jesus,' Deborah said, and she was clearly a little shocked. Even by Miami standards, this was a bit much.

'And Halpern doesn't remember any of that part. He gets blackouts under stress, the file says. It makes sense. The blackouts were probably a conditioned response to the repeated trauma,' I said. 'That can happen.'

'Well, fuck,' Deborah said, and I inwardly applauded her elegance. 'So he forgets shit. You have to admit that fits. The girl tries to frame him for rape, and he's already worried about tenure – so he gets stressed and kills her without knowing it.'

'A couple of other things,' I said, and I admit that I enjoyed the drama of the moment perhaps a little more than was necessary. 'To begin with, the death of his parents.'

'What about it?' she said, quite clearly lacking any theatrical pleasure at all.

'Their heads were cut off,' I said. 'And then the house was torched.'

Deborah straightened up. 'Shit,' she said.

'I thought so, too.'

'Goddamn, that's *great*, Dex,' she said. 'We have his ass.'

'Well,' I said, 'it certainly fits the pattern.'

'It sure as hell does,' she said. 'So did he kill his parents?'

I shrugged. 'They couldn't prove anything. If they could, Halpern would have been committed. It was so violent that nobody could believe a kid had done it. But they're pretty sure that he was there, and at least saw what happened.'

She looked at me hard. 'So what's wrong with that? You still think he didn't do it? I mean, you're having one of your hunches here?'

It stung a lot more than it should have, and I closed my eyes for a moment. There was still nothing there except dark and empty. My famous hunches were, of course, based on things whispered to me by the Dark Passenger, and in its absence I had nothing to go on. 'I'm not having hunches lately,' I admitted. 'There's just something that bothers me about this. It just—'

I opened my eyes and Deborah was staring at me. For the first time today there was something in her expression beyond bubbly happiness, and for a moment I thought she was going to ask me what

151

that meant and was I all right. I had no idea what I would say if she did, since the Dark Passenger was not something I had ever talked about, and the idea of sharing something that intimate was very unsettling.

'I don't know,' I said weakly. 'It doesn't seem right.'

Deborah smiled gently. I would have felt more at ease if she had snarled and told me to fuck off, but she smiled and reached a hand across the desk to pat mine. 'Dex,' she said softly, 'the hard evidence is more than enough. The background fits. The motive is good. You admit you're not having one of your . . . hunches.' She cocked her head to the side, still smiling, which made me even more uneasy. 'This one is righteous, Bro. Whatever is bothering you, don't pin it on this. He did it, we got him, that's it.' She let go of my hand before either one of us could burst into tears. 'But I'm a little worried about you.'

'I'm fine,' I said, and it sounded false even to me.

Deborah looked at me for a long moment, and then stood up. 'All right,' she said. 'But I'm here for you if you need me.' And she turned and walked away.

Somehow I slogged through the gray soup of the rest of the day and made it all the way home to Rita's at the end of the day, where the soup gelled into an aspic of sensory deprivation. I don't know what we had for dinner, or what anyone might have said. The only thing I could bring myself to listen for was the sound of the Passenger rushing back in, and this sound did not come. And so I swam through the evening on automatic pilot and finally went to bed, still completely wrapped up in Dull Empty Dexter.

It surprised me a great deal to learn it, but sleep is not automatic for humans, not even for the semi-human I was becoming. The old me, Dexter of the Darkness, had slept perfectly, with great ease, simply lying down, closing his eyes, and thinking, 'One two three GO.' Presto, sleep-o.

But the New Model Dexter had no such luck.

I tossed, I turned, I commanded my pitiful self to go immediately to sleep with no further dithering, and all to no avail. I could not sleep. I could only lie there wide-eyed and wonder why.

And as the night dragged on, so did the terrible, dreary introspection. Had I been misleading myself my entire life? What if I was not Dashing Slashing Dexter and his Canny Sidekick the Passenger? What if I was, in fact, actually only a Dark Chauffeur, allowed to live in a small room at the big house in exchange for driving the master on his appointed rounds? And if my services were no longer required, what could I possibly be now that the boss had moved away? Who was I if I was no longer me?

It was not a happy thought, and it did not make me happy. It also did not help me sleep. Since I had already tossed and turned exhaustively, without getting exhausted, I now concentrated on rolling and pitching, with much the same result. But finally, at around 3:30 A.M., I must have hit on the right combination of pointless movement and I dropped off at last into a shallow uncomfortable sleep.

The sound and smell of bacon cooking woke me up. I glanced at the clock – it was 8:32, later than I ever sleep. But of course it was Saturday morning. Rita had allowed me to doze on in my miserable unconsciousness. And now she would reward my return to the land of the waking with a bountiful breakfast. Yahoo.

Breakfast did, in fact, take some of the sourness out of me. It is very hard to maintain a really good feeling of utter depression and total personal worthlessness when you are full of food, and I gave up trying halfway through an excellent omelet.

Cody and Astor had naturally been awake for hours – Saturday morning was their unrestricted television time, and they usually took advantage of it to watch a series of cartoon shows that would certainly have been impossible before the discovery of LSD. They did not even notice me when I staggered past them on my way to the kitchen, and they stayed glued to the image of a talking kitchen utensil while I finished my break-fast, had a final cup of coffee, and decided to give life one more day to get its act together.

'All better?' Rita asked as I put down my coffee mug.

'It was a very nice omelet,' I said. 'Thank you.'

She smiled and lunged up out of her chair to give me a peck on the cheek before flinging all the dishes in the sink and starting to wash them. 'Remember you said you'd take Cody and Astor somewhere this morning,' she said over the sound of running water.

'I said that?'

'Dexter, you know I have a fitting this morning. For my wedding gown. I told you that weeks ago, and you said fine, you would take care of the kids while I went over to Susan's for the fitting, and then I really need to go to the florist's and see about some arrangements, even Vince offered to help me with that, he says he has a friend?'

'I doubt that,' I said, thinking of Manny Borque. 'Not Vince.'

'But I said no thanks. I hope that was all right?'

'Fine,' I said. 'We have only one house to sell to pay for things.'

'I don't want to hurt Vince's feelings and I'm sure his friend is wonderful, but I have been going to Hans for flowers since forever, and he would be brokenhearted if I went somewhere else for the wedding.'

'All right,' I said. 'I'll take the kids.'

I had been hoping for a chance to devote some serious time to my own personal misery and find a way to start on the problem of the absent Passenger. Failing that, it would have been nice just to relax a little bit, perhaps even catch up on some of the precious sleep I had lost the night before, as was my sacred right.

It was, after all, a Saturday. Many well-regarded religions and labor unions have been known to recommend that Saturdays are for relaxation and personal growth; for spending time away from the hectic hurly-burly, in well-earned rest and recreation. But Dexter was more or less a family man nowadays, which changes everything, as I was learning. And with Rita spinning around making wedding preparations like a tornado with blond bangs, it was a clear imperative for me to scoop up Cody and Astor and take them away from the pandemonium to the shelter of some activity sanctioned by society as appropriate for adult-child bonding time.

After a careful study of my options, I chose the Miami Museum of Science and Planetarium. After all, it would be crowded with other family groups, which would maintain my disguise – and start them on theirs as well. Since they were planning to embark on the Dark Trail, they needed to begin right away to understand the notion that the more abnormal one is, the more important it is to appear normal.

And going to the museum with Doting Daddy Dexter was supremely normal-appearing for all three of us. It had the added cachet of being something that was officially Good for Them, a very big advantage, no matter how much that notion made them squirm.

So I loaded the three of us into my car and headed north on U.S. 1, promising the whirling Rita that we would return safely for dinner. I drove us through Coconut Grove and just before the Rickenbacker Causeway turned into the parking lot of the museum in question. We did not go gentle into that good museum, however. In the parking lot, Cody got out of the car and simply stood there. Astor looked at him for a moment, and then turned to me. 'Why do we have to go in there?' she said.

'It's educational,' I told her.

'Ick,' she said, and Cody nodded.

'It's important for us to spend time together,' I said.

'At a *museum*?' Astor demanded. 'That's *pathetic*.'

'That's a lovely word,' I said. 'Where did you get it?'

'We're *not* going in there,' she said. 'We want to *do* something.'

'Have you ever been to this museum?'

'No,' she said, drawing the word out into three contemptuous syllables as only a ten-year-old girl can.

'Well, it might surprise you,' I said. 'You might actually learn something.'

'That's not what we want to learn,' she said. 'Not at a *museum*.'

'What is it you think you want to learn?' I said, and even I was impressed by how very much like a patient adult I sounded.

157

Astor made a face. 'You know,' she said. 'You said you'd show us stuff.'

'How do you know I'm not?' I said.

She looked at me uncertainly for a moment, then turned to Cody. Whatever it was they said to each other, it didn't require words. When she turned back to me a moment later, she was all business, totally self-assured. 'No way,' she said.

'What do you know about the stuff I'm going to show you?'

'*Dex*ter,' she said. 'Why else did we ask you to show us?'

'Because you don't know anything about it and I do.'

'Duh-uh.'

'Your education begins in that building,' I said with my most serious face. 'Follow me and learn.' I looked at them for a moment, watched their uncertainty grow, then I turned and headed for the museum. Maybe I was just cranky from a night of lost sleep, and I was not sure they would follow, but I had to set down the ground rules right away. They had to do it my way, just as I had come to understand so long ago that I had to listen to Harry and do it his way.

CHAPTER 15

Being fourteen years old is never easy, even for artificial humans. It's the age where biology takes over, and even when the fourteen-year-old in question is more interested in clinical biology than the sort more popular with his classmates at Ponce de Leon Junior High, it still rules with an iron hand.

One of the categorical imperatives of puberty that applies even to young monsters is that nobody over the age of twenty knows anything. And since Harry was well over twenty at this point, I had gone into a brief period of rebellion against his unreasonable restraints on my perfectly natural and wholesome desires to hack my school chums into little bits.

Harry had laid out a wonderfully logical plan to get me squared away, which was his term for making things – or people – neat and orderly. But there is nothing logical about a fledgling Dark Passenger flexing its wings for the first time and beating them against the bars of the cage, yearning to fling itself into the free air and fall on its prey like a sharp steel thunderbolt.

Harry knew so many things I needed to learn to become safely and quietly me, to turn me from a wild, blossoming monster into the Dark Avenger: how to act human, how to be certain and careful, how to clean up afterward. He knew all these things as only an old cop could know them. I understood this, even then – but it all seemed so dull and unnecessary.

And Harry couldn't really know everything, after all. He could not know, for example, about Steve Gonzalez, a particularly charming example of pubescent humanity who had earned my attention.

Steve was larger than me, and at a year or two older; he already had something on his upper lip that he referred to as a mustache. He was in my PE class and felt it his God-given duty to make my life miserable whenever possible. If he was right, God must have been very pleased with the effort he put into it.

This was long before Dexter became the Living Ice Cube, and a certain amount of heated and very hard feeling built up inside. This seemed to please Steve and urge him on to greater heights of creativity in his persecution of the simmering young Dexter. We both knew this could end only one way, but alas for him, it was not the way Steve had in mind.

And so one afternoon an unfortunately industrious janitor stumbled into the biology lab at Ponce de Leon to find Dexter and Steve sorting out their personality conflict. It was not quite the classical middle-school face-off of filthy words and swinging fists, although I believe that might have been what Steve had in mind. But he had not reckoned with confronting the young Dark Passenger, and so the janitor found Steve securely taped to the table with a swatch of gray duct tape over his mouth, and Dexter standing above him with a scalpel, trying to remember what he had learned in biology class the day they dissected the frog.

Harry came to get me in his police cruiser, in uniform. He listened to the outraged assistant principal, who described the scene, quoted the student handbook, and demanded to know what Harry was going to do about it. Harry just looked at the assistant principal until the man's words dribbled away into silence. He looked at him a moment longer, for effect, and then he turned his cold blue eyes on me.

'Did you do what he says you did, Dexter?' he asked me.

There was no possibility of evasion or falsehood in the grip of that stare. 'Yes,' I said, and Harry nodded.

'You see?' the assistant principal said. He thought he was going to say more, but Harry turned the look back on him and he fell silent again.

Harry looked back at me. 'Why?' he said.

'He was picking on me.' That sounded somewhat

feeble, even to me, so I added, 'A lot. All the time.'

'And so you taped him to a table,' he said, with very little inflection.

'Uh-huh.'

'And you picked up a scalpel.'

'I wanted him to stop,' I said.

'Why didn't you tell somebody?' Harry asked me.

I shrugged, which was a large portion of my working vocabulary in those days.

'Why didn't you tell me?' he asked.

'I can take care of it,' I said.

'Looks like you didn't take care of it so well,' he said.

There seemed to be very little I could do, so naturally enough I chose to look at my feet. They apparently had very little to add to the discussion, however, so I looked up again. Harry still watched me, and somehow he no longer needed to blink. He did not seem angry, and I was not really afraid of him, and that somehow made it even more uncomfortable.

'I'm sorry,' I said at last. I wasn't sure if I meant it – for that matter, I'm still not sure I can really be sorry for anything I do. But it seemed like a very politic remark, and nothing else burbled up in my teenaged brain, simmering as it was with an oatmeal-thick sludge of hormones and un-certainty. And although I am sure Harry didn't believe that I was sorry, he nodded again.

'Let's go,' he said.

'Just a minute,' the assistant principal said. 'We still have things to discuss.'

'You mean the fact that you let a known bully push my boy to this kind of confrontation because of poor supervision? How many times has the other boy been disciplined?'

'That's not the point—' the assistant principal tried to say.

'Or are we talking about the fact that you left scalpels and other dangerous equipment unsecured and easily available to students in an unlocked and unsupervised classroom?'

'Really, Officer—'

'I tell you what,' Harry said. 'I promise to overlook your extremely poor performance in this matter, if you agree to make a real effort to improve.'

'But this boy—' he tried to say.

'I will deal with this boy,' Harry said. 'You deal with fixing things so I don't have to call in the school board.'

And that, of course, was that. There was never any question of contradicting Harry, whether you were a murder suspect, the president of the Rotary Club, or a young errant monster. The assistant principal opened and closed his mouth a few more times, but no actual words came out, just a sort of sputtering sound combined with throat-clearing. Harry watched him for a moment, and then turned to me. 'Let's go,' he said again.

Harry was silent all the way out to the car, and it was not a chummy silence. He did not speak as we drove away from the school and turned north on Dixie Highway – instead of heading around the school in the other direction, Granada to Hardee and over to our little house in the Grove. I looked at him as he made his turn, but he still had nothing to say, and the expression on his face did not seem to encourage conversation. He looked straight ahead at the road, and drove – fast, but not so fast he had to turn on the siren.

Harry turned left on 17th Avenue, and for a few moments I had the irrational thought that he was taking me to the Orange Bowl. But we passed the turnoff for the stadium and kept going, over the Miami River and then right on North River Drive, and now I knew where we were going but I didn't know why. Harry still hadn't said a word or looked in my direction, and I was beginning to feel a certain oppression creeping into the afternoon that had nothing to do with the storm clouds that were beginning to gather on the horizon.

Harry parked the cruiser and at last he spoke. 'Come on,' he said. 'Inside.' I looked at him, but he was already climbing out of the car, so I got out, too, and followed him meekly into the detention center.

Harry was well known here, as he was everywhere a good cop might be known. He was followed by calls of 'Harry!' and 'Hey, Sarge!' all the way through the receiving area and down the hall to the cell block. I simply trudged behind him as my sense of grim foreboding grew. Why had

Harry brought me to the jail? Why wasn't he scolding me, telling me how disappointed he was, devising harsh but fair punishment for me?

Nothing he did or refused to say offered me any clues. So I trailed along behind. We were stopped at last by one of the guards. Harry took him to one side and spoke quietly; the guard looked over at me, nodded, and led us to the end of the cell block. 'Here he is,' the guard said. 'Enjoy yourself.' He nodded at the figure in the cell, glanced at me briefly, and walked away, leaving Harry and me to resume our uncomfortable silence.

Harry did nothing to break the silence at first. He turned and stared into the cell, and the pale shape inside moved, stood up, and came to the bars. 'Why it's Sergeant Harry!' the figure said happily. 'How are you, Harry? So *nice* of you to drop by.'

'Hello, Carl,' Harry said. At last he turned to me and spoke. 'This is Carl, Dexter.'

'What a handsome lad you are, Dexter,' Carl said. 'Very pleased to meet you.'

The eyes Carl turned on me were bright and empty, but behind them I could almost see a huge dark shadow, and something inside me twitched and tried to slink away from the larger and fiercer thing that lived there beyond the bars. He was not in himself particularly large or fierce-looking – he was even pleasant in a very superficial way, with his neat blond hair and regular features – but there was something about him that made me very uneasy.

'They brought Carl in yesterday,' Harry said. 'He's killed eleven people.'

'Oh, well,' Carl said modestly, 'more or less.'

Outside the jail, the thunder crashed and the rain began. I looked at Carl with real interest; now I knew what had unsettled my Dark Passenger. We were just starting out, and here was somebody who had already been there and back, on eleven occasions, more or less. For the first time I understood how my classmates at Ponce might feel when they came face-to-face with an NFL quarter-back.

'Carl enjoys killing people,' Harry said matter-of-factly. 'Don't you, Carl?'

'It keeps me busy,' Carl said happily.

'Until we caught you,' Harry said bluntly.

'Well, yes, there is that of course. Still . . .' he shrugged and gave Harry a very phony-looking smile, 'it was fun while it lasted.'

'You got careless,' Harry said.

'Yes,' Carl said. 'How could I know the police would be so very thorough?'

'How do you do it?' I blurted out.

'It's not so hard,' Carl said.

'No, I mean— Um, like *how*?'

Carl looked at me searchingly, and I could almost hear a purring coming from the shadow just past his eyes. For a moment our eyes locked and the world was filled with the black sound of two predators meeting over one small, helpless prey. 'Well, well,' Carl said at last. 'Can it really be?' He turned to Harry just as I was beginning to squirm. 'So I'm supposed to be an object lesson, is that it, Sergeant? Frighten your boy onto the straight and narrow path to godliness?'

Harry stared back, showing nothing, saying nothing.

'Well, I'm afraid I have to tell you that there is no way off this particular path, poor dear Harry. When you are on it, you are on it for life, and possibly beyond, and there is nothing you or I or the dear child here can do about it.'

'There's one thing,' Harry said.

'Really,' Carl said, and now a slow black cloud seemed to be rising up around him, coalescing on the teeth of his smile, spreading its wings out toward Harry, and toward me. 'And what might that be, pray tell?'

'Don't get caught,' Harry said.

For a moment the black cloud froze, and then it drew back and vanished. 'Oh my God,' Carl said. 'How I wish I knew how to laugh.' He shook his head slowly, from side to side. 'You're serious, aren't you? Oh my God. What a wonderful dad you are, Sergeant Harry.' And he gave us such a huge smile that it almost looked real.

Harry turned his full ice-blue gaze on me now.

'He got caught,' Harry said to me, 'because he didn't know what he was doing. And now he will go to the electric chair. Because he didn't know what the *police* were doing. Because,' Harry said without raising his voice at all and without blinking, 'he had no training.'

I looked at Carl, watching us through the thick bars with his too-bright dead empty eyes. Caught. I looked back at Harry. 'I understand,' I said.

And I did.

That was the end of my youthful rebellion.

And now, so many years later – wonderful years, filled with slicing and dicing and not getting caught – I truly knew what a remarkable gamble Harry had taken by introducing me to Carl. I could never hope to measure up to his performance – after all, Harry did things because he had *feelings* and I never would – but I could follow his example and make Cody and Astor toe the line. I would gamble, just as Harry had.

They would follow or not.

CHAPTER 16

They followed.

The museum was crowded with groups of curious citizens in search of knowledge – or a bathroom, apparently. Most of them were between the ages of two and ten, and there seemed to be about one adult for every seven children. They moved like a great colorful flock of parrots, swooping back and forth through the exhibits with a loud cawing sound that, in spite of the fact that it was in at least three languages, all sounded the same. The international language of children.

Cody and Astor seemed slightly intimidated by the crowd and stayed close to me. It was a pleasant contrast to the spirit of Dexterless adventure that seemed to rule them the rest of the time, and I tried to take advantage of it by steering them immediately to the piranha exhibit.

'What do they look like?' I asked them.

'Very bad,' Cody said softly, staring unblinking at the many teeth the fish displayed.

'Those are piranha,' Astor said. 'They can eat a whole cow.'

169

'If you were swimming and you saw piranha, what would you do?' I asked them.

'Kill them,' said Cody.

'There's too many,' Astor said. 'You should run away from them, and not go anywhere near.'

'So anytime you see these wicked-looking fish you will either try to kill them or run away from them?' I said. They both nodded. 'If the fish were really smart, like people, what would they do?'

'Wear a disguise,' Astor giggled.

'That's right,' I said, and even Cody smiled. 'What kind of disguise would you recommend? A wig and a beard?'

'Dex-ter,' Astor said. 'They're fish. Fish don't wear beards.'

'Oh,' I said. 'So they would still want to look like fish?'

'Of course,' she said, as if I was too stupid to understand big words.

'What kind of fish?' I said. 'Great big ones? Like sharks?'

'Normal,' Cody said. His sister looked at him for a moment, and then nodded.

'Whatever there's lots of in the area,' she said. 'Something that won't scare away what they want to eat.'

'Uh-huh,' I said.

They both looked at the fish in silence for a moment. It was Cody who first got it. He frowned and looked at me. I smiled encouragingly. He whispered something to Astor, who looked startled.

She opened her mouth to say something, and then stopped.

'Oh,' she said.

'Yes,' I said. 'Oh.'

She looked at Cody, who looked up again from the piranha. Again, they didn't say anything aloud, but there was an entire conversation. I let it run its course, until they looked up at me. 'What can we learn from piranha?' I said.

'Don't look ferocious,' Cody said.

'Look like something normal,' Astor said grudgingly. 'But Dexter, fish aren't people.'

'That's exactly right,' I said. 'Because people survive by recognizing things that look dangerous. And fish get caught. We don't want to.' They looked at me solemnly, then back at the fish. 'So what else have we learned today?' I asked after a moment.

'Don't get caught,' Astor said.

I sighed. At least it was a start, but there was much work yet to do. 'Come on,' I said. 'Let's see some of the other exhibits.'

I was not really very familiar with the museum, perhaps because until recently I'd had no children to drag in there. So I was definitely improvising, looking for things that might get them started toward thinking and learning the right things. The piranha had been a stroke of luck, I admit – they had simply popped into view and my giant brain had supplied the correct lesson. Finding the next piece of happy coincidence was not as easy, and it was half an hour of trudging grimly through the murderous crowd of kids and their vicious parents before we came to the lion exhibit.

Once again, the ferocious appearance and reputation proved irresistible to Cody and Astor, and they came to a halt in front of the exhibit. It was a stuffed lion, of course, what I think they call a diorama, but it held their attention. The male lion stood proudly over the body of a gazelle, mouth wide and fangs gleaming. Beside him were two females and a cub. There was a two-page explanation that went with the exhibit, and about halfway down the second page I found what I needed.

'Well now,' I said brightly. 'Aren't we glad we're not lions?'

'No,' said Cody.

'It says here,' I said, 'that when a male lion takes over a lion family—'

'It's called a *pride*, Dexter,' Astor said. 'It was in *Lion King*.'

'All right,' I said. 'When a new daddy lion takes over a pride, he kills all the cubs.'

'That's horrible,' Astor said.

I smiled to show her my sharp teeth. 'No, it's perfectly natural,' I said. 'To protect his own and make sure that it's *his* cubs that rule the roost. Lots of predators do that.'

'What does that have to do with us?' Astor said. 'You're not going to kill us when you marry Mom, are you?'

'Of course not,' I said. 'You are my cubs now.'

'Then so what?' she said.

I opened my mouth to explain to her and then felt all the air rush out of me. My mouth hung open but I couldn't speak, because my brain was whirling with a thought so far-fetched that I didn't even bother to deny it. *Lots of predators do that*, I heard myself say. *To protect his own*, I had said.

Whatever made me a predator, its home was in the Dark Passenger. And now something had scared away the Passenger. Was it possible that, that—

That what? A new daddy Passenger was threatening *my* Passenger? I had run into many people in my life who had the shadow of something similar to mine hung over them, and nothing had ever happened with them except mutual recognition and a bit of inaudible snarling. This was too stupid even to think about – Passengers didn't have daddies.

Did they?

'Dexter,' Astor said. 'You're scaring us.'

I admit that I was scaring me, too. The thought that the Passenger could have a parent stalking it with lethal intentions was appallingly stupid – but then, after all, where had the Passenger really come from? I was reasonably sure that it was more than a psychotic figment of my disordered brain. I was not schizophrenic – both of us were sure of that. The fact that it was now gone proved that it had an independent existence.

And this meant that the Passenger had come from somewhere. It had existed before me. It had a source, whether you called it a parent or anything else.

'Earth to Dexter,' Astor said, and I realized that I still stood in front of them frozen in my unlikely, foolish openmouthed pose like a pedantic zombie.

'Yes,' I said stupidly, 'I was just thinking.'

'Did it hurt a lot?' she said.

I closed my mouth and looked at her. She was facing me with her look of ten-year-old disgust at how dumb grown-ups can be, and this time I agreed with her. I had always taken the Passenger for granted, so much so that I had never really wondered where it had come from, or how it had come to be. I had been smug, fatuously content to share space with it, simply glad to be me and not some other, emptier mortal, and now, when a little self-knowledge might have saved the day, I was struck dumb. Why had I never thought of any of these things before? And why did I have to choose now as the first time, in the presence of a sarcastic child? I had to devote some time and thought to this – but of course, this was neither the time nor the place.

'Sorry,' I said. 'Let's go see the planetarium.'

'But you were going to tell us why lions are important,' she said.

In truth, I could no longer remember why lions were important. But happily for my image, my cell phone began to chatter before I could admit it. 'Just a minute,' I said, and I pulled the phone from its holster. I glanced at it and saw that it was Deborah. And after all, family is family, so I answered.

'They found the heads,' she said.

It took me a moment to figure out what she meant, but Deborah was hissing in my ear and I realized some sort of response was called for. 'The heads? From the two bodies over at the university?' I said.

Deborah made an exasperated hissing noise and said, 'Jesus, Dex, there aren't that many missing heads in town.'

'Well, there's city hall,' I said.

'Get your ass over here, Dexter. I need you.'

'But Deborah, it's Saturday, and I'm in the middle of—'

'Now,' she said, and hung up.

I looked at Cody and Astor and pondered my quandary. If I took them home it would be at least an hour before I got back to Debs, and in addition we would lose our precious Saturday quality time together. On the other hand, even I knew that taking children to a homicide scene might be considered a little bit eccentric.

But it would also be educational. They needed to be impressed with just how through the police are when dead bodies turn up, and this was as good an opportunity as any. On balance, even taking into consideration that my dear sister might have a semi-ballistic reaction, I decided it would be best simply to pile into the car and take them to their first investigation.

'All right,' I said to them as I reholstered my phone. 'We have to go now.'

'Where?' Cody said.

'To help my sister,' I said. 'Will you remember what we learned today?'

'Yes, but this is just a *museum*,' Astor said. 'It's not what we want to learn.'

'Yes, it is,' I said. 'And you have to trust me, and do it my way, or I'm not going to teach you.' I leaned down to where I could look them both in the eyes. 'Not doodly-squat,' I said.

Astor frowned. 'Dex-terrrr,' she said.

'I mean it. It has to be my way.'

Once again she and Cody locked glances. After a moment he nodded, and she turned back to me. 'All right,' she said. 'We promise.'

'We'll wait,' Cody said.

'We understand,' Astor said. 'When can we start the cool stuff?'

'When I say,' I said. 'Anyway, right now we have to go.'

She switched immediately back to snippy ten-year-old. 'Now where do we have to go?'

'I have to go to work,' I said. 'So I'm taking you with me.'

'To see a *body*?' she asked hopefully.

I shook my head. 'Just the head,' I said.

She looked at Cody and shook her head. 'Mom won't like it.'

'You can wait in the car if you want to,' I said.

'Let's go,' said Cody, his longest speech all day. We went.

CHAPTER 17

Deborah was waiting at a modest $2 million house on a private cul-de-sac in Coconut Grove. The street was sealed off from just inside the guard booth to the house itself, about halfway down on the left, and a crowd of indignant residents stood around on their carefully manicured lawns and walkways, fuming at the swarm of low-rent social undesirables from the police department who had invaded their little paradise. Deborah was in the street instructing a videographer in what to shoot and from what angles. I hurried over to join her, with Cody and Astor trailing along right behind.

'What the hell is that?' Deborah demanded, glaring from the kids to me.

'They are known as children,' I told her. 'They are often a byproduct of marriage, which may be why you are unfamiliar with them.'

'Are you off your fucking nut bringing them here?' she snapped.

'You're not supposed to say that word,' Astor told Deborah with a glare. 'You owe me fifty cents for saying it.'

Deborah opened her mouth, turned bright red, and closed it again. 'You gotta get them outta here,' she finally said. 'They shouldn't see this.'

'We *want* to see it,' Astor said.

'Hush,' I told them. 'Both of you.'

'Jesus Christ, Dexter,' Deborah said.

'You told me to come right away,' I said. 'I came.'

'I can't play nursemaid to a couple of kids,' Deborah said.

'You don't have to,' I said. 'They'll be fine.'

Deborah stared at the two of them; they stared back. Nobody blinked, and for a moment I thought my dear sister would chew off her lower lip. Then she shook herself. 'Screw it,' she said. 'I don't have time for a hassle. You two wait over there.' She pointed to her car, which was parked across the street, and grabbed me by the arm. She dragged me toward the house where all the activity was humming. 'Lookit,' she said, and pointed at the front of the house.

On the phone, Deborah had told me they found the heads, but in truth it would have taken a major effort to miss them. In front of the house, the short driveway curled through a pair of coral-rock gateposts before puddling into a small courtyard with a fountain in the middle. On top of each gatepost was an ornate lamp. Chalked on the driveway between the posts was something that looked like the letters MLK, except that it was in a strange script that I did not recognize. And to make sure that no one spent too

178

long puzzling out the message, on top of each gatepost—

Well. Although I had to admit the display had a certain primitive vigor and an undeniable dramatic impact, it was really far too crude for my taste. Even though the heads apparently had been carefully cleaned, the eyelids were gone and the mouths had been forced into a strange smile by the heat, and it was not pleasant. Certainly no one on-site asked my opinion, but I have always felt that there should be no leftovers. It's untidy, and it shows a lack of a real workmanlike spirit. And for these heads to be left so conspicuously – this was mere showing off, and demonstrated an unrefined approach to the problem. Still, there's no accounting for taste. I'm always willing to admit that my technique is not the only way. And as always in aesthetic matters, I waited for some small sibilant whisper of agreement from the Dark Passenger – but of course, there was nothing.

Not a murmur, not a twitch of the wing, not a peep. My compass was gone, leaving me in the very unsettling position of needing to hold my own hand.

Of course, I was not completely alone. There was Deborah beside me, and I became aware that as I was pondering the matter of my shadow companion's disappearance, she was speaking to me.

'They were at the funeral this morning,' she said. 'Came back and this was waiting for them.'

'Who are they?' I asked, nodding at the house.

Deborah jabbed me in the ribs with her elbow. It hurt. 'The family, asshole. The Ortega family. What did I just say?'

'So this happened in daylight?' For some reason, that made it seem a little more disturbing.

'Most of the neighbors were at the funeral, too,' she said. 'But we're still looking for somebody who might have seen something.' She shrugged. 'We might get lucky. Who knows.'

I did not know, but for some reason I did not think that anything connected to this would bring us luck. 'I guess this creates a little doubt about Halpern's guilt,' I said.

'It damned well does not,' she said. 'That asshole is guilty.'

'Ah,' I said. 'So you think that somebody else found the heads, and, uh . . .'

'Fucking hell, I don't know,' she said. 'Somebody must be working with him.'

I just shook my head. That didn't make any sense at all, and we both knew it. Somebody capable of conceiving and performing the elaborate ritual of the two murders would almost have to do it alone. Such acts were so highly personal, each small step the acting out of some unique inner need, that the idea of two people sharing the same vision was almost pure nonsense. In a weird way, the ceremonial display of the heads fit in with the way the bodies had been left – two pieces of the same ritual.

'That doesn't seem right,' I said.

'Well then, what does?'

180

I looked at the heads, perched so carefully atop the lamps. They had of course been burned in the fire that had toasted the bodies, and there were no traces of blood visible. The necks appeared to have been cut very neatly. Other than that, I had no keen insight into anything at all – and yet there was Deborah, staring at me expectantly. It's difficult to have a reputation for being able to see into the still heart of the mystery when all that notoriety rests on the shadowy guidance of an interior voice that was, at the moment, somewhere else altogether. I felt like a ventriloquist's dummy, suddenly called upon to perform the whole act alone.

'Both the heads are here,' I said, since I clearly had to say something. 'Why not at the other girl's house? The one with the boyfriend?'

'Her family lives in Massachusetts,' Deborah said. 'This was easier.'

'And you checked him out, right?'

'Who?'

'The dead girl's boyfriend,' I said slowly and carefully. 'The guy with the tattoo on his neck.'

'Jesus Christ, Dexter, of course we're checking him out. We're checking out everybody who came within half a mile of these girls in their whole fucking sad little lives, and you—' She took a deep breath, but it didn't seem to calm her down very much. 'Listen, I don't really need any help with the basic police work, okay? What I need help with is the weird creepy shit you're supposed to know about.'

181

It was nice to confirm my identity as the Weird Creepy Shit King, but I did have to wonder how long it would last without my Dark Crown. Still, with my reputation on the line I had to venture some kind of insightful opinion, so I took a small bloodless stab at it.

'All right,' I said. 'Then from a weird creepy point of view, it doesn't make sense to have two different killers with the same ritual. So either Halpern killed 'em and somebody found the heads and thought, what the hell, I'll hang 'em up – or else the wrong guy is in jail.'

'Fuck that,' she said.

'Which part?'

'All of it, goddamn it!' she said. 'Neither one of those choices is any better.'

'Well, shit,' I said, surprising us both. And since I felt cranky beyond endurance with Deborah, and with myself, and with this whole burned-and-headless thing, I took the only logical, reasonable course. I kicked a coconut.

Much better. Now my foot hurt, too.

'I'm checking Goldman's background,' she said abruptly, nodding at the house. 'So far, he's just a dentist. Owns an office building in Davie. But this – it smells like the cocaine cowboys. And that doesn't make sense, either. Goddamn it, Dexter,' she said. 'Give me something.'

I looked at Deborah with surprise. Somehow she had brought it around so it was back in my lap again, and I had absolutely nothing beyond a very strong hope that Goldman would turn out to be a drug lord who was only disguised as a dentist. 'I have come up empty,' I said, which was sad but far too true.

'Aw, crap,' she said, looking past me to the edge of the gathering crowd. The first of the news vans had arrived, and even before the vehicle had come to a full stop the reporter leaped out and began poking at his cameraman, prodding him into position for a long shot. 'Goddamn it,' Deborah said, and hurried over to deal with them.

'That guy is scary, Dexter,' said a small voice behind me, and I turned quickly around. Once again, Cody and Astor had snuck up on me unobserved. They stood together, and Cody inclined his head toward the small crowd that had gathered on the far side of the crime-scene tape.

'Which guy is scary?' I said, and Astor said, 'There. In the orange shirt. Don't make me point, he's *looking*.'

I looked for an orange shirt in the crowd and saw only a flash of color at the far end of the cul-de-sac as someone ducked into a car. It was a small blue car, not a white Avalon – but I did notice a familiar dab of additional color dangling from the rearview mirror as the car moved out onto the main road. And although it was difficult to be sure, I was relatively confident that it was a University of Miami faculty parking pass.

I turned back to Astor. 'Well, he's gone now,' I said. 'Why did you say he was scary?'

'*He* says so,' Astor said, pointing to Cody, and Cody nodded.

'He was,' Cody said, barely above a whisper. 'He had a big shadow.'

'I'm sorry he scared you,' I said. 'But he's gone now.'

Cody nodded. 'Can we look at the heads?'

Children are so interesting, aren't they? Here Cody had been frightened by something as insubstantial as somebody's shadow, and yet he was as eager as I'd ever seen him to get a closer look at a concrete example of murder, terror, and human mortality. Of course I didn't blame him for wanting a peek, but I didn't think I could openly allow it. On the other hand, I had no idea how to explain all of this to them, either. I am told that the Turkish language, for example, has subtleties far beyond what I can imagine, but English was definitely not adequate for a proper response.

Happily for me, Deborah came back just then, muttering, 'I will never complain about the captain again.' That seemed highly unlikely, but it did not seem politic to say so. 'He can *have* those blood-sucking bastards from the press.'

'Maybe you're just not a people person,' I said.

'Those assholes aren't people,' she said. 'All they want is to get some goddamned pictures of their perfect fucking haircuts standing in front of the heads, so they can send their tape to the network. What kind of animal wants to see this?'

Actually, I knew the answer to that one, since I was

shepherding two of them at the moment and, truth be told, might be considered one myself. But it did seem like I should avoid this question and try to keep our focus on the problem at hand. So I pondered whatever it was that had made Cody's scary guy seem scary, and the fact that he'd had what looked very much like a university parkingpermit.

'I've had a thought,' I said to Deborah, and the way her head snapped around you might have thought I'd told her she was standing on a python. 'It doesn't really fit with your dentist-as-drug-lord theory,' I warned her.

'Out with it,' she said through her teeth.

'Somebody was here, and he scared the kids. He took off in a car with a faculty parking tag.'

Deborah stared at me, her eyes hard and opaque. 'Shit,' she said softly. 'The guy Halpern said, what's his name?'

'Wilkins,' I said.

'No,' she said. 'Can't be. All because the kids say somebody scared them? No.'

'He has a motive,' I said.

'To get tenure, for Christ's sake? Come on, Dex.'

'We don't have to think it's important,' I said. '*They* do.'

'So to get tenure,' she said, shaking her head, 'he breaks into Halpern's apartment, steals his clothes, kills two girls—'

'And then steers us to Halpern,' I said, remembering how he had stood there in the hall and suggested it.

185

Deborah's head jerked around to face me. 'Shit,' she said. 'He did do that, didn't he? Told us to go see Halpern.'

'And however feeble tenure might seem as a motive,' I said, 'it makes more sense than Danny Rollins and Ted Bundy getting together on a little project, doesn't it?'

Deborah smoothed down the back of her hair, a surprisingly feminine gesture for someone I had come to think of as Sergeant Rock. 'It might,' she said finally. 'I don't know enough about Wilkins to say for sure.'

'Shall we go talk to him?'

She shook her head. 'First I want to see Halpern again,' she said.

'Let me get the kids,' I said.

Naturally enough, they were not anywhere near where they should have been. But I found them easily enough; they had wandered over to get a better look at the two heads, and it may have been my imagination, but I thought I could see a small gleam of professional appreciation in Cody's eyes.

'Come on,' I told them, 'we have to get going.' They turned away and followed me reluctantly, but I did hear Astor muttering under her breath, 'Better than a stupid museum anyway.'

From the far edge of the group that had gathered to see the spectacle he had watched, careful to be just one of the staring crowd, no different from all the rest of them, and unobserved in any specific

186

way. It was a risk for the Watcher to be there at all – he could well be recognized, but he was willing to take the chance. And of course, it was gratifying to see the reaction to his work; a small vanity but one he allowed himself.

Besides, he was curious to see what they would make of the one simple clue he had left. The other was clever – but so far he had ignored it, walking right past and allowing his coworkers to photograph it and examine it. Perhaps he should have been a little more blatant – but there was time to do this right. No hurry at all, and the importance of getting the other ready, taking him when it was all just right – that outweighed everything else.

The Watcher moved a little closer, to study the other, perhaps see some sign as to how he was reacting so far. Interesting to bring those children with him. They didn't seem particularly disturbed by the sight of the two heads. Perhaps they were used to such things, or—

No. It was not possible.

Moving with the greatest possible care, he edged closer, still trying to work his way near with the natural ebb and flow of the onlookers, until he got to the yellow tape at a point as close to the children as he could get.

And when the boy looked up and their eyes met, there was no longer any possibility of mistake.

For a moment their gaze locked and all sense of time was lost in the whir of shadowy wings. The boy simply stood there and stared at him with recognition – not of who he was but of what, and his small dark wings fluttered in panicked fury. The Watcher could not help himself; he moved closer, allowing the boy to see him and the nimbus of dark power he carried. The boy showed no fear – simply looked back at him and showed his own power. Then the boy turned away and took his sister's hand, and the two of them trotted over to the other.

Time to leave. The children would certainly point him out, and he did not want his face seen, not yet. He hurried back to the car and drove away, but not with anything like worry. Not at all. If anything, he was more pleased than he had a right to be.

It was the children, of course. Not just that they would tell the other, and move him a few small steps further into the necessary fear. But also because he really liked children. They were wonderful to work with, they broadcast emotions that were so very powerful, and raised the whole energy of the event to a higher plane.

Children – wonderful.

This was actually starting to be enjoyable.

For a while, it was enough to ride in the monkey-things and help them kill. But even this grew dull with the simple repetition, and every now and then IT felt again that there had to be something more. There was that tantalizing twitch of something indefinable at the moment of the kill, the sense that something stirred toward waking and then settled back down again, and IT wanted to know what that was.

But no matter how many times, no matter how many different monkey-things, IT could never get any closer to that feeling, never push in far enough to find out what it was. And that made IT want to know all the more.

A great deal of time went by, and IT began to turn sour again. The monkey-things were just too simple, and whatever IT did with them was not enough. IT began to resent their stupid, pointless, endlessly repeating existence. IT lashed out at them once or twice, wanting to punish them for their dumb, unimaginative suffering, and IT drove IT's host to kill entire families, whole tribes of the things. And as they all died, that wonderful hint of something else would hang there just out of reach and then settle back down again into slumber.

It was furiously frustrating; there had to be a way to break through, find out what that elusive something was and pull it into existence.

And then at last, the monkey-things began to change. It was very slow at first, so slow that IT didn't even realize what was happening until the process was well under way. And one wonderful day, when IT went into a new host, the thing stood up on its back legs and, as IT still wondered what was happening, the thing said, 'Who are you?'

The extreme shock of this moment was followed by an even more extreme pleasure.

IT was no longer alone.

CHAPTER 18

The ride to the detention center went smoothly, but with Deborah driving that merely meant that no one was severely injured. She was in a hurry, and she was first and foremost a Miami cop who had learned to drive from Miami cops. And that meant she believed that traffic was fluid in nature and she sliced through it like a hot iron in butter, sliding into gaps that weren't really there, and making it clear to the other drivers that it was either move or die.

Cody and Astor were very pleased, of course, from their securely seat-belted position in the backseat. They sat as straight as possible, craning upward to see out. And rarest of all, Cody actually smiled briefly when we narrowly missed smashing into a 350-pound man on a small motorcycle.

'Put on the siren,' Astor demanded.

'This isn't a goddamned game,' Deborah snarled.

'Does it have to be a goddamned game for the siren?' Astor said, and Deborah turned bright red and yanked the wheel hard to bring us off U.S.

1, just barely missing a battered Honda riding on four doughnut tires.

'Astor,' I said, 'don't say that word.'

'She says it all the time,' Astor said.

'When you are her age, you can say it, too, if you want to,' I said. 'But not when you're ten years old.'

'That's stupid,' she said. 'If it's a bad word it doesn't matter how old you are.'

'That's very true,' I said. 'But I can't tell Sergeant Deborah what to say.'

'That's stupid,' Astor repeated, and then switched directions by adding, 'Is she really a sergeant? Is that better than a policeman?'

'It means she's the boss policeman,' I said.

'She can tell the ones in the blue suits what to do?'

'Yes,' I said.

'And she gets to have a gun, too?'

'Yes.'

Astor leaned forward as far as the seat belt would let her, and stared at Deborah with something approaching respect, which was not an expression I saw on her face very often. 'I didn't know girls could have a gun and be the boss policeman,' she said.

'Girls can do any god – anything boys can do,' Deborah snapped. 'Usually better.'

Astor looked at Cody, and then at me. 'Anything?' she said.

'Almost anything,' I said. 'Professional football is probably out.'

'Do you shoot people?' Astor asked Deborah.

'For Christ's sake, Dexter,' Deborah said.

'She shoots people sometimes,' I told Astor, 'but she doesn't like to talk about it.'

'Why not?'

'Shooting somebody is a very private thing,' I said, 'and I think she feels that it isn't anybody else's business.'

'Stop talking about me like I'm a lamp, for Christ's sake,' Deborah snapped. 'I'm sitting right here.'

'I know that,' Astor said. 'Will you tell us about who you shot?'

For an answer, Deborah squealed the car through a sharp turn, into the parking lot, and rocked to a stop in front of the center. 'We're here,' she said, and jumped out as if she was escaping a nest of fire ants. She hurried into the building and as soon as I got Cody and Astor unbuckled, we followed at a more leisurely pace.

Deborah was still speaking with the sergeant on duty at the desk, and I steered Cody and Astor to a pair of battered chairs. 'Wait here,' I said. 'I'll be back in a few minutes.'

'Just *wait*?' Astor said, with outrage quivering in her voice.

'Yes,' I said. 'I have to go talk to a bad guy.'

'Why can't we go?' she demanded.

'It's against the law,' I said. 'Now wait here like I said. Please.'

They didn't look terribly enthusiastic, but at

192

least they didn't leap off the chairs and charge down the hallway screaming. I took advantage of their cooperation and joined Deborah.

'Come on,' she said, and we headed to one of the interview rooms down the hall. In a few minutes a guard brought Halpern in. He was handcuffed, and he looked even worse than he had when we brought him in. He hadn't shaved and his hair was a rat's nest, and there was a look in his eyes that I can only describe as haunted, no matter how clichéd that sounds. He sat in the chair where the guard nudged him, perching on the edge of the seat and staring at his hands as they lay before him on the table.

Deborah nodded to the guard, who left the room and stood in the hall outside. She waited for the door to swing closed and then turned her attention to Halpern. 'Well, Jerry,' she said, 'I hope you had a good night's rest.'

His head jerked as if it had been yanked upward by a rope, and he goggled at her. 'What – what do you mean?' he said.

Debs raised her eyebrows. 'I don't mean anything, Jerry,' she said mildly. 'Just being polite.'

He stared at her for a moment and then dropped his head again. 'I want to go home,' he said in a small, shaky voice.

'I'm sure you do, Jerry,' Deborah said. 'But I can't let you go right now.'

He just shook his head, and muttered something inaudible.

'What's that, Jerry?' she asked in the same kind, patient voice.

'I said, I don't think I did anything,' he said, still without looking up.

'You don't *think* so?' she asked him. 'Shouldn't we be kind of sure about that before we let you go?'

He raised his head to look at her, very slowly this time. 'Last night . . .' he said. 'Something about being in this place . . .' He shook his head. 'I don't know. I don't know,' he said.

'You've been in a place like this before, haven't you, Jerry? When you were young,' Deborah said, and he nodded. 'And this place made you remember something?'

He jerked as if she'd spit in his face. 'I don't – it isn't a memory,' he said. 'It was a dream. It had to be a dream.'

Deborah nodded very understandingly. 'What was the dream about, Jerry?'

He shook his head and stared at her with his jaw hanging open.

'It might help you to talk about it,' she said. 'If it's just a dream, what can it hurt?' He kept shaking his head. 'What was the dream about, Jerry?' she said again, a little more insistently, but still very gently.

'There's a big statue,' he said, and he stopped shaking his head and looked surprised that words had come out.

'All right,' Deborah said.

'It – it's really big,' he said. 'And there's a . . . a . . . it has a fire burning in its belly.'

'It has a belly?' Deborah said. 'What kind of statue is it?'

'It's so big,' he said. 'Bronze body, with two arms held out, and the arms are moving down, to . . .' He trailed off, and then mumbled something.

'What did you say, Jerry?'

'He said it has a bull's head,' I said, and I could feel all the hairs on the back of my neck standing straight out.

'The arms come down,' he said. 'And I feel . . . really happy. I don't know why. Singing. And I put the two girls into the arms. I cut them with a knife, and they go up to the mouth, and the arms dump them in. Into the fire . . .'

'Jerry,' Debs said, even more gently, 'your clothes had blood on them, and they'd been singed.' He didn't say anything, and she went on. 'We know you have blackouts when you're feeling too much stress,' she said. He stayed quiet. 'Isn't it just possible, Jerry, that you had one of these black-outs, killed the girls, and came home? Without knowing it?'

He began shaking his head again, slowly and mechanically.

'Can you give me a better suggestion?' she said.

'Where would I find a statue like that?' he said. 'That's – how could I, what, find the statue, and build the fire inside it, and get the girls there, and – how could that be possible? How could I do all that and not know it?'

Deborah looked at me, and I shrugged. It was

195

a fair point. After all, there must surely be some practical limit to what you can do while sleep-walking, and this did seem to go a little beyond that.

'Then where did the dream come from, Jerry?' she said.

'Everybody has dreams,' he said.

'And how did the blood get on your clothes?'

'Wilkins did it,' he said. 'He had to, there's no other answer.'

There was a knock on the door and the sergeant came in. He bent over and spoke softly into Deborah's ear, and I leaned closer to hear. 'This guy's lawyer is making trouble,' he said. 'He says now that the heads turned up while his client is in here, he has to be innocent.' The sergeant shrugged. 'I can't keep him outta here,' he said.

'All right,' Debs said. 'Thanks, Dave.' He shrugged again, straightened, and left the room.

Deborah looked at me. 'Well,' I said, 'at least it doesn't seem too easy anymore.'

She turned back to Halpern. 'All right, Jerry,' she said. 'We'll talk some more later.' She stood up and walked out of the room and I followed.

'What do we think about that?' I asked her.

She shook her head. 'Jesus, Dex, I don't know. I need a major break here.' She stopped walking and turned to face me. 'Either the guy really did this in one of his blackouts, which means he set the whole thing up without really knowing, which is impossible.'

'Probably,' I said.

'Or else somebody else went to a shitload of trouble to set it up and frame him, and timed it just right to match one of his blackouts.'

'Which is also impossible,' I said helpfully.

'Yeah,' she said. 'I know.'

'And the statue with the bull's head and the fire in its belly?'

'Fuck,' she said. 'It's just a dream. Has to be.'

'So where were the girls burned?'

'You want to show me a giant statue with a bull's head and a built-in barbecue? Where do you hide that? You find it and I'll believe it's real,' she said.

'Do we have to release Halpern now?' I asked.

'No, goddamn it,' she snarled. 'I still got him on resisting arrest.' And she turned away and walked back toward the receiving area.

Cody and Astor were sitting with the sergeant when we got back out to the entryway, and even though they had not remained where I told them to, I was so grateful that they had not set anything on fire that I let it go. Deborah watched impatiently while I collected them, and we all headed out the door together. 'Now what?' I said.

'We have to talk to Wilkins, of course,' Deborah said.

'And do we ask him if he has a statue with a bull's head in his backyard?' I asked her.

'No,' she said. 'That's bullshit.'

'That's a bad word,' said Astor. 'You owe me fifty cents.'

'It's getting late,' I said. 'I have to get the kids home before their mother barbecues me.'

Deborah looked at Cody and Astor for a long moment, then up at me. 'All right,' she said.

CHAPTER 19

I did manage to get the kids home before Rita went over the edge, but it was a very close call that was not made any easier when she found out that they had been to see severed heads. Still, they were obviously unbothered and even excited about their day, and Astor's new determination to be a Mini-Me to my sister Deborah seemed to distract Rita from anything approaching actual wrath. After all, an early career choice could save a lot of time and bother later.

It was clear that Rita had a full head of steam and we were in for Babblefest. Normally I would simply smile and nod and let her run on. But I was in no mood for anything that smacked of normal. For the last two days I had wanted nothing but a quiet place and time to try to figure out where my Passenger had gone, and I had instead been pulled in every other direction possible by Deborah, Rita, the kids, even my job, of all things. My disguise had taken over from the thing it was supposed to be hiding, and I did not like it. But if I could make it past Rita and out the door, I would finally have some time to myself.

199

And so, pleading important case work that could not wait for Monday morning, I slid out the door and drove in to the office, enjoying the relative peace and calm of Miami traffic on a Saturday night.

For the first fifteen minutes of the drive I could not lose the feeling that I was being followed. Ridiculous, I know, but I had no experience with being alone in the night and it made me feel very vulnerable. Without the Passenger I was a tiger with a dull nose and no fangs. I felt slow and stupid, and the skin on my back would not stop crawling. It was an overall feeling of impending creepiness, the sense that I needed to circle around and sniff the back trail, because something was lurking there hungrily. And tickling at the edges of all that was an echo of that strange dream music, making my feet twitch in an involuntary way, as if they had someplace to go without me.

It was a terrible feeling, and if only I had been capable of empathy, I'm sure I might have had a moment of awful revelation, wherein I flung a hand to my forehead and sank to the ground, murmuring anguished regrets over all the times I had done the stalking and caused this dreadful feeling in others. But I am not built for anguish – at least, not my own – and so all I could think about was my very large problem. My Passenger was gone, and I was empty and defenseless if somebody really was tailing me.

It had to be mere imagination. Who would stalk

Dutiful Dexter, plodding through his completely normal artificial existence with a happy smile, two children, and a new mortgage to a caterer? Just to be sure, I glanced into the rearview mirror.

No one of course; no one lurking with an ax and a piece of pottery with Dexter's name on it. I was turning stupid in my lonely dotage.

A car was on fire on the shoulder of the Palmetto Expressway, and most of the traffic was dealing with the congestion by either roaring around it on the left shoulder or leaning on the horn and shouting. I got off and drove past the warehouses near the airport. At a storage place just off 69th Avenue a burglar alarm was clattering endlessly, and three men were loading boxes into a truck without any appearance of haste. I smiled and waved; they ignored me.

It was a feeling I was getting used to – everyone was ignoring poor empty Dexter lately, except, of course, whoever it was that had either been following me or not really following me at all.

But speaking of empty, the way I had weaseled out of a confrontation with Rita, smooth as it had been, had left me without dinner, and this is not something I willingly tolerate. Right now I wanted to eat almost as much as I wanted to breathe.

I stopped at a Pollo Tropical and picked up half a chicken to take with me. The smell instantly filled the car, and the last couple of miles it was all I could do to keep the car on the road instead of screeching to a halt and ripping at the chicken with my teeth.

It finally overwhelmed me in the parking lot, and as I walked in the door I had to fumble out my credentials with greasy fingers, nearly dropping the beans in the process. But by the time I settled in at my computer, I was a much happier boy and the chicken was no more than a bag of bones and a pleasant memory.

As always, with a full stomach and a clean conscience I found it much easier to shift my powerful brain into high gear and think about the problem. The Dark Passenger was missing; that seemed to imply that it had some kind of independent existence without me. That meant it must have come from somewhere and, quite possibly, gone back there. So my first problem was to learn what I could about where it came from.

I knew very well that mine was not the only Passenger in the world. Over the course of my long and rewarding career I had encountered several other predators wrapped in the invisible black cloud that indicated a hitchhiker like mine. And it stood to reason that they had originated somewhere and sometime, and not just with me and in my own time. Shamefully enough, I had never wondered why, or where these inner voices came from. Now, with the whole night stretching ahead of me in the peace and quiet of the forensics lab, I could rectify this tragic oversight.

And so without any thought of my own personal safety, I dashed fearlessly onto the Internet. Of course, there was nothing helpful when I searched

'Dark Passenger.' That was, after all, my private term. I tried it anyway, just to be safe, and found nothing more than a few online games and a couple of blogs that someone really should report to the proper authorities, whoever was in charge of policing teenage angst.

I searched for 'interior companion,' 'inside friend,' and even 'spirit guide.' Once again there were some very interesting results that made one wonder what this tired old world was coming to, but nothing that illuminated my problem. But as far as I know there has never been only one of anything, and the odds were that I was simply failing to come up with the correct search terms to find what I needed.

Very well: 'Inner guide.' 'Internal adviser.' 'Hidden helper.' I went through as many combinations of these as I could think of, switching around the adjectives, running through lists of synonyms, and always marveling at how New Age pseudo-philosophy had taken over the Internet. And still I came up with nothing more sinister than a way to tap my powerful subconscious to make a killing in real estate.

There was, however, one very interesting reference to Solomon, of biblical fame, which claimed that the old wise guy had made secret references to some kind of inner king. I searched for a few tidbits of information on Solomon. Who would have guessed that this Bible stuff was interesting and relevant? But apparently when we think of him as being a wise, jolly old guy with a beard who offered to cut a baby in half just for laughs, we are missing out on all the good parts.

For example, Solomon built a temple to something called Moloch, apparently one of the naughty elder gods, and he killed his brother because 'wickedness' was found inside him. I could certainly see that, from a biblical perspective, interior wickedness might be a fine description of a Dark Passenger. But if there was a connection here, did it really make sense that someone with an 'inner king' would kill somebody inhabited by wickedness?

It was making my head spin. Was I to believe that King Solomon himself actually had a Dark Passenger of his own? Or because he was supposedly one of the Bible's good guys, should I interpret it to mean that he found one in his brother and killed him because of it? And contrary to what we had all been led to believe, did he really mean it when he offered to cut the baby in half?

Most important of all, did it really matter what had happened several thousand years ago on the far side of the world? Even supposing that King Solomon had one of the original Dark Passengers, how did that help me get back to being lovable deadly me? What did I actually *do* with all this fascinating historical lore? None of it told me where the Passenger came from, what it was, or how to get it back.

I was at a loss. All right, then, it was clearly time to give up, accept my fate, throw myself on the mercy of the court, assume the role of Dexter, quiet family man and former Dark Avenger. Resign myself to the idea that I would never again feel the hard cool touch of the moonlight on my electrified nerve endings as I slid through the night like the avatar of cold, sharp steel.

I tried to think of something to inspire me to even greater heights of mental effort in my investigation, but all I came up with was a piece of a Rudyard Kipling poem: 'If you can keep your head when all about you are losing theirs,' or words to that effect. It didn't seem like it was enough. Perhaps Ariel Goldman and Jessica Ortega should have memorized Kipling. In any case, my search had taken me no place helpful.

Fine. What else could someone call the Passenger? 'Sardonic commentator,' 'warning system,' 'inside cheerleader.' I checked them all. Some of the results for inside cheerleader were really quite startling, but had nothing to do with my search.

I tried 'watcher,' 'interior watcher,' 'dark watcher,' 'hidden watcher.'

One last long shot, possibly having to do with the fact that my thoughts were once again turning toward food, but quite justified nevertheless: 'hungry watcher.'

Again, the results were mostly New Age blather. But one blog caught my eye, and I clicked on it. I read the opening paragraph and, although I did not actually say 'Bingo,' that was certainly the gist of what I thought.

'Once again into the night with the Hungry Watcher,' it began. 'Stalking the dark streets that teem with prey, riding slowly through the waiting feast and feeling the pull of the tide of blood that will soon rise to cover us with joy . . .'

Well. The prose was somewhat purple, perhaps. And the part about the blood was a little bit icky. But that aside, it was a pretty good description of how I felt when I went off on one of my adventures. It seemed likely that I had found a kindred spirit.

I read on. It was all consistent with the experience as I knew of it, cruising through the night with hungry anticipation as a sibilant inner voice whispered guidance. But then, when the narrative came to the point where I would have pounced and slashed, this narrator instead made a reference to 'the others,' followed by three figures from some alphabet I didn't recognize.

Or did I?

Feverishly, I scrabbled across my desk for the folder holding the file for the two headless girls. I yanked out the stack of photographs, flipped through them – and there it was.

Chalked on the driveway at Dr Goldman's house, the same three letters, looking like a misshapen MLK.

I glanced up at my computer screen: it was a match, no question about it.

This was way too much to be a coincidence. It clearly meant something very important; perhaps it was even the key to understanding the entire mess. Yes, highly significant, with just one small footnote: Significant of what? What did it mean?

On top of everything else, why was this particular clue afflicting me? I had come here to work on my own personal problem of a missing Passenger – had come late at night so I would not be harried by my sister or other demands of work. And now, apparently, if I wanted to solve my problem I would have to do it by working on Deborah's case. How come nothing was fair anymore?

Well, if there was any real reward for complaining I hadn't seen it so far, in a life filled with suffering and verbal skill. So I might as well take what was offered and see where it led.

First, what language was the script? I was reasonably certain it wasn't Chinese or Japanese – but what about some other Asian alphabet I knew nothing about? I pulled up an online atlas and began checking off countries: Korea, Cambodia, Thailand. None of them had an alphabet that was even close. What did that leave? Cyrillic? Easy enough to check. I pulled up a page containing the whole alphabet. I had to stare at it for a long time; some of the letters seemed close, but in the end I concluded that it was not a match.

What then? What did that leave? What would somebody really smart do next, somebody like who I had once been, or even somebody like that all-time champion of bright guys, King Solomon?

A small beeping sound began to chirp in the

back of my brain, and I listened to it for a moment before I answered it. Yes, that's right, I said King Solomon. The guy from the Bible with an inner king. What? Oh, really? A connection, you say? You think so?

A long shot, but easy enough to check, and I did. Solomon would have spoken ancient Hebrew, of course, which was simple to find on the Web. And it looked very little like the characters I had found. So that was that, and there was no connection: ipso facto, or some other equally compelling Latin saying.

But hold on: Didn't I remember that the original language of the Bible was not Hebrew but something else? I beat my gray cells brutally, and they finally came out with it. Yes, it had been something I remembered from that unimpeachable scholarly source, *Raiders of the Lost Ark*. And the language I was looking for was Aramaic.

Once again, it was easy to find a Web site eager to teach us all to write Aramaic. And as I looked at it, I became eager to learn, because there was no doubt about it – the three letters were an exact match. And they were, in fact, the Aramaic counterparts of MLK, just the way they looked.

I read on. Aramaic, like Hebrew, did not use vowels. Instead, you had to supply them yourself. Very tricky, really, because you had to know what the word was before you could read it. Therefore, MLK could be milk or milik or malik or any other combination, and none of them made sense. At least not to me, which seemed like the important thing. But I doodled anyway, trying to make sense of the letters. Milok. Molak. Molek—

Once again something flickered in the back of my brain and I grabbed at it, pulled it forward into the light, and looked it over. It was King Solomon again. Just before the part where he killed his brother for having wickedness inside, he had built a temple to Moloch. And of course, the preferred alternative spelling for Moloch was Molek, known as the detestable god of the Ammonites.

This time I searched 'Moloch worship,' scanning through a dozen irrelevant Web sites before hitting a few that told me the same things: the worship was characterized by an ecstatic loss of control and ended with a human sacrifice. Apparently the people were whipped into a frenzy until they didn't realize that little Jimmy had somehow been killed and cooked, not necessarily in that order.

Well, I don't really understand ecstatic loss of control, even though I have been to football games at the Orange Bowl. So I admit I was curious: How did they work that trick? I read a little closer, and found that apparently there was music involved, music so compelling that the frenzy was almost automatic. How this happened was a little ambiguous – the clearest reading I found, from an Aramaic text translated with lots of footnotes, was that 'Moloch sent music unto them.' I supposed that meant a band of his priests would march through the streets with drums and trumpets . . .

Why drums and trumpets, Dexter?

Because that was what I was hearing in my sleep. Drums and trumpets rising into a glad chorus of singing and the feeling that pure eternal joy was right outside the door.

Which seemed like a pretty good working definition of ecstatic loss of control, didn't it?

All right, I reasoned: just for the sake of argument, let's say Moloch has returned. Or maybe he never went away. So a three-thousand-year-old detestable god from the Bible was sending music in order to, um – what, exactly? Steal my Dark Passenger? Kill young women in Miami, the modern Gomorrah? I even dragged in my earlier insight from the museum and tried to fit it into the puzzle: so Solomon had the original Dark Passenger, which had now come to Miami, and, like a male lion taking over a pride, was therefore trying to kill the Passengers already here, because, um . . . Why exactly?

Or was I really supposed to believe that an Old Testament bad guy was coming out of time to get me? Wouldn't it make more sense simply to reserve myself a rubber room right now?

I pushed at it from every side and still came up with nothing. Possibly my brain was starting to fall apart, too, along with the rest of my life. Maybe I was just tired. Whatever the case, none of it made sense. I needed to know more about Moloch. And because I was sitting in front of the computer, I wondered if Moloch had his own Web site.

It took only a moment to find out, so I typed it in, went down the list of self-important self-pitying blogs, online fantasy games, and arcane paranoid fantasies until I found one that looked likely. When I clicked on the link, a picture began to form very slowly, and as it did—

The deep, powerful beat of the drum, insistent horns rising behind the pulsing rhythm to a point that swells until it can no longer hold back the voices which break out in anticipation of a gladness beyond knowing – it was the music I had heard in my sleep.

Then the slow blossom of a smoldering bull's head, there in the middle of the page, with two upraised hands beside it and the same three Aramaic letters above.

And I sat and stared and blinked with the cursor, still feeling the music crash through me and lift me toward the hot glorious heights of an unknown ecstasy that promised me all the blinding delight ever possible in a world of hidden joy. For the first time in my memory, as these passionate strange sensations washed over and through me and finally out and away – for the first time ever I felt something new, different, and unwelcome.

I was afraid.

I could not say why, or of what, which made it much worse, a lonely unknown fear that roiled through me and echoed off the empty places and drove away everything but the picture of that bull's head and the fear.

This is nothing, Dexter, I told myself. *An animal picture and some random notes of not terribly good music.* And I agreed with myself completely – but I could not make my hands listen to reason and move off my lap. Something about this crossover between the supposedly unconnected worlds of sleep and waking made telling them apart impossible, as if anything that could show up in my sleep and then appear on my screen at work was too powerful to resist and I had no chance of fighting it, had simply to watch as it dragged me down and under into the flames.

There was no black, mighty voice inside me to turn me into steel and fling me like a spear at whatever this was. I was alone, afraid, helpless, and clueless; Dexter in the dark, with the bogeyman and all his unknown minions hiding under the bed and getting ready to pull me out of this world and into the burning land of shrieking, terror-filled pain.

With a motion that was far from graceful I lunged across my desk and yanked the computer's power cord from the wall and, breathing rapidly and looking like someone had attached electrodes to my muscles, I jerked backward into my chair again, so quick and clumsy that the plug on the end of the cord whipped back and snapped me on the forehead just above the left eyebrow.

For several minutes I did nothing but breathe

and watch as the sweat rolled off my face and plopped onto my desk. I had no idea why I had leaped off my chair like a gaffed barracuda and yanked the cord out of the wall, beyond the fact that for some reason it had felt like I had to do it or die, and I couldn't understand where that notion came from, either, but come it had, barreling out of the new darkness between my ears and crushing me with its urgency.

And so I sat in my quiet office and gaped at a dead screen, wondering who I was and what had just happened.

I was never afraid. Fear was an emotion and Dexter did not have them. To be afraid of a Web site was so far beyond stupid and pointless that there were no adjectives for it. And I did not act irrationally, except when imitating human beings.

So why had I pulled the plug, and why were my hands trembling, all from a cheerful little tune and a cartoon cow?

There were no answers, and I was no longer sure I wanted to find them.

I drove home, convinced that I was being followed, even though the rearview mirror stayed empty the whole way.

The other really was quite special, resilient in a way that the Watcher had not seen in quite some time. This was proving to be far more interesting than some of the ones in the past. He began to feel something that might even be called kinship with the other. Sad, really. If only things had worked out differently. But there was a kind of beauty to the inevitable fate of the other, and that was good, too.

Even this far behind the other's car, he could see the signs of nerves starting to fray: speeding up and slowing down, fiddling with the mirrors. Good. Uneasy was just the beginning. He needed to move the other far beyond uneasy, and he would. But first it was essential to make sure the other knew what was coming. And so far, in spite of the clues, he did not seem to have figured it out.

Very well, then. The Watcher would simply repeat the pattern until the other recognized just what sort of power was after him. After that, the other would have no choice. He would come like a happy lamb to the slaughter.

Until then, even the watching had purpose. Let him know he was watched. It would do him no good, even if he saw the face watching him.

Faces can change. But the watching would not.

CHAPTER 20

Of course there was no sleep for me that night. The next day, Sunday, passed in a haze of fatigue and anxiety. I took Cody and Astor to a nearby park and sat on a bench while I tried to make sense of the pile of unco-operative information and conjecture I had come up with so far. The pieces refused to come together into any kind of picture that made sense. Even if I hammered them into a semi-coherent theory, it told me nothing that would help me understand how to find my Passenger.

The best I could come up with was a sort of half-formed notion that the Dark Passenger and others like it had been hanging around for at least three thousand years. But why mine should flee from any other was impossible to say – espe-cially since I had encountered others before with no more reaction than raised hackles. My notion of the new daddy lion seemed particu-larly far-fetched in the pleasant sunlight of the park, against the background of the children twittering threats at one another. Statistically speaking, about half of them had new daddies, based on the divorce rate, and they seemed to be thriving.

I let despair wash over me, a feeling that seemed slightly absurd in the lovely Miami afternoon. The Passenger was gone, I was alone, and the only solution I could come up with was to take lessons in Aramaic. I could only hope that a chunk of frozen waste-water from a passing airplane would fall on my head and put me out of my misery. I looked up hopefully, but there, too, I was out of luck.

Another semi-sleepless night, broken only by a recurrence of the strange music that came into my sleep and woke me as I sat up in bed to go to it. I had no idea why it seemed like such a good idea to follow the music, and even less idea where it wanted to take me, but apparently I was going anyway. Clearly I was falling apart, sliding rapidly downhill into gray, empty madness.

Monday morning a dazed and battered Dexter staggered into the kitchen, where I was immediately and violently assaulted by Hurricane Rita, who charged at me waving a huge stack of papers and CDs. 'I need to know what you think,' she said, and it struck me that this was something she definitely did *not* need to know, considering the deep bleakness of my thoughts. But before I could summon even a mild objection she had hurled me into a kitchen chair and began flinging the documents around.

'These are the flower arrangements that Hans wants to use,' she started, showing me a series of pictures that were, in fact, floral in nature. 'This is for the altar. And it's maybe a little too, oh, I don't know,' she said desperately. 'Is anybody going to make jokes about too much white?'

Although I am known for a finely tuned sense of humor, very few jokes based on the color white sprang to mind, but before I could reassure her on the subject, Rita was already flipping the pages.

'Anyway,' she said, 'this is the individual table setting. Which hopefully goes with what Manny Borque is doing. Maybe we should get Vince to check it with him?'

'Well,' I said.

'Oh good lord, look at the time,' she said, and before I could speak even one more syllable she had dropped a pile of CDs in my lap. 'I've narrowed it down to six bands,' she said. 'Can you listen to these today and let me know what you think? Thanks, Dex,' she went on relentlessly, leaning to plant a kiss on my cheek and then heading for the door, already moving on to the next item on her checklist. 'Cody?' she called. 'It's time to go, sweetie. Come on.'

There was another three minutes of commotion, the highlights of which were Cody and Astor sticking their heads in the kitchen door to say good-bye, and then the front door slammed and all was silent.

And in the silence I thought I could almost hear, as I had heard in the night, the faint echo of the music. I knew I should leap from my chair and charge out the door with my saber clamped firmly between my teeth – charge into the bright light of day and find this thing, whatever it was, beard it in its den and slay it – but I could not.

The Moloch Web site had stuck its fear into me, and even though I knew it was foolish, wrong, counterproductive, totally non-Dexter in every way, I could not fight it. Moloch. Just a silly ancient name. An old myth that had disappeared thousands of years ago, torn down with Solomon's temple. It was nothing, a figment from prehistoric imaginations, less than nothing – except that I was afraid of it.

There seemed nothing else to do except to stumble through the day with my head down and hope that it didn't get me, whatever it was. I was bone tired, and maybe that was adding to my sense of helplessness. But I didn't think so. I had the feeling that a very bad thing was circling closer with its nose full of my scent, and I could already feel its sharp teeth in my neck. All I could hope for was to make its sport last a little longer, but sooner or later I would feel its claws on me and then I, too, would bleat, beat my heels in the dust, and die. There was no fight left in me; there was, in fact, almost nothing at all left in me, except a kind of reflex humanity that said it was time to go to work.

I picked up Rita's stack of CDs and slogged out the door. And as I stood in the doorway of the house, turning the key to lock the front door, a white Avalon very slowly pulled away from the curb and drove off with a lazy insolence that cut through all my fatigue and despair and sliced right into me with a jolt of sheer terror that rocked me back against the door as the CDs slipped from my fingers and crashed onto the walk.

The car motored slowly up the street to the stop sign. I watched, nerveless and numb. And as its brake lights flicked off and it started up and through the intersection, a small piece of Dexter woke up, and it was very angry.

It might have been the absolute bold uncaring disrespect of the Avalon's behavior, and it might have been that all I really needed was the jolt of adrenaline to supplement my morning coffee. Whatever it was, it filled me with a sense of righteous indignation, and before I could even decide what to do I was already doing it, running down the driveway to my car and leaping into the driver's seat. I jammed the key into the ignition, fired up the engine, and raced after the Avalon.

I ignored the stop sign, accelerated through the intersection, and caught sight of the car as it turned right a few blocks ahead. I went much faster than I should have and saw him turn left toward U.S. 1. I closed the gap and sped up, frantic to catch him before he got lost in the rush-hour traffic.

I was only a block or so back when he turned north on U.S. 1 and I followed, ignoring the squealing brakes and the deafening chord of horn

219

music from the other motorists. The Avalon was about ten cars ahead of me now, and I used all my Miami driving skills to get closer, concentrating only on the road and ignoring the lines that separated the lanes, even failing to enjoy the wonderful creativity of the language that followed me from the surrounding cars. The worm had turned, and although it might not have all its teeth, it was ready for battle, however it was that worms fought. I was angry – another novelty for me. I had been drained of all my darkness and pushed into a bright drab corner where all the walls were closing in, but enough was enough. It was time for Dexter to fight back. And although I did not really know what I planned to do when I caught up with the other car, I was absolutely going to do it.

I was half a block back when the Avalon's driver became aware of me and sped up immediately, slipping into the far left lane into a space so tight that the car behind him slammed on its brakes and spun sideways. The two cars behind it smashed into its exposed side and a great roar of horns and brakes hammered at my ears. I found just enough room to my right to squeak through around the crash and then over to the left again in the now-open far lane. The Avalon was a block ahead and picking up speed, but I put the pedal down and followed.

For several blocks the gap between us stayed about the same. Then the Avalon caught up with the traffic that was ahead of the accident and I got a bit closer, until I was only two cars behind, close enough to see a pair of large sunglasses looking back at me in the side mirror. And as I surged up to within one car length of his bumper, he suddenly yanked his steering wheel hard to the left, bouncing his car up onto the median strip and sliding sideways down into traffic on the other side. I was past him before I could even react. I could almost hear mocking laughter drifting back at me as he trundled off toward Homestead.

But I refused to let him go. It was not that catching the other car might give me some answers, although that was probably true. And I was not thinking of justice or any other abstract concept. No, this was pure indignant anger, rising from some unused interior corner and flowing straight out of my lizard brain and down to my knuckles. What I really wanted to do was pull this guy out of his rotten little car and smack him in the face. It was an entirely new sensation, this idea of inflicting bodily harm in the heat of anger, and it was intoxicating, strong enough to shut down any logical impulses that might be left in me and it sent me across the median in pursuit.

My car made a terrible crunching noise as it bounced up onto the median and then down on the other side, and a large cement truck missed flattening me by only about four inches, but I was off again, heading after the Avalon in the lighter southbound traffic.

Far ahead of me there were several spots of moving white color, any one of which might have been my target. I stomped down on the gas and followed.

The gods of traffic were kind to me, and I zipped through the steadily moving cars for almost half a mile before I hit my first red light. There were several cars in each lane halted obediently at the intersection and no way around them – except to repeat my car-crunching trick of banging up onto the median strip. I did. I came down off the narrow end of the median and into the intersection just in time to cause severe inconvenience to a bright yellow Hummer that was foolishly trying to use the roads in a rational way. It gave a manic lurch to avoid me, and very nearly succeeded; there was only the lightest of thuds as I bounced neatly off its front bumper, through the intersection, and onward, followed by yet another blast of horn music and yelling.

The Avalon would be a quarter of a mile ahead if it was still on U.S. 1, and I did not wait for the distance to grow. I chugged on in my trusty, banged-up little car, and after only half a minute I was in sight of two white cars directly ahead of me – one of them a Chevy SUV and the other a minivan. My Avalon was nowhere to be seen.

I slowed just for a moment – and out of the corner of my eye I saw it again, edging around behind a grocery store in a strip mall parking lot off to the right. I slammed my foot down onto the gas pedal and slewed across two lanes of traffic and into the parking lot. The driver of the other car saw me coming; he sped up and pulled out onto the street running perpendicular to U.S. 1, racing away to the east as fast as he could go. I hurried through the parking lot and followed.

He led me through a residential area for a mile or so, then around another corner and past a park where a day-care program was in full swing. I got a little closer – just in time to see a woman holding a baby and leading two other children step into the road in front of us.

The Avalon accelerated up and onto the side-walk and the woman continued to move slowly across the road looking at me as if I was a bill-board she couldn't read. I swerved to go behind her, but one of her children suddenly darted back-ward right in front of me and I stood on the brake. My car went into a skid, and for a moment it looked as if I would slide right into the whole slow, stupid cluster of them as they stood there in the road, watching me with no sign of interest. But my tires bit at last, and I managed to spin the wheel, give it a little bit of gas, and skid through a quick circle on the lawn of a house across the street from the park. Then I was back onto the road in a cloud of crabgrass, and after the Avalon, now farther ahead.

The distance stayed about the same for several more blocks before I got my lucky break. Ahead of me the Avalon roared through another stop sign, but this time a police cruiser pulled out after it, turned on the siren, and gave chase. I wasn't sure if I should be glad of the company or jealous of the competition, but in any case it was much easier to follow the flashing lights and siren, so I continued to slog along in the rear.

The two other cars went through a quick series of turns, and I thought I might be getting a little closer, when suddenly the Avalon disappeared and the cop car slid to a halt. In just a few seconds I was up beside the cruiser and getting out of my car.

In front of me the cop was running across a close-cropped lawn marked with tire tracks that led around behind a house and into a canal. The Avalon was settling down into the water by the far side and, as I watched, a man climbed out of the car through the window and swam the few yards to the opposite bank of the canal. The cop hesitated on our side and then jumped in and swam to the half-sunk car. As he did, I heard the sound of heavy tires braking fast behind me. I turned to look.

A yellow Hummer rocked to a stop behind my car and a red-faced man with sandy hair jumped out and started to yell at me. 'You cocksucker son of a bitch!' he hollered. 'You dinged up my car! What the hell you think you're doing?'

Before I could answer, my cell phone rang. 'Excuse me,' I said, and oddly enough the sandy-haired man stood there quietly as I answered the phone.

'Where the hell are you?' Deborah demanded.

'Cutler Ridge, looking at a canal,' I said.

It gave her pause for a full second before she said, 'Well, dry off and get your ass over to the campus. We got another body.'

CHAPTER 21

It took me a few minutes to disengage myself from the driver of the yellow Hummer, and I might have been there still if not for the cop who had jumped into the canal. He finally climbed out of the water and came over to where I stood listening to a nonstop stream of threats and obscenities, none very original. I tried to be polite about it – the man obviously had a great deal to get off his chest, and I certainly didn't want him to sustain psychological damage by repressing it – but I did have some urgent police business to attend to, after all. I tried to point that out, but apparently he was one of those individuals who could not yell and listen to reason at the same time.

So the appearance of an unhappy and extremely wet cop was a welcome interruption to a conversation that was verging on tedious and one-sided. 'I would really like to know what you find out about the driver of that car,' I said to the cop.

'I bet you would,' he said. 'Can I see some ID, please?'

'I have to get to a crime scene,' I said.

'You're at one,' he told me. So I showed him my credentials and he looked at them very carefully, dripping canal water onto the laminated picture. Finally he nodded and said, 'Okay, Morgan, you're out of here.'

From the Hummer driver's reaction you might have thought the cop had suggested setting the Pope on fire. 'You can't let that son of a bitch just go like that!' he screeched. 'That goddamn asshole dinged up my car!'

And the cop, bless him, simply stared at the man, dripped a little more water, and said, 'May I see your license and registration, sir?' It seemed like a wonderful exit line, and I took advantage of it.

My poor battered car was making very unhappy noises, but I put it on the road to the university anyway – there really was no other choice. No matter how badly damaged it was, it would have to get me there. And it made me feel a certain kinship with my car. Here we were, two splendidly built pieces of machinery, hammered out of our original beautiful condition by circumstances beyond our control. It was a wonderful theme for self-pity, and I indulged it for several minutes. The anger I had felt only a few minutes ago had leeched away, dripped onto the lawn like canal water off the cop. Watching the Avalon's driver swim to the far side, climb out, and walk away had been in the same spirit as everything else lately; get a little bit close and then have the rug pulled out from under your feet.

And now there was a new body, and we hadn't even figured out what to do about the others yet. It was making us look like the greyhounds at a dog track, chasing after a fake rabbit that is always just a little bit too far ahead, jerked tantalizingly away every time the poor dog thinks he's about to get it in his teeth.

There were two squad cars at the university ahead of me, and the four officers had already cordoned off the area around the Lowe Art Museum and pushed back the growing crowd. A squat, powerful-looking cop with a shaved head came over to meet me, and pointed toward the back of the building.

The body was in a clump of vegetation behind the gallery. Deborah was talking to someone who looked like a student, and Vince Masuoka was squatting beside the left leg of the body and poking carefully with a ballpoint pen at something on the ankle. The body could not be seen from the road, but even so you could not really say it had been hidden. It had obviously been roasted like the others, and it was laid out just like the first two, in a stiff formal position, with the head replaced by a ceramic bull's head. And once again, as I looked at it I waited by reflex for some reaction from within. But I heard nothing except the gentle tropical wind blowing through my brain. I was still alone.

As I stood in huffish thought, Deborah came roaring over to me at full volume. 'Took you long enough,' she snarled. 'Where have you been?'

'Macramé class,' I said. 'It's just like the others?'

'Looks like it,' she said. 'What about it, Masuoka?'

'I think we got a break this time,' Vince said.

'About fucking time,' Deborah said.

'There's an ankle bracelet,' Vince said. 'It's made of platinum, so it didn't melt off.' He looked up at Deborah and gave her his terribly phony smile. 'It says Tammy on it.'

Deborah frowned and looked over to the side door of the gallery. A tall man in a seersucker jacket and bow tie stood there with one of the cops, looking anxiously at Deborah. 'Who's that guy?' she asked Vince.

'Professor Keller,' he told her. 'Art history teacher. He found the body.'

Still frowning, Deborah stood up and beckoned the uniformed cop to bring the professor over.

'Professor . . . ?' Deborah said.

'Keller. Gus Keller,' the professor said. He was a good-looking man in his sixties with what looked like a dueling scar on his left cheek. He didn't appear to be about to faint at the sight of the body.

'So you found the body here,' Deb said.

'That's right,' he said. 'I was coming over to check on a new exhibit – Mesopotamian art, actually, which is interesting – and I saw it here in the shrubbery.' He frowned. 'About an hour ago, I guess.'

Deborah nodded as if she already knew all that, even the Mesopotamian part, which was a standard cop trick designed to make people eager to add new details, especially if they might be a little bit guilty. It didn't appear to work on Keller. He simply stood and waited for another question, and Deborah stood and tried to think of one. I am justly proud of my hard-earned artificial social skills, and I didn't want the silence to turn awkward, so I cleared my throat, and Keller looked at me.

'What can you tell us about the ceramic head?' I asked him. 'From the artistic point of view.' Deborah glared at me, but she may have been jealous that I thought of the question instead of her.

'From the artistic point of view? Not much,' Keller said, looking down at the bull's head by the body. 'It looks like it was done in a mold, and then baked in a fairly primitive kiln. Maybe even just a big oven. But historically, it's much more interesting.'

'What do you mean interesting?' Deborah snapped at him, and he shrugged.

'Well, it's not perfect,' Keller said. 'But some-body tried to recreate a very old stylized design.'

'How old?' Deborah said. Keller raised an eyebrow and shrugged, as if to say she had asked the wrong question, but he answered.

'Three or four thousand years old,' he said.

'That's very old,' I offered helpfully, and they both looked at me, which made me think I ought to add something halfway clever, so I said, 'And what part of the world would it be from?'

Keller nodded. I was clever again. 'Middle East,'

he said. 'We see a similar motif in Babylonia, and even earlier around Jerusalem. The bull head appears to be attached to the worship of one of the elder gods. A particularly nasty one, really.'

'Moloch,' I said, and it hurt my throat to say that name.

Deborah glared at me, absolutely certain now that I had been holding out on her, but she looked back at Keller as he continued to talk.

'Yes, that's right,' he said. 'Moloch liked human sacrifice. Especially children. It was the standard deal: sacrifice your child and he would guarantee a good harvest, or victory over your enemies.'

'Well, then, I think we can look forward to a very good harvest this year,' I said, but neither one of them appeared to think that was worth even a tiny smile. Ah well, you do what you can to bring a little cheer into this dreary world, and if people refuse to respond to your efforts it's their loss.

'What's the point of burning the bodies?' Deborah demanded.

Keller smiled briefly, kind of a professorial thanks-for-asking smile. 'That's the whole key to the ritual,' he said. 'There was a huge bull-headed statue of Moloch that was actually a furnace.'

I thought of Halpern and his 'dream.' Had he known about Moloch beforehand, or had it come to him the way the music came to me? Or was Deborah right all along and he had actually been to the statue and killed the girls – as unlikely as that seemed now?

'A furnace,' said Deborah, and Keller nodded. 'And they toss the bodies in there?' she said, with an expression that indicated she was having trouble believing it, and it was all his fault.

'Oh, it gets much better than that,' Keller said. 'They delivered the miracle in the ritual. Very sophisticated flummery, in fact. But that's why Moloch had such lasting popularity – it was convincing, and it was exciting. The statue had arms that stretched out to the congregation. When you placed the sacrifice in his arms, Moloch would appear to come to life and eat the sacrifice – the arms would slowly raise up the victim and place it in his mouth.'

'And into the furnace,' I said, not wanting to be left out any longer, 'while the music played.'

Deborah looked at me strangely, and I realized that no one else had mentioned music, but Keller shrugged it off and answered.

'Yes, that's right. Trumpets and drums, singing, all very hypnotic. Climaxing as the god lifted the body up to its mouth and dropped it. Into the mouth and you fall down into the furnace. Alive. It can't have been much fun for the victim.'

I believed what Keller said – I heard the soft throb of the drums in the distance, and it wasn't much fun for me, either.

'Does anybody still worship this guy?' Deborah asked.

Keller shook his head. 'Not for two thousand years, as far as I know,' he said.

'Well then, what the hell,' Deborah said. 'Who's doing this?'

'It isn't any kind of secret,' Keller said. 'It's a pretty well-documented part of history. Anybody could have done a little research and found out enough to do something like this.'

'But why would they?' Deborah said.

Keller smiled politely. 'I'm sure I don't know,' he said.

'So what the hell good does any of that do me?' she said, with a tone that suggested it was Keller's job to come up with an answer.

He gave her a kindly professor smile. 'It never hurts to know things,' he said.

'For instance,' I said, 'we know that somewhere there must be a big statue of a bull with a furnace inside.'

Deborah snapped her head around so that she faced me.

I leaned close to her and said softly, 'Halpern.' She blinked at me and I could see she hadn't thought of that yet.

'You think it wasn't a dream?' she demanded.

'I don't know what to think,' I said. 'But if somebody is doing this Moloch thing for real, why wouldn't he do it with all the proper equipment?'

'Goddamn it,' Deborah said. 'But where could you hide something like that?'

Keller coughed with a certain delicacy. 'I'm afraid there's more to it than that,' he said.

233

'Like what?' Deborah demanded.

'Well, you'd have to hide the smell, too,' he said. 'The smell of cooking human bodies. It lingers, and it's rather unforgettable.' He sounded a little bit embarrassed and he shrugged.

'So we're looking for a gigantic *smelly* statue with a furnace inside,' I said cheerfully. 'That shouldn't be too hard to find.'

Deborah glared at me, and once again I had to feel a little disappointed at her heavy-handed approach to life – especially since I would almost certainly join her as a permanent resident in the Land of Gloom if the Dark Passenger refused to behave and come out of hiding.

'Professor Keller,' she said, turning away from me and completing the abandonment of her poor brother, 'is there anything else about this bull shit that might help us?'

It was certainly a clever enough remark to be encouraging, and I almost wished I had said it, but it appeared to have no effect on Keller, nor even on Deborah herself, who looked as though she was unaware that she had said something notable. Keller merely shook his head.

'It's not really my area, I'm afraid,' he said. 'I know just a little background stuff that affects the art history. You might check with somebody in philosophy or comparative religion.'

'Like Professor Halpern,' I whispered again, and Deborah nodded, still glaring.

She turned to go and luckily remembered her

manners just in time; she turned back to Keller and said, 'You've been very helpful, Dr Keller. Please let me know if you think of anything else.'

'Of course,' he said, and Debs grabbed my arm and propelled me onward.

'Are we going back to the registrar's office?' I asked politely as my arm went numb.

'Yeah,' she said. 'But if there's a Tammy enrolled in one of Halpern's classes, I don't know what I'm going to do.'

I pulled the tattered remnants of my arm from her grip. 'And if there isn't?'

She just shook her head. 'Come on,' she said.

But as I passed by the body once more, something clutched at the leg of my pants, and I looked down.

'Ahk,' Vince said to me. He cleared his throat. 'Dexter,' he said, and I raised an eyebrow. He flushed and let go of my pants. 'I have to talk to you,' he said.

'By all means,' I said. 'Can it wait?'

He shook his head. 'It's pretty important,' he said.

'Well, all right then.' I took the three steps back to where he was still squatting beside the body. 'What is it?'

He looked away, and as unlikely as it was that he would show real emotion, his face flushed even more. 'I talked to Manny,' he said.

'Wonderful. And yet you still have all your limbs,' I said.

'He, ahm,' Vince said. 'He wants to make a few changes. Ahm. In the menu. Your menu. For the wedding.'

'Aha,' I said, in spite of how corny it sounds to say 'Aha' when you are standing beside a dead body. I just couldn't help myself. 'By any chance, are these expensive changes?'

Vince refused to look up at me. He nodded his head. 'Yes,' he said. 'He said he's had an inspiration. Something really new and different.'

'I think that's terrific,' I said, 'but I don't think I can afford inspiration. We'll have to tell him no.'

Vince shook his head again. 'You don't understand. He only called because he *likes* you. He says the contract allows him to do whatever he wants.'

'And he wants to raise the price a wee bit?'

Vince was definitely blushing now. He mumbled a few syllables and tried to look away even further. 'What?' I asked him. 'What did you say?'

'About double,' he said, very quietly, but at least audible.

'Double,' I said.

'Yes.'

'That's $500 a plate,' I said.

'I'm sure it will be very nice,' said bright-red Vince.

'For $500 a plate it had better be more than nice. It had better park the cars, mop the floor, and give all the guests a back rub.'

'This is cutting-edge stuff, Dexter. You'll probably get your wedding in a magazine.'

'Yes, and it will probably be *Bankruptcy Today*. We have to talk to him, Vince.'

He shook his head and continued to look at the grass. 'I can't,' he said.

Humans are wonderful combinations of silly, ignorant, and dumb, aren't they? Even the ones who are pretending most of the time, like Vince. Here he was, a fearless forensic tech, actually within inches of a gruesomely murdered body that had no more effect on him than a tree stump, and yet he was paralyzed with terror at the thought of facing a tiny man who sculpted chocolate for a living.

'All right,' I said. 'I'll talk to him myself.'

He looked up at me at last. 'Be careful, Dexter,' he said.

CHAPTER 22

I caught up with Deborah as she was turning her car around, and happily, she paused long enough for me to climb in for a ride to the registrar's office. She had nothing to say on the short drive over, and I was too preoccupied with my own problems to care.

A quick search of the records with my new friend at the registrar's office turned up no Tammy in any of Halpern's classes. But Deborah, who had been pacing back and forth while she waited, was ready for that. 'Try last semester,' she said. I did; again nothing.

'All right,' she said with a frown. 'Then try Wilkins's classes.'

It was a lovely idea, and to prove it, I got an immediate hit: Ms Connor was in Wilkin's seminar on situational ethics.

'Right,' Deborah said. 'Get her address.'

Tammy Connor lived in a residential hall that was only moments away, and Deborah wasted no time in getting us over there and parking illegally in front of it. She was out of the car and marching toward the front door before I could even get my door open, but I followed along as quickly as I could.

The room was on the third floor. Deborah chose to vault up the stairs two at a time rather than waste time pushing the button for an elevator, and since this left me with not enough breath to complain about it, I didn't. I got there just in time to see the door to Tammy's room swing open to reveal a stocky girl with dark hair and glasses. 'Yes?' she said, frowning at Deborah.

Debs showed her badge and said, 'Tammy Connor?'

The girl gasped and put a hand to her throat. 'Oh, God, I knew it,' she said.

Deborah nodded. 'Are you Tammy Connor, miss?'

'No. No, of course not,' the girl said. 'Allison, her roommate.'

'Do you know where Tammy is, Allison?'

The girl inhaled her lower lip and chewed it while shaking her head vigorously. 'No,' she said.

'How long has she been gone?' Deborah asked.

'Two days.'

'Two days?' Deborah said, raising her eyebrows. 'Is that unusual?'

Allison looked like she was going to chew her lip off, but she kept gnawing on it, pausing only long enough to blurt out, 'I'm not supposed to say anything.'

Deborah stared at her for a long moment before finally saying, 'I think you're going to have to say something, Allison. We think Tammy may be in a lot of trouble.'

That seemed to me a very understated way of saying that we thought she was dead, but I let it go by, since it was obviously having a profound effect on Allison.

'Oh,' she said, and started jiggling up and down. 'Oh, oh, I just *knew* this would happen.'

'What is it that you think happened?' I asked her.

'They got caught,' she said. 'I told her.'

'I'm sure you did,' I said. 'So why not tell us, too?'

She hopped a little faster for a moment. 'Oh,' she said again and then warbled, 'she's having an affair with a professor. Oh, God, she'll *kill* me for this!'

Personally, I didn't think Tammy would be killing anybody, but just to be sure I said, 'Did Tammy wear any jewelry?'

She looked at me like I was crazy. 'Jewelry?' she said, as if the word was in some foreign language – Aramaic, perhaps.

'Yes, that's right,' I said encouragingly. 'Rings, bracelets – anything like that?'

'You mean like her platinum anklet?' Allison said, very obligingly, I thought.

'Yes, exactly like that,' I said. 'Did it have any markings on it?'

'Uh-huh, her name,' she said. 'Oh, God, she'll be so *pissed* at me.'

240

'Do you know which professor she was having an affair with, Allison?' Deborah said.

Allison went back to shaking her head. 'I really shouldn't tell,' she said.

'Was it Professor Wilkins?' I said, and even though Deborah glared at me, Allison's reaction was much more gratifying.

'Oh God,' she said. 'I swear I never said.'

One call on the cell phone got us the address in Coconut Grove where Dr Wilkins made his humble home. It was in a section called The Moorings, which meant that either my alma mater was paying professors a great deal more than they used to, or else Professor Wilkins had independent means. As we turned onto the street, the after-noon rain started, blowing across the road in slanted sheets, then slowing to a trickle, then picking up again.

We found the house easily. The number was on the yellow seven-foot wall that surrounded the house. A wrought-iron gate blocked off the driveway. Deborah pulled up in front and parked in the street, and we climbed out and looked through the gate. It was a rather modest home, no more than 4,000 square feet, and situated at least seventy-five yards from the water, so perhaps Wilkins wasn't really all that wealthy.

As we peeked in, looking for some way to signal the house that we had arrived and wished to enter, the front door swung open and a man came out, wearing a bright yellow rain suit. He headed for the car parked in the drive, a blue Lexus.

Deborah raised her voice and called out, 'Professor? Professor Wilkins?'

The man looked up at us from under the hood of his rain suit. 'Yes?'

'Can we speak to you for a moment, please?' Deborah said.

He walked toward us slowly, head cocked at Deborah on a slight angle. 'That depends. Who is us?'

Deborah reached into her pocket for her badge and Professor Wilkins paused cautiously, no doubt worried that she might pull out a hand grenade.

'Us is the police,' I reassured him.

'Is we?' he said, and he turned toward me with a half smile that froze when he saw me, flickered, and then resumed as a very poor fake smile. Since I am an expert on faking emotions and expressions I was in absolutely no doubt about it – the sight of little old me had startled him somehow, and he was covering it by pretending to smile. But why? If he was guilty, surely the thought of police at the gate would be worse than Dexter at the door. But instead he looked at Deborah and said, 'Oh, yes, we met once before, outside my office.'

'That's right,' said Deborah as she finally fished out her badge.

'I'm sorry, will this take long? I'm kind of in a hurry,' he said.

'We have just a couple of questions, Professor,' Deborah said. 'It will take only a minute.'

'Well,' he said, looking from the badge to my face and then quickly away again. 'All right.' He opened the gate and held it wide. 'Would you like to come in?'

Even though we were already soaked to the skin, it seemed like a pretty good idea to get out of the rain, and we followed Wilkins through the gate, up the driveway, and into his house.

The interior of the house was done in a style I recognized as classic Coconut Grove Rich Person Casual. I had not seen an example like this since I was a boy, when Miami Vice Modern took over as the area's dominant decorative pattern. But this was old school, bringing back the memory of when the area was called Nut Grove because of its loose, Bohemian flavor.

The floors were reddish-brown tile and shiny enough to shave in, and there was a conversation area consisting of a leather couch and two matching chairs off to the right beside a large picture window. Next to the window was a wet bar with a large, glassed-in, temperature-controlled wine cabinet and an abstract painting of a nude on the wall next to it.

Wilkins led us past a pair of potted plants and over to the couch, and hesitated a couple of steps in front of it. 'Ah,' he said, pushing back the hood from his rain jacket, 'we're kind of wet for the leather furniture. Can I offer you a barstool?' He gestured toward the bar.

I looked at Deborah, who shrugged. 'We can stand,' she said. 'This will only take a minute.'

'All right,' Wilkins said. He folded his arms and smiled at Deborah. 'What's so important that they send someone like you, in this weather?' he said.

Deborah flushed slightly, whether from irritation or something else I couldn't tell. 'How long have you been sleeping with Tammy Connor?' Deborah said.

Wilkins lost his happy expression and for a moment there was a very cold, unpleasant look on his face. 'Where did you hear that?' he said.

I could see that Deborah was trying to push him off-balance just a bit, and since that is one of my specialties I chimed in. 'Will you have to sell this place if you don't get tenure?' I said.

His eyes snapped to mine, and there was nothing at all pleasant about the look he gave me. He kept his tongue in his mouth, too. 'I should have known,' he said. 'So this was Halpern's jailhouse confession, was it? Wilkins did it.'

'So you didn't have an affair with Tammy Connor?' Deborah said.

Wilkins looked back to her again and, with a visible effort, regained his relaxed smile. He shook his head. 'I'm sorry,' he said. 'I can't get used to you as the tough one. I guess that's a pretty successful technique for you two, hmm?'

'Not so far,' I said. 'You haven't answered any of the questions.'

He nodded. 'All right,' he said. 'And did Halpern

tell you he broke into my office? I found him hiding under my desk. God knows what he was doing there.'

'Why do you think he broke into your office?' Deborah asked.

Wilkins shrugged. 'He said I sabotaged his paper.'

'Did you?'

He looked at her, and then over to me for an unpleasant moment, then back to Deborah. 'Officer,' he said, 'I am trying very hard to co-operate here. But you've accused me of so many different things I'm not sure which one I'm supposed to answer.'

'Is that why you haven't answered any of them?' I asked.

Wilkins ignored me. 'If you can tell me how Halpern's paper and Tammy Connor fit together, I'll be happy to help any way I can. But otherwise, I've got to get going.'

Deborah looked at me, whether for advice or because she was tired of looking at Wilkins, I couldn't tell, so I gave her my very best shrug, and she looked back at Wilkins. 'Tammy Connor is dead,' she said.

'Oh, my,' Wilkins said. 'How did it happen?'

'The same way as Ariel Goldman,' Debs said.

'And you knew them both,' I added helpfully.

'I imagine that dozens of people knew them both. Including Jerry Halpern,' he said.

'Did Professor Halpern kill Tammy Connor,

Professor Wilkins?' Deborah asked him. 'From the detention center?'

He shrugged. 'I'm only saying that he knew them, too.'

'And did he have an affair with her, too?' I asked.

Wilkins smirked. 'Probably not. Not with Tammy, anyway.'

'What does that mean, Professor?' Deborah asked.

Wilkins shrugged. 'Just rumors, you know. The kids talk. Some of them think Halpern is gay.'

'Less competition for you,' I said. 'Like with Tammy Connor.'

Wilkins scowled at me and I'm sure I would have been intimidated if I was a university sophomore. 'You need to make up your mind whether I killed my students or screwed them,' he said.

'Why not both?'

'Did you go to college?' he demanded.

'Why yes, I did,' I said.

'Then you ought to know that a certain type of girl sexually pursues her professors. Tammy was over eighteen, and I'm not married.'

'Isn't it a little bit unethical to have sex with a student?' I said.

'Ex-student,' he snapped. 'I dated her after the class last semester. There's no law against dating an ex-student. Especially if she throws herself at you.'

'Nice catch,' I said.

'Did you sabotage Professor Halpern's paper?' Deborah said.

Wilkins looked back at Deborah and smiled again. It was wonderful to watch somebody almost as good as I am at switching emotions so quickly. 'Detective, do you see a pattern here?' he said. 'Listen, Jerry Halpern is a brilliant guy, but . . . not exactly stable? And with all the pressure on him right now, he's just decided that I am a whole conspiracy to get him, all by myself.' He shrugged. 'I don't think I'm quite that good,' he said with a little smile. 'At least, not at conspiracy.'

'So you think Halpern killed Tammy Connor and the others?' Deborah said.

'I didn't say that,' he said. 'But hey, he's the psycho. Not me.' He made a step toward the door and raised an eyebrow at Deborah. 'And now, if you don't mind, I really have to get going.'

Deborah handed him a business card. 'Thank you for your time, Professor,' she said. 'If you think of anything that might help, please give me a call.'

'I certainly will,' he said, giving her the kind of smile that killed disco and placing a hand on her shoulder. She managed not to flinch. 'I really hate to throw you back out into the rain, but . . .'

Deborah moved, very willingly I thought, out from under his hand and toward the door. I followed. Wilkins herded us out the door and through the gate, and then climbed into his car, backed out of the driveway, and drove away. Debs stood in the rain and watched him go, which I am sure she intended to make Wilkins nervous enough to leap from the car and confess, but considering the weather it struck me as excessive zeal. I got into the car and waited for her.

When the blue Lexus had vanished Deborah finally got in beside me. 'Guy gives me the fucking creeps,' she said.

'Do you think he's the killer?' I asked. It was a strange feeling for me, not knowing, and wondering if somebody else had seen behind the predator's mask.

She shook her head with irritation. Water flew off her hair and hit me. 'I think he's a fucking creep,' she said. 'What do you think?'

'I'm pretty sure you're right,' I said.

'He didn't mind admitting his affair with Tammy Connor,' she said. 'So why lie and say she was in his class *last* semester?'

'Reflex?' I said. 'Because he's up for tenure?'

She drummed her fingers on the steering wheel, and then leaned forward decisively and started the car. 'I'm putting a tail on him,' she said.

CHAPTER 23

A copy of an incident report lay on my desk when I finally got to work, and I realized that someone expected me to be a productive drone today, in spite of it all. So much had happened in the last few hours that it was hard to adjust to the idea that most of the workday was still looming over me with its long sharp teeth, so I went for a cup of coffee before submitting to servitude. I had half hoped that someone might have brought in some doughnuts or cookies, but of course it was a foolish thought. There was nothing but a cup and a half of burned, very dark coffee. I poured some into a cup – leaving the rest for someone truly desperate – and slogged back to my desk.

I picked up the report and began to read. Apparently someone had driven a vehicle belonging to a Mr Darius Starzak into a canal and then fled the scene. Mr Starzak himself was thus far unavailable for questioning. It took me several long moments of blinking and sipping the vile coffee to realize that this was the report of my incident this morning, and several minutes longer to decide what to do about it.

To have the name of the car's owner was little enough to go on – almost nothing, since the odds were good that the car was stolen. But to assume that and do nothing was worse than trying it and coming up empty, so I went to work once again on my computer.

First, the standard stuff: the car's registration, which showed an address off Old Cutler Road in a somewhat pricey neighborhood. Next, the police records: traffic stops, outstanding warrants, child support payments. There was nothing. Mr Starzak was apparently a model citizen who'd had no contact at all with the long arm of the law.

All right then; the name itself, 'Darius Starzak.' Darius was not a common name – at least, not in the United States. I checked immigration records. And surprisingly, I got a hit right away.

First of all, it was Dr Starzak, not Mister. He held a Ph.D. in religious philosophy from Heidelberg University, and until a few years ago had been a tenured professor at the University of Kraków. A little more digging revealed that he had been fired for some kind of uncertain scandal. Polish is not really one of my stronger languages, although I can say kielbasa when ordering lunch at a deli. But unless the translation was completely off, Starzak had been fired for membership of an illegal society.

The file did not mention why a European scholar who had lost his job for such an obscure reason would want to follow me and then drive his car into a canal. It seemed like a significant omission.

Nevertheless, I printed the picture of Starzak from the immigration file. I squinted at the photo, trying to imagine it half hidden by the large sunglasses I had seen in the Avalon's side mirror. It could have been him. It could also have been Elvis. And as far as I knew, Elvis had just as much reason to follow me as Starzak.

I went a little deeper. It isn't easy for a forensics wonk to access Interpol without an official reason, even when he is charming and clever. But after playing my online version of dodgeball for a few minutes, I got into the central records, and here things became more interesting.

Dr Darius Starzak was on a special watch list in four countries, not including the States, which explained why he was here. Although there was no proof that he had done anything, there were suspicions that he knew more than he would say about the traffic in war orphans from Bosnia. And the file casually mentioned that, of course, it is impossible to account for the whereabouts of such children. In the language of official police documents, that meant that somebody thought he might be killing them.

I should have filled up with a great thrill of cold glee as I read this, a wicked gleam of sharp anticipation – but there was nothing, not the dullest echo of the smallest spark. Instead, I felt a very small return of the human-style anger I had felt this morning when Starzak was following me. It was not an adequate replacement for the surge of dark, savage certainty from the Passenger that I had been used to, but at least it was something.

Starzak had been doing bad things to children, and he – or someone using his car, at least – had tried to do them to me. All right then. So far I had been battered back and forth like a Ping-Pong ball, and I had been content to take it, passively and without complaint, sucked into a vacuum of miserable submission because I had been deserted by the Dark Passenger. But here was something I could understand and, better, act upon.

The Interpol file told me that Starzak was a bad man, exactly the kind of person I normally tried to find in pursuit of my hobby. Someone had followed me in his car, and then gone to the extreme measure of driving his car into a canal to escape. It was possible that someone had stolen the car and Starzak was completely innocent. I didn't think so, and the Interpol report argued against it. But just to be sure I checked the stolen vehicle reports. There was no listing for Starzak or his car.

All right: I was sure it had been him, and this confirmed his guilt. I knew what to do about this: Just because I was alone inside, did that have to mean I couldn't do it?

The warm glow of certainty flickered under the anger and brought it to a slow, confident simmer. It was not the same as the gold-standard sureness I had always received from the Passenger, but it was certainly more than a hunch. This was right,

I was sure. If I did not have the kind of solid proof I usually had, too bad. Starzak had escalated the situation to a point where I had no doubt, and he had moved himself to the top of my list. I would find him and turn him into a bad memory and a drop of dried blood in my little rosewood box.

And since I was running on emotion for the first time anyway, I allowed a small feeble flicker of hope to bloom. It might well be that dealing with Starzak and doing all the things I had never before done alone might bring back the Dark Passenger. I knew nothing about how these things worked, but it made a certain kind of sense, didn't it? The Passenger had always been there urging me on – wouldn't it just possibly show up if I created the kind of situation it needed? And wasn't Starzak right in front of me and practically begging to be dealt with?

And if the Passenger didn't come back, why shouldn't I begin to be me by myself? I was the one who did the heavy lifting – couldn't I carry on with my vocation, even in my empty state?

All the answers clicked up an angry red 'yes.' And for a moment I paused and waited automatically for the accustomed answering hiss of pleasure from the shadowy inside corner – but of course, it did not come.

Never mind. I could do this alone.

I had been working at night a good deal lately, so there was no surprise at all on Rita's face when I told her after dinner that I had to go back to the office. Of course, I was not off the hook with Cody and Astor, who wanted to come with me and do something interesting, or at least stay home and play kick the can. But after some minor wheedling and a few vague threats I plucked them off me and slid out the door into the night. My night, my last remaining friend, with its feeble half-moon flickering in a dull soggy sky.

Starzak lived in an area with a gate, but a minimum-wage guard in a little hut is really much better at raising property values than it is at keeping out someone with Dexter's experience and hunger. And even though it meant a little bit of a hike after I left my car up the road from the guardhouse, the exercise was welcome. I'd had too many late nights, too many sour mornings lately, and it felt good to be up on my legs and moving toward a worthwhile goal.

I circled slowly through the neighborhood, finding Starzak's address and moving on past as if I was no more than a neighbor out for an evening constitutional. There was a light on in the front room and a single car in the driveway; it had a Florida plate that said Manatee County on the bottom. There are only 300,000 people living in Manatee County, and at least twice that many cars on the road that claim to be from there. It's a rental-car trick, designed to disguise the fact that the driver has rented a car and is therefore a tourist and a legitimate target for any predator with a yen for easy prey.

I felt a small surge of hot anticipation. Starzak was home, and the fact that he had a rental car made it more likely that he was the one who had driven his car into the canal. I moved past the house, alert for any sign that I had been seen. I saw nothing, and heard only the faint sound of a TV somewhere nearby.

I circled the block and found a house with no lights on and hurricane shutters up, a very good sign that no one was home. I moved through the darkened yard and up to the tall hedge that separated it from Starzak's house. I slipped into a gap in the shrubbery, slid the clean mask over my face, pulled on gloves, and waited as my eyes and ears adjusted. And as I did it occurred to me just how ridiculous I would look if someone saw me. I had never worried about that before; the Passenger's radar is excellent and always gave me warning of unwanted eyes. But now, without any interior help, I felt naked. And as that feeling washed over me, it left another in its wake: sheer, helpless stupidity.

What was I doing? I was violating nearly every rule I had lived by, coming here spontaneously, without my usual careful preparation, without any real proof, and without the Passenger. It was madness. I was just asking to be discovered, locked up, or hacked to bits by Starzak.

I closed my eyes and listened to the novel emotions gurgling through me. Feeling – what authentic human fun. Next I could join a bowling league. Find a chat room online and talk about

New Age self-help and alternative herbal medicine for hemorrhoids. Welcome to the human race, Dexter, the endlessly futile and pointless human race. We hope you will enjoy your short and painful stay.

I opened my eyes. I could give up, accept the fact that Dexter's day was done. Or – I could go through with this, whatever the risks, and reassert the thing that had always been me. Take action that would either bring back the Passenger or start me on the path to living without it. If Starzak was not an absolute certainly, he was close, I was here, and this was an emergency.

At least it was a clear choice, something I hadn't had in quite some time. I took a deep breath and moved as silently as I could through the hedge and into Starzak's yard.

I kept to the shadows and got to the side of the house where a door opened into the garage. It was locked – but Dexter laughs at locks, and I did not need any help from the Passenger to open this one and step into the dark garage, quietly closing the door behind me. There was a bicycle along the far wall, and a workbench with a very neat set of hanging tools. I made a mental note and crossed the garage to the door that led into the house and paused there for a long moment with my ear against the door.

Above the faint hum of air-conditioning, I heard a TV and nothing else. I listened a little longer to be sure, and then very carefully eased open the door. It was unlocked and opened smoothly and without sound, and I was into Starzak's house as silent and dark as one of the shadows.

I slipped down a hallway toward the purple glow of the TV, keeping myself pressed against the wall, painfully aware that if he was behind me for some reason I was brilliantly backlit. But as I came in sight of the TV, I saw a head rising above the back of a sofa and I knew I had him.

I held my noose of fifty-pound-test fishing line ready in my hand and stepped closer. A commercial came on and the head moved slightly. I froze, but he moved his head back to center again and I was across the room and on him, my noose whistling around his neck and sliding tight just above his Adam's apple.

For a moment he thrashed in a very gratifying way, which only pulled the noose tighter. I watched him flop and grab at his throat, and while it was enjoyable I did not feel the same cold, savage glee that I was used to at such moments. Still, it was better than watching the commercial, and I let him go on until his face started to turn purple and the thrashing subsided into a helpless wobble.

'Be still and be quiet,' I said, 'and I will let you breathe.'

It was very much to his credit that he understood at once and stopped his feeble floundering. I eased off on the noose just a bit and listened while he forced in a breath. Just one – and then

I tightened up again and pulled him to his feet. 'Come,' I said, and he came.

I stood behind him, keeping the pressure on the line just tight enough so that he could breathe a little if he tried really hard, and I led him down the hall to the back of the house and into the garage. As I pushed him to the workbench he went down to one knee, either a stumble or a foolish attempt to escape. Either way, I was in no mood for it, and I pulled hard enough to make his eyes bulge out and watched as his face got dark and he slumped over on the floor, unconscious.

Much easier for me. I got his dead weight up onto the workbench and duct-taped securely into place while he still wallowed in gape-mouthed unconsciousness. A thin stream of drool ran from one corner of his mouth and his breath came very rough, even after I loosened the noose. I looked down at Starzak, taped to the table with his unlovely face hanging open, and I thought, as I never had before, this is what we all are. This is what it comes to. A bag of meat that breathes, and when that stops, nothing but rotting garbage.

Starzak began to cough, and more phlegm dribbled from his mouth. He pushed against the duct tape, found he could not move, and fluttered open his eyes. He said something incomprehensible, composed of far too many consonants, and then rolled his eyes back and saw me. Of course he could not see my face through my mask, but I got the very unsettling feeling that he recognized me anyway. He moved his mouth a few times, but said nothing until he finally rolled his eyes back down to point at his feet and said in a dry and raspy voice with a Central European accent, but very little of the expected emotion in it, 'You are making a very large mistake.'

I searched for an automatic sinister reply, and found nothing.

'You will see,' he said in his terrible flat and raw voice. 'He will get you anyway, even without me. It is too late for you.'

And there it was. As close to a confession as I needed that he had been following me with sinister intent. But all I could think to say was, 'Who is he?'

He forgot he was taped to the bench and tried to shake his head. It didn't work, but it didn't seem to bother him much, either. 'They will find you,' he repeated. 'Soon enough.' He twitched a little, as if he was trying to wave a hand, and said, 'Go ahead. Kill me now. They will find you.'

I looked down at him, so passively taped and ready for my special attentions, and I should have been filled with icy delight at the job ahead of me – and I was not. I was not filled with anything except emptiness, the same feeling of hopeless futility that had come over me while I waited outside the house.

I shook myself out of the funk and taped Starzak's mouth shut. He flinched a little, but other than that he continued to look straight away, with no show of any kind of emotion.

I raised my knife and looked down at my unmoving and unmoved prey. I could still hear his awful wet breath rattling in and out through his nostrils and I wanted to stop it, turn out his lights, shut down this noxious thing, cut it into pieces and seal them into neat dry garbage bags, unmoving chunks of compost that would no longer threaten, no longer eat and excrete and flail around in the patternless maze of human life—

And I could not.

I called silently for the familiar rush of dark wings to sweep out of me and light up my knife with the wicked gleam of savage purpose, and nothing came. Nothing moved within me at the thought of doing this sharp and necessary thing I had done so happily so many times. The only thing that welled up inside me was emptiness.

I lowered the knife, turned away, and walked out into the night.

CHAPTER 24

Somehow I pulled myself out of bed and went in to work the next day, in spite of the gnawing sense of dull despair that bloomed in me like a brittle garden of thorns. I felt wrapped in a fog of dull pain that hurt only enough to remind me that it, too, was without purpose, and there seemed no point to going through the empty motions of breakfast, the long slow drive to work, no reason at all beyond the slavery of habit. But I did it, allowing muscle memory to push me all the way into the chair at my desk, where I sat, turned on the computer, and let the day drag me off into gray drudgery.

I had failed with Starzak. I was no longer me, and had no idea who or what I was.

Rita was waiting for me at the door when I got home with a look of anxious annoyance on her face.

'We need to decide about the band,' she said. 'They may already be booked.'

'All right,' I said. Why not decide about bands? It was as meaningful as anything else.

'I picked up all the CDs from where you dropped

261

them yesterday,' she said, 'and sorted them by price.'

'I'll listen to them tonight,' I said, and although Rita still seemed peeved, eventually the evening routine took over and calmed her down, and she settled into cooking and cleaning while I listened to a series of rock bands playing 'Chicken Dance' and 'Electric Slide.' I'm sure that ordinarily it would have been as much fun as a toothache, but since I couldn't think of anything else in the world worth doing, I labored through the whole stack of CDs and soon it was time for bed again.

At 1 A.M. the music came back to me, and I don't mean 'Chicken Dance.' It was the drums and trumpets, and a chorus of voices came with them and rolled through my sleep, lifting me up into the heavens, and I woke up on the floor with the memory of it still echoing in my head.

I lay on the floor for a long time, unable to form any truly coherent thought about what it meant, but afraid to go to sleep in case it should come back again. Eventually I did get into bed, and I suppose I even slept, since I opened my eyes to sunlight and sound coming from the kitchen.

It was a Saturday morning, and Rita made blueberry pancakes, a very welcome nudge back to everyday life. Cody and Astor piled into the flapjacks with enthusiasm, and on any normal morning I would not have held back either. But today was not a normal morning.

It is difficult to understate how large the shock must be to put Dexter off his feed. I have a very fast metabolism, and require constant fuel in order to maintain the wonderful device that is me, and Rita's pancakes fully qualify as high-test unleaded. And yet, time and again I found myself staring at the fork as it wavered halfway between the plate and my mouth, and I was unable to muster the necessary enthusiasm for completing the motion and putting in food.

Soon enough, everyone else was finished with the meal, and I was still staring at half a plate of food. Even Rita noticed that all was not well in Dexter's Domain.

'You've hardly touched your food,' she said. 'Is something wrong?'

'It's this case I'm working on,' I said, at least half truthfully. 'I can't stop thinking about it.'

'Oh,' she said. 'You're sure that . . . I mean, is it very violent?'

'It's not that,' I said, wondering what she wanted to hear. 'It's just . . . very puzzling.'

Rita nodded. 'Sometimes if you stop thinking about something for a while, the answer comes to you,' she said.

'Maybe you're right,' I said, which was probably stretching the truth.

'Are you going to finish your breakfast?' she said.

I stared down at my plate with its pile of half-eaten pancakes and congealed syrup. Scientifically speaking, I knew they were still delicious, but at the moment they seemed about as appealing as old wet newspaper. 'No,' I said.

Rita looked at me with alarm. When Dexter does not finish his breakfast, we are in uncharted territory. 'Why don't you take your boat out?' she said. 'That always helps you relax.' She came over and put a hand on me with aggressive concern, and Cody and Astor looked up with the hope of a boat ride written on their faces, and it was suddenly like being in quicksand.

I stood up. It was all too much. I could not even meet my own expectations, and to be asked to deal with all theirs too was suffocating. Whether it was my failure with Starzak, the pursuing music, or being sucked down into family life, I could not say. Maybe it was the combination of all of them, pulling me apart with wildly opposite gravities and sucking the pieces into a whirlpool of clinging normalcy that made me want to scream, and at the same time left me unable even to whimper. Whatever it was, I had to get out of here.

'I have an errand I have to run,' I said, and they all looked at me with wounded surprise.

'Oh,' Rita said. 'What kind of errand?'

'Wedding business,' I blurted out, without any idea what I was going to say next, but trusting the impulse blindly. And happily for me, at least one thing went right, because I remembered my conversation with the blushing, groveling Vince Masuoka. 'I have to talk to the caterer.'

264

Rita lit up. 'You're going to see Manny Borque? Oh,' she said. 'That's really—'

'Yes, it is,' I assured her. 'I'll be back later.' And so at the reasonable Saturday-morning time of fifteen minutes before ten o'clock, I bid a fond farewell to dirty dishes and domesticity, and climbed into my car. It was an unusually calm morning on the roads, and I saw no violence or crime of any kind as I drove to South Beach, which was almost like seeing snow at the Fontaine-bleau. Things being what they were for me lately, I kept an eye on the rearview mirror. For just a minute I thought that a little red Jeep-style car was following me, but when I slowed down it went right past me. The traffic stayed light, and it was still only ten fifteen when I had parked my car, rode up in the elevator, and knocked on Manny Borque's door.

There was a very long spell of utter silence, and I knocked again, a little more enthusiastically this time. I was about to try a truly rousing salute on the door when it swung open and an exceedingly bleary and mostly naked Manny Borque blinked up at me. 'Jesus' tits,' he croaked. 'What time is it?'

'Ten fifteen,' I said brightly. 'Practically time for lunch.'

Perhaps he wasn't really awake, or perhaps he thought it was so funny it was worth saying again, but in any case he repeated himself: 'Jesus' tits.'

'May I come in?' I asked him politely, and he

blinked a few more times and then pushed the door open all the way.

'This better be good,' he said, and I followed him in, past the hideous art-thing in his foyer and on to his perch by the window. He hopped up onto his stool, and I sat on the one opposite.

'I need to talk to you about my wedding,' I said, and he shook his head very grumpily and squealed out, 'Franky!' There was no answer and he leaned on one tiny hand and tapped the other on the table. 'That little bitch had better – Goddamn it, *Franky!*' he called out in something like a very high-pitched bellow.

A moment later there was a scurrying sound from the back of the apartment, and then a young man came out, pulling a robe closed as he hurried in and brushing back his lank brown hair as he came to a halt in front of Manny. 'Hi,' he said. 'I mean, you know. Good morning.'

'Get coffee very quickly,' Manny said without looking up at him.

'Um,' Franky said. 'Sure. Okay.' He hesitated for half a second, just long enough to give Manny time to fling out his minuscule fist and shriek, 'Now, goddamn it!' Franky gulped and lurched away toward the kitchen, and Manny went back to leaning his full eighty-five pounds of towering grumpiness on his fist and closing his eyes with a sigh, as though he were tormented by number-less hordes of truly idiotic demons.

Since it seemed obvious that there could be no

possibility of conversation without coffee, I looked out the window and enjoyed the view. There were three large freighters on the horizon, sending up plumes of smoke, and closer in to shore a good scattering of pleasure boats, ranging from the multimillion-dollar playtoys headed for the Bahamas all the way down to a cluster of Wind-surfers in close to the beach. A bright yellow kayak was off-shore, apparently heading out to meet the freighters. The sun shone, the gulls flew by searching for garbage, and I waited for Manny to receive his transfusion.

There was a shattering crash from the kitchen, and Franky's muted wail of 'Oh, *shit.*' Manny tried to close his eyes tighter, as if he could seal out all the agony of being surrounded by terrible stupidity. And only a few minutes later, Franky arrived with the coffee service, a silver semi-shapeless pot and three squat stoneware cups, perched on a transparent platter shaped like an artist's palette.

With trembling hands Franky placed a cup in front of Manny and poured it full. Manny took a tiny sip, sighed heavily without any sense of relief, and opened his eyes at last. 'All right,' he said. And turning to Franky, he added, 'Go clean up your hideous mess, and if I step on broken glass later, I swear to *God* I will disembowel you.' Franky stumbled away, and Manny took another microscopic sip before turning his bleary glare on me. 'You want to talk about your wedding,' he said as if he couldn't really believe it.

'That's right,' I said, and he shook his head.

'A nice-looking man like you,' he said. 'Why on *earth* would you want to get married?'

'I need the tax break,' I said. 'Can we talk about the menu?'

'At the crack of dawn, on a Saturday? No,' he said. 'It's a horrible, pointless, primitive ritual,' and I assumed he was talking about the wedding rather than the menu, although with Manny one really couldn't be sure. 'I am truly appalled that anyone would *willingly* go through with it. But,' he said, waving his hand dismissively, 'at least it gives me a chance to experiment.'

'I wonder if it might be possible to experiment a little cheaper.'

'It might be,' he said and for the first time he showed his teeth, but it could only be called a smile if you agree that torturing animals is funny, 'but it just won't happen.'

'Why not?'

'Because I've already decided what I want to do, and there's nothing you can do to stop me.'

To be perfectly truthful there were several things I could think of to stop him, but none of them – enjoyable as they might be – would pass the strict guidelines of the Harry Code, and so I could not do them. 'I don't suppose sweet reason would have any effect?' I asked hopefully.

He leered at me. 'How sweet did you have in mind?' he said.

'Well, I was going to say please and smile a lot,' I said.

'Not good enough,' he said. 'Not by a great deal.'

'Vince said you were guessing five hundred dollars a plate?'

'I don't *guess*,' he snarled. 'And I don't give a *shit* about counting your fucking pennies.'

'Of course not,' I said, trying to soothe him a bit. 'After all, they're not your pennies.'

'Your girlfriend signed the fucking contract,' he said. 'I can charge you anything I fucking feel like.'

'But there must be something I can do to get the price down a little?' I said hopefully.

His snarl loosened into his patented leer again. 'Not in a chair,' he said.

'Then what can I do?'

'If you mean what can you do to get me to change my mind, nothing. Not a thing in the world. I have people lined up around the block trying to hire me – I am booked two years in advance, and I am doing you a very large favor.' His leer widened into something almost supernatural. 'So prepare yourself for a miracle. And a very hefty bill.'

I stood up. The little gnome was obviously not going to bend in the least, and there was nothing I could do about it. I really wanted to say something like 'You haven't heard the last of me,' but there didn't seem much point to that either. So I just smiled back, said, 'Well then,' and walked out of the apartment. As the door closed behind me, I could hear him, already squealing at Franky,

'For Christ's sake move your big ass and get all that shit off my fucking *floor*.'

As I walked toward the elevator I felt an icy steel finger brush the back of my neck and for just a moment I felt a faint stirring, as if the Dark Passenger had put one toe in the water and run away after seeing that it was too cold. I stopped dead and slowly looked around me in the hallway.

Nothing. Down at the far end a man was fumbling with the newspaper in front of his door. Otherwise, the hall was empty. I closed my eyes for just a moment. *What?* I asked. But there was no answer. I was still alone. And unless somebody was glaring at me through a peephole in one of the doors, it had been a false alarm. Or, more likely, wishful thinking.

I got in the elevator and went down.

As the elevator door slid shut the Watcher straightened up, still holding the newspaper from where he had taken it off the mat. It was a good piece of camouflage, and it might work again. He stared down the hall and wondered what was so interesting in that other apartment, but it didn't really matter. He would find out. Whatever the other had been doing, he would find out.

He counted slowly to ten and then sauntered down the hallway to the apartment the other had visited. It would only take a moment to find out why he had gone in there. And then—

The Watcher had no real idea what was really

going through the other's mind right now, but it was not happening fast enough. It was time for a real push, something to break the other out of his passivity. He felt a rare pulse of playfulness welling up through the dark cloud of power, and he heard the flutter of dark wings inside.

CHAPTER 25

In my lifelong study of human beings, I have found that no matter how hard they might try, they have found no way yet to prevent the arrival of Monday morning. And they do try, of course, but Monday always comes, and all the drones have to scuttle back to their dreary workaday lives of meaningless toil and suffering.

That thought always cheers me up, and because I like to spread happiness wherever I go, I did my small part to cushion the blow of unavoidable Monday morning by arriving at work with a box of doughnuts, all of which vanished in what can only be called an extremely grumpy frenzy before I reached my desk. I doubted very seriously that anyone had a better reason than I did for feeling surly, but you would not have known it to watch them all snatching at my doughnuts and grunting at me.

Vince Masuoka seemed to be sharing in the general feeling of low-key anguish. He stumbled into my cubbyhole with a look of horror and wonderment on his face, an expression that must have indicated something very moving because it looked almost real. 'Jesus, Dexter,' he said. 'Oh, Jesus Christ.'

'I tried to save you one,' I said, thinking that with that much anguish he could only be referring to the calamity of facing an empty doughnut box. But he shook his head.

'Oh, Jesus, I can't believe it. He's dead!'

'I'm sure it had nothing to do with the doughnuts,' I said.

'My God, and you were going to see him. Did you?'

There comes a point in every conversation where at least one of the people involved has to know what is being talked about, and I decided that point had arrived.

'Vince,' I said, 'I want you to take a deep breath, start all over from the top, and pretend you and I speak the same language.'

He stared at me as if he was a frog and I was a heron. 'Shit,' he said. 'You don't know yet, do you? Holy shit.'

'Your language skills are deteriorating,' I said. 'Have you been talking to Deborah?'

'He's *dead*, Dexter. They found the body late last night.'

'Well, then, I'm sure he'll stay dead long enough for you to tell me what in the hell you're talking about.'

Vince blinked at me, his eyes suddenly huge and moist. 'Manny Borque,' he breathed. 'He was murdered.'

I will admit to having mixed reactions. On the one hand, I was certainly not sorry to have somebody else take the little troll out of the picture in a way I was unable to do for ethical reasons. But on the other hand, now I needed to find another caterer – and oh, yes, I would probably have to give a statement of some kind to the detective in charge. Annoyance fought it out with relief, but then I remembered that the doughnuts were gone, too.

And so the reaction that won out was irritation at all the bother this was going to cause. Still, Harry had schooled me well enough to know that this is not really an acceptable reaction to display when one hears of the death of an acquaintance. So I did my best to push my face into something resembling shock, concern, and distress. 'Wow,' I said. 'I had no idea. Do they know who did it?'

Vince shook his head. 'The guy had no enemies,' he said, and he didn't seem aware of how unlikely his statement sounded to anyone who had ever met Manny. 'I mean, everybody was just in *awe* of him.'

'I know,' I said. 'He was in magazines and everything.'

'I can't believe anybody would do that to him,' he said.

In truth, I couldn't believe it had taken so long for somebody to do that to him, but it didn't seem like the politic thing to say. 'Well, I'm sure they'll figure it out. Who's assigned to the case?'

Vince looked at me like I had asked him if he thought the sun might come up in the morning. 'Dexter,' he said wonderingly, 'his head was cut off. It's just like the three over at the university.'

When I was young and trying hard to fit in, I played football for a while, and one time I had been hit hard in the stomach and couldn't breathe for a few minutes. I felt a little bit like that now.

'Oh,' I said.

'So naturally they've given it to your sister,' he said.

'Naturally.' A sudden thought hit me, and because I am a lifelong devotee of irony, I asked him, 'He wasn't cooked, too, was he?'

Vince shook his head. 'No,' he said.

I stood up. 'I better go talk to Deborah,' I said.

Deborah was not in any mood to talk when I arrived at Manny's apartment. She was bending over Camilla Figg, who was dusting for prints around the legs of the table by the window. She didn't look up, so I peeked into the kitchen, where Angel-no-relation was bent over the body.

'Angel,' I said, and I found some difficulty believing my eyes, so I asked him, 'Is that really a girl's head there?'

He nodded and poked at the head with a pen. 'Your sister says, prolly the girl from the Lowe Museum,' he said. 'They put it here because this guy is such a *bugero*.'

I looked down at the two cuts, one just above the shoulders, the other just below the chin. The

275

one on the head matched what we had seen before, done with neatness and care. But the one on the body that was presumably Manny was much rougher, as if it had been hurried. The edges of the two cuts were pushed together carefully, but of course they did not quite mesh. Even on my own, with no dark interior muttering, I could tell that this was different somehow, and one small cold finger crawling across the back of my neck suggested that the difference might be very import-ant – maybe even to my current troubles – but beyond that vague and unsatisfying ghost of a hint, there was nothing for me here but uneasiness.

'Is there another body?' I asked him, remembering poor bullied Franky.

Angel shrugged without looking up. 'In the bedroom,' he said. 'Just with a butcher knife stuck in him. They left his head.' He sounded a little offended that someone would go to all that trouble and leave the head, but other than that he seemed to have nothing to tell me, so I walked away, over to where my sister was now squatting beside Camilla.

'Good morning, Debs,' I said, with a cheerful-ness I did not feel at all, and I was not the only one, because she didn't even look up at me.

'Goddamn it, Dexter,' she said. 'Unless you have something really good for me, stay the fuck away.'

'It isn't all that good,' I said. 'But the guy in the bedroom is named Franky. This one here is Manny Borque, who has been in a number of magazines.'

276

'How the fuck would you know that?' she said.

'Well, it's a little awkward,' I said, 'but I may have been one of the last people to see this guy alive.'

She straightened up. 'When,' she said.

'Saturday morning. Around ten thirty. Right here.' And I pointed to the coffee cup that was still on top of the table. 'Those are my prints.'

Deborah was looking at me with disbelief and shaking her head. 'You *knew* this guy,' she said. 'He was a friend of yours?'

'I hired him to cater my wedding,' I said. 'He was supposed to be very good at it.'

'Uh-huh,' she said. 'So what were you doing here on a Saturday morning?'

'He raised the price on me,' I said. 'I wanted to talk him down.'

She looked around the apartment and glanced out the window at the million-dollar view. 'What was he charging?' she said.

'Five hundred dollars a plate,' I said.

Her head snapped around to face me again. 'Jesus fuck,' she said. 'For what?'

I shrugged. 'He wouldn't tell me, and he wouldn't lower the price.'

'Five hundred dollars a *plate?*' she said.

'It is a little high, isn't it? Or should I say, it *was.*'

Deborah chewed on her lip for a long moment without blinking, and then she grabbed me by the arm and pulled me away from Camilla. I could still see one small foot sticking out of the kitchen door where the dear departed had met his untimely end, but Deborah led me away from it and over to the far end of the room.

'Dexter,' she said, 'promise me you didn't kill this guy.'

As I have mentioned before, I do not have real emotions. I have practiced long and hard to react the way human beings would react in almost every possible situation – but this one caught me by surprise. What is the correct facial expression for being accused of murder by your sister? Shock? Anger? Disbelief? As far as I knew, this wasn't covered in any of the textbooks.

'Deborah,' I said. Not tremendously clever, but it was all I could think of.

'Because you don't get a free pass with me,' she said. 'Not for something like this.'

'I would never,' I said. 'This is not . . .' I shook my head, and it really seemed so unfair. First the Dark Passenger left me, and now my sister and my wits had apparently fled, too. All the rats were swimming away as the good ship Dexter slid slowly under the waves.

I took a deep breath and tried to organize the crew to bail out a little. Deborah was the only person on earth who knew what I really was, and even though she was still getting used to the idea, I had thought she understood the very careful boundaries set up by Harry, and understood, too, that I would never cross them. Apparently I was wrong. 'Deborah,' I said. 'Why would I—'

'Cut the crap,' she snapped. 'We both know you could have done it. You were here at the right time. And you have a pretty good motive, to get out of paying him like fifty grand. It's either that or I believe some guy in jail did it.'

Because I am an artificial human, I am also extremely clearheaded most of the time, uncluttered by emotions. But I felt as if I was trying to see through quicksand. On the one hand, I was surprised and a little disappointed that she thought I might have done something this sloppy. On the other hand, I wanted to reassure her that I hadn't. And I wanted to say that if I had done this, she would never have found out about it, but that didn't seem quite diplomatic. So I took another deep breath and settled for, 'I promise.'

My sister looked at me long and hard. 'Really,' I said.

She finally nodded. 'All right,' she said. 'You better be telling me the truth.'

'I am,' I said. 'I didn't do this.'

'Uh-huh,' she said. 'Then who did?'

It really isn't fair, is it? I mean, this whole life thing. Here I was, still defending myself from an accusation of murder – from my own foster flesh and blood! – and at the same time being asked to solve the crime. I had to admire the mental agility that allowed Deborah to perform that kind of cerebral tumbling act, but I also had to wish she would direct her creative thinking at somebody else.

'I don't know who did this,' I said. 'And I don't – I'm not getting any, um, ideas about it.'

She stared at me very hard indeed. 'Why should I believe that, either?' she said.

'Deborah,' I said, and I hesitated. Was this the time to tell her about the Dark Passenger and its present absence? There was a very uncomfortable series of sensations sloshing through me, somewhat like the onset of the flu. Could these be emotions, pounding at the defenseless coastline of Dexter, like huge tidal waves of toxic sludge? If so, it was no wonder humans were such miserable creatures. This was an awful experience.

'Listen, Deborah,' I said again, trying to think of a way to start.

'I am listening, for Christ's sake,' she said. 'But you're not saying anything.'

'It's hard to say,' I said. 'I've never said it before.'

'This would be a great time to start.'

'I, uh – I have this thing inside me,' I said, aware that I sounded like a complete idiot and feeling a strange heat rising into my cheeks.

'What do you mean,' she demanded. 'You've got cancer?'

'No, no, it's— I hear, um— It tells me things,' I said. For some reason I had to look away from Deborah. There was a photograph of a naked man's torso on the wall; I looked back to Deborah.

'Jesus,' she said. 'You mean you hear voices? Jesus Christ, Dex.'

'No,' I said. 'It's not like hearing voices. Not exactly.'

'Well then what the fuck?' she said.

I had to look at the naked torso again, and then blow out a large breath before I could look back at Deborah. 'When I get one of my hunches about, you know. At a crime scene,' I said. 'It's because this . . . thing is telling me.' Deborah's face was frozen over, completely immobile, as if she was listening to a confession of terrible deeds; which she was, of course.

'So it *tells* you, what?' she said. 'Hey, somebody who thinks he's Batman did this.'

'Kind of,' I said. 'Just, you know. The little hints I used to get.'

'Used to get,' she said.

I really had to look away again. 'It's gone, Deborah,' I said. 'Something about all this Moloch stuff scared it away. That's never happened before.'

She didn't say anything for a long time, and I saw no reason to say it for her.

'Did you ever tell Dad about this voice?' she said at last.

'I didn't have to,' I said. 'He already knew.'

'And now your voices are gone,' she said.

'Just one voice.'

'And that's why you're not telling me anything about all this.'

'Yes.'

Deborah ground her teeth together loud enough for me to hear them. Then she released a large breath without unlocking her jaw. 'Either you're lying to me because you did this,' she hissed at me, 'or you're telling the truth and you're a fucking psycho.'

'Debs—'

'Which one do you think I want to believe, Dexter? Huh? Which one?'

I don't believe I have felt real anger since I was an adolescent, and it may be that even then I was not able to feel the real thing. But with the Dark Passenger gone and me slipping down the slope into genuine humanity, all the old barriers between me and normal life were fading, and I felt something now that must have been very close to the real thing. 'Deborah,' I said, 'if you don't trust me and you want to think I did this, then I don't give a rat's ass which one you believe.'

She glared at me, and for the very first time, I glared back.

Finally she spoke. 'I still have to report this,' she said. 'Officially, you can't come anywhere near this for now.'

'Nothing would make me happier,' I said. She stared at me for a moment longer, then made her mouth very small and returned to Camilla Figg. I watched her back for a moment, and then headed for the door.

There was really no point in hanging around, especially since I had been told, officially and unofficially, that I was not welcome. It would be nice to say that my feelings were hurt, but surprisingly, I was still too angry to feel miffed. And in truth, I have always been so shocked that anyone could really like me that it was almost a relief to see Deborah taking a sensible attitude for once.

It was all good all the time for Dexter, but for some reason, it didn't really feel like a very large victory as I headed for the door and exile.

I was waiting for the elevator to arrive when I was blindsided by a hoarse shout of 'Hey!'

I turned and saw a grim, very angry old man racing at me wearing sandals and black socks that came up almost to his knobby old knees. He also wore baggy shorts and a silk shirt and an expression of completely righteous wrath. 'Are you the police?' he demanded.

'Not all of them,' I said.

'What about my goddamn paper?' he said.

Elevators are so slow, aren't they? But I do try to be polite when it is unavoidable, so I smiled reassuringly at the old lunatic. 'You didn't like your paper?' I asked.

'I didn't *get* my goddamn paper!' he shouted at me, turning a light purple from the effort. 'I called and I told you people and the colored girl on the phone said to call the newspaper! I watch the kid *steal* it, and she hangs up on me!'

'A kid stole your newspaper,' I said.

'What the hell did I just say?' he said, and he was getting a little bit shrill now, which did nothing to make waiting for the elevator any more enjoyable.

'Why the hell do I pay my taxes, to hear her say that? And she *laughs* at me, goddamn it!'

'You could get another paper,' I said soothingly.

It didn't seem to soothe him. 'What the hell is that, get another paper? Saturday morning, in my pajamas, and I should get another paper? Why can't you people just catch the criminals?'

The elevator made a muted *ding* sound to announce its arrival at last, but I was no longer interested, because I had a thought. Every now and then I do have thoughts. Most of them never make it all the way to the surface, probably because of a lifetime of trying to seem human. But this one came slowly up and, like a gas bubble bursting through mud, popped brightly in my brain. 'Saturday morning?' I said. 'Do you remember what time?'

'Of course I remember what time! I told them when I called, ten thirty, on a Saturday morning, and the kid is stealing my paper!'

'How do you know it was a kid?'

'I watched through the peephole, that's how!' he yelled at me. 'I should go out in the hall without looking, the job you people do? Forget it!'

'When you say "kid,"' I said, 'how old do you mean?'

'Listen, mister,' he said, 'to me, everybody under seventy is a kid. But this kid was maybe twenty, and he had a backpack on like they all wear.'

'Can you describe this kid?' I asked.

'I'm not blind,' he said. 'He stands up with my

paper, he's got one of those goddamn tattoos they all have now, right on the back of his neck!'

I felt little metal fingers flutter across the back of my neck and I knew the answer, but I asked anyway. 'What kind of tattoo?'

'Stupid thing, one of those Jap symbols. We beat the crap out of the Japs so we could buy their cars and tattoo their goddamn scribbles on our kids?'

He seemed to be only warming up, and while I really admired the fact that he had such terrific stamina at his age, I felt it was time to turn him over to the proper authorities as constituted by my sister, which lit up in me a small glow of satisfaction, since it not only gave her a suspect better than poor Disenfranchised Dexter but also inflicted this beguiling old poop on her as a small measure of punishment for suspecting me in the first place. 'Come with me,' I said to the old man.

'I'm not going anywhere,' he said.

'Wouldn't you like to talk to a real detective?' I said, and the hours of practice I had spent on my smile must have paid off, because he frowned, looked around him, and then said, 'Well, all right,' and followed me all the way back to where Sergeant Sister was snarling at Camilla Figg.

'I told you to stay away,' she said, with all the warmth and charm I had come to expect from her.

'Okay,' I said. 'Shall I take the witness away with me?'

Deborah opened her mouth, then closed and

opened it a few more times, as if she was trying to figure out how to breathe like a fish.

'You can't – it isn't – Goddamn it, Dexter,' she said at last.

'I can, it is, and I'm sure he will,' I said. 'But in the meantime, this nice old gentleman has something interesting to tell you.'

'Who the hell are you to call me old?' he said.

'This is Detective Morgan,' I told him. 'She's in charge here.'

'A girl?' he snorted. 'No wonder they can't catch anybody. A girl detective.'

'Be sure to tell her about the backpack,' I told him. 'And the tattoo.'

'What tattoo?' she demanded. 'What the hell are you talking about?'

'The mouth on you,' the old man said. 'Shame!'

I smiled at my sister. 'Have a nice chat,' I said.

CHAPTER 26

I could not be sure that I was officially invited back to the party, but I didn't want to go so far away that I missed the chance to graciously accept my sister's apology. So I went to loiter just inside the front door of the former Manny Borque's apartment, where I could be noticed at the appropriate time. Unfortunately, the killer had not stolen the giant artistic ball of animal vomit on the pedestal by the door. It was still there, right in the middle of my loitering grounds, and I was forced to look at it while I waited.

I was wondering how long it would take Deborah to ask the old man about the tattoo and then make the connection. Even as I wondered, I heard her raise her voice in official ritual words of dismissal, thanking the old man for his help and instructing him to call if he thought of anything else. And then the two of them came toward the door, Deborah holding the old man firmly by the elbow and steering him out of the apartment.

'But what about my paper, miss?' he protested as she opened the door.

'It's Sergeant Miss,' I told him, and Deborah glared at me.

'Call the paper,' she told him. 'They'll give you a refund.' And she practically hurled him out the door, where he stood for a moment trembling with anger.

'The bad guys are winning!' he shouted, and then, happily for us, Deborah closed the door.

'He's right, you know,' I said to her.

'Well, you don't have to look so goddamned happy about it,' she said.

'And you, on the other hand, might try looking a lot happier,' I said. 'It's him, the boyfriend, what's his name.'

'Kurt Wagner,' she said.

'Very good,' I said. 'Due diligence. Kurt Wagner it is, and you know it.'

'I don't know shit,' she said. 'It could still be a coincidence.'

'Sure, it could be,' I said. 'And there's even a mathematical chance that the sun will come up in the west, but it's not very likely. And who else do you have?'

'That fucking creep, Wilkins,' she said.

'Somebody's been watching him, right?'

She snorted. 'Yeah, but you know what these guys are like. They take a nap, or take a dump, and swear the guy was never out of their sight. Meantime, the guy they're supposed to watch is out chopping up cheerleaders.'

'So you really still think he could be the killer?

288

Even when this kid was here at exactly the same time Manny was killed?'

'You were here at the same time,' she said. 'And this one's not like the others. More like a cheap copy.'

'Then how did Tammy Connor's head get here?' I said. 'Kurt Wagner is doing this, Debs, he has to be.'

'All right,' she said. 'He probably is.'

'Probably?' I said, and I really was surprised. Everything pointed to the kid with the neck tattoo, and Deborah was dithering.

She looked at me for a long moment, and it was not a look of warm, loving filial affection. 'It still might be you,' she said.

'By all means, arrest me,' I said. 'That would be the smart thing to do, wouldn't it? Captain Matthews will be happy because you made an arrest, and the media will love you for busting your brother. Terrific solution, Deborah. It will even make the real killer happy.'

Deborah said nothing, just turned and walked away. After thinking about it for a moment, I realized what a good idea that was. So I did it, too, and walked away in the opposite direction, out of the apartment and back to work.

The rest of my day was far more fulfilling. Two bodies, male, Caucasian, had been found in a BMW parked on the shoulder of the Palmetto Expressway. When somebody tried to steal the car, they found the bodies and phoned it in – after removing the sound system and the airbags. The apparent cause of death was multiple gunshot wounds. The newspapers are fond of using the phrase 'gangland style' for killings that show a certain neatness and economy. We would not be searching for any gangs this time. The two bodies and the inside of the car had been quite literally hosed with lead and spurting blood, as though the killer had trouble figuring out which end of the gun to hold on to. Judging from the bullet holes in the windows, it was a miracle that no passing motorists had been shot as well.

A busy Dexter should be a happy Dexter, and there was enough awful dried blood in the car and on the surrounding pavement to keep me occupied for hours, but not surprisingly I was still not happy. I had such a large number of hideous things happening to me, and now there was this disagreement with Debs. It was not really accurate to say that I loved Deborah, since I am incapable of love, but I was used to her, and I would rather have her around and reasonably content with me.

Other than a few ordinary sibling squabbles when we were younger, Deborah and I had rarely had any serious disagreements, and I was a bit surprised to find out that this one bothered me a great deal. In spite of the fact that I am a soulless monster who enjoys killing, it stung to have her think of me that way, especially since I had given my word of honor as an ogre that I was entirely innocent, at least in this case.

I wanted to get along with my sister, but I was also miffed that she seemed a little too enthusiastic about her role as a representative of the Full Majesty of the Law, and not quite willing enough as my sidekick and confidante.

Of course it made sense for me to be wasting my perfectly good indignation on this, since there was nothing else at all to occupy my attention at the time – things like weddings, mysterious music, and missing Passengers always sort themselves out, right? And blood spatter is a simple craft that requires minimal concentration. To prove it, I let my thoughts wander as I mentally wallowed in my sad state, and because of it I slipped in the congealed blood and went down to one knee on the roadside by the BMW.

The shock of contact with the road was immediately echoed by an interior shock, a jolt of fear and cold air going through me, rising up from the awful sticky mess and straight into my empty self, and it was a long moment before I could breathe again. Steady, Dexter, I thought. This is just a small, painful reminder of who you are and where you came from, brought on by stress. It has nothing to do with operatic cattle.

I managed to stand up without whimpering, but my pants were torn, my knee hurt, and one leg of the pants was covered with the vile half-dry blood.

I really don't like blood. And to look down and see it actually on my clothes, actually *touching* me,

291

and on top of the complete turmoil my life had become and the great empty Passenger-less pit I had fallen into – the blood completed the circuit. These were definitely emotions I was feeling now, and they were not pleasant. I felt myself shudder and I nearly shouted, but I managed, just barely, to contain myself, clean up, and soldier on.

I did not feel much better, but I made it through the day by changing into the extra set of clothing that wise blood-spatter techs keep handy, and it was finally time to head home.

As I drove south to Rita's on Old Cutler a little red Geo got on my bumper and would not back off. I watched in the mirror, but I could not see the driver's face, and I wondered if I had done something I wasn't aware of to make him or her angry. I was very tempted to step on the brakes and let the chips fall where they might, but I was not yet so completely frazzled as to believe that wrecking my car would make anything better. I tried to ignore the other car, just one more semi-insane Miami driver with a mysterious hidden agenda.

But it stayed with me, inches away, and I began to wonder what that agenda might be. I sped up. The Geo sped up and stayed right on my bumper.

I slowed down; so did the Geo.

I moved across two lanes of traffic, leaving a chorus of angry horns and upraised fingers in my wake. The Geo followed.

Who was it? What did they want with me? Was

it possible that Starzak knew that it was me who had taped him up, and now he was coming after me in a different car, determined to revenge himself on me? Or was it someone else this time – and if so, who? Why? I could not bring myself to believe that Moloch was driving the car behind me. How could an ancient god even get a learner's permit? But somebody was back there, clearly planning to stay with me for a while, and I had no idea who. I found myself flailing for an answer, reaching for something that was no longer there, and the sense of loss and emptiness amplified my uncertainty and anger and uneasiness, and I realized my breath was hissing in and out between clenched teeth and my hands were clenched on the wheel and covered with a chilly sheen of sweat, and I thought, that's enough.

And as I mentally prepared myself to slam on the brakes and leap out of the car to smash this other driver's face into a red pulp, the red Geo suddenly slid off my bumper and turned right, vanishing down a side street into the Miami night.

It had been nothing after all, just a perfectly normal rush-hour psychosis. Another average crazed Miami driver, killing the boredom of the long drive home by playing tag with the car in front.

And I was nothing more than a dazed, battered, paranoid former monster with his hands clenched and his teeth grinding together.

I went home.

★ ★ ★

The Watcher dropped away and then circled back. He moved through the traffic invisible to the other now, and turned down the street to the house well behind the other. He had enjoyed tailing him so closely, forcing a display of mild panic. He had provoked the other in order to gauge his readiness, and what he found was very satisfying. It was a finely balanced process, to push the other precisely into the right frame of mind. He had done it many times before, and he knew the signs. Jumpy, but not quite on the ragged edge where he needed to be, not yet.

It was clearly time to accelerate things.

Tonight would be very special.

CHAPTER 27

Dinner was ready when I got to Rita's house. Considering what I had gone through and what I was thinking about it, you might have thought that I would never eat again. But as I walked in the front door I was assaulted by the aroma; Rita had made roast pork, broccoli, and rice and beans, and there are very few things in this world that compare to Rita's roast pork. And so it was a somewhat mollified Dexter who finally pushed the plate away and rose from the table. And in truth, the rest of the evening was mildly soothing as well. I played kick the can with Cody and Astor and the other neighborhood children until it was bedtime, and then Rita and I sat on the couch and watched a show about a grumpy doctor before turning in for the night.

Normality wasn't all bad, not with Rita's roast pork in it, and Cody and Astor to keep me interested. Perhaps I could live vicariously through them, like an old baseball player who becomes a coach when his playing days are over. They had so much to learn, and in teaching them I could relive my fading days of glory. Sad, yes, but it was at least a small compensation.

And as I drifted off to sleep, in spite of the fact that I really do know better, I caught myself thinking that maybe things weren't that bad after all.

That foolish notion lasted until midnight, when I woke up to see Cody standing at the foot of the bed. 'Somebody's outside,' he said.

'All right,' I said, feeling half asleep and not at all curious about why he needed to tell me that.

'They want in,' he said.

I sat up. 'Where?' I said.

Cody turned and headed into the hallway and I followed. I was half convinced that he had simply had a bad dream, but after all, this was Miami and these things have been known to happen, although certainly seldom more than five or six hundred times on any given night.

Cody led me to the door to the backyard. About ten feet from the door he stopped dead, and I stopped with him.

'There,' Cody said softly.

There indeed. It was not a bad dream, or at least not the kind you need to be asleep to have.

The doorknob was moving, wiggling as someone on the outside tried to turn it.

'Wake up your mom,' I whispered to Cody. 'Tell her to call 9-1-1.' He looked up at me as if he was disappointed that I wasn't going to charge out the door with a hand grenade and take care of things myself, but then he turned and walked back down the hall toward the bedroom.

I approached the door, quietly and cautiously. On the wall beside it was a switch that turned on a floodlight which illuminated the backyard. As I reached for the switch, the doorknob stopped turning. I turned the light on anyway.

Immediately, as if the switch had caused it to happen, something began to thump on the front door.

I turned and ran for the front of the house – and halfway there Rita stepped into the hall and crashed into me. 'Dexter,' she said. 'What – Cody said—'

'Call the cops,' I told her. 'Someone is trying to break in.' I looked behind her at Cody. 'Get your sister and all of you get into the bathroom. Lock the door.'

'But who would – we're not—' Rita said.

'Go,' I told her, and pushed past her to the front door.

Once again I flipped on the outside light, and once again the sound stopped immediately.

Only to start up again down the hall, apparently on the kitchen window.

And naturally enough when I ran into the kitchen the sound had already stopped, even before I turned on the overhead light.

I slowly approached the window over the sink and carefully peeked out.

Nothing. Just the night and the hedge and the neighbor's house and nothing else whatsoever.

I straightened up and stood there for a moment, waiting for the noise to start up again at some other corner of the house. It didn't. I realized I was holding my breath, and I let it out. Whatever it was, it had stopped. It was gone. I unclenched my fists and took a deep breath.

And then Rita screamed.

I turned around fast enough to twist my ankle, but still hobbled for the bathroom as quickly as I could. The door was locked, but from inside I could hear something scrabbling at the window. Rita shouted, 'Go away!'

'Open the door,' I said, and a moment later Astor opened it wide.

'It's at the window,' she said, rather calmly I thought.

Rita was standing in the middle of the bathroom with her clenched fists raised to her mouth. Cody stood in front of her protectively holding the toilet plunger, and they were both staring at the window.

'Rita,' I said.

She turned to me with her eyes wide and filled with fear. 'But what do they want?' she demanded, as if she thought I could tell her. And perhaps I could have, in the ordinary course of things – 'ordinary' being defined as the entire previous portion of my life, when I had my Passenger to keep me company and whisper terrible secrets. But as it was, I only knew they wanted in and I did not know why.

I also did not know what they wanted, but it didn't seem quite as important at the moment as the fact that they obviously wanted something and thought we had it. 'Come on,' I said. 'Everybody out of here.' Rita turned to look at me, but Cody stood his ground. 'Move,' I said, and Astor took Rita by the hand and hurried through the door. I put a hand on Cody's shoulder and pushed him after his mother, gently prying the plunger from his hands, and then I turned to face the window.

The noise continued, a hard scratching that sounded like someone was trying to claw through the glass. Without any real conscious thought I stepped forward and whacked the window with the rubber head of the toilet plunger.

The sound stopped.

For a long moment there was no sound except for my breathing, which I realized was somewhat fast and ragged. And then, not too far away, I heard a police siren cutting through the silence. I backed out of the bathroom, watching the window.

Rita sat on the bed with Cody on one side of her and Astor on the other. The children seemed quite calm, but Rita was clearly on the edge of hysteria. 'It's all right,' I said. 'The cops are almost here.'

'Will it be Sergeant Debbie?' Astor asked me, and she added hopefully, 'Do you think she'll shoot somebody?'

'Sergeant Debbie is in bed, asleep,' I said. The siren was near now, and with a squeal of tires it came to a stop in front of our house and wound its way down through the scale to a grumbling halt. 'They're here,' I told them, and Rita lunged up off the bed and grabbed the children by the hand.

The three of them followed me out of the bedroom, and by the time we got to the front door there was already a knock sounding on the wood, polite but firm. Still, life teaches us caution, so I called out, 'Who is it?'

'This is the police,' a stern masculine voice said. 'We have a report of a possible break-in.' It sounded authentic, but just to be sure, I left the chain on as I opened the door and looked out. Sure enough, there were two uniformed cops standing there, one looking at the door and one turned away, looking out into the yard and the street.

I closed the door, took the chain off, and reopened it. 'Come in, Officer,' I said. His name tag said Ramirez, and I realized I knew him slightly. But he made no move to enter the house; he simply stared down at my hand.

'What kind of emergency is this, chief?' he said, nodding at my hand. I looked and realized I was still holding the toilet plunger.

'Oh,' I said. I put the plunger behind the door in the umbrella stand. 'Sorry. That was for self-defense.'

'Uh-huh,' Ramirez said. 'Guess it would depend what the other guy had.' He stepped forward into the house, calling over his shoulder to his partner, 'Take a look around the yard, Williams.'

'Yo,' said Williams, a wiry black man of about forty. He walked down into the yard and disappeared around the corner of the house.

Ramirez stood in the center of the room, looking at Rita and the kids. 'So, what's the story here?' he asked, and before I could answer he squinted at me. 'I know you from somewhere?' he said.

'Dexter Morgan,' I said. 'I work in forensics.'

'Right,' he said. 'So what happened here, Dexter?'

I told him.

CHAPTER 28

The cops stayed with us for about forty minutes. They looked around the yard and the surrounding neighborhood and found nothing, which did not seem to surprise them, and which truthfully was not a great shock to me, either. When they were done looking Rita made them coffee and fed them some oatmeal cookies she had made.

Ramirez was certain it had been a couple of kids trying to get some kind of reaction from us, and if so they had certainly succeeded. Williams tried very hard to be reassuring, telling us it was just a prank and now it was over, and as they were leaving Ramirez added that they would drive by a few times the rest of the night. But even with these soothing words still fresh, Rita sat in the kitchen with a cup of coffee for the rest of the night, unable to get back to sleep. For my part, I tossed and turned for more than three minutes before I drifted back to slumberland.

And as I flew down the long black mountain into sleep, the music started up again. And there was a great feeling of gladness and then heat on my face . . .

And somehow I was in the hallway, with Rita shaking me and calling my name. 'Dexter, wake up,' she said. 'Dexter.'

'What happened?' I said.

'You were sleepwalking,' she said. 'And singing. Singing in your sleep.'

And so rosy-fingered dawn found both of us sitting at the kitchen table, drinking coffee. When the alarm finally went off in the bedroom, she got up to turn it off and came back and looked at me. I looked back, but there didn't seem to be anything to say, and then Cody and Astor came into the kitchen, and there was nothing more we could do except stumble through the morning routine and head for work, automatically pretending that everything was exactly the way it should be.

But of course it wasn't. Someone was trying to get into my head, and they were succeeding far too well. And now they were trying to get into my house, and I didn't even know who it was, or what they wanted. I had to assume that somehow it was all connected to Moloch, and the absence of my Presence.

The bottom line was that somebody was trying to do something to me, and they were getting closer and closer to doing it.

I found myself unwilling to consider the idea that a real live ancient god was trying to kill me. To begin with, they don't exist. And even if they did, why would one bother with me? Clearly some human being was using the whole Moloch thing as a costume in order to feel more powerful and important, and to make his victims believe he had special magical powers.

Like the ability to invade my sleep and make me hear music, for instance? A human predator couldn't do that. And it couldn't scare away the Dark Passenger, either.

The only possible answers were impossible. Maybe it was just the crippling fatigue, but I couldn't think of any others that weren't.

When I arrived at work that morning, I had no chance to think of anything better, because there was an immediate call to a double homicide in a quiet marijuana house in the Grove. Two teenagers had been tied up, cut up, and then shot several times each, just for good measure. And although I am certain that I should have considered this a terrible thing, I was actually very grateful for the opportunity to view dead bodies that were not cooked and beheaded. It made things seem normal, even peaceful, for just a little while. I sprayed my luminol hither and yon, almost happy to perform a task that made the hideous music recede for a little while.

But it also gave me time to ponder, and this I did. I saw scenes like this every day, and nine times out of ten the killers said things like 'I just snapped' or 'By the time I knew what I was doing it was too late.' All grand excuses, and it had seemed a bit amusing to me, since I always knew what I was doing, which was why I did it.

And at last a thought wandered in – I had found myself unable to do anything at all to Starzak without my Dark Passenger. This meant that my talent was in the Passenger, not in me by myself. Which could mean that all these others who 'snapped' were temporarily playing host to something similar, couldn't it?

Until now, mine had never left me; it was permanently at home with me, not wandering around in the streets hitchhiking with the first bad-tempered wretch that wandered by.

All right, put that aside for the time being. Let's just assume that some Passengers wander and some of them nest. Could this account for what Halpern had described as a dream? Could something go into him, make him kill two girls, and then take him home and tuck him into bed before leaving?

I didn't know. But I did know that if that idea held water, I was in a lot deeper than I had imagined.

By the time I got back to my office it was past time for lunch, and there was a call waiting from Rita to remind me that I had a 2:30 appointment with her minister. And by 'minister' I don't mean the kind with a position in the cabinet of a foreign government. As unlikely as it seems, I mean the kind of minister you will find in a church, if you are ever compelled to visit one for some reason. For my part, I have always assumed that if there is any kind of God at all He would never let something

305

like me flourish. And if I am wrong, the altar might crack and fall if I went inside a church.

But my sensible avoidance of religious buildings was at an end now, since Rita wanted her very own minister to perform our wedding ceremony, and apparently he needed to check my human credentials before agreeing to the assignment. Of course, he hadn't done a very good job of it the first time, since Rita's first husband had been a crack addict who regularly beat her, and the reverend had somehow failed to detect that. And if the minister had missed something that obvious before, the odds of him doing better with me were not very good at all.

Still, Rita set great store by the man, so away we went to an ancient coral-rock church on an overgrown lot in the Grove, only half a mile from the homicide scene I had worked that morning. Rita had been confirmed there, she told me, and had known the minister for a very long time. Apparently that was important, and I supposed it should be, considering what I knew about several men of God who had come to my attention through my hobby. My former hobby, that is.

Reverend Gilles was waiting for us in his office – or is it called a cloister, or a retreat, or something like that? Rectory always sounded to me like a place where you would find a proctologist. Perhaps it was a sacristy – I admit that I am not up on my terminology here. My foster mother, Doris, did try to get me to church when I was young, but after a couple of regrettable incidents it became apparent that it wasn't going to stick, and Harry intervened.

The reverend's study was lined with books that had improbable titles offering no doubt very sound advice on dealing with things God would really prefer you to avoid. There were also a few that offered insight into a woman's soul, although it did not specify which woman, and information on how to make Christ work for you, which I hoped did not mean at minimum wage. There was even one on Christian chemistry, which seemed to me to be stretching the point, unless it gave a recipe for the old water-into-wine trick.

Much more interesting was a book with Gothic script on the binding. I turned my head to read the title; mere curiosity, but when I read it I felt a jolt go through me as if my esophagus had suddenly filled with ice.

Demonic Possession: Fact or Fancy? it said, and as I read the title I distinctly heard the far-off sound of a nickel dropping.

It would be very easy for an outside observer to shake his head and say, Yes, obviously, Dexter is a dull boy if he has never thought of that. But the truth is, I had not. Demon has so many negative connotations, doesn't it? And as long as the Presence was present, there seemed no need to define it in those arcane terms. It was only now that it was gone that I required some explanation. And why not this one? It was a bit old-fashioned, but its very hoariness seemed to argue that there might be something to it, some connection that went back to the nonsense with Solomon and Moloch and all the way up to what was happening to me today.

Was the Dark Passenger really a demon? And did the Passenger's absence mean it had been cast out? If so, by what? Something overwhelmingly good? I could not recall encountering anything like that in the last, oh, lifetime or so. Just the opposite, in fact.

But could something very very bad cast out a demon? I mean, what could be worse than a demon? Perhaps Moloch? Or could a demon cast itself out for some reason?

I tried to comfort myself with the thought that at least I had some good questions now, but I didn't feel terribly comforted, and my thoughts were interrupted when the door opened and the Right Reverend Gilles breezed in, beaming and muttering, 'Well, well.'

The reverend was about fifty and seemed well fed, so I suppose the tithing business was working. He came right to us and gave Rita a hug and a peck on the cheek, before turning to offer me a hearty masculine handshake.

'Well,' he said, smiling cautiously at me. 'So you're Dexter.'

'I suppose I am,' I said. 'I just couldn't help it.'

He nodded, almost as if I had made sense. 'Sit down, please, relax,' he said, and he moved around behind the desk and sat in a large swivel chair.

I took him at his word and leaned back in the red leather chair opposite his desk, but Rita perched nervously on the edge of her identical seat.

'Rita,' he said, and he smiled again. 'Well, well. So you're ready to try again, are you?'

'Yes, I – that's just – I mean, I think so,' Rita said, blushing furiously. 'I mean, yes.' She looked at me with a bright red smile and said, 'Yes, I'm ready.'

'Good, good,' he said, and he switched his expression of fond concern over to me. 'And you, Dexter. I would really like to know a little bit about you.'

'Well, to begin with, I'm a murder suspect,' I said modestly.

'Dexter,' Rita said, and impossibly turned even redder.

'The police think you killed somebody?' Reverend Gilles asked.

'Oh, they don't all think that,' I said. 'Just my sister.'

'Dexter works in forensics,' Rita blurted out. 'His sister is a detective. He just – he was only kidding about the other part.'

Once again he nodded at me. 'A sense of humor is a big help in any relationship,' he said.

He paused for a moment, looked very thoughtful and even more sincere, and then said, 'How do you feel about Rita's children?'

'Oh, Cody and Astor *adore* Dexter,' Rita said, and she looked very happy that we were no longer talking about my status as a wanted man.

'But how does Dexter feel about *them*?' he insisted gently.

'I like them,' I said.

Reverend Gilles nodded and said, 'Good. Very good. Sometimes children can be a burden. Especially when they're not yours.'

'Cody and Astor are very good at being a burden,' I said. 'But I don't really mind.'

'They're going to need a lot of mentoring,' he said, 'after all they went through.'

'Oh, I mentor them,' I said, although I thought it was probably a good idea not to be too specific, so I just added, 'They're very eager to be mentored.'

'All right,' he said. 'So we'll see those kids here at Sunday school, right?' It seemed to me to be a bald-faced attempt to blackmail us into providing future recruits to fill his collection basket, but Rita nodded eagerly, so I went along with it. Besides, I was reasonably sure that whatever anyone might say, Cody and Astor would find their spiritual comfort somewhere else.

'Now, the two of you,' he said, leaning back in his chair and rubbing the back of one hand with the palm of the other. 'A relationship in today's world needs a strong foundation in faith,' he said, looking at me expectantly. 'Dexter? How about it?'

Well, there it was. You have to believe that sooner

or later a minister will find a way to twist things around so they fall into his area. I don't know if it's worse to lie to a minister than to anyone else, but I did want to get this interview over quickly and painlessly, and could that possibly happen if I told the truth? Suppose I did and said something like, Yes, I have a great deal of faith, Reverend – in human greed and stupidity, and in the sweetness of sharp steel on a moonlit night. I have faith in the dark unseen, the cold chuckle from the shadows inside, the absolute clarity of the knife. Oh, yes, I have faith, Reverend, and beyond faith – I have certainty, because I have seen the bleak bottom line and I know it is real; it's where I live.

But really, that was hardly calculated to reassure the man, and I surely didn't need to worry about going to hell for telling a lie to a minister. If there actually is a hell, I already have a front-row seat. So I merely said, 'Faith is very important,' and he seemed to be happy with that.

'Great, okay,' he said, and he glanced covertly at his watch. 'Dexter, do you have any questions about our church?'

A fair question, perhaps, but it took me by surprise, since I had been thinking of this interview as my time for answering questions, not asking them. I was perfectly ready to be evasive for at least another hour – but really, what was there to ask about? Did they use grape juice or wine? Was the collection basket metal or wood? Was dancing a sin? I was just not prepared. And yet he seemed like he was truly interested in knowing. So I smiled reassuringly back at Reverend Gilles and said, 'Actually, I'd love to know what you think about demonic possession.'

'Dexter!' Rita gulped with a nervous smile. 'That's not— You can't really—'

Reverend Gilles raised a hand. 'It's all right, Rita,' he said. 'I think I know where Dexter's coming from.' He leaned back in the chair and nodded, favoring me with a pleasant and knowing smile. 'Been quite a while since you've been to church, Dexter?'

'Well, actually, it has,' I said.

'I think you'll find that the new church is quite a good fit for the modern world. The central truth of God's love doesn't change,' he said. 'But sometimes our understanding of it can.' And then he actually winked at me. 'I think we can agree that demons are for Halloween, not for Sunday service.'

Well, it was nice to have an answer, even if it wasn't the one I was looking for. I hadn't really expected Reverend Gilles to pull out a grimoire and cast a spell, but I admit it was a little disappointing. 'All right, then,' I said.

'Any other questions?' he asked me with a very satisfied smile. 'About our church, or anything about the ceremony?'

'Why, no,' I said. 'It seems very straightforward.'

'We like to think so,' he said. 'As long as we put Christ first, everything else falls into place.'

'Amen,' I said brightly. Rita gave me a bit of a look, but the reverend seemed to accept it.

'All right, then,' he said, and he stood up and held out his hand, 'June twenty-fourth it is.' I stood up, too, and shook his hand. 'But I expect to see you here before then,' he said. 'We have a great contemporary service at ten o'clock every Sunday.' He winked and gave my hand an extra-manly squeeze. 'Gets you home in time for the football game.'

'That's terrific,' I said, thinking how nice it is when a business anticipates the needs of its customers.

He dropped my hand and grabbed Rita, wrapping her up in a full embrace. 'Rita,' he said. 'I'm so happy for you.'

'Thank you,' Rita sobbed into his shoulder. She leaned against him for a moment longer and snuffled, and then stood upright again, rubbing her nose and looking at me. 'Thank you, Dexter,' she said. For what I don't know, but it's always nice to be included.

CHAPTER 29

For the first time in quite a while I was actually anxious to get back to my cubicle. Not because I was pining for blood spatter – but because of the idea that had descended on me in Reverend Gilles's study. Demonic possession. It had a certain ring to it. I had never really felt possessed, although Rita was certainly staking her claim. But it was at least some kind of explanation with a degree of history attached, and I was very eager to pursue it.

First I checked my answering machine and e-mail: no messages except a routine departmental memo on cleaning up the coffee area. No abject apology from Debs, either. I made a few careful calls and found that she was out trying to round up Kurt Wagner, which was a relief, since it meant she wasn't following me.

Problem solved and conscience clear, I began looking into the question of demonic possession. Once again, good old King Solomon figured prominently. He had apparently been quite cozy with a number of demons, most of whom had improbable names with several z's in them. And he had ordered them about like indentured servants, forcing them to fetch and tote and build his great temple, which was a bit of a shock, since I had always heard that the temple was a good thing, and surely there must have been some kind of law in place about demon labor. I mean, if we get so upset about illegal immigrants picking the oranges, shouldn't all those God-fearing patriarchs have had some kind of ordinance against demons?

But there it was in black and white. King Solomon had consorted with them quite comfortably, as their boss. They didn't like being ordered around, of course, but they put up with it from him. And that raised the interesting thought that perhaps someone else was able to control them, and was trying to do so with the Dark Passenger, who had therefore fled from involuntary servitude. I paused and thought about that.

The biggest problem with that theory was that it did not fit in with the overwhelming sense of mortal danger that had flooded through me from the very first, even when the Passenger had still been on board. I can understand reluctance to do unwanted work as easily as the next guy, but that had nothing to do with the lethal dread that this had raised in me.

Did that mean the Passenger was not a demon? Did it mean that what was happening to me was mere psychosis? A totally imagined paranoid fantasy of pursuing bloodlust and approaching horror?

And yet, every culture in the world throughout

history seemed to believe that there was something to the whole idea of possession. I just couldn't get it to connect in any way to my problem. I felt like I was onto something, but no great thought emerged.

Suddenly it was five thirty, and I was more than usually anxious to flee from the office and head for the dubious sanctuary of home.

The next afternoon I was in my cubicle, typing up a report on a very dull multiple killing. Even Miami gets ordinary murders, and this was one of them – or three and a half of them, to be precise, since there were three bodies in the morgue and one more in intensive care at Jackson Memorial. It was a simple drive-by shooting in one of the few areas of the city with low property values. There was really no point in spending a great deal of my time on it, since there were plenty of witnesses and they all agreed that someone named 'Motherfucker' had done the deed.

Still, forms must be observed, and I had spent half a day on the scene making sure that no one had jumped out of a doorway and hacked the victims with a hedge clipper while they were being shot from a passing car. I was trying to think of an interesting way to say that the blood spatter was consistent with gunfire from a moving source, but the boredom of it all was making my eyes cross, and as I stared vacantly at the screen, I felt a ringing rise in my ears and change to the clang of gongs and the night music came again, and the plain white of the word-processing page seemed suddenly to wash over with awful wet blood and spill out across me, flood the office, and fill the entire visible world. I jumped out of my chair and blinked a few times until it went away, but it left me shaking and wondering what had just happened.

It was starting to come at me in the full light of day, even sitting at my desk at police headquarters, and I did not like that at all. Either it was getting stronger and closer, or I was going right off the deep end and into complete madness. Schizophrenics heard voices – did they ever hear music, too? And did the Dark Passenger qualify as a voice? Had I been completely insane all this time and was just now coming to some kind of crazy final episode in the artificial sanity of Dubious Dexter?

I didn't think that was possible. Harry had gotten me squared away, made sure that I fit in just right – Harry would have known if I was crazy, and he had told me I was not. Harry was never wrong. So it was settled and I was fine, just fine, thank you.

So why did I hear that music? Why was my hand shaking? And why did I need to cling to a ghost to keep from sitting on the floor and flipping my lips with an index finger?

Clearly no one else in the building heard anything – it was just me. Otherwise the halls would be filled with people either dancing or screaming. No, fear had crawled into my life, slinking after me faster than I could run, filling the huge empty space inside me where the Passenger had once snuggled down.

I had nothing to go on; I needed some outside information if I hoped to understand this. Plenty of sources believed that demons were real – Miami was filled with people who worked hard to keep them away every day of their lives. And even though the *babalao* had said he wanted nothing to do with this whole thing, and had walked away from it as rapidly as he could, he had seemed to know what it was. I was fairly sure that Santeria allowed for possession. But never mind: Miami is a wonderful and diverse city, and I would certainly find some other place to ask the question and get an entirely different answer – perhaps even the one I was looking for. I left my cubicle and headed for the parking lot.

The Tree of Life was on the edge of Liberty City, an area of Miami that is not a good place for tourists from Iowa to visit late at night. This particular corner had been taken over by Haitian immigrants, and many of the buildings had been painted in several bright colors, as if there was not enough of one color to go around. On some of the buildings there were murals depicting Haitian country life. Roosters seemed to be prominent, and goats.

Painted on the outside wall of the Tree of Life there was a large tree, appropriately enough, and under it was an elongated image of two men pounding on some tall drums. I parked right in front of the shop and went in through a screen door that rang a small bell and then banged behind me. In the back, behind a curtain of hanging beads, a woman's voice called out something in Creole, and I stood by the glass counter and waited. The store was lined with shelves that contained numerous jars filled with mysterious things, liquid, solid, and uncertain. One or two of them seemed to be holding things that might once have been alive.

After a moment, a woman pushed through the beads and came into the front of the store. She appeared to be about forty and reed thin, with high cheekbones and a complexion like sun-bleached mahogany. She wore a flowing red-and-yellow dress, and her head was wrapped in a matching turban. 'Ah,' she said with a thick Creole accent. She looked me over with a very doubtful expression and shook her head slightly. 'How I can help you, sir?'

'Ah, well,' I said, and I more or less stumbled to a halt. How, after all, did one begin? I couldn't really say that I thought I used to be possessed and wanted to get the demon back – the poor woman might throw chicken blood at me.

'Sir?' she prompted impatiently.

'I was wondering,' I said, which was true enough, 'do you have any books on possession by demons? Er – in English?'

She pursed her lips with great disapproval and shook her head vigorously. 'It is not the demons,' she said. 'Why do you ask this – are you a reporter?'

'No,' I said. 'I'm just, um, interested. Curious.'

'Curious about the *voudoun*?' she said.

'Just the possession part,' I said.

'Huh,' she said, and if possible her disapproval grew even more. 'Why?'

Someone very clever must already have said that when all else fails, try the truth. It sounded so good that I was sure I was not the first to think of it, and it seemed like the only thing I had left. I gave it a shot.

'I think,' I said, 'I mean, I'm not sure. I think I may have been possessed. A while ago.'

'Ha,' she said. She looked at me long and hard, and then shrugged. 'May be,' she said at last. 'Why do you say so?'

'I just, um . . . I had the feeling, you know. That something else was, ah. Inside me? Watching?'

She spat on the floor, a very strange gesture from such an elegant woman, and shook her head. 'All you blancs,' she said. 'You steal us and bring us here, take everythin' from us. And then when we make somethin' from the nothin' you give us, now you want to be part of that, too. Ha.' She shook her finger at me, for all the world like a second-grade teacher with a bad student. 'You listen, blanc. If the spirit enters you, you would know. This is not somethin' like in a movie. It is a very great blessing, and,' she said with a mean smirk, 'it does not happen to the blancs.'

'Well, actually,' I said.

'Non,' she said. 'Unless you are willing, unless you ask for the blessing, it does not come.'

'But I *am* willing,' I said.

'Ha,' she said. 'It never come to you. You waste my time.' And she turned around and walked through the bead curtains to the back of the store.

I saw no point in waiting around for her to have a change of heart. It didn't seem likely to happen – and it didn't seem likely that voodoo had any answers about the Dark Passenger. She had said it only comes when called, and it was a blessing. At least that was a different answer, although I did not remember ever calling the Dark Passenger to come in – it was just always there. But to be absolutely sure, I paused at the curb outside the store and closed my eyes. *Please come back in*, I said.

Nothing happened. I got in my car and went back to work.

What an interesting choice, the Watcher thought. Voodoo. There was a certain logic to the idea, of course, he could not deny that. But what was really interesting was what it showed about the other. *He was moving in the right direction – and he was very close.*

And when his next little clue turned up, the other would be that much closer. The boy had been so panicky, he had almost wriggled away. But he had not; he had been very helpful and he was now on his way to his dark reward.

Just like the other was.

CHAPTER 30

I had barely settled back into my chair when Deborah came into my little cubicle and sat in the folding chair across from my desk.

'Kurt Wagner is missing,' she said.

I waited for more, but nothing came, so I just nodded. 'I accept your apology,' I said.

'Nobody's seen him since Saturday afternoon,' she said. 'His roommate says he came in acting all freaked out, but wouldn't say anything. He just changed his shoes, and left, and that's it.' She hesitated, and then added, 'He left his backpack.'

I admit I perked up a little at that. 'What was in it?' I asked.

'Traces of blood,' she said, as if she was admitting she had taken the last cookie. 'It matches Tammy Connor's.'

'Well then,' I said. It didn't seem right to say anything about the fact that she'd had somebody else do the blood work. 'That's a pretty good clue.'

'Yeah,' she said. 'It's him. It has to be him. So he did Tammy, took the head in his backpack and did Manny Borque.'

'It does look like that,' I said. 'That's a shame

– I was just getting used to the idea that I was guilty.'

'It makes no fucking sense,' Deborah complained. 'The kid's a good student, on the swimming team, good family – all of that.'

'He was such a nice guy,' I said. 'I can't believe he did all those horrible things.'

'All right,' Deborah said. 'I know it, goddamn it. Total cliché. But what the hell – the guy kills his own girlfriend, sure. Maybe even her room-mate, because she saw it. But why everybody else? And all that crap with burning them, and the bulls' heads, what is it, Mollusk?'

'Moloch,' I said. 'Mollusk is a clam.'

'Whatever,' she said. 'But it makes no sense, Dex. I mean . . .' She looked away, and for a moment I thought she was going to apologize after all. But I was wrong. 'If it does make sense,' she said, 'it's *your* kind of sense. The kind of thing you know about.' She looked back at me, but she still seemed to be embarrassed. 'That's, you know – I mean, is it, um – did it come back? Your, uh . . .'

'No,' I said. 'It didn't come back.'

'Well,' she said, 'shit.'

'Did you put out a BOLO on Kurt Wagner?' I asked.

'I know how to do my job, Dex,' she said. 'If he's in the Miami-Dade area, we'll get him, and FDLE has it, too. If he's in Florida, somebody'll find him.'

'And if he's not in Florida?'

323

She looked hard at me, and I saw the beginnings of the way Harry had looked before he got sick, after so many years as a cop: tired, and getting used to the idea of routine defeat. 'Then he'll probably get away with it,' she said. 'And I'll have to arrest you to save my job.'

'Well, then,' I said, trying hard for cheerfulness in the face of overwhelming grim grayness, 'let's hope he drives a very recognizable car.'

She snorted. 'It's a red Geo, one of those mini-Jeep things.'

I closed my eyes. It was a very odd sensation, but I felt all the blood in my body suddenly relocating to my feet. 'Did you say red?' I heard myself ask in a remarkably calm voice.

There was no answer, and I opened my eyes. Deborah was staring at me with a look of suspicion so strong I could almost touch it.

'What the hell is that,' she said. 'One of your voices?'

'A red Geo followed me home the other night,' I said. 'And then somebody tried to break into my house.'

'Goddamn it,' she snarled at me, 'when the fuck were you going to tell me all this?'

'Just as soon as you decided you were speaking to me again,' I said.

Deborah turned a very gratifying shade of crimson and looked down at her shoes. 'I was busy,' she said, not very convincingly.

'So was Kurt Wagner,' I said.

'All right, Jesus,' she said, and I knew that was all the apology I would ever get. 'Yeah, it's red. But shit,' she said, still looking down, 'I think that old man was right. The bad guys are winning.'

I didn't like seeing my sister this depressed. I felt that some cheery remark was called for, something that would lift the gloom and bring a song back to her heart, but alas, I came up empty. 'Well,' I said at last, 'if the bad guys really are winning, at least there's plenty of work for you.'

She looked up at last, but not with anything resembling a smile. 'Yeah,' she said. 'Some guy in Kendall shot his wife and two kids last night. I get to go work on that.' She stood up, straightening slowly into something that at least resembled her normal posture. 'Hooray for our side,' she said, and walked out of my office.

From the very beginning it was an ideal partnership. The new things had self-awareness, and that made manipulating them much easier – and much more rewarding for IT. They killed one another much more readily, too, and IT did not have to wait long at all for a new host – nor to try again to reproduce. IT eagerly drove IT's host to a killing, and IT waited, longing to feel the strange and wonderful swelling.

But when the feeling came, it simply stirred slowly, tickled IT with a tendril of sensation, and then vanished without blossoming and producing offspring.

IT was puzzled. Why didn't reproduction work this time? There had to be a reason, and IT was orderly and efficient in IT's search for the answer. Over many years, as the new things changed and grew, IT experimented. And gradually IT found the conditions that made reproduction work. It took quite a few kills before IT was satisfied that IT had found the answer, but each time IT duplicated the final formula, a new awareness came into being and fled into the world in pain and terror, and IT was satisfied.

The thing worked best when the hosts were off-balance a bit, either from the drinks they had begun to brew or from some kind of trance state. The victim had to know what was coming, and if there was an audience of some kind, their emotions fed into the experience and made it even more powerful.

Then there was fire – fire was a very good way to kill the victims. It seemed to release their essence all at once in a great shrieking jolt of spectacular energy.

And finally, the whole thing worked better with the young ones. The emotions all around were so much stronger, especially in the parents. It was wonderful beyond anything else IT could imagine.

Fire, trance, young victims. A simple formula.

IT began to push the new hosts to create a way to establish these conditions permanently. And the hosts were surprisingly willing to go along with IT.

CHAPTER 31

When I was very young I once saw a variety act on TV. A man put a bunch of plates on the end of a series of supple rods, and kept them up in the air by whipping the rods around to spin the plates. And if he slowed down or turned his back, even for a moment, one of the plates would wobble and then crash to the ground, followed by all the others in series.

That's a terrific metaphor for life, isn't it? We're all trying to keep our plates spinning in the air, and once you get them up there you can't take your eyes off them and you have to keep chugging along without rest. Except that in life, somebody keeps adding more plates, hiding the rods, and changing the law of gravity when you're not looking. And so every time you think you have all your plates spinning nicely, suddenly you hear a hideous clattering crash behind you and a whole row of plates you didn't even know you had begins to hit the ground.

Here I had stupidly assumed that the tragic death of Manny Borque had given me one less plate to worry about, since I could now proceed to cater the wedding as it should be done, with $65 worth of cold cuts and a cooler full of soda. I could concentrate on the very real and important problem of putting me back together again. And so thinking all was quiet on the home front, I turned my back for just a moment and was rewarded with a spectacular crash behind me.

The metaphorical plate in question shattered when I came into Rita's house after work. It was so quiet that I assumed no one was home, but a quick glance inside showed something far more disturbing. Cody and Astor sat motionless on the couch, and Rita was standing behind them with a look on her face that could easily turn fresh milk into yogurt.

'Dexter,' she said, and the tromp of doom was in her voice, 'we need to talk.'

'Of course,' I said, and as I reeled from her expression, even the mere thought of a light-hearted response shriveled into dust and blew away in the icy air.

'These children,' Rita said. Apparently that was the entire thought, because she just glared and said no more.

But of course, I knew which children she meant, so I nodded encouragingly. 'Yes,' I said.

'Ooh,' she said.

Well, if it was taking Rita this long to form a complete sentence, it was easy to see why the house had been so quiet when I walked in. Clearly the lost art of conversation was going to need a little boost from Diplomatic Dexter if we were ever going to get more than seven words out in time for dinner. So I plunged straight in with my well-known courage. 'Rita,' I said, 'is there some kind of problem?'

'Ooh,' she said again, which was not encouraging.

Well really, there's only so much you can do with monosyllables, even if you are a gifted conversationalist like me. Since there was clearly no help coming from Rita, I looked at Cody and Astor, who had not moved since I came in. 'All right,' I said. 'Can you two tell me what's wrong with your mother?'

They exchanged one of their famous looks, and then turned back to me. 'We didn't mean to,' Astor said. 'It was an accident.'

It wasn't much, but at least it was a complete sentence. 'I'm very glad to hear it,' I said. '*What* was an accident?'

'We got caught,' Cody said, and Astor poked him with an elbow.

'We didn't *mean to*,' she repeated with emphasis, and Cody turned to look at her before he remembered what they had agreed on; she glared at him and he blinked once before slowly nodding his head at me.

'Accident,' he said.

It was nice to see that the party line was firmly in place behind a united front, but I was still no closer to knowing what we were talking about, and we had been talking about it, more or less, for several minutes – time being a large factor, since the dinner hour was approaching and Dexter does require regular feeding.

'That's all they'll say about it,' Rita said. 'And it is nowhere *near* enough. I don't see *how* you could possibly tie up the Villegas' cat by accident.'

'It didn't die,' Astor said in the tiniest voice I had ever heard her use.

'And what were the hedge clippers for?' Rita demanded.

'We didn't use them,' Astor said.

'But you were going to, weren't you?' Rita said.

Two small heads swiveled to face me, and a moment later, Rita's did, too.

I am sure it was completely unintentional, but a picture was beginning to emerge of what had happened, and it was not a peaceful still life. Clearly the youngsters had been attempting an independent study without me. And even worse, I could tell that somehow it had become my problem; the children expected me to bail them out, and Rita was clearly prepared to lock and load and open fire on me. Of course it was unfair; all I had done so far was come home from work. But as I have noticed on more than one occasion, life itself is unfair, and there is no complaint department, so we might as well accept things the way they happen, clean up the mess, and move on.

Which is what I attempted to do, however futile

I suspected it would be. 'I'm sure there's a very good explanation,' I said, and Astor brightened immediately and began to nod vigorously.

'It was an accident,' she insisted happily.

'Nobody ties up a cat, tapes it to a workbench, and stands over it with hedge clippers by *accident!*' Rita said.

To be honest, things were getting a little complicated. On the one hand, I was very pleased to get such a clear picture at last of what the problem was. But on the other hand, we seemed to have strayed into an area that could be somewhat awkward to explain, and I could not help feeling that Rita might be a little bit better off if she remained ignorant of these matters.

I thought I had been clear with Astor and Cody that they were not to fly solo until I had explained their wings to them. But they had obviously chosen not to understand and, even though they were suffering some very gratifying consequences for their action, it was still up to me to get them out of it. Unless they could be made to understand that they absolutely must not repeat this – and must not stray from the Harry Path as I put their feet upon it – I was happy to let them twist in the wind indefinitely.

'Do you know that what you did is wrong?' I asked them. They nodded in unison.

'Do you know *why* it is wrong?' I said.

Astor looked very uncertain, glanced at Cody, and then blurted out, 'Because we got caught!'

'There now, you see?' said Rita, and a hysterical edge was creeping into her voice.

'Astor,' I said, looking at her very carefully and not really winking, 'this is not the time to be funny.'

'I'm glad somebody thinks this is funny,' Rita said. 'But I don't happen to think so.'

'Rita,' I said, with all the soothing calm I could muster, and then, using the smooth cunning I had developed in my years as an apparently human adult, I added, 'I think this might be one of those times that Reverend Gilles was talking about, where I need to mentor.'

'Dexter, these two have just – I don't have any idea – and you—!' she said, and even though she was close to tears, I was happy to see that at least her old speech patterns were returning. Just as happily, a scene from an old movie popped into my head in the nick of time, and I knew exactly what a real human being was supposed to do.

I walked over to Rita and, with my very best serious face, I put a hand on her shoulder.

'Rita,' I said, and I was very proud of how grave and manly my voice sounded, 'you are too close to this, and you're letting your emotions cloud your judgment. These two need some firm perspective, and I can give it to them. After all,' I said as the line came to me, and I was pleased to see that I hadn't lost a step, 'I have to be their father now.'

I should have guessed that this would be the remark that pushed Rita off the dock and into the lake of tears; and it was, because immediately after I said it, her lips began to tremble, her face lost all its anger, and a rivulet began to stream down each cheek.

'All right,' she sobbed, 'please, I – just talk to them.' She snuffled loudly and hurried from the room.

I let Rita have her dramatic exit and gave it a moment to sink in before I walked back around to the front of the couch and stared down at my two miscreants. 'Well,' I said. 'What happened to We understand, We promise, We'll wait?'

'You're taking too long,' said Astor. 'We haven't done anything except the once, and besides, you're not always right and we think we shouldn't have to wait anymore.'

'I'm ready,' Cody said.

'Really,' I said. 'Then I guess your mother is the greatest detective in the world, because you're ready and she caught you anyway.'

'Dex-terrrr,' Astor whined.

'No, Astor, you quit talking and just listen to me for a minute.' I stared at her with my most serious face, and for a moment I thought she was going to say something else but then a miracle took place right there in our living room. Astor changed her mind and closed her mouth.

'All right,' I said. 'I have said from the very beginning that you have to do it my way. You don't have to believe I'm always right,' and Astor made a sound, but didn't say anything. 'But you have to do what I say. Or I will not help you, and you will end up in jail. There is no other way. Okay?'

It is quite possible that they didn't know what to do with this new tone of voice and new role. I was no longer Playtime Dexter, but something very different, Dexter of Dark Discipline, which they had never seen before. They looked at each other uncertainly so I pushed a little more.

'You got caught,' I said. 'What happens when you get caught?'

'Time out?' Cody said uncertainly.

'Uh-huh,' I said. 'And if you're thirty years old?'

For possibly the first time in her life, Astor had no answer, and Cody had already used up his two-word quota for the time being. They looked at each other, and then they looked at their feet.

'My sister, Sergeant Deborah, and I spend all day catching people who do this kind of stuff,' I said. 'And when we catch them, they go to prison.' I smiled at Astor. 'Time out for grown-ups. But a lot worse. You sit in a little room the size of your bathroom, locked in, all day and all night. You pee in a hole in the floor. You eat moldy garbage, and there are rats and lots of cockroaches.'

'We know what prison is, Dexter,' she said.

'Really? Then why are you in such a hurry to get there?' I said. 'And do you know what Old Sparky is?'

Astor looked at her feet again; Cody hadn't looked up yet.

'Old Sparky is the electric chair. If they catch

you, they strap you into Old Sparky, put some wires on your head, and fry you up like bacon. Does that sound like fun?'

They shook their heads, no.

'So the very first lesson is not to get caught,' I said. 'Remember the piranhas?' They nodded. 'They look ferocious, so people know they're dangerous.'

'But Dexter, we don't look ferocious,' Astor said.

'No, you don't,' I said. 'And you don't want to. We are supposed to be people, not piranhas. But the idea is the same, to look like something you are not. Because when something bad happens, that's who everyone will look for first – the ferocious people. You need to look like sweet, lovable, normal children.'

'Can I wear makeup?' Astor asked.

'When you're older,' I said.

'You say that about *everything*!' she said.

'And I mean it about everything,' I said. 'You got caught this time because you went off on your own and didn't know what you were doing. You didn't know what you were doing because you didn't listen to me.'

I decided the torture had gone on long enough and I sat down on the couch in between them. 'No more doing anything without me, okay? And when you promise this time, you better mean it.'

They both looked slowly up at me and then nodded. 'We promise,' Astor said softly, and Cody, even softer, echoed, 'Promise.'

'Well then,' I said. I took their hands and we shook solemnly.

'Good,' I said. 'Now let's go apologize to your mom.' They both jumped up, radiating relief that the hideous ordeal was over, and I followed them out of the room, closer to feeling self-satisfied than I could remember feeling before.

Maybe there was something to this whole fatherhood thing after all.

CHAPTER 32

Sun Tzu, a very smart man, in spite of the fact that he has been dead for so long, wrote a book called *The Art of War*, and one of the many clever observations he made in the book was that every time something awful happens, there's a way to turn it to your advantage, if you just look at things properly. This is not New Age California Pollyanna thinking, insisting that if life gives you lemons you can always make Key Lime pie. It is, rather, very practical advice that comes in handy a lot more than you might think.

At the moment, for instance, my problem was how to continue training Cody and Astor in the Harry Way now that they had been busted by their mother. And in looking for a solution I remembered good old Sun Tzu and tried to imagine what he might have done. Of course, he had been a general, so he probably would have attacked the left flank with cavalry or something, but surely the principles were the same.

So as I led Cody and Astor to their weeping mother I was beating the bushes in the dark forest of Dexter's brain for some small partridge of an idea that the old Chinese general might approve of. And just as the three of us trickled to a halt in front of sniffling Rita, the idea popped out, and I grabbed it.

'Rita,' I said quietly, 'I think I can stop this before it gets out of hand.'

'You heard what – This is already out of hand,' she said, and she paused for a large snuffle.

'I have an idea,' I said. 'I want you to bring them down to me at work tomorrow, right after school.'

'But that isn't – I mean, didn't it all start because—'

'Did you ever see a TV show called *Scared Straight*?' I said.

She stared at me for a moment, snuffled again, and looked at the two kids.

And that is why, at three thirty the next afternoon, Cody and Astor were taking turns peering into a microscope in the forensics lab. 'That's a *hair*?' Astor demanded.

'That's right,' I said.

'It looks *gross*!'

'Most of the human body is gross, especially if you look at it under a microscope,' I told her. 'Look at the one next to it.'

There was a studious pause, broken only once when Cody yanked on her arm, and she pushed him away and said, 'Stop it, Cody.'

'What do you notice?' I asked.

'They don't look the same,' she said.

'They're not,' I said. 'The first one is yours. The other one is mine.'

She continued to look for a moment, then straightened up from the eyepiece. 'You can tell,' she said. 'They're different.'

'It gets better,' I told her. 'Cody, give me your shoe.'

Cody very obligingly sat on the floor and pried off his left sneaker. I took it from him and held out a hand. 'Come with me,' I said. I helped him to his feet and he followed me, hopping one-footed to the closest countertop. I lifted him onto a stool and held up the shoe so he could see the bottom. 'Your shoe,' I said. 'Clean or dirty?'

He peered at it carefully. 'Clean,' he said.

'So you would think,' I said. 'Watch this.' I took a small wire brush to the tread of his shoe, carefully scraping out the nearly invisible gunk from between the ridges of the tread into a petri dish. I lifted a small sample of it onto a glass slide and took it back over to the microscope. Astor immediately crowded in to look, but Cody hopped over quickly. 'My turn,' he said. 'My shoe.' She looked at me and I nodded.

'It's his shoe,' I said. 'You can see right after.' She apparently accepted the justice of that, as she stepped back and let Cody climb onto the stool. I looked into the eyepiece to focus it, and saw that the slide was everything I could hope for. 'Aha,' I said, and stepped back. 'Tell me what you see, young Jedi.'

Cody frowned into the microscope for several minutes, until Astor's jiggling dance of impatience became so distracting that we both looked at her. 'That's long enough,' she said. 'It's my turn.'

'In a minute,' I said, and I turned back to Cody. 'Tell me what you saw.'

He shook his head. 'Junk,' he said.

'Okay,' I said. 'Now I'll tell you.' I looked into the eyepiece again and said, 'First off, animal hair, probably feline.'

'That means cat,' Astor said.

'Then there's some soil with a high nitrogen content – probably potting soil, like you'd use for houseplants.' I spoke to him without looking up. 'Where did you take the cat? The garage? Where your mom works on her plants?'

'Yes,' he said.

'Uh-huh. I thought so.' I looked back into the microscope. 'Oh – look there. That's a synthetic fiber, from somebody's carpet. It's blue.' I looked at Cody and raised an eyebrow. 'What color is the carpet in your room, Cody?'

His eyes were wide-open round as he said, 'Blue.'

'Yup. If I wanted to get fancy I'd compare this to a piece I took from your room. Then you would be cooked. I could prove that it was you with the cat.' I looked back into the eyepiece again. 'My goodness, somebody had pizza recently – oh, and there's a small chunk of popcorn, too. Remember the movie last week?'

'Dexter, I wanna see,' Astor whined. 'It's my turn.'

'All right,' I said, and I set her on a stool next to Cody's so she could peer into the microscope.

'I don't see popcorn,' she said immediately.

'That round, brownish thing up in the corner,' I said. She was quiet for a minute, and then looked up at me.

'You can't really tell all that,' she said. 'Not just looking in the microscope.'

I am happy to admit that I was showing off, but after all, that's what this whole episode was about, so I was prepared. I grabbed a three-ring note-book I had prepared and laid it open on the counter. 'I can, too,' I said. 'And a whole lot more. Look.' I turned to a page that had photos of several different animal hairs, carefully selected to show the greatest variety. 'Here's the cat hair,' I said. 'Completely different from goat, see?' I flipped the page. 'And carpet fibers. Nothing like these from a shirt and this one from a wash-cloth.'

The two of them crowded together and stared at the book, flipping through the ten or so pages I had put together to show them that, yes indeed, I really can tell all that. It was carefully arranged to make forensics look just a tiny bit more all-seeing and all-powerful than the Wizard of Oz, of course. And to be fair, we really can do most of what I showed them. It never actually seems to do much good in catching any bad guys, but why should I tell them that and spoil a magical afternoon?

'Look back in the microscope,' I told them after a few minutes. 'See what else you can find.' They did so, very eagerly, and seemed quite happy at it for a while.

When they finally looked up at me I gave them a cheerful smile and said, 'All this from a clean shoe.' I closed the book and watched the two of them think about this. 'And that's just using the microscope,' I said, nodding around the room at the many gleaming machines. 'Think what we can figure out if we use all the fancy stuff.'

'Yeah, but we could go barefoot,' Astor said.

I nodded as if what she had said made sense. 'Yes, you could,' I said. 'And then I could do something like this – give me your hand.'

Astor eyed me for a few seconds as if she was afraid I would cut her arm off, but then she held it out slowly. I held it and, using a fingernail clipper from my pocket, I scraped under her fingernails. 'Wait until you see what you have here,' I said.

'But I washed my hands,' Astor said.

'Doesn't matter,' I told her. I put the small specks of stuff onto another glass slide and fixed it to the microscope. 'Now then,' I said.

CLUMP.

It really is a bit melodramatic to say that we all froze, but there it is – we did. They both looked up at me and I looked back at them and we all forgot to breathe.

CLUMP.

The sound was getting closer and it was very hard to remember that we were in police headquarters and perfectly safe.

'Dexter,' Astor said in a slightly quavery voice.

'We are in police headquarters,' I said. 'We're perfectly safe.'

CLUMP.

It stopped, very close. The hair went up on the back of my neck and I turned toward the door as it swung slowly open.

Sergeant Doakes. He stood there in the doorway, glaring, which seemed to have become his permanent expression. 'You,' he said, and the sound was nearly as unsettling as his appearance as it rolled out of his tongue-less mouth.

'Why yes, it is me,' I said. 'Good of you to remember.'

He clumped one more step into the room and Astor scrambled off her stool and scurried to the windows, as far away from the door as she could get. Doakes paused and looked at her. Then his eyes swung back to Cody, who slid off his stool and stood there unblinking, facing Doakes.

Doakes stared at Cody, Cody stared back, and Doakes made what I can only call a Darth Vader intake of breath. Then he swung his head back to me and clumped one rapid step closer, nearly losing his balance. 'You,' he said again, hissing it this time. 'Kigs!'

'Kigs?' I said, and I really was puzzled and not trying to provoke him. I mean, if he insisted on stomping around and frightening children, the least he could do is carry a notepad and pencil to communicate with.

Apparently that thoughtful gesture was beyond him, though. Instead he gave another Darth Vader breath and slowly pointed his steel claw at Cody. 'Kigs,' he said again, his lips drawn back in a snarl.

'He means me,' Cody said. I turned to him, surprised to hear him speak with Doakes right there, like a nightmare come to life. But of course, Cody didn't have nightmares. He simply looked at Doakes.

'What about you, Cody?' I said.

'He saw my shadow,' Cody said.

Sergeant Doakes took another wobbly step toward me. His right claw snapped, as if it had decided on its own to attack me. 'You. Goo. Gik.'

It was becoming apparent that he had something on his mind, but it was even clearer that he ought to stick with the silent glaring, since it was nearly impossible to understand the gooey syllables that came from his damaged mouth.

'Wuk. You. Goo,' he hissed, and it was such a clear condemnation of all that was Dexter, I at last understood that he was accusing me of something.

'What do you mean?' I said. 'I didn't do anything.'

'Goy,' he said, pointing again at Cody.

'Why, yes,' I said. 'Methodist, actually.' I admit that I deliberately misunderstood him: he was saying 'boy' and it came out 'goy' because he had no tongue, but really, one can only take so much. It should have been painfully clear to Doakes that his attempts at vocal communication were having very limited success, and yet he insisted on trying. Didn't the man have any sense of decorum at all?

Happily for all of us, we were interrupted by a clatter in the hallway and Deborah rushed into the room. 'Dexter,' she said. She paused as she took in the wild tableau of Doakes with claw upraised against me, Astor cringing against the window, and Cody lifting a scalpel off the bench to use against Doakes. 'What the hell,' Deborah said. 'Doakes?'

He very slowly let his arm drop, but he did not take his eyes off me.

'I've been looking for you, Dexter. Where were you?'

I was grateful enough for her timely entry that I did not point out how foolish her question was. 'Why, I was right here, educating the children,' I said. 'Where were you?'

'On my way to the Dinner Key,' she said. 'They found Kurt Wagner's body.'

CHAPTER 33

Deborah hurled us through traffic at Evel Knievel-over-the-canyon speeds. I tried to think of a polite way to point out that we were going to see a dead body that would probably not escape, so could she please slow down, but I could not come up with any phrase that would not cause her to take her hands off the wheel and put them around my neck.

Cody and Astor were too young to realize that they were in mortal danger, and they seemed to be enjoying themselves thorougly in the backseat, even getting into the spirit of things by happily returning the greetings of the other motorists by raising their own middle fingers in unison each time we cut off somebody.

There was a three-car pileup on U.S. 1 at LeJeune which slowed traffic for a few moments and we were forced to cut our pace to a crawl. Since I no longer had to spend all my breath suppressing screams of terror, I tried to find out from Deborah exactly what we were racing to see.

'How was he killed?' I asked her.

346

'Just like the others,' she said. 'Burned. And there's no head on the body.'

'You're sure this is Kurt Wagner?' I asked her.

'Can I prove it? Not yet,' she said. 'Am I sure? Shit yes.'

'Why?'

'They found his car nearby,' she said.

I was quite sure that normally I would understand exactly why somebody seemed to have a fetish for the heads, and know where to find them and why. But of course, now that I was all alone on the inside there was no more normal.

'This doesn't make any sense, you know,' I said.

Deborah snarled and hammered the heel of her hand on the steering wheel. 'Tell me about it,' she said.

'Kurt must have done the other victims,' I said.

'So who killed him? His scoutmaster?' she said, leaning on the horn and pulling around the traffic snarl into the oncoming lane. She swerved toward a bus, stomped on the gas, and wove through traffic for fifty yards until we were past the pileup. I concentrated on remembering to breathe and reflecting that we were all certain to die someday anyway, so in the big picture what did it really matter if Deborah killed us? It was not terribly comforting, but it did keep me from screaming and diving out the car window until Deborah pulled back into the correct lane on the far side of U.S. 1.

'That was fun,' said Astor. 'Can we do that again?'

347

Cody nodded enthusiastically.

'And we could put on the siren next time,' Astor said. 'How come you don't use the siren, Sergeant Debbie?'

'Don't call me Debbie,' Deborah snapped. 'I just don't like the siren.'

'Why not?' Astor insisted.

Deborah blew out a huge breath and glanced at me out of the corner of her eye. 'It's a fair question,' I said.

'It makes too much noise,' Deborah said. 'Now let me drive, okay?'

'All right,' Astor said, but she didn't sound convinced.

We drove in silence all the way to Grand Avenue, and I tried to think about it by myself – clearly enough to come up with anything that might help. I didn't, but I did think of one thing worth mentioning.

'What if Kurt's murder is just a coincidence?' I said.

'Even you can't really believe that,' she said.

'But if he was on the run,' I said, 'maybe he tried to get a fake ID from the wrong people, or get smuggled out of the country. There are plenty of bad guys he could run into under the circumstances.'

It didn't really sound likely, even to me, but Deborah thought about it for a few seconds anyway, chewing on her lower lip and absent-mindedly blasting the horn as she pulled around a courtesy van from one of the hotels.

'No,' she said at last. 'He was cooked, Dexter. Like the first two. No way they could copy that.'

Once again I was aware of a small stirring in the bleak emptiness inside, the area once inhabited by the Dark Passenger. I closed my eyes and tried to find some shred of my once-constant companion, but there was nothing. I opened my eyes in time to see Deborah accelerate around a bright red Ferrari.

'People read the newspapers,' I said. 'There are always copycat killings.'

She thought some more, and then shook her head. 'No,' she said at last. 'I don't believe in coincidence. Not with something like this. Cooked and headless both, and it's a coincidence? No way.'

Hope always dies hard, but even so I had to admit that she was probably right. Beheading and burning were not really standard procedures for the normal, blue-collar killer, and most people would be far more likely simply to clonk you on the head, tie an anchor to your feet, and fling you into the bay.

So in all likelihood, we were on our way to see the body of somebody we were sure was a killer, and he had been killed the same way as his own victims. If I had been my cheerful old self, I would certainly have enjoyed the delicious irony, but in my present condition it seemed like just another annoying affront to an orderly existence.

But Deborah gave me very little time to reflect and become grumpy; she whipped through the traffic in the center of Coconut Grove and pulled into the parking area beside Bayfront Park, where the familiar circus was already under way. Three police cruisers were pulled up, and Camilla Figg was dusting for fingerprints on a battered red Geo parked at one of the meters – presumably Kurt Wagner's car.

I got out and looked around, and even without an inner voice whispering clues, I noticed right away that there was something wrong with this picture. 'Where's the body?' I asked Deborah.

She was already walking toward the gate of the yacht club. 'Out on the island,' she said.

I blinked and got out of the car. For no reason I could name, the thought of the body on the island raised the hair on the back of my neck, but as I looked out over the water for the answer, all I got was the afternoon breeze that blew across the pines on the barrier islands of Dinner Key and straight through the emptiness inside me.

Deborah jogged me with her elbow. 'Come on,' she said.

I looked in the backseat at Cody and Astor, who had just now mastered the intricacies of the seat-belt release and were trickling out of the car. 'Stay here,' I said to them. 'I'll be back in a little while.'

'Where are you going?' Astor said.

'I have to go out to that island,' I said.

'Is there a dead person there?' she asked me.

'Yes,' I said.

She glanced at Cody, then back at me. 'We want to go,' she said.

'No, absolutely not,' I said. 'I got in enough trouble the last time. If I let you see another dead body your mother would turn me into one, too.'

Cody thought that was very funny and he made a small noise and shook his head.

I heard a shout and looked through the gate into the marina. Deborah was already at the dock, about to step into the police boat tied up there. She waved an arm at me and yelled, 'Dexter!'

Astor stomped her foot to get my attention, and I looked back at her. 'You have to stay here,' I said, 'and I have to go now.'

'But Dexter, we want to ride on the boat,' she said.

'Well, you can't,' I said. 'But if you behave I'll take you on my boat this weekend.'

'To see a dead person?' Astor said.

'No,' I said. 'We're not going to see any more dead bodies for a while.'

'But you promised!' she said.

'Dexter!' Deborah yelled again. I waved at her, which did not seem to be the response she was looking for, because she beckoned furiously at me.

'Astor, I have to go,' I said. 'Stay here. We'll talk about this later.'

'It's always later,' she muttered.

On the way through the gate I paused and spoke to the uniformed cop there, a large heavy man with black hair and a very low forehead. 'Could you keep one eye on my kids there?' I asked him.

He stared at me. 'What am I, day-care patrol?'

'Just for a few minutes,' I said. 'They're very well behaved.'

'Lookit, sport,' he said, but before he could finish his sentence there was a rustle of movement and Deborah was beside us.

'God*damn* it, Dexter!' she said. 'Get your ass on the boat!'

'I'm sorry,' I said. 'I have to find somebody to watch the kids.'

Deborah ground her teeth together. Then she glanced at the big cop and read his name tag. 'Suchinsky,' she said. 'Watch the fucking kids.'

'Aw, come on, Sarge,' he said. 'Jesus Christ.'

'Stick with the kids, goddamn it,' she said. 'You might learn something. Dexter – get on the goddamn boat, now!'

I turned meekly and hurried for the goddamn boat. Deborah strode past me and was already seated when I jumped on, and the cop driving the boat headed for one of the smaller islands, weaving between the anchored sailboats.

There are several small islands on the outside of Dinner Key Marina that provide protection from wind and wave, one of the things that makes it such a good anchorage. Of course, it's only good under ordinary circumstances, as the islands themselves proved. They were littered with broken boats and other maritime junk deposited by the many recent hurricanes, and every now and then a squatter would set up housekeeping, building a shack from shattered boat parts.

The island we headed for was one of the smaller ones. Half of a forty-foot sports fisherman lay on the beach at a crazy angle, and the pine trees inland of the beach were hung with chunks of Styrofoam, tattered cloth, and wispy shreds of plastic sheeting and garbage bags. Other than that, it was just the way the Native Americans had left it, a peaceful little chunk of land covered with Australian pines, condoms, and beer cans.

Except, of course, for Kurt Wagner's body, which had most likely been left by someone other than Native Americans. It was lying in the center of the island in a small clearing, and like the others, it had been arranged in a formal pose, with the arms folded across the chest and the legs pressed together. The body was headless and unclothed, charred from being burned, very much like the others – except that this time there had been a small addition. Around the neck was a leather string holding a pewter medallion about the size of an egg. I leaned closer to look; it was a bull's head.

Once again I felt a strange twinge in the emptiness, as if some part of me were recognizing that this was significant, but didn't know why or how to express it – not alone, not without the Passenger.

Vince Masuoka was squatting next to the body examining a cigarette butt and Deborah knelt down beside him. I circled them one time, looking at it from all angles: Still Life with Cops. I was hoping, I suppose, that I would find a small but significant clue. Perhaps the killer's driver's license, or a signed confession. But there was nothing of the kind, nothing but sand, pockmarked from countless feet and the wind.

I went down on one knee beside Deborah. 'You looked for the tattoo, right?' I asked her.

'First thing,' Vince said. He extended a rubber-gloved hand and lifted the body slightly. There it was, half covered with sand but still visible, only the upper edge of it cut off and left, presumably, with the missing head.

'It's him,' Deborah said. 'The tattoo, his car is at the marina – it's him, Dexter. And I wish I knew what the hell that tattoo meant.'

'It's Aramaic,' I said.

'How the fuck would you know that?' Deborah said.

'My research,' I said, and I squatted down next to the body. 'Look.' I picked a small pine twig out of the sand and pointed with it. Part of the first letter was missing, cut off along with the head, but the rest was plainly visible and matched my language lesson. 'There's the *M*, what's left of it. And the *L*, and the *K*.'

'What the hell does that mean?' Deborah demanded.

'Moloch,' I said, feeling a small irrational chill just saying the word here in the bright sunshine. I tried to shake it off, but a feeling of uneasiness stayed behind. 'Aramaic has no vowels. So *MLK* spells Moloch.'

'Or milk,' Deborah said.

'Really, Debs, if you think our killer would tattoo *milk* on his neck, you need a nap.'

'But if Wagner is Moloch, who killed him?'

'Wagner kills the others,' I said, trying very hard to sound thoughtful and confident at the same time, a difficult task. 'And then, um . . .'

'Yeah,' she said. 'I already figured out "um."'

'And you're watching Wilkins.'

'We're watching Wilkins, for Christ's sake.'

I looked at the body again, but there was nothing else on it to tell me more than I knew, which was almost nothing. I could not stop my brain from going in a circle; if Wagner had been Moloch, and now Wagner was dead, and killed by Moloch . . .

I stood up. For a moment I felt dizzy, as if bright lights were crashing in on me, and in the distance I heard that awful music beginning to swell up into the afternoon and for just that moment I could not doubt that somewhere nearby the god was calling me – the real god himself and not some psychotic prankster.

I shook my head to silence it and nearly fell over. I felt a hand grabbing my arm to steady me, but whether it was Debs, Vince, or Moloch himself, I couldn't tell. From far away a voice was calling my name, but it was singing it, the cadence rising up to the far-too-familiar rhythm of that music. I closed my eyes and felt heat on my face and the music got louder. Something shook me and I opened my eyes.

The music stopped. The heat was just the Miami sun, with the wind whipping in the clouds of an afternoon squall. Deborah held both my elbows and shook me, saying my name over and over patiently.

'Dexter,' she said. 'Hey Dex, come on. Dexter. Dexter.'

'Here I am,' I said, although I was not entirely sure of that.

'You okay, Dex?' she said.

'I think I stood up too fast,' I said.

She looked dubious. 'Uh-huh,' she said.

'Really, Debs, I'm fine now,' I said. 'I mean, I think so.'

'You think so,' she said.

'Yes. I mean, I just stood up too fast.'

She looked at me a moment longer, then let go and stepped back. 'Okay,' she said. 'Then if you can make it to the boat, let's get back.'

It may be that I was still dizzy, but there seemed to be no sense in her words, almost as if they were just made-up syllables. 'Get back?' I said.

'Dexter,' she said. 'We got six bodies, and our only suspect is on the ground here with no head.'

'Right,' I said, and I heard a faint drumbeat under my voice. 'So where are we going?'

Deborah balled up her fists and clenched her teeth. She looked down at the body, and for a moment I thought she was actually going to spit. 'What about the guy you chased into the canal?' she said at last.

'Starzak? No, he said . . .' I stopped myself from finishing, but not quite soon enough, because Deborah pounced.

'He *said*? When did you talk to him, goddamn it?'

To be fair to me, I really was still a little bit dizzy, and I had not thought before I spoke, and now I was in a somewhat awkward spot. I could not very well tell my sister that I had spoken to him just the other night when I had taped him to his workbench and tried to cut him up into small neat pieces. But the blood must have been flowing back into my brain, because I very quickly said, 'I mean, he *seemed*,' I said. 'He seemed to be just a . . . I don't know,' I said. 'I think it was personal, like I cut him off in traffic.'

Deborah looked at me angrily for a moment, but then she seemed to accept what I had said, and she turned away and kicked at the sand. 'Well, we got nothing else,' she said. 'It won't hurt to check him out.'

It didn't seem like a really good idea to tell her that I already had checked him out quite thoroughly, far beyond the boundaries of normal police routine, so I just nodded in agreement.

CHAPTER 34

There was not a great deal more worth seeing on the little island. Vince and the other forensic nerds would spot anything else worth the trouble, and our presence would only hamper them. Deborah was impatient and wanted to rush back to the mainland to intimidate suspects. So we walked to the beach and boarded the police launch for the short trip back across the harbor to the dock. I felt a little better when I climbed onto the dock and walked back to the parking lot.

I didn't see Cody and Astor, so I went over to Officer Low Forehead. 'The kids are in the car,' he told me before I could speak. 'They wanted to play cops and robbers with me, and I didn't sign up for day care.'

Apparently he was convinced that his line about day care was so sidesplittingly funny that it was worth repeating, so rather than risk having him say it again, I simply nodded, thanked him, and went over to Deborah's car. Cody and Astor were not visible until I was practically on top of the car, and for a moment I wondered which car they were in. But then I saw them, crouching down in the backseat, looking at me with very wide eyes. I tried to open the door, but it was locked. 'Can I come in?' I called through the glass.

Cody fumbled with the lock, and then swung the door open.

'What's up?' I asked them.

'We saw the scary guy,' Astor said.

At first I had no idea what she meant by that, and so I really couldn't say why I felt the sweat start rolling down my back. 'What do you mean, the scary guy?' I said. 'You mean that policeman over there?'

'Dex-terrr,' Astor said. 'Not dumb, *scary*. Like when we saw the heads.'

'The *same* scary guy?'

They exchanged another look, and Cody shrugged. 'Kind of,' Astor said.

'He saw my shadow,' Cody said in his soft, husky voice.

It was good to hear the boy open up like this, and even better, now I knew why the sweat was running down my back. He had said something about his shadow before, and I had ignored it. Now it was time to listen. I climbed into the backseat with them.

'How do you know he saw your shadow, Cody?'

'He *said* so,' Astor said. 'And Cody could see *his*.'

Cody nodded, without taking his eyes off my face, looking at me with his usual guarded expression that showed nothing. And yet I could tell that he trusted me to take care of whatever this was. I wished I could share his optimism.

'When you say your shadow,' I asked him carefully, 'do you mean the one on the ground that the sun makes?'

Cody shook his head.

'You have another shadow besides that,' I said.

Cody looked at me like I had asked him if was wearing pants, but he nodded. 'Inside,' he said. 'Like you used to have.'

I sat back against the seat and pretended to breathe. 'Inside shadow.' It was a perfect description – elegant, economical, and accurate. And to add that I used to have one gave it a poignancy which I found quite moving.

Of course, being moved really serves no useful purpose, and I usually manage to avoid it. In this case, I mentally shook myself and wondered what had happened to the proud towers of Castle Dexter, once so lofty and festooned with silk banners of pure reason. I remembered very well that I used to be smart, and yet here I was ignoring something important, ignoring it for far too long. Because the question was not what was Cody talking about. The real puzzle was why I had failed to understand him before.

Cody had seen another predator and recognized him when the dark thing inside him heard the roar of a fellow monster, just as I had known others when my Passenger was at home. And this other had recognized Cody for what he was in exactly the same way. But why that should frighten Cody and Astor into hiding in the car—

'Did the man say anything to you?' I asked them.

'He gave me this,' Cody said. He held out a buff-colored business card and I took it from him.

On the card was a stylized picture of a bull's head, exactly like the one I had just seen around the neck of Kurt's body out on the island. And underneath it was a perfect copy of Kurt's tattoo: MLK.

The front door of the car opened and Deborah hurled herself behind the wheel. 'Let's go,' she said. 'Get in your seat.' She slammed the key into the ignition and had the car started before I could even inhale to speak.

'Wait a minute,' I said after I managed to find a little air to work with.

'I don't *have* a goddamned minute,' she said. 'Come on.'

'He was here, Debs,' I said.

'For Christ's sake, Dex, *who* was here?'

'I don't know,' I admitted.

'Then how the fuck do you know he was here?'

I leaned forward and handed her the card. 'He left this,' I said.

Deborah took the card, glanced at it, and then dropped it on the seat as if it was made out of cobra venom. 'Shit,' she said. She turned off the car's engine. 'Where did he leave it?'

'With Cody,' I said.

She swiveled her head around and looked at the three of us, one after the other. 'Why would he leave it with a kid?' she asked.

'Because—' Astor said, and I put a hand on her mouth.

'Don't interrupt, Astor,' I said, before she could say anything about seeing shadows.

She took a breath, but then she thought better of it and just sat there, unhappy at being muzzled but going along with it for the time being. We sat there for a moment, the four of us, one big unhappy extended family.

'Why not stick it on the windshield, or send it in the mail?' Deborah said. 'For that matter, why the hell give us the damn thing at all? Why even have it printed, for Christ's sake?'

'He gave it to Cody to intimidate us,' I said. 'He's saying, "See? I can get to you where you're vulnerable."'

'Showing off,' Deborah said.

'Yes,' I said. 'I think so.'

'Well goddamn it, that's the first thing he's done that made any sense at all.' She slapped the heels of her hands on the steering wheel. 'He wants to play catch-me-if-you-can like all the other psychos, then by God I can play that game, too. And I'll catch the son of a bitch.' She looked back at me. 'Put that card in an evidence bag,' she said, 'and try to get a description from the kids.' She opened the car door, vaulted out, and went over to talk to the big cop, Suchinsky.

362

'Well,' I said to Cody and Astor, 'can you remember what this man looked like?'

'Yes,' said Astor. 'Are we really going to play with him like your sister said?'

'She didn't mean "play" like you play kick the can,' I said. 'It's more like he's daring us to try to catch him.'

'Then how is that different from kick the can?' she said.

'Nobody gets killed playing kick the can,' I told her. 'What did this man look like?'

She shrugged. 'He was old.'

'You mean, really old? White hair and wrinkles?'

'No, you know. Old like you,' she said.

'Ah, you mean *old*,' I said, feeling the icy hand of mortality brush its fingers across my forehead and leave feebleness and shaky hands in its wake. It was not a promising start toward getting a real description, but after all, she was ten years old and all grown-ups are equally uninteresting. It was clear the Deborah had made the smart move by choosing to speak to Officer Dim instead. This was hopeless. Still, I had to try.

A sudden inspiration hit me – or at any rate, considering my current lack of brain power, something that would have to stand in for inspiration. It would at least make sense if the scary guy had been Starzak, coming back after me. 'Anything else about him you remember? Did he have an accent when he spoke?'

She shook her head. 'You mean like French or

something? No, he just talked regular. Who's Kurt?'

It would be an exaggeration to say that my little heart went flipflop at her words, but I certainly felt some kind of internal quiver. 'Kurt is the dead guy I just looked at. Why do you want to know?'

'The man said,' Astor said. 'He said someday Cody would be a much better helper than Kurt.'

A sudden, very cold chill rolled through Dexter's interior climate. 'Really,' I said. 'What a nice man.'

'He wasn't nice at all, Dexter, we told you. He was scary.'

'But what did he look like, Astor?' I said without any real hope. 'How can we find him if we don't know what he looks like?'

'You don't have to catch him, Dexter,' she said, with the same mildly irritated tone of voice. 'He said you'll find him when the time is right.'

The world stopped for a moment, just long enough for me to feel drops of ice water shoot out of all my pores as if they were spring-loaded. 'What exactly did he say?' I asked her when things started up again.

'He said to tell you you'll find him when the time is right,' she said. 'I just said.'

'How did he say it?' I said. '"Tell Daddy?" "Tell that man?" What?'

She sighed again. 'Tell *Dexter*,' she said, slowly so I would understand. 'That's you. He said, "Tell Dexter he'll find me when the time is right."'

I suppose I should have been even more scared.

But strangely enough, I wasn't. Instead, I felt better. Now I knew for sure – someone really was stalking me. Whether a god or a mortal, it didn't matter anymore, and he would come get me when the time was right, whatever that meant.

Unless I got him first.

It was a silly thought, straight out of a high-school locker room. I had so far shown absolutely no ability to stay even half a step ahead of whoever this was, let alone find him. I'd done nothing but watch as he stalked me, scared me, chased me, and drove me into a state of dark dithering unlike anything I had ever experienced before.

He knew who, what, and where I was. I didn't even know what he looked like. 'Please, Astor, this is important,' I said. 'Was he real tall? Did he have a beard? Was he Cuban? Black?'

She shrugged. 'Just, you know,' she said, 'a white man. He had glasses. Just a regular man. You know.'

I didn't know, but I was saved from admitting it when Deborah yanked open the driver's door and slid back into the car. 'Jesus Christ,' she said. 'How can a man be that dumb and still tie his own shoes?'

'Does that mean Officer Suchinsky didn't have a lot to say?' I asked her.

'He had plenty to say,' Deborah said. 'But it was all brain-dead bullshit. He thought the guy might have been driving a green car, and that's about it.'

'Blue,' Cody said, and we all looked at him. 'It was blue.'

'Are you sure?' I asked him, and he nodded.

'So do I believe a little kid?' Deborah asked. 'Or a cop with fifteen years on the force and nothing in his head but shit?'

'You shouldn't keep saying those bad words,' Astor said. 'That's five and a half dollars you owe me. And anyway, Cody's right, it was a blue car. I saw it, too, and it was blue.'

I looked at Astor, but I could feel the pressure of Deborah's stare on me and I turned back to her.

'Well?' she said.

'Well,' I said. 'Without the bad words, these are two very sharp kids, and Officer Suchinsky will never be invited to join Mensa.'

'So I'm supposed to believe them,' she said.

'I do.'

Deborah chewed on that for a moment, literally moving her mouth around as if she was grinding some very tough food. 'Okay,' she said at last. 'So now I know he's driving a blue car, just like one out of every three people in Miami. Tell me how that helps me.'

'Wilkins drives a blue car,' I said.

'Wilkins is under surveillance, goddamn it,' she said.

'Call them.'

She looked at me, chewed on her lip, and then picked up her radio and stepped out of the car.

She talked for a moment, and I heard her voice rising. Then she said another of her very bad words, and Astor looked at me and shook her head. And then Deborah slammed herself back into the car.

'Son of a bitch,' she said.

'They lost him?'

'No, he's right there, at his house,' she said. 'He just pulled in and went in the house.'

'Where did he go?'

'They don't know,' she said. 'They lost him on the shift change.'

'What?'

'DeMarco was coming in as Balfour was punching out,' she said. 'He slipped away while they were changing. They swear he wasn't gone more than ten minutes.'

'His house is a five-minute drive from here.'

'I know that,' she said bitterly. 'So what do we do?'

'Keep them watching Wilkins,' I said. 'And in the meantime, you go talk to Starzak.'

'You're coming with me, right?' she said.

'No,' I said, thinking that I certainly didn't want to see Starzak, and that for once I had a perfect excuse in place. 'I have to get the kids home.'

She gave me a sour look. 'And what if it isn't Starzak?' she said.

I shook my head. 'I don't know,' I said.

'Yeah,' she said. 'I don't know either.' She started the engine. 'Get in your seat.'

CHAPTER 35

It was well past five o'clock by the time we got back to headquarters and so, in spite of some very sour looks from Deborah, I loaded Cody and Astor into my own humble vehicle and headed for home. They remained subdued for most of the ride, apparently still a little bit shaken by their encounter with the scary guy. But they were resilient children, which was amply demonstrated by the fact that they could still talk at all, considering what their biological father had done to them. So when we were only about ten minutes from the house Astor began to return to normal.

'I wish you would drive like Sergeant Debbie,' she said.

'I would rather live a little longer,' I told her.

'Why don't you have a siren?' she demanded. 'Didn't you want one?'

'You don't get a siren in forensics,' I said. 'And no, I never wanted one. I would rather keep a low profile.'

In the rearview mirror I could see her frown. 'What does that mean?' she asked.

'It means I don't want to draw attention to myself,'

I said. 'I don't want people to notice me. That's something you two have to learn about,' I added.

'Everybody else wants to be noticed,' she said. 'It's like all they ever do, is do stuff so everybody will look at them.'

'You two are different,' I said. 'You will always be different, and you will never be like everybody else.' She didn't say anything for a long time and I glanced at her in the mirror. She was looking at her feet. 'That's not necessarily a bad thing,' I said. 'What's another word for normal?'

'I don't know,' she said dully.

'Ordinary,' I said. 'Do you really want to be ordinary?'

'No,' she said, and she didn't sound quite so unhappy. 'But then if we're not ordinary, people will notice us.'

'That's why you have to learn to keep a low profile,' I said, secretly pleased at the way the conversation had worked around to prove my point. 'You have to pretend to be *really* normal.'

'So we shouldn't ever let anybody know we're different,' she said. 'Not anybody.'

'That's right,' I said.

She looked at her brother, and they had another of those long silent conversations. I enjoyed the quiet, just driving through the evening congestion and feeling sorry for myself.

After a few minutes Astor spoke up again. 'That means we shouldn't tell Mom what we did today,' she said.

'You can tell her about the microscope,' I said.

'But not the other stuff?' Astor said. 'The scary guy and riding with Sergeant Debbie?'

'That's right,' I said.

'But we're never supposed to tell a lie,' she said. 'Especially to our own mother.'

'That's why you don't tell her anything,' I said. 'She doesn't need to know things that will make her worry too much.'

'But she loves us,' Astor said. 'She wants us to be happy.'

'Yes,' I said. 'But she has to think you are happy in a way she can understand. Otherwise *she* can't be happy.'

There was another long silence before Astor finally said, just before we turned onto their street, 'Does the scary guy have a mother?'

'Almost certainly,' I said.

Rita must have been waiting right inside the front door, because as we pulled up and parked the door swung open and she came out to meet us. 'Well, hello,' she said cheerfully. 'And what did you two learn today?'

'We saw dirt,' Cody said. 'From my shoe.'

Rita blinked. 'Really,' she said.

'And there was a piece of popcorn, too,' Astor said. 'And we looked in the microphone and we could tell where we had been.'

'Micro*scope*,' Cody said.

'Whatever,' Astor shrugged. 'But you could tell whose hair it was, too. And if it was a goat or a rug.'

'Wow,' Rita said, looking somewhat over-whelmed and uncertain, 'I guess you had quite a time then.'

'Yes,' Cody said.

'Well then,' Rita said. 'Why don't you two get started on homework, and I'll get you a snack.'

'Okay,' Astor said, and she and Cody scurried up the walk and into the house. Rita watched them until they went inside, and then she turned to me and held onto my elbow as we strolled after them.

'So it went well?' she asked me. 'I mean, with the – they seemed very, um . . .'

'They are,' I said. 'I think they're beginning to understand that there are consequences for fooling around like that.'

'You didn't show them anything too grim, did you?' she said.

'Not at all. Not even any blood.'

'Good,' she said, and she leaned her head on my shoulder, which I suppose is part of the price you have to pay when you are going to marry someone. Perhaps it was simply a public way to mark her territory, in which case I guess I should be very happy that she chose not to do so with the traditional animal method. Anyway, displaying affection through physical contact is not some-thing I really understand, and I felt a bit awkward, but I put an arm around her, since I knew that was the correct human response, and we followed the kids into the house.

★   ★   ★

I'm quite sure it isn't right to call it a dream. But in the night the sound came into my poor battered head once again, the music and chanting and the clash of metal I had heard before, and there was the feeling of heat on my face and a swell of savage joy rising from the special place inside that had been empty for so long now. I woke up standing by the front door with my hand on the doorknob, covered with sweat, content, fulfilled, and not at all uneasy as I should have been.

I knew the term 'sleepwalking,' of course. But I also knew from my freshman psychology class that the reasons someone sleepwalks are usually not related to hearing music. And I also knew in the deepest level of my being that I should be anxious, worried, crawling with distress at the things that had been happening in my unconscious brain. They did not belong there, it was not possible that they could be there – and yet, there they were. And I was glad to have them. That was the most frightening thing of all.

The music was not welcome in the Dexter Auditorium. I did not want it. I wanted it to go away. But it came, and it played, and it made me supernaturally happy against my will and then dumped me by the front door, apparently trying to get me outside and—

And what? It was a jolt of monster-under-the-bed thought straight from the lizard brain, but . . .

Was it a random impulse, uncharted movement by my unconscious mind, that got me out of bed and down the hall to the door? Or was something trying to get me to open the door and go outside? He had told the kids I would find him when the time was right – was this the right time?

Did someone want Dexter alone and unconscious in the night?

It was a wonderful thought, and I was terribly proud to have it, because it meant that I had clearly suffered brain damage and could no longer be held responsible. Once again I was blazing new trails in the territory of stupid. It was impossible, idiotic, stress-induced hysteria. No one on earth could possibly have so much time to throw away; Dexter was not important enough to anyone but Dexter. And to prove it, I turned on the floodlight over the front porch and opened the door.

Across the street and about fifty feet to the west a car started up and drove away.

I closed the door and double-locked it.

And now it was my turn once more to sit up at the kitchen table, sipping coffee and pondering life's great mystery.

The clock said 3:32 when I sat down, and 6:00 when Rita finally came into the room.

'Dexter,' she said with an expression of soporific surprise on her face.

'In the flesh,' I said, and it was exceedingly difficult for me to maintain my artificially cheerful facade.

She frowned. 'What's wrong?'

'Nothing at all,' I said. 'I just couldn't sleep.'

Rita bent her face down toward the floor and shuffled over to the coffeemaker and poured herself a cup. Then she sat across the table from me and took a sip. 'Dexter,' she said, 'it's perfectly normal to have reservations.'

'Of course,' I said, with absolutely no idea what she meant, 'otherwise you don't get a table.'

She shook her head slightly with a tired smile. 'You know what I mean,' she said, which was not true. 'About the wedding.'

A small bleary light went on in the back of my head, and I very nearly said *Aha*. Of course the wedding. Human females were obsessive on the subject of weddings, even it if wasn't their own. When it was, in fact, their own, the idea of it took over every moment of waking and sleeping thought. Rita was seeing everything that happened through a pair of wedding-colored glasses. If I could not sleep, that was because of bad dreams brought on by our upcoming wedding.

I, on the other hand, was not similarly afflicted. I had a great deal of important stuff to worry about, and the wedding was something that was on automatic pilot. At some point I would show up, it would happen, and that would be that. Clearly this was not a viewpoint I could invite Rita to share, no matter how sensible it seemed to me. No, I had to come up with a plausible reason for my sleeplessness, and in addition I needed to reassure her of my enthusiasm for the wonderful looming event.

I looked around the room for a clue, and finally saw something in the two lunch boxes stacked beside the sink. A great place to start: I reached deep into the dregs of my soggy brain and pulled out the only thing I could find there that was less than half wet. 'What if I'm not good enough for Cody and Astor?' I said. 'How can I be their father when I'm really not? What if I just can't do it?'

'Oh, Dexter,' she said. 'You're a wonderful father. They absolutely love you.'

'But,' I said, struggling for both authenticity and the next line, 'but they're little now. When they get older. When they want to know about their *real* father—'

'They know all they'll ever need to know about that sonofabitch,' Rita snapped. It surprised me: I had never heard her use rough language before. Possibly she never had, either, because she began to blush. 'You are their real father,' she said. 'You are the man they look up to, listen to, and love. You are exactly the father they need.'

I suppose that was at least partly true, since I was the only one who could teach them the Harry Way and other things they needed to know, though I suspected this was not exactly what Rita had in mind. But it didn't seem politic to bring that up, so I simply said, 'I really want to be good at this. I can't fail, even for a minute.'

'Oh, Dex,' she said, 'people fail all the time.' That was very true. I had noticed many times before that failure seemed to be one of the identifying characteristics of the species. 'But we keep trying, and it comes out all right in the end. Really. You're going to be great at this, you'll see.'

'Do you really think so?' I said, only mildly ashamed of the disgraceful way I was hamming it up.

'I *know* so,' she said, with her patented Rita smile. She reached across the table and clutched at my hand. 'I won't let you fail,' she said. 'You're mine now.'

It was a bold claim, flinging the Emancipation Proclamation aside like that and saying she owned me. Still, it seemed to close off an awkward moment comfortably, so I let it slide. 'All right,' I said. 'Let's have breakfast.'

She cocked her head to one side and looked at me for a moment, and I was aware that I must have hit a false note, but she just blinked a few times before she said, 'All right,' and got up and began to cook breakfast.

The other had come to the door in the night, and then slammed it in fear – there was no mistaking that part. He had felt fear. He heard the call and came, and he was afraid. And so the Watcher had no doubt about it.

It was time.

Now.

CHAPTER 36

I was bone weary, confused, and, worst of all, still frightened. Every lighthearted blast of the horn had me leaping against the seat belt and searching for a weapon to defend myself, and every time an innocent car pulled up to within inches of my bumper I found myself glaring into the mirror, waiting for an unusually hostile movement or a burst of the hateful dream music flung at my head.

Something was after me. I still didn't know why or what, beyond a vague connection to an ancient god, but I knew it was after me, and even if it could not catch me right away, it was wearing me down to the point where surrender would seem like a relief.

What a frail thing a human being is – and without the Passenger, that is all I was, a poor imitation of a human being. Weak, soft, slow and stupid, unseeing, unhearing and unaware, helpless, hopeless, and harried. Yes, I was almost ready to lie down and let it run over me, whatever it was. Give in, let the music wash over me and take me away into the joyful fire and the blank bliss of death. There would be no struggle, no negotiation, nothing but an end to all that is Dexter. And after a few more nights like the one just past, that would be fine with me.

Even at work there was no relief. Deborah was lurking in wait, and pounced after I had barely stepped out of the elevator.

'Starzak is missing,' she said. 'Couple of days of mail in the box, newspapers in the drive— He's gone.'

'But that's good news, Debs,' I said. 'If he ran, doesn't that prove he's guilty?'

'It doesn't prove shit,' she said. 'The same thing happened to Kurt Wagner, and he showed up dead. How do I know that won't happen to Starzak?'

'We can put out a BOLO,' I said. 'We might get to him first.'

Deborah kicked the wall. 'Goddamn it, we haven't gotten to anything first, or even on time. Help me out here, Dex,' she said. 'This thing is driving me nuts.'

I could have said that it was doing far more than that to me, but it didn't seem charitable. 'I'll try,' I said instead, and Deborah slouched away down the hall.

I was not even into my cubicle when Vince Masuoka met me with a massive fake frown 'Where are the doughnuts?' he said accusingly.

'What doughnuts?' I said.

'It was your turn,' he said. 'You were supposed to bring doughnuts today.'

'I had a rough night,' I said.

'So now we're all going to have a rough morning?' he demanded. 'Where's the justice in that?'

'I don't do justice, Vince,' I said. 'Just blood spatter.'

'Hmmph,' he said. 'Apparently you don't do doughnuts, either.' And he stalked away with a nearly convincing imitation of righteous indignation, leaving me to reflect that I could not remember another occasion when Vince had gotten the best of me in any kind of verbal interchange. One more sign that the train had left the station. Could this really be the end of the line for poor Decaying Dexter?

The rest of the workday was long and awful, as we have always heard that workdays are supposed to be. This had never been the case for Dexter; I have always kept busy and artificially cheerful in my job, and never watched the clock or complained. Perhaps I had enjoyed work because I was conscious of the fact that it was part of the game, a piece of the Great Joke of Dexter putting one over and passing for human. But a really good joke needs at least one other in on it, and since I was alone now, bereft of my inner audience, the punch line seemed to elude me.

I plodded manfully through the morning, visited a corpse downtown, and then came back for a pointless round of lab work. I finished out the day by ordering some supplies and finishing a report. As I was tidying up my desk to go home, my telephone rang.

'I need your help,' my sister said brusquely.

379

'Of course you do,' I said. 'Very good of you to admit it.'

'I'm on duty until midnight,' she said, ignoring my witty and piquant sally, 'and Kyle can't get the shutters up by himself.'

So often in this life I find myself halfway through a conversation and realizing I don't know what I'm talking about. Very unsettling, although if everybody else would realize the same thing, particularly those in Washington, it would be a much better world.

'Why does Kyle need to get the shutters up at all?' I asked.

Deborah snorted. 'Jesus Christ, Dexter, what do you do all day? We've got a hurricane coming in.'

I might well have said that whatever else I do all day, I don't have the leisure to sit around and listen to the Weather Channel. Instead, I just said, 'A hurricane, really. How exciting. When did this happen?'

'Try to get there around six. Kyle will be waiting,' she said.

'All right,' I said. But she had already hung up.

Since I speak fluent Deborah, I suppose I should have accepted her telephone call as a kind of formal apology for her recent pointless hostility. Quite possibly she had come to accept the Dark Passenger, especially since it was gone. This should have made me happy. But considering the day I had been having, it was just one more splinter under the fingernail for poor Downtrodden Dexter. On top of that, it seemed like sheer effrontery for a

380

hurricane to pick this moment for its pointless harassment. Was there no end to the pain and suffering I would be forced to endure?

Ah well, to exist is to wallow in misery. I headed out the door for my date with Deborah's paramour.

Before I started my car, however, I placed a call to Rita, who would be very nearly home now by my calculations.

'Dexter,' she answered breathlessly, 'I can't remember how much bottled water we have and the lines at Publix are all the way out into the parking lot.'

'Well then we'll just have to drink beer,' I said.

'I think we're okay on the canned food, except that beef stew has been there for two years,' she said, apparently unaware that anyone else might have said something. So I let her rattle on, hoping she would slow down eventually. 'I checked the flashlights two weeks ago,' she said. 'Remember, when the power went out for forty minutes? And the extra batteries are in the refrigerator, on the bottom shelf at the back. I have Cody and Astor with me now, there's no after-school program tomorrow, but somebody at school told them about Hurricane Andrew and I think Astor is a little frightened, so maybe when you get home you could talk to them? And explain that it's like a big thunderstorm and we'll be all right, there's just going to be a lot of wind and noise and the lights will go out for a little while. But if you see a store on the way home that isn't too crowded be sure to stop and get some bottled water, as much as you can get. And some ice, I think the cooler is still on the shelf above the washing machine, we can fill it with ice and put in the perishables. Oh – what about your boat? Will it be all right where it is, or do you need to do something with it? I think we can get the things out of the yard before dark, I'm sure we'll be fine, and it probably won't hit here anyway.'

'All right,' I said. 'I'll be a little late getting home.'

'All right. Oh – look at that, the Winn-Dixie store doesn't look too bad. I guess we'll try to get in, there's a parking spot. Bye!'

I would never have thought it possible, but Rita had apparently learned to get by without breathing. Or perhaps she only had to come up for air every hour or so, like a whale. Still, it was an inspiring performance, and after witnessing it, I felt far better prepared to put up shutters with my sister's one-handed boyfriend. I started the car and slid out into traffic.

If rush-hour traffic is utter mayhem, then rush-hour traffic with a hurricane coming is end-of-the-world, we're-all-going-to-die-but-you-go-first insanity. People were driving as if they positively had to kill everyone else who might come between them and getting their plywood and batteries. It was not a terribly long drive to Deborah's little house in Coral Gables, but when I finally pulled into her driveway I felt as if I had survived an Apache manhood ordeal.

As I climbed out of the car, the front door of the house swung open and Chutsky came out. 'Hey, buddy,' he called. He gave me a cheerful wave with the steel hook where his left hand used to be and came down the walkway to meet me. 'I really appreciate the help. This goddamned hook makes it kind of tough to put the wing nuts on.'

'And even harder to pick your nose,' I said, just a little irritated by his cheerful suffering.

But instead of taking offense, he laughed. 'Yeah. And a whole lot harder to wipe my ass. Come on. I got all the stuff out in back.'

I followed him around to the back of the house, where Deborah had a small overgrown patio. But to my great surprise, it was no longer overgrown. The trees that had hung over the area were trimmed back, and the weeds growing up between the flagstones were all gone. There were three neatly pruned rosebushes and a bank of ornamental flowers of some kind, and a neatly polished barbecue grill stood in one corner.

I looked at Chutsky and raised an eyebrow.

'Yeah, I know,' he said. 'It's maybe a little bit gay, right?' He shrugged. 'I get real bored sitting around here healing, and anyway I like to keep things neatened up a little more than your sister.'

'It looks very nice,' I said.

'Uh-huh,' he said, as if I really had accused him of being gay. 'Well, let's get this done.' He nodded toward a stack of corrugated steel leaning against the side of the house – Deborah's hurricane shutters. The Morgans were second-generation Floridians, and Harry had raised us to use good shutters. Save a little money on the shutters, spend a lot more replacing the house when they failed.

The downside to the high quality of Deborah's shutters, though, was that they were very heavy and had sharp edges. Thick gloves were necessary – or in Chutsky's case, one glove. I'm not sure he appreciated the cash he was saving on gloves, though. He seemed to work a little harder than he had to, in order to let me know that he was not really handicapped and didn't actually need my help.

At any rate, it was only about forty minutes before we had all the shutters in their tracks and locked on. Chutsky took a last look at the ones that covered the French doors of the patio and, apparently satisfied with our outstanding craftsmanship, he raised his left arm to wipe the sweat from his brow, catching himself at the very last moment before he rammed the hook through his cheek. He laughed a little bitterly, staring at the hook.

'I'm still not used to this thing,' he said, shaking his head. 'I wake up in the night and the missing knuckle itches.'

It was difficult to think of anything clever or even socially acceptable to say to that. I had never read anywhere what to say to someone speaking of having feeling in his amputated hand. Chutsky seemed to feel the awkwardness, because he gave me a small dry snort of non-humorous amusement.

'Hey, well,' he said, 'there's still a couple of kicks left in the old mule.' It seemed to me an unfortunate choice of words, since he was also missing his left foot, and any kicking at all seemed out of the question. Still, I was pleased to see him coming out of his depression, so it seemed like a good thing to agree with him.

'No one ever doubted it,' I said. 'I'm sure you're going to be fine.'

'Uh-huh, thanks,' he said, not very convincingly. 'Anyway, it's not you I have to convince. It's a couple of old desk jockeys inside the Beltway. They've offered me a desk job, but . . .' He shrugged.

'Come on now,' I said. 'You can't really want to go back to the cloak-and-dagger work, can you?'

'It's what I'm good at,' he said. 'For a while there, I was the very best.'

'Maybe you just miss the adrenaline,' I said.

'Maybe,' he said. 'How about a beer?'

'Thank you,' I said, 'but I have orders from on high to get bottled water and ice before it's all gone.'

'Right,' he said. 'Everybody's terrified they might have to drink a mojito without ice.'

'It's one of the great dangers of a hurricane,' I said.

'Thanks for the help,' he said.

★   ★   ★

If anything, traffic was even worse as I headed for home. Some of the people were hurrying away with their precious sheets of playwood tied to their car roofs as if they had just robbed a bank. They were angry from the tension of standing in line for an hour wondering if someone would cut in front of them and whether there would be anything left when it was their turn.

The rest of the people on the road were on their way to take their places in these same lines and hated everyone who had gotten there first and maybe bought the last C battery in Florida.

Altogether, it was a delightful mixture of hostility, rage, and paranoia, and it should have cheered me up immensely. But any hope of good cheer vanished when I found myself humming something, a familiar tune that I couldn't quite place, and couldn't stop humming. And when I finally did place it, all the joy of the festive evening was shattered.

It was the music from my sleep.

The music that had played in my head with the feeling of heat and the smell of something burning. It was plain and repetitive and not a terribly catchy bit of music, but here I was humming it to myself on South Dixie Highway, humming and feeling comfort from the repeating notes as if it was a lullaby my mother used to sing.

And I still didn't know what it meant.

I am sure that whatever was happening in my subconscious was caused by something simple, logical, and easy to understand. On the other hand, I just couldn't think of a simple, logical, and easy-to-understand reason for hearing music and feeling heat on my face in my sleep.

My cell phone started to buzz, and since traffic was crawling along anyway, I answered it.

'Dexter,' Rita said, but I barely recognized her voice. She sounded small, lost, and completely defeated. 'It's Cody and Astor,' she said. 'They're gone.'

Things were really working out quite well. The new hosts were wonderfully cooperative. They began to gather, and with a little bit of persuasion, they easily came to follow IT's suggestions about behavior. And they built great stone buildings to hold IT's offspring, dreamed up elaborate ceremonies with music to put them in a trance state, and they became so enthusiastically helpful that for a while there were just too many of them to keep up with. If things went well for the hosts, they killed a few of their number out of gratitude. If things went badly, they killed in the hope that IT would make things better. And all IT had to do was let it happen.

And with this new leisure, IT began to consider the result of IT's reproductions. For the first time, when the swelling and bursting came, IT reached out to the newborn, calming it down, easing its fear, and sharing consciousness. And the newborn responded with gratifying eagerness, quickly and happily learning all that IT had to teach and gladly joining in. And then there were four of them, then

387

eight, sixty-four – and suddenly it was too much. With that many, there was simply not enough to go around. Even the new hosts began to balk at the number of victims they needed.

IT was practical, if nothing else. IT quickly realized the problem, and solved it – by killing almost all of the others IT had spawned. A few escaped, out into the world, in search of new hosts. IT kept just a few with IT, and things were under control at last.

Sometime later, the ones who fled began to strike back. They set up their rival temples and rituals and sent their armies at IT, and there were so many. The upheaval was enormous and lasted a very long time. But because IT was the oldest and most experienced, IT eventually vanquished all the others, except for a few who went into hiding.

The others hid in scattered hosts, keeping a low profile, and many survived. But IT had learned over the millennia that it was important to wait. IT had all the time there was, and IT could afford to be patient, slowly hunt out and kill the ones who fled, and then slowly, carefully, build back up the grand and wonderful worship of ITself.

IT kept IT's worship alive; hidden, but alive.

And IT waited for the others.

CHAPTER 37

As I know very well, the world is not a nice place. There are numberless awful things that can happen, especially to children: they can be taken by a stranger or a family friend or a divorced dad; they can wander away and vanish, fall in a sinkhole, drown in a neighbor's pool – and with a hurricane coming there were even more possibilities. The list is limited only by their imaginations, and Cody and Astor were quite well supplied with imagination.

But when Rita told me they were gone, I did not even consider sinkholes or traffic accidents or motorcycle gangs. I knew what had happened to Cody and Astor, knew it with a cold, hard certainty that was more clear and positive than anything the Passenger had ever whispered to me. One thought burst in my head, and I never questioned it.

In the half a second it took to register Rita's words my brain flooded with small pictures: the cars following me, the night visitors knocking on the doors and windows, the scary guy leaving his calling card with the kids, and, most convincingly, the searing statement uttered by Professor

Keller: 'Moloch liked human sacrifice. Especially children.'

I did not know why Moloch wanted my children in particular, but I knew without the slightest doubt that he, she, or it had them. And I knew that this was not a good thing for Cody and Astor.

I lost no time getting home, swerving through the traffic like the Miami native I am, and in just a few minutes I was out of the car. Rita stood in the rain at the end of the driveway, looking like a small, desolate mouse.

'Dexter,' Rita said, with a world of emptiness in her voice. 'Please, oh God, Dexter, find them.'

'Lock the house,' I said, 'and come with me.'

She looked at me for a moment as if I had said to leave the kids and go bowling. 'Now,' I said. 'I know where they are, but we need help.'

Rita turned and ran to the house and I pulled out my cell phone and dialed.

'What,' Deborah answered.

'I need your help,' I said.

There was a short silence and then a hard bark of not-amused laughter. 'Jesus Christ,' she said. 'There's a hurricane coming in, the bad guys are lined up five deep all over town waiting for the power to go out, and you need my help.'

'Cody and Astor are gone,' I said. 'Moloch has them.'

'Dexter,' she said.

'I have to find them fast, and I need your help.'

'Get over here,' she said.

As I put my phone away Rita came splattering down the sidewalk through the puddles that were already forming. 'I locked up,' she said. 'But Dexter, what if they come back and we're gone?'

'They won't come back,' I said. 'Not unless we bring them back.' Apparently that was not the reassuring remark she was hoping for. She stuffed a fist into her mouth and looked like she was trying very hard not to scream. 'Get in the car, Rita,' I said. I opened the door for her and she looked at me over her half-digested knuckles. 'Come on,' I said, and she finally climbed in. I got behind the wheel, started up, and nosed the car out of the driveway.

'You said,' Rita stammered, and I was relieved to notice that she had removed the fist from her mouth, 'you said you know where they are.'

'That's right,' I said, turning onto U.S. 1 without looking and accelerating through the thinning traffic.

'Where are they?' she asked.

'I know who has them,' I said. 'Deborah will help us find out where they went.'

'Oh God, Dexter,' Rita said, and she began to weep silently. Even if I wasn't driving I wouldn't know what to do or say about that, so I simply concentrated on getting us to headquarters alive.

A telephone rang in a very comfortable room. It did not give out an undignified chirping, or a salsa tune, or even a fragment of Beethoven, as modern cell phones do. Instead, it purred with a simple old-fashioned sound, the way telephones are supposed to ring.

And this conservative sound went well with the room, which was elegant in a very reassuring way. It contained a leather couch and two matching chairs, all worn just enough to give the feeling of a favourite pair of shoes. The telephone sat on a dark mahogany end table on the far side of the room, next to a bar made of matching wood.

Altogether the room had the relaxed and timeless feel of a very old and well-established gentlemen's club, except for one detail: the wall space between the bar and the couch was taken up by a large wooden case with a glass front, looking something like a cross between a trophy case and a shelf for rare books. But instead of flat shelves, the case was fitted with hundreds of felt-lined niches. Just over half of them cradled a skull-sized ceramic of a bull's head.

An old man entered the room, without haste, but also without the careful hesitance of frail old age. There was a confidence in his walk that is usually found only in much younger men. His hair was white and full and his face was smooth, as if it had been polished by the desert wind. He walked to the telephone like he was quite sure that whoever was calling would not hang up until he answered, and apparently he was right, since it was still ringing when he lifted the receiver.

'Yes,' he said, and his voice, too, was much

younger and stronger than it should have been. As he listened he picked up a knife that lay on the table beside the telephone. It was of ancient bronze. The pommel was curved into a bull's head, the eyes set with two large rubies, and the blade was traced with gold letters that looked very much like *MLK*. Like the old man, the knife was much older than it looked, and far stronger. He idly ran a thumb along the blade as he listened, and a line of blood rose up on his thumb. It didn't seem to affect him. He put the knife down.

'Good,' he said. 'Bring them here.' He listened again for a moment, idly licking the blood from his thumb. 'No,' he said, running his tongue along his lower lip. 'The others are already gathering. The storm won't affect Moloch, or his people. In three thousand years, we've seen far worse, and we're still here.'

He listened again for a moment before interrupting with just a trace of impatience. 'No,' he said. 'No delays. Have the Watcher bring him to me. It's time.'

The old man hung up the telephone and stood for a moment. Then he picked up the knife again, and an expression grew on his smooth old face.

It was almost a smile.

The wind and the rain were gusting fiercely but only occasionally, and most of Miami was already off the roads and filling out insurance claim forms for the damage they planned to have, so the traffic was not bad. One very intense blast of wind nearly pushed us off the expressway, but other than that it was a quick trip.

Deborah was waiting for us at the front desk. 'Come to my office,' she said, 'and tell me what you know.' We followed her to the elevator and went up.

'Office' was a bit of an exaggeration for the place where Deborah worked. It was a cubicle in a room with several others just like it. Crammed into the space was a desk and chair and two folding chairs for guests, and we settled in. 'All right,' she said. 'What happened?'

'They . . . I sent them out into the yard,' Rita said. 'To get all their toys and things. For the hurricane.'

Deborah nodded. 'And then?' she prompted.

'I went in to put away the hurricane supplies,' she said. 'And when I came out they were gone. I didn't – it was only a couple of minutes, and they . . .' Rita put her face in her hands and sobbed.

'Did you see anyone approach them?' Deborah asked. 'Any strange cars in the neighborhood? Anything at all?'

Rita shook her head. 'No, nothing, they were just gone.'

Deborah looked at me. 'What the hell, Dexter,' she said. 'That's it? The whole story? How do you know they're not playing Nintendo next door?'

'Come on, Deborah,' I said. 'If you're too tired to work, tell us now. Otherwise, stop the crap. You know as well as I do—'

'I don't know anything like it, and neither do you,' she snapped.

'Then you haven't been paying attention,' I said, and I found that my tone was sharpening to match hers, which was a bit of a surprise. Emotion? Me? 'That business card he left with Cody tells us everything we need to know.'

'Except where, why, and who,' she snarled. 'And I'm still waiting to hear some hints about that.'

Even though I was perfectly prepared to snarl right back at her, there was really nothing to snarl. She was right. Just because Cody and Astor were missing, that didn't mean we suddenly had new information that would lead us to our killer. It only meant that the stakes were considerably higher, and that we were out of time.

'What about Wilkins?' I demanded.

She waved a hand. 'They're watching him,' she said.

'Like last time?'

'Please,' Rita interrupted, with a rough edge of hysteria creeping into her voice, 'what are you talking about? Isn't there some way to just – I mean, anything . . . ?' Her voice trailed off into a new round of sobs, and Deborah looked from her to me. 'Please,' Rita wailed.

As her voice rose it echoed into me and seemed to drop one final piece of pain into the empty dizziness inside me that blended in with the faraway music.

I stood up.

I felt myself sway slightly and heard Deborah say my name, and then the music was there, soft but insistent, as if it had always been there, just waiting for a moment when I could hear it without distraction, and as I turned my focus on the thrum of the drums it called me, called as I knew it had been calling all along, but more urgently now, rising closer to the ultimate ecstasy and telling me to come, follow, go this way, come to the music.

And I remember being very glad about that, that the time was here at last, and even though I could hear Deborah and Rita speaking to me it didn't seem that anything they had to say could be terribly important, not when the music was calling and the promise of perfect happiness was here at last. So I smiled at them and I think I even said, 'Excuse me,' and I walked out of the room, not caring about their puzzled faces. I went out of the building, and to the far side of the parking lot where the music was coming from.

A car was waiting for me there, which made me even happier, and I hurried over to it, moving my feet to the beautiful flow of the music, and when I got there the back door of the car swung open and then I don't remember anything at all.

CHAPTER 38

I had never been so happy.

The joy came at me like a comet, blazing huge and ponderous through a dark sky and whirling toward me at inconceivable speed, swirling in to consume me and carry me away into a boundless universe of rapture and all-knowing unity, love, and understanding – bliss without end, in me and of me and all around me forever.

And it whirled me across the trackless night sky in a warm, blinding blanket of jubilant love and rocked me in a cradle of endless joy, joy, joy. As I spun higher and faster and even more replete with every possible happiness, a great slamming sound rolled across me and I opened my eyes in a small dark room with no windows and a very hard concrete floor and walls and no idea of where it was or how I got there. A single small light burned above the door, and I was lying on the floor in the dim glow it cast.

The happiness was gone, all of it, and nothing welled up to replace it other than a sense that wherever I might be, nobody had in mind restoring either my joy or my freedom. And although there were no bulls' heads anywhere in the room, ceramic or otherwise, and there were no old Aramaic magazines stacked on the floor, it was not hard to add it all up. I had followed the music, felt ecstasy, and lost conscious control. And that meant that the odds were very good that Moloch had me, whether he was real or mythical.

Still, better not to take things for granted. Perhaps I had sleepwalked my way into a storage room somewhere, and getting out was simply a matter of turning the knob on the door. I got to my feet with a little difficulty – I felt groggy and a bit wobbly, and I guessed that whatever had brought me here, some kind of drug had been part of the process. I stood for a moment and concentrated on getting the room to hold still, and after a few deep breaths I succeeded. I took one step to the side and touched a wall: very solid concrete blocks. The door felt almost as thick and was solidly locked; it didn't even rattle when I punched my shoulder against it. I walked one time around the small room – really, it was no more than a large closet. There was a drain in the center of the room, and that was the only feature or furnishing that I could see. This did not seem particularly encouraging, since it meant that either I was supposed to use the drain for personal tasks or else I was not expected to be here long enough to need a toilet. If that was the case, I had trouble believing that an early exit would be a good thing for me.

Not that there was anything I could do about it, whatever plans were being made for me. I had read *The Count of Monte Cristo* and *The Prisoner of Zenda,* and I knew that if I could get hold of something like a spoon or a belt buckle it would be easy enough to dig my way out in the next fifteen years or so. But they had thoughtlessly failed to provide me with a spoon, whoever they were, and my belt buckle had apparently been appropriated, too. This told me a great deal about them, at least. They were very careful, which probably meant experienced, and they lacked even the most basic sense of modesty, since they were clearly not concerned in the least that my pants might fall down without a belt. However, I still had no idea who they might be or what they might want with me.

None of this was good news.

And none of it offered any clue at all as to what I could do about it, except sit on the cold concrete floor and wait.

So I did.

Reflection is supposed to be good for the soul. Throughout history, people have tried to find peace and quiet, time all to themselves with no distractions, just so they can reflect. And here I was with exactly that – peace and quiet with no distractions, but I nevertheless found it very difficult to lean back in my comfy cement room and let the reflections come and do good for my soul.

To begin with, I wasn't sure I had a soul. If

I did, what was it thinking to allow me to do such terrible things for so many years? Did the Dark Passenger take the place of the hypothetical soul that humans were supposed to have? And now that I was without it, would a real one grow and make me human after all?

I realized that I was reflecting anyway, but somehow that failed to create any real sense of fulfillment. I could reflect until my teeth fell out and it was not going to explain where my Passenger had gone – or where Cody and Astor were. It was also not going to get me out of this little room.

I got up again and circled the room, slower this time, looking for any small weakness. There was an air-conditioning vent in one corner – a perfect way to escape, if only I had been the size of a ferret. There was an electric outlet on the wall beside the door. That was it.

I paused at the door and felt it. It was very heavy and thick, and offered me not the tiniest bit of hope that I could break it, pick the lock, or otherwise open it without the assistance of either explosives or a road grader. I looked around the room again, but didn't see either one lying in a corner.

Trapped. Locked in, captured, sequestered, in durance vile – even synonyms didn't make me feel any better. I leaned my cheek against the door. What was the point in hoping, really? Hoping for what? Release back into the world where I no longer had any purpose? Wasn't it better for all concerned that Dexter Defeated simply vanish into oblivion?

Through the thickness of the door I heard something, some high-pitched noise approaching outside. And as the sound got closer I recognized it: a man's voice, arguing with another, higher, insistent voice that was very familiar.

Astor.

'Stupid!' she said, as they came even with my door. 'I don't have to . . .' And then they were gone.

'Astor!' I shouted as loud as I could, even though I knew she would never hear me. And just to prove that stupidity is ubiquitous and consistent, I slammed on the door with both hands and yelled it again. 'Astor!'

There was no response at all, of course, except for a faint stinging sensation on the palms of my hands. Since I could not think of anything else to do, I slid down to the floor, leaned against the door, and waited to die.

I don't know how long I sat there with my back against the door. I admit that sitting slumped against the door was not terribly heroic. I know I should have jumped to my feet, pulled out my secret decoder ring, and chewed through the wall with my secret radioactive powers. But I was drained. To hear Astor's defiant small voice on the other side of the door had hammered in what felt like the last nail. There was no more Dark Knight. There was nothing left of me but the envelope, and it was coming unglued.

So I sat, slumped, sagged against the door, and nothing happened. I was in the middle of planning how to hang myself from the light switch on the wall when I felt a kind of scuffling on the other side of the door. Then someone pushed on it.

Of course I was in the way and so naturally enough it hurt, a severe pinch right in the very back end of my human dignity. I was slow to react, and they pushed again. It hurt again. And blossoming up from the pain, shooting out of the emptiness like the first flower of spring, came something truly wonderful.

I got mad.

Not merely irritated, narked by someone's thoughtless use of my backside as a doorstop. I got truly angry, enraged, furious at the lack of any consideration for *me*, the assumption that I was a negligible commodity, a thing to be locked in a room and shoved around by anyone with an arm and a short temper. Never mind that only moments ago I had held the same low opinion of me. That didn't matter at all – I was mad, in the classic sense of being half crazed, and without thinking anything other than that, I shoved back against the door as hard as I could.

There was a little bit of resistance, and then the latch clicked shut. I stood up, thinking, *There!* – without really knowing what that meant. And as I glared at the door it began to open again, and once more I heaved against it, forcing it closed. It was wonderfully fulfilling, and I felt better than

I had in quite some time, but as some of the pure blind anger leached out of me it occurred to me that as relaxing as door thumping was, it was slightly pointless, after all, and sooner or later it would have to end in my defeat, since I had no weapons or tools of any kind, and whoever it was on the other side of the door was theoretically unlimited in what they could bring to the task.

As I thought this, the door banged partially open again, stopping when it hit my foot, and as I banged back automatically I had an idea. It was stupid, pure James Bond escapism, but it just might possibly work, and I had absolutely nothing to lose. With me, to think is to explode into furious action, and so even as I thumped the door shut with my shoulder, I stepped to the side of the doorframe and waited.

Sure enough, only a moment later the door thumped open, this time with no resistance from me, and as it swung wide to slam against the wall an off-balance man in some kind of uniform stumbled in after it. I grabbed at his arm and managed to get a shoulder instead, but it was enough, and with all my strength I pivoted and shoved him headfirst into the wall. There was a gratifying thump, as if I had dropped a large melon off the kitchen table, and he bounced off the wall and fell face-first onto the concrete floor.

And lo, there was Dexter reborn and triumphant, standing proudly on both feet, with the body of his enemy stretched supine at his feet, and an open door leading to freedom, redemption, and then perhaps a light supper.

I searched the guard quickly, removing a ring of keys, a large pocketknife, and an automatic pistol that he would probably not need anytime soon, and then I stepped cautiously into the hall, closing the door behind me. Somewhere out here, Cody and Astor waited, and I would find them. What I would do then I didn't know, but it didn't matter. I would find them.

CHAPTER 39

The building was about the size of a large Miami Beach house. I prowled cautiously through a long hallway that ended at a door similar to the one I had just played bull-in-the-ring with. I tiptoed up and put my ear against it. I didn't hear anything at all, but the door was so thick that this meant almost nothing.

I put my hand on the knob and turned it very slowly. It wasn't locked, and I pushed the door open.

I peeked carefully around the edge of the door and saw nothing that ought to cause alarm other than some furniture that looked like real leather – I made a mental note to report it to PETA. It was quite an elegant room, and as I opened the door farther I saw a very nice mahogany bar in the far corner.

But much more interesting was the trophy case beside the bar. It stretched along the wall for twenty feet, and behind the glass, just visible, I could see row after row of what seemed to be assorted ceramic bulls' heads. Each piece shone under its own mini-spotlight. I did not count, but there had to be more than a hundred of them. And before I could move into the room I heard a voice, as cold and dry as it could be and still be human.

'Trophies,' and I jumped, turning the gun toward the sound. 'A memorial wall dedicated to the god. Each represents a soul we have sent to him.' An old man sat there, simply looking at me, but seeing him was almost a physical blow. 'We create a new one for each sacrifice,' he said. 'Come in, Dexter.'

The old man didn't seem very menacing. In fact, he was nearly invisible, sitting back as he was in one of the large leather chairs. He got up slowly, with an old man's care, and turned a face on me that was as cold and smooth as river rock.

'We have been waiting for you,' he said, although as far as I could tell he was alone in the room, except for the furniture. 'Come in.'

I really don't know if it was what he said, or the way he said it – or something else entirely. In any case, when he looked directly at me I suddenly felt like there was not enough air in the room. All the mad dash of my escape seemed to bleed out of me and puddle around my ankles, and a great clattering emptiness tore through me, as though there was nothing in the world but pointless pain, and he was its master.

'You've caused us a great deal of trouble,' he said quietly.

'That's some consolation,' I said. It was very

hard to say, and sounded feeble even to me, but at least it made the old man look a little bit annoyed. He took a step toward me, and I found myself trying to shrink away. 'By the way,' I said, hoping to appear nonchalant about the fact that I felt like I was melting, 'who are us?'

He cocked his head to one side. 'I think you know,' he said. 'You've certainly been looking at us long enough.' He took another step forward and my knees wobbled slightly. 'But for the sake of a pleasant conversation,' he said, 'we are the followers of Moloch. The heirs of King Solomon. For three thousand years, we have kept the god's worship alive and guarded his traditions, and his power.'

'You keep saying "we,"' I said.

He nodded, and the movement hurt me. 'There are others here,' he said. 'But the we is, as I am sure you are aware, Moloch. He exists inside me.'

'So *you* killed those girls? And followed me around?' I said, and I admit I was surprised to think of this elderly man doing all that.

He actually smiled, but it was humorless and didn't make me feel any better. 'I did not go in person, no. It was the Watchers.'

'So – you mean, it can leave you?'

'Of course,' he said. 'Moloch can move between us as he wishes. He's not one person, and he's not *in* one person. He's a god. He goes out of me and into some of the others for special errands. To watch.'

'Well, it's wonderful to have a hobby,' I said. I wasn't really sure where our conversation was going, or if my precious life was about to skid to a halt, so I asked the first question that sprung to mind. 'Then why did you leave the bodies at the university?'

'We wanted to find you, naturally.' The old man's words froze me to the spot.

'You had come to our attention, Dexter,' he continued, 'but we had to be sure. We needed to observe you to see if you would recognize our ritual or respond to our Watcher. And, of course, it was convenient to lead the police to concentrate on Halpern,' he said.

I didn't know where to begin. 'He's not one of you?' I said.

'Oh, no,' the old man said pleasantly. 'As soon as he's released from police custody he'll be over there, with the others.' He nodded toward the trophy case, filled with ceramic bulls' heads.

'Then he really didn't kill the girls.'

'Yes, he did,' he said. 'While he was being persuaded from the inside by one of the Children of Moloch.' He cocked his head to one side. 'I'm sure you of all people can understand that, can't you?'

I could, of course. But it didn't answer any of the main questions. 'Can we please go back to where you said I had "come to your attention"?' I asked politely, thinking of all the hard work I put into keeping a low profile.

The man looked at me as though I had an excep-
tionally thick head. 'You killed Alexander
Macauley,' he said.

Now the tumblers fell into the weakened steel
lock that was Dexter's brain. 'Zander was one of
you?'

He shook his head slightly. 'A minor helper. He
supplied material for our rites.'

'He brought you the winos, and you killed them,'
I said.

He shrugged. 'We practice sacrifice, Dexter, not
killing. In any case, when you took Zander, we
followed you and discovered what you are.'

'What am I?' I blurted, finding it slightly exhil-
arating to think that I stood face-to-face with
someone who could answer the question I had
pondered for most of my slash-happy life. But
then my mouth went dry, and as I awaited his
answer a sensation bloomed inside me that felt an
awful lot like real fear.

The old man's glare turned sharp. 'You're an aberration,' he said. 'Something that shouldn't exist.'

I will admit that there have been times when I
would agree with that thought, but right now was
not one of them. 'I don't want to seem rude,' I
said, 'but I like existing.'

'That is no longer your choice,' he said. 'You
have something inside you that represents a threat
to us. We plan to get rid of it, and you.'

'Actually,' I said, sure he was talking about my
Dark Passenger, 'that thing is not there anymore.'

409

'I know that,' he said, a little irritably, 'but it originally came to you because of great traumatic suffering. It is attuned to you. But it is also a bastard child of Moloch, and that attunes *you* to *us*.' He waved a finger at me. 'That's how you were able to hear the music. Through the connection made by your Watcher. And when we cause you sufficient agony in a very short time, it will come back to you, like a moth to a flame.'

I really didn't like the sound of that, and I could see that our conversation was sliding rapidly out of my control, but just in time I remembered that I did, after all, have a gun. I pointed it at the old man and drew myself up to my full quivering height.

'I want my children,' I said.

He didn't seem terribly concerned about the pistol aimed at his navel, which to me seemed like pushing the envelope of self-confidence. He even had a large wicked-looking knife on one hip, but he made no move to touch it.

'The children are no longer your concern,' he said. 'They belong to Moloch now. Moloch likes the taste of children.'

'Where are they?' I said.

He waved his hand dismissively. 'They're right here on Toro Key, but you're too late to stop the ritual.'

Toro Key was far from the mainland and completely private. But in spite of the fact that it's generally a great pleasure to learn where you are, this time it raised a number of very sticky questions – like, where were Cody and Astor, and how would I prevent life as I knew it from ending momentarily?

'If you don't mind,' I said, and I wiggled the pistol, just so he would get the point, 'I think I'll collect them and go home.'

He didn't move. He just looked at me, and from his eyes I could very nearly see enormous black wings beating out and into the room, and before I could squeeze the trigger, breathe, or blink, the drums began to swell, insisting on the beat that was embedded in me already, and the horns rose with the rhythm, leading the chorus of voices up and into happiness, and I stopped dead in my tracks.

My vision seemed normal, and my other senses were unimpaired, but I could not hear anything but the music, and I could not do anything except what the music told me to do. And it told me that just outside this room true happiness was waiting. It told me to come and scoop it up, fill my hands and heart with bliss everlasting, joy to the end of all things, and I saw myself turning toward the door, my feet leading me to my happy destiny.

The door swung open as I approached it, and Professor Wilkins came in. He was carrying a gun, too, and he barely glanced at me. Instead, he nodded at the old man and said, 'We're ready.' I could barely hear him through the wild flush of feeling and sound welling up, and I moved eagerly toward the door.

Somewhere deep beneath all this was the tiny shrill voice of Dexter, screaming that things were not as they should be and demanding a change in direction. But it was such a small voice, and the music was so large, bigger than everything else in this endlessly wonderful world, and there was never any real question about what I was going to do.

I stepped toward the door in rhythm to the ubiquitous music, dimly aware that the old man was moving with me, but not really interested in that fact or any other. I still had the gun in my hand – they didn't bother to take it from me, and it didn't occur to me to use it. Nothing mattered but following the music.

The old man stepped around me and opened the door, and the wind blew hot in my face as I stepped out and saw the god, the thing itself, the source of the music, the source of everything, the great and wonderful bull-horned fountain of ecstasy there ahead of me. It towered above everything else, its great bronze head twenty-five feet high, its powerful arms held out to me, a wonderful hot glow burning in its open belly. My heart swelled and I moved toward it, not really seeing the handful of people standing there watching, even though one of those people was Astor. Her eyes got big when she saw me, and her mouth moved, but I could not hear what she said.

And tiny Dexter deep inside me screamed louder, but only just loud enough to be heard, and not even close to loud enough to be obeyed. I walked on toward the god, seeing the glow from the fire inside it, watching the flames in its belly flicker and jump with the wind that whipped around us. And when I was as close as I could get, standing right beside the open furnace of its belly, I stopped and waited. I did not know what I was waiting for, but I knew that it was coming and it would take me away to wonderful forever, so I waited.

Starzak came into view, and he was holding Cody by the hand, dragging him along to stand near us, and Astor was struggling to get away from the guard beside her. It didn't matter, though, because the god was there and its arms were moving down now, outspread and reaching to embrace me and clasp me in its warm, beautiful grip. I quivered with the joy of it, no longer hearing the shrill, pointless voice of protest from Dexter, hearing nothing at all but the voice of the god calling from the music.

The wind whipped the fire into life, and Astor thumped against me, bumping me into the side of the statue and the great heat coming from the god's belly. I straightened up with only a moment of annoyance and once more watched the miracle of the god's arms coming down, the guard moving Astor forward to share the bronze embrace, and then there was the smell of something burning and a blaze of pain along my legs and I looked down to see that my pants were on fire.

413

The pain of the fire on my legs jolted through me with the shriek of a hundred thousand outraged neurons, and the cobwebs were instantly cleared away. Suddenly the music was just noise from a loudspeaker, and this was Cody and Astor here beside me in very great danger. It was as if a hole had opened up in a dam and Dexter came pouring back in through it. I turned to the guard and yanked him away from Astor. He gave me a look of blank surprise and pitched over, grabbing my arm as he fell and pulling me down onto the ground with him. But at least he fell away from Astor, and the ground jarred the knife out of his hand. It bounced along to me and I picked it up and holstered it snugly in the guard's solar plexus.

Then the pain in my legs went up a notch and I quickly concentrated on extinguishing my smoldering pants, rolling and slapping at them until they were no longer burning. And while it was a very good thing not to be on fire anymore, it was also several seconds of time that allowed Starzak and Wilkins to come charging toward me. I grabbed the pistol from the ground and lurched to my feet to face them.

A long time ago, Harry had taught me to shoot. I could almost hear his voice now as I moved into my firing stance, breathed out, and calmly squeezed the trigger. Aim for the center and shoot twice. Starzak goes down. Move your aim to Wilkins, repeat. And then there were bodies on the ground, and a terrible scramble of the

414

remaining onlookers running for safety, and I was standing beside the god, alone in a place that was suddenly very quiet except for the wind. I turned to see why.

The old man had grabbed Astor and was holding her by the neck, with a grip much more powerful than seemed possible with his frail body. He pushed her close to the open furnace. 'Drop the gun,' he said, 'or she burns.'

I saw no reason to doubt that he would do as he said, and I saw no sign of any way to stop him, either. Everyone living had scattered, except for us.

'If I drop the gun,' I said, and I hoped I sounded reasonable, 'how do I know you won't put her in the fire anyway.'

He snarled at me, and it still caused a twinge of agony. 'I'm not a murderer,' he said. 'It has to be done right or it's just killing.'

'I'm not sure I can see a difference,' I said.

'You wouldn't. You're an aberration,' he said.

'How do I know you won't kill us all anyway?' I said.

'You're the one I need to feed to the fire,' he said. 'Drop the gun and you can save this girl.'

'Not terribly convincing,' I said, stalling for time, hoping for that time to bring something.

'I don't need to be,' he said. 'This isn't a stalemate – there are other people on this island, and they'll be back out here soon. You can't shoot them all. And the god is still here. But since you obviously need convincing, how about if I slice your girl a few times and let the blood flow persuade you?' He reached down to his hip, found nothing, and frowned. 'My knife,' he said, and then his expression of puzzlement blossomed into one of great astonishment. He gaped at me without saying a thing, simply holding his mouth wide open as if he was about to sing an aria.

And then he dropped to his knees, frowned, and pitched forward onto his face, revealing a knife blade protruding from his back – and also revealing Cody, standing behind him, smiling slightly as he watched the old man fall, and then looking up at me.

'Told you I was ready,' he said.

CHAPTER 40

The hurricane turned north at the last minute and ended up hitting us with nothing but a lot of rain and a little wind. The worst of the storm passed far to the north of Toro Key, and Cody, Astor, and I spent the remainder of the night locked in the elegant room with the couch in front of one door and a large overstuffed chair in front of the other. I called Deborah on the phone I found in the room, and then made a small bed out of cushions behind the bar, thinking that the thick mahogany would provide additional protection if it was needed.

It wasn't. I sat with my borrowed pistol all night, watching the doors, and watching the kids sleep. And since nobody disturbed us, that was really not enough to keep a full-grown brain alive, so I thought, too.

I thought about what I would say to Cody when he woke up. When he put the knife into the old man he had changed everything. No matter what he thought, he was not ready merely because of what he had done. He had actually made things harder for himself. The road was going to be a long tough one for him, and I didn't know if I was good enough to keep his feet on it. I was not Harry, could never be anything like Harry. Harry had run on love, and I had a completely different operating system.

And what was that now? What was Dexter without Darkness?

How could I hope to live at all, let alone teach the children how to live, with a gaping gray vacuum inside me? The old man had said the Passenger would come back if I was in enough pain. Did I have to physically torture myself to call it home? How could I do that? I had just stood in burning pants watching Astor nearly thrown into a fire, and that hadn't been enough to bring back the Passenger.

I still didn't have any answers when Deborah arrived at dawn with the SWAT team and Chutsky. They found no one left on the island, and no clues as to where they might have gone. The bodies of the old man, Wilkins, and Starzak were tagged and bagged, and we all clambered onto the big Coast Guard helicopter to ride back to the mainland. Cody and Astor were thrilled of course, although they did an excellent job of pretending not to be impressed. And after all the hugs and weeping showered on them by Rita, and the general happy air of a job well done among the rest of them, life went on.

Just that: life went on. Nothing new happened, nothing within me was resolved, and no new direction revealed itself. It was simply a resumption of an aggressively plain ordinary existence that did more to grind me down further than all the physical pain in the world could have done. Perhaps the old man had been right – perhaps I had been an aberration. But I was not even that any longer.

I felt deflated. Not merely empty but *finished* somehow, as if whatever I came into the world to do was done now, and the hollow shell of me was left behind to live on the memories.

I still craved an answer to the personal absence that plagued me, and I had not received it. It now seemed likely that I never would. In my numbness I could never feel a pain deep enough to bring home the Dark Passenger. We were all safe and the bad guys were dead or gone, but somehow that didn't seem to be about *me*. If that sounds selfish, I can only say that I have never pretended to be anything else but completely self-centered – at least not unless someone was watching. Now, of course, I would have to learn to truly *live* the part, and the notion filled me with a distant, weary loathing that I couldn't shake off.

The feeling stayed with me over the next few days, and finally faded into the background just enough that I began to accept it as my new permanent lot. Dexter Downtrodden. I would learn to walk stooped over, and dress all in gray, and children everywhere would play mean little tricks on me because I was so sad and dreary. And finally, at some pathetic old age, I would simply fall over unnoticed and let the wind blow my dust into the street.

Life went on. Days blended into weeks. Vince Masuoka went into a furious frenzy of activity, finding a new more reasonable caterer, fitting me for my tuxedo, and, eventually, when the wedding day itself came, getting me to the overgrown church in Coconut Grove on time.

So I stood there at the altar, listening to the organ music and waiting with my new numb patience for Rita to sashay down the aisle and into permanent bondage with me. It was a very pretty scene, if only I had been able to appreciate it. The church was full of nicely dressed people – I never knew Rita had so many friends! Perhaps now I should try to collect some, too, to stand beside me in my new gray, pointless life. The altar was overflowing with flowers, and Vince stood at my side, sweating nervously and spasmodically wiping his hands on his pants legs every few seconds.

Then there was a louder blare from the organ, and everyone in the church stood up and faced backward. And here they came: Astor in the lead, in her beautiful white dress, her hair done in sausage curls and an enormous basket of flowers in her hands. Next came Cody in his tiny tuxedo, his hair plastered to his head, holding the small velvet cushion with the rings on it.

Last of all came Rita. As I saw her and the children, I seemed to see the whole drab agony of my

420

new life parading toward me, a life of PTA meetings and bicycles, mortgages and Neighborhood Watch meetings, and Boy Scouts, Girl Scouts, soccer and new shoes and braces. It was an entire lifeless, colorless secondhand existence, and the torment of it was blindingly sharp, almost more than I could bear. It washed over me with exquisite agony, a torture worse than anything I had ever felt, a pain so bitter that I closed my eyes—

And then I felt a strange stirring inside, a kind of surging fulfillment, a feeling that things were just the way they should be, now and evermore, world without end; that what was brought together here must never be rent asunder.

And marveling at this sensation of rightness, I opened my eyes and turned to look at Cody and Astor as they climbed the steps to stand beside me. Astor looked so radiantly happy, an expression beyond any I had ever seen from her, and it filled me with a sense of comfort and rightness. And Cody, so dignified with his small careful steps, very solemn in his quiet way. I saw that his lips were moving in some secret message for me, and I gave him a questioning glance. His lips moved again and I bent just a little to hear him.

'Your shadow,' he said. 'It's back.'

I straightened slowly and closed my eyes for the merest moment. Just long enough to hear the hushed sibilance of a welcome-home chuckle.

The Passenger had returned.

I opened my eyes, back again to the world as it

should be. No matter that I stood surrounded by flowers and light and music and happiness, nor that Rita was now climbing the steps intent on clamping herself to me forevermore. The world was whole once again, just as it should be. A place where the moon sung hymns and the darkness below it murmured perfect harmony broken only by the counterpoint of sharp steel and the joy of the hunt.

No more gray. Life had returned to a place of bright blades and dark shadows, a place where Dexter hid behind the daylight so that he could leap out of the night and be what he was meant to be: Dexter the Avenger, Dark Driver for the thing once more inside.

And I felt a very real smile spread across my face as Rita stepped up to stand beside me, a smile that stayed with me through all the pretty words and hand-holding, because once more, forever and always, I could say it again.

I do. And yes, I will, I really will.

And soon.

EPILOGUE

Far above the aimless scurrying of the city IT watched, and IT waited. There was plenty to see, as always, and IT was in no hurry. IT had done this many times before, and would do so again, endlessly and forever. That was what IT was for. Right now there were so many different choices to consider, and no reason to do anything but consider them until the right one was clear. And then IT would start again, gather the faithful, give them their bright miracle, and IT would feel once more the wonder and joy and swelling rightness of their pain.

All that would come again. It was just a matter of waiting for the right moment.

And IT had all the time in the world.